"Fire the UAEPs!" the commodore shouted.

"Fire the UAEPs!" Sir Grumdish repeated. "Aye!"

Just as the ship began to settle back into the water, it lurched backward. Twin forty-foot-long sprays of glistening water erupted from the bow, and from them shot two enormous arrows, directly at the minotaur vessel.

The pirates spun round in surprise at the sudden appearance of the *Indestructible* less than a hundred yards off their starboard rail. Half panicked by the sight, their crew tried to swing their catapult around and bring it to bear on the gnomes' submersible, but their efforts were wasted. One UAEP swept through them, scattering them across the decks and knocking not a few overboard. The other UAEP struck home in the mast, thudding into the hard timber and splitting it from base to wind-bellied topsail.

The minotaur captain, seeing the steel-headed ram jutting out from the bow of the *Indestructible*, recognized the hopelessness of the situation. Already, the mainmast of the pirate galley was cracking under the weight of the sails and push of the wind. He swept out his scimitar and roared in a bestial voice, "She's gonna ram us! Prepare to board and take 'em, lads!"

The DRAGONLANCE Saga

. . . and more than one hundred other
DRAGONLANCE® novels and anthologies
by dozens of authors.

CONUNDRUM

JEFF CROOK

CONUNDRUM

©2001 Wizards of the Coast, Inc.

Distributed in the United States by Holtzbrinck Publishing. Distributed in Canada by Fenn Ltd.

Distributed to the hobby, toy, and comic trade in the United States and Canada by regional distributors.

Distributed worldwide by Wizards of the Coast, Inc. and regional distributors.

Cover art by Matt Stawicki
First Printing: December 2001
Library of Congress Catalog Card Number: 2001089487

9 8 7 6 5 4 3 2 1

ISBN: 0-7869-1949-3
UK ISBN: 0-7869-2661-9
620-T21949

U.S., CANADA,
ASIA, PACIFIC, & LATIN AMERICA
Wizards of the Coast, Inc.
P.O. Box 707
Renton, WA 98057-0707
+ 1-800-324-6496

EUROPEAN HEADQUARTERS
Wizards of the Coast, Belgium
P.B. 2031
2600 Berchem
Belgium
+ 32-70-23-32-77

Visit our web site at **www.wizards.com/dragonlance**

INTRODUCTION

Although the events described in this report are true, the dialogue has been slowed to protect the sanity of the reader.

—The Literary Treasures and
Racial Heritage Guild of Mount Nevermind

CHAPTER
I

As they strolled along the strand, the gnome in the red jumpsuit with gold braids on the sleeves led the way with a purposeful (if short-legged) stride. The other two—a shorter gnome similarly dressed, and a green-vested kender—followed behind, delighting each other by singing the opposing parts in the accidental decapitation scene of the gnomish opera *In the Hall of the Mountain Dwarf*, otherwise known as *The Nibelugnut*. The shorter gnome roared the role of Turpidus, the dwarf toolmaker, while the kender's shrill (though not unlovely) tones told of the dismay of the lovely and hapless Jadander as the vegetable polisher escapes her control and careens through the marketplace of Thorbardin.

"Thy hand, Jadander?" Turpidus laments as his bearded head wags free of his neck. "Oh! Lay me in the earth."

The shorter gnome was dressed like his fellow—a tight red jumpsuit of close-knit material, with gold braids circling the cuffs, and the Tarbrush-and-Bilgepump symbol of the Maritime Sciences Guild sewn over his left breast pocket. He differed from the taller gnome only in his height, the amount of white hair on his rather bulbous head, and the variety of things protruding from the dozen or so pockets covering every available inch of free space on his jumpsuit. Where his companion's pockets were nearly empty, except for a small, clever whistle neatly outlined on his right buttocks as he walked, the shorter gnome's pockets were bulging with scrolls, papers, parchments, quills, pens, compasses, as well as what appeared to be an astrolabe.

The kender wore a pair of faded yellow leggings tucked into his boots and a furry green vest, which he asserted was made from the hide of a behemoth. As he strode bouncingly along, his kender throat warbling with Jadander's lamentations, he absentmindedly spun the inevitable weapon of the kender race—a hoopak staff. Its copper-shod tip glinted circles in the light of the westering sun, now beginning its descent toward the ocean.

Ahead rose the dry, rocky hills of northern Sancrist Isle, and beyond the hills, a single mountain: Mount Nevermind, home of the gnomes of western Krynn.

Their path along the beach did not lead toward the mountain. It led instead toward a pile of black boulders that split the beach like a wall, from the hills down into the surf, and around which the turbid ocean crashed and foamed. Tiny red crabs danced along the flat wet edges of the surf, back and forth, back and forth, waving their big pinchers over their backs.

Jadander's solo having come to an end, the kender immediately launched into a frighteningly realistic imitation of a gnomish bladder horn playing the old sailor's ditty "Merry It Is," but only a few ear-shattering notes into his tune, his voice trailed off into a sigh of wonder. His companions stopped, and the shorter gnome pointed toward the distant rocks.

From beyond the black, seaweed-draped boulders shot a small dark object, roughly spherical and trailing a beard of fire. They heard a faint roar, like a great army cheering its champion as he rides out to deliver a challenge. The object scribed a perfect parabola out over the surging waves and fell with a thunderous splash a quarter mile out to sea. A little puff of steam marked the place where it fell. The cheering passed into groans of disappointment, which eventually tapered off into the percussion noises of hammers and the sighing of saws.

"There they are," the shorter gnome stated, lowering his hand. The three started forward again, but without musical accompaniment.

They continued along the beach, the taller gnome in the lead, his compatriot immediately behind him, the green-vested kender bringing up a meandering rear guard. The kender strayed this way and that to inspect an unusually shaped bit of driftwood, chase a red crab, or pick up a seashell and drop it into one of his bulging pouches.

"Is there any buried treasure along this beach?" he asked as they neared the boulders amid the continuing sounds of construction.

"No," the lead gnome answered.

"How do you know? Have you searched? There might have been pirates once. . . ."

"There are no pirates in these waters," the taller gnome answered without turning. His thin white hair stirred restlessly in the wind as he walked.

"Smugglers, then," the kender pressed, "or shipwrecks."

"Actually, we don't allow shipwrecks along this shore any longer," the shorter gnome explained. "We've sunk a variety of safety precautions into the seabed offshore, which should prevent any future disasters."

The hammering and sawing stopped, and with a much louder cheer, another dark flaming object climbed heavenward beyond the boulders. This one was bigger, and scribed a higher, grander curve against the sky before it, too, crashed into the sea a quarter mile out. The cheers tapered off into groans. Soon came more hammering and sawing.

Where the enormous black boulders marched down into the surf, the beach narrowed to less than fifty paces from the stony feet of the hills to the water at low tide. The sand here was smooth, flat, wet from the receding tide and the constant spray from the boulders, and made for easy walking. The sounds of hammering and sawing echoed noisily from the cliffs beyond the black rocks.

Suddenly, two black-armored warriors appeared from between a pair of boulders. By the skull designs on their armor and on the horses' tack and barding, they appeared to be Knights of Neraka. Formerly known as Knights of Takhisis, they were the evil counterparts to the noble and goodly Knights of Solamnia. They spurred their horses directly at the three companions, their faces twisted into hideous grins. The two gnomes quickly scuttled crabwise out of the way, dragging the reluctant kender with them, while the horses thundered past, flinging gouts of wet sand from their hooves, and galloped off into the distance, vanishing around a bend in the coastline.

The kender lay on the wet sand staring after the Knights before finally rising and brushing off his elbows. "You'd think they were trying to trample us on purpose," he said. He settled his pouches about his waist and picked up his hoopak from where it had been smashed into the sand by a heavy, iron-shod hoof.

"They mostly don't even notice we are here," the shorter gnome said. "Mostly."

"Except when they want something from us," the other added grimly as they continued on their way.

Upon closer inspection, it became apparent that the black boulders, which had appeared from a distance to be

5

almost touching, were in fact widely separated, with numerous small tidal pools lying between them. The hoof-prints of the Knights' horses were plainly visible in the sand, as were the thousands of faint, spindly prints of the hundreds of birds—mostly plovers, spoonbills and waders—now working the pools.

But what most interested the three, drawing gasps of delight from the kender and nods of approval from the gnomes, was the scene spreading beyond the boulders. The hills drew back from the beach and climbed ever higher. This left a wide, sandy bay, like a great amphitheater, walled on the northern side by tall cliffs that were home to many thousands of gulls. Hundreds of gnomes could be seen scurrying all over this beach and the surrounding hillsides, some dragging freshly cut trees down from the hills, others hauling barrels from a ship beached in the surf, still others busily quarrying huge stones from the nearby sea-washed cliff. More labored to haul the quarried stones on giant rafts through the breakers, while yet more were involved in constructing the wildest collection of catapults and ballista ever before assembled in one place. Each catapult was bigger than the last, with the one currently under construction the biggest of them all. Beside this colossal catapult lay a stone nearly as big as a house.

Nearer to the observers of this circus-like scene stood a party-colored canopy, its ropes staked out in the sand near the water's edge. Beneath it, a gathering of Knights of Neraka, their squires and horses, keenly observed the gnomes' activities. It appeared to be the scene of a siege, yet there was nothing to besiege. No castle crouched on yonder beetling cliffs. While they watched, a catapult loosed a flaming stone out to sea. Hundreds of gnomes stopped their work to stand and cheer, only to groan with disappointment when the stone struck the sea in a mighty splash a good half-mile from shore. Only the Knights seemed pleased with this result, for there was a general round of nodding, backslapping, laughing and pointing at the spot where the stone sank. The gnomes returned to their business. Hammers rapped and saws snored, ropes creaked and chisels rang against stone.

"It looks like things are going well," the taller gnome observed as he looked over the chaotic scene.

"Indeed," his shorter companion concurred. "I suspect the professor has nearly completed his studies."

"What're they doing?" the kender asked. "Testing new weapons?"

"Don't be ridiculous. The professor is studying the buoyancy of very large hot stones," the taller gnome answered as he strode off in the direction of the Knights' tent.

"Good evening," the tall gnome said to the Knight who stopped them outside the tent when it became apparent that they intended to enter. "We are here to see Sir Wolhelm."

The Knight eyed the kender dubiously and maintained his position in front of the gnome, his mailed hand resting firmly on the sword at his hip.

"I am Commodore Brigg, of the Maritime Sciences Guild," the tall gnome said. "My compatriot here is Navigator Snork, also of the Maritime Sciences Guild."

The shorter gnome bowed, taking care to clap a hand over those pockets most likely to spill their contents. The kender stepped forward and extended his small sun-browned hand in greeting.

"This is Razmous Pinchpocket, cartographer and chief acquisitions officer for the maiden voyage of the MNS *Indestructible*," the commodore said. The Knight glared at the kender's hand as if it were a snake, his fingers twitching round the hilt of his sword.

"How do you do?" Razmous asked, edging closer to the Knight and eyeing the large leather pouch at his belt.

The Knight took a cautious step back in the sand and gripped his sword more tightly. "What do you want here?" he demanded. "Go on. Be on your way before I have you arrested . . . and searched!" This last comment was directed at the kender, whose innocent smile collapsed into an injured pout.

"We have been summoned here, Sir Knight!" Commodore Brigg snapped as he stepped closer, forcing the Knight to take another retreating step.

"Sure. Right." The Knight chuckled, half-drawing his sword.

"Sir Morsed, who is that?" a booming, basso voice called from the group of black-armored figures beneath the canopy.

"Some gnome," the Knight answered over his shoulder. "Claims to be a Commodore Brigg."

"Show him in, please."

A smug smile spread across the commodore's face, parting his white beard like a knife-stroke.

"He's got a kender, sir," the Knight warned, still not sheathing his weapon.

There was no immediate response, rather some muttering and restless shifting among the tent's occupants. Finally, the baritone voice said, "Very well. Show them in." At the same time, most of the Knights and squires departed the tent, many leading their steeds as well, as if they feared the kender might find some way to pocket a warhorse.

This left just a few Knights remaining, their horses forming a restless wall between the open back of the tent and the sea. The largest and most important-looking of the Knights sat on a campstool behind a low table, on top of which was spread a profusion of papers and scrolls, enough to cause even the mildest kender heart to flutter with greedy longings. The Knight absently stroked his thick black beard as he pored over some calculation and made notations into a dog-eared book resting on his lap. Beside him stood a studious young Knight, dressed in long gray robes and holding a tablet to his chest. A few others lounged about the tent, warily eyeing the approaching kender but continuing their conversations, which seemed mostly concerned with weight ratios, torsion strength, terminal velocities, and conic sections of a plane.

The area beneath the tent was strewn with straw and smelled strongly of horses, oiled leather, and stale sweat. By the crumpled blankets lying in the corners it appeared the Knights had been here many days. Large canvas rolls, secured with straps to the underside of the canopy's eaves, probably served as walls that could be let down at night to keep out the wind and elements.

"This is half command post, half bedroom, and half barn," Navigator Snork muttered distastefully as they entered.

"Be quiet," the commodore whispered. They stopped before Sir Wolhelm, and Commodore Brigg bowed low, sweeping the floor at his feet with one hand.

"Sir Wolhelm, my companions and—"

The Knight silenced him with an impatient wave, then continued scribbling in his book. the commodore's lips set into a hard frown, but he said nothing. Navigator Snork sucked his teeth and listened to his belly growl; it was well past lunchtime. After scanning the contents of the tabletop and finding nothing but schematics, Razmous's periwinkle eyes wandered around the interior of the tent, a bored expression settling into the delicate lines and wrinkles of his face. He absently chewed the brown tip of his topknot and fiddled with the things in his pouches. His gaze finally came to rest on one of the horses. The great black beast stamped and snorted nervously, its one visible red-rimmed eye glaring at the kender in alarm.

Without warning, a third gnome scurried into the tent, crossed to the table, and irritably shoved its contents onto the floor. From under his arm, he drew a soggy ream of drawings and schematics and flopped them onto the cleared space. Like Commodore Brigg and Navigator Snork, this gnome was short. He could have passed without ducking beneath the belly of any one of the Knights' warhorses, and he had a large, bulbous brown head scantily covered by a few thin wisps of downy white hair. From his jaws sprouted a thick tangle of curly white beard. What distinguished him most was his mode of dress. He wore a tan coverall buttoned up the back like a child's pajamas, which was dark with seawater all the way up to his armpits. Over the right breast pocket was sewn the rock-and-pick symbol of the Geological Sciences Guild, but the blue background of the patch indicated that he was a marine geology specialist—a rare specialization for a mountain-dwelling race. Behind one large, sunburned ear protruded a pencil, another peeked from the curls of his beard, and a third was clamped firmly between his strong white teeth, giving him something of a snarling appearance. He looked round the table for a moment, then turned to the kender and held out one stubby-fingered hand, palm upward.

"You haven't got a pencil, have you?" he asked.

"I don't know," Razmous answered with delight. "Let me see!" He flopped to the ground and upended his pouches.

Sir Wolhelm rose in alarm. "See here now, Professor—" he began.

Commodore Brigg perked up. "Professor? Professor Hap-Troggensbottle?"

"At your service, sir!" the newcomer declared without hesitation, bowing low.

The commodore grabbed his hand and shook it heartily. They embraced, slapping each other on the back like two people trying to put out a fire.

"See here . . ." the Knight leader said.

"Commodore Brigg of the MNS *Indestructible*," the commodore said as they parted. "Navigator Snork, and Chief Acquisitions Officer Razmous Pinchpocket."

"How do you do?" the kender said from where he had chased something under the table. The Knights leaped back, clutching at their money pouches.

Snork bowed, then tugged his beard in respect. The professor made a rude noise with his lips. Snork bowed again, blushing with pride.

The professor turned back to Commodore Brigg. "The *Indestructible*, eh? Isn't that a . . ."

"A Class C Submersible Deepswimmer, yes," the commodore answered for him.

"Ah, so that is why you are here."

"We would like to invite you—" Commodore Brigg began.

Sir Wolhelm cut him off angrily. "I am in charge here! There will be no inviting without my say so."

"Yes, of course," the commodore bowed. Professor Hap-Troggensbottle nodded his reluctant assent.

The leader of the Knights resumed his seat behind the table, settling himself onto the tiny stool with as much dignity as he could muster, and glared around the tent. "Now," he said, his black beard bristling, "Professor Hap-Troggensbottle, you are hereby *ordered* by the Knights of Neraka, the rightful rulers-regent of Mount Nevermind for His Inestimable Majesty Pyrothraxus the dragon, to undertake the voyage of the MNS *Indestructible*, representing the interests of the Knighthood and of Mount Nevermind in all matters of a geologic question."

Out on the beach, another of the catapults fired its load out to sea, forcing a pause. Commodore Brigg took this opportunity to resume the conversation.

"We know of your life quest to discover why small rocks, and even big rocks, sink, while really big rocks like islands and continents float. We intend to subnavigate the continent of Ansalon," said Commodore Brigg, "to complete the great voyage begun by the MNS *Polywog*, which nearly ended in disaster, some twenty-five years ago."

"It is *ordered*, by the Knights of Neraka," Sir Wolhelm continued with a warning glance at the commodore, "that the legendary Sub-Ansalonian Passage between Mount Nevermind in the west and Winston's Tower in the east be located and—"

"The first attempt nearly ended in disaster," Navigator Snork chimed in. "The MNS *Polywog* actually succeeded in completing the west-to-east leg of the journey. Fortunately, on the return leg, the ship was lost, and the crew has not been seen since. So this still leaves the east-to-west leg of the journey to complete the life quest. Chief Acquisitions Officer Razmous"—a slight bow from same—"is vital to the success of this mission, as he claims to be in possession of a copy of the map left at Winston's Tower before the *Polywog* began its return voyage."

"Yes, I have it here somewhere," the kender declared from under the table.

"The kender has the long-lost map?" Sir Wolhelm exclaimed, forgetting that he had been interrupted again. He glared under the table, but the kender had vanished.

"Yes, of course. And he is a most qualified cartographer," Commodore Brigg asserted.

"The gods help you," the young Knight in the gray robes sighed.

With a puzzled look at this remark, Commodore Brigg

continued, "We intend to sail round the northern shore of Ansalon until we reach the Blood Sea of Istar. We'll stop off in Flotsam to replenish our supplies—"

"I have additions to those orders," Sir Wolhelm inserted hastily, while still searching beneath the table for the kender. The young Gray Robe read from his tablet. "When you reach the city of Flotsam, you are ordered take on board the Thorn Knight, Sir Tanar Lobcrow, and extend him every courtesy."

The gnomes exchanged puzzled looks.

"Whatever for?" the commodore exclaimed. "I have no need of a sorcerer. My crew list is already completed."

"You are so *ordered*, Brigg," Sir Wolhelm said. "If you want the Knights of Neraka to finance this excursion of yours, as agreed, you must abide by our terms. We want one of our own on this voyage, but we'll not needlessly risk the life of even one Knight until you have proved you can sail your ship from here to Flotsam."

"I assure you, Sir Wolhelm, the MNS *Indestructible will* reach Flotsam," the commodore responded in insulted tones. "However, my ship is not built to accommodate individuals of your . . . your . . ." he paused, waving his hand vaguely toward the Knight Commander.

"Stature," Snork whispered.

"Stature!" Commodore Brigg snapped. "Yes, that's it. This is a gnome-built ship built for gnomes, and, well, the occasional kender. Your Knight will be most uncomfortable, rest assured. One might even say cramped. We've agreed to turn over all logs, maps, records and so forth, upon our successful return. That should be sufficient. I should think that would satisfy your . . . how shall we say? . . . curiosity about our venture."

The Knight's face darkened, and the muscles along his jaw began to quiver. "There is no point in arguing. You have been ordered to take Sir Tanar aboard at Flotsam, and that is what you shall do. Sir Tanar will see that you do not accidentally get lost along the way and, for example, fall into the hands of any Knights of Solamnia."

"Very well," the commodore sighed. Obviously flustered, he turned back to the professor. "As I was saying, we will put into port at Flotsam. From there, we sail to the center of the Blood Sea, dive to the bottom, and enter the chasm that once led to the Abyss. In the wall of this deep crevasse is an opening, a cave, from which the *Polywog* emerged all those years ago at the end of their legendary west-to-east journey. We should emerge in the New Sea somewhere near the Isle of Schallsea."

"Sounds impossible," the professor said while gnawing thoughtfully on the pencil in his mouth.

"Perhaps—but let me remind you that no one is going anywhere until these ordinance experiments are completed," Sir Wolhelm said.

The professor's eyes narrowed beneath his shaggy white brows. "These may be ordinance experiments to you Knights, but they are scientific experiments to me," he snarled. "Need I remind you that my life quest is to unravel the mystery of buoyant stone? And these experiments, I tell you, are a complete failure!" He stabbed his pencil into the ream of wet schematics he had thrown onto the table upon first entering the tent. Then he drew the pencil from his beard, hurled it to the ground and stomped on it vehemently.

"Every time we come up with a useful, time-saving device you military types twist our machines to your own evil uses!" he shouted while stomping around the tent. "Take the gnomeflinger, for instance, designed to transport gnomes to the various levels within the central shaft of Mount Nevermind. You use it to hurl rocks to batter down the walls of your enemies. Or the cheese-holer, an ingenious device designed to put the holes in cheese, yet you make it an instrument of torture! Science has ever been the pawn of the military!"

Sir Wolhelm rose, his face scarlet with rage, but fortunately whatever he was about to say was interrupted by the young Thorn Knight. "Come now, Professor. They haven't been a complete waste of time. And there is still the last and greatest of your experiments—Big Bertrem." He pointed out over the sands toward the catapult of truly monstrous proportions, requiring the pulley systems of three normal catapults just to draw, and a crew of well over two hundred gnomes. The stone currently being loaded onto it was easily large enough to knock a dragon out of the sky.

"Well, hmm, true, I would like to see Big Bertrem fired, just once," the professor said dreamily, his pique momentarily forgotten. He reached twitchingly for the pencil behind his ear, then spun back to the table and began scribbling calculations of the tangents of imaginary circles.

The Knights nodded and smiled to one another over the gnomes' heads.

By the time the sun had dropped an hour closer to the horizon, the gargantuan ballista was ready. From their vantage point in the tent, Commodore Brigg and Navigator Snork could see the professor scurrying about in its shadow, shouting last-minute orders. Someone lit the stone with a torch, setting fire to the tar covering every inch of its surface. As the flames blazed up, gnomes scattered in all directions, leaving the professor alone by the catapult's release. In the light of the westering sun, they saw an axe rise up, then flash down. A report like the cracking of a whip echoed against the cliffs. There followed a tremendous bone-shaking thud, and a wave of sand spread like ripples in a pond away from Big Bertrem. The throwing arm rose slowly, bending under the weight of the massive flaming stone, but then counterweights swung into place, and a gout of steam escaped from what appeared to be a smokestack. Two giant flywheels, attached to the fulcrum post, began to whirl faster and faster. The throwing arm of the catapult hesitated for a moment, like a diver taking a deep breath before leaping, and then the entire contraption flipped over backwards, pivoting around a point in space centered on the house-sized stone. The spinning fly wheels dug in, throwing up a huge fountain of sand that instantly buried three dozen members of the Mishaps Guild who were rushing in to record and measure the event as it was happening. Meanwhile, the flywheels found purchase in the sand and the thing began to move. Its steam whistle screaming, the monstrous catapult tore across the beach and up into the hills beyond, where it sailed over the crest of a ridge and disappeared in a cloud of dust, rocks, and uprooted trees.

Within moments, Professor Hap-Troggensbottle appeared from the wreckage down the beach, a bit battered but alive. His eyes beamed with delight. He approached the tent, slapping sand and dust from his beard and eyebrows. A pencil, snapped cleanly in two, dangled behind his ear.

"I'm tempted to think you did that on purpose," Sir Wolhelm accused as he emerged from the tent.

"I assure you, I could not produce that result again unless I tried," the professor answered as he approached Commodore Brigg. "Now, what is the status of your ship? Are we prepared to disembark?"

"Yes," the commodore harrumphed, "except we are still looking for the security officer. We were hoping to get a Knight—a real Knight and not some blasted sorcerer. The name we have is Sir Grumdish. Do you know him?"

"Grumdish?" Sir Wolhelm snorted as he approached. "Never heard of him."

His aide-de-camp, the young Thorn Knight, leaned over and whispered something into his commander's ear. Sir Wolhelm's eyes narrowed. "Him!"

He turned to Commodore Brigg, smiling wolfishly. "Yes, of course. Take him with you. By all means. Sir Jarnett will show you to him. He isn't far." He strode away, calling for the squires to saddle Sir Jarnett's horse.

Within moments, a seemingly reluctant Sir Jarnett was mounted and leading the three gnomes and their kender companion up into the hills, taking a path not far from the one trailblazed moments before by Big Bertrem. When they had gone, a squire approached and reported that Sir Wolhelm's warhorse was missing. The Knight eyed the hills suspiciously, considering whether to send a patrol to arrest the kender, but then he shook his head in disbelief, silently reprimanding himself. "Not even a kender," he muttered.

CHAPTER
2

The stream was no wider than an oxcart and shallow enough for a gnome to ford with his pants rolled up, if he didn't mind cold piggies. The clear, icy water sprang in a noisy gush from the hillside at the edge of the meadow, then galloped and purled through a copse of oak, elm, and walnut trees. A few squirrels scampered and leaped in the evening shadows beneath the eaves of the trees.

Where the stream emerged from the trees, someone had built a small wooden bridge. A little-used path, leading from the beach to Mount Nevermind in the distance, crossed the stream at this bridge. It was at this place that Sir Grumdish had taken his stand.

As they entered the meadow valley, Commodore Brigg and his companions, including Sir Jarnett, found the Knight sitting his massive charger beside the bridge, as still and solid as a carving of weathered stone. He wore the armor and livery of a Knight of the Rose, but his armor was oddly antique even by generous standards. Though polished to a glassy sheen, his armor appeared dented in several places, while unaccountable bulges showed in others. The roses, kingfishers, and crowns on his breastplate

CONUNDRUM

looked worn and tired. At his side hung an enormous two-handed sword in a battered scabbard. In his left hand, he held a great kite shield painted with a golden cog at the fess point. Propped on his right stirrup and steadied by his right hand was an long, white jousting lance with a red pennant near its silver tip rippling in the evening breeze.

Of his features, little could be discerned, except for a bit of white moustache hair dangling from beneath the bucket helm that completely covered his head. A thin, V-shaped slit in the front of the helm allowed for vision and a modicum of air. Like the rest of his antique armor, the helm exhibited signs of both carelessness and loving care. It was as battered as it was outdated, but otherwise shone like a mirror in the westering sun.

His horse was a massive beast, but even an untrained eye could see, upon closer inspection, that this was no warhorse. With its big heavy withers, dangling lips and dull eyes, it looked more a beer-wagon horse than the fearless steed of a renowned and fearless Knight of the Rose.

Sir Jarnett walked his horse across the meadow, the gnomes and the kender spreading in his wake, their eyes wide with curiosity. Surely these two sworn enemies—a Knight of Solamnia and a Knight of Neraka—could not meet but that blows would soon begin to rain. But as they drew closer, Sir Grumdish did not move or speak. Razmous began to suspect that he had fallen asleep, what with the buzzing of the flies and the purling of the stream and the warm sun shining through his visor. The kender was just stooping for a stone to plink off the Knight's helm and wake him when a voice rang out, high and challenging, muffled but echoing, like a bee in a pipe.

"Halt! Fare thee nary closer, lest ye care to tilt with me for the road, sirrah," Sir Grumdish cried in some semblance of the ancient language of chivalry.

Sir Jarnett stopped his horse and waited for the others

to catch up. They gathered round him, their attention focused on the Knight.

"Well, there he is," Sir Jarnett said with a bored yawn. "He's all yours." So saying, he turned his horse and rode away.

"Halt, miscreant Knight!" Sir Grumdish cried as he bounced angrily in the saddle. His horse took a ponderous step onto the bridge. It creaked ominously under its massive weight.

"Halt, coward Knight! Stand to and fewter thy lance!" Sir Grumdish continued as his mount crossed the bridge in a slow rumble of hooves and cracking wood. "Onward! Run hard, run free, my brave heart, my bonnie steed!" He rocked in the saddle, trying to urge his mount into something resembling a gallop.

Slowly, ponderous and unstoppable as a glacier, the great beast did manage to lift its head and come into the bit. Its broad back became like the rolling deck of a ship, and its rider a cargo broken free of its moorings. Sir Grumdish slipped backwards onto the horse's withers and began to bounce, his feet in the stirrups and his elbows sticking straight out at the apex of each soaring bound, as though about to take flight. As he scrabbled clumsily at the reins, trying to maintain his seat, his shield sailed free like a pie plate in the wind, then his lance came loose and performed three cartwheels across the meadow before its point stabbed into the sandy soil and it jerked to a quivering stop, upright, like a flagpole. Sir Grumdish rode past it, shouting, "Whoa . . . Bright . . . Dancer!"

Then the saddle girth snapped.

Saddle and rider bounced once last time on the horse's pumpkin-colored rump, then rose together, a little too slowly for belief, while the horse galloped out from beneath them. At the top of their arcing flight, Sir Grumdish kicked free of the stirrups, and he and the saddle parted ways, like an apple sliced in half by the trick swordsman at the fair.

The bonnie Knight struck the ground with a clang— and broke cleanly in two at the waist. His top half bounded along the path of the still-galloping horse, arms flailing, and a startling stream of curses and exclamations of pain flowed from within the helm. His bottom half bounced to its feet and began running in a large but ever tightening circle, like the proverbial chicken. The Knight's horse continued obliviously across the meadow and vanished into the undergrowth of the trees beyond.

The top half of the Knight finally rolled to a stop, expelling during its last few revolutions a gnome (whole and uninjured except for his pride) wearing only a dirty white loincloth and a rag wound turbanlike around his enormous bald brown head. As soon as he regained his feet, the gnome dove on top of the still-thrashing upper half of his armor, reached inside, and with a curse worthy of a dwarf, twisted some knob that shut the thing off. The arms fell to each side, limp and dead, while the gnome collapsed across the breastplate, exhausted.

The legs continued their mad scamper around the meadow, passing the two gnomes and their kender companion, who watched them with something combining curiosity, amusement, and horror. Commodore Brigg snapped a short command, and Razmous dropped his hoopak and chased after the legs. But once he had caught up with the Knight's legs, he didn't quite know what to do with them, so he ran alongside, hopping up and down to try to see into the waist for the switch or lever to shut them off. Finally, finding no other solution, he threw his arms around the knees and tackled them. Legs and kender went down together in a scrabble of dust.

The legs continued to thrash, flinging up large tufts of grass and odd items from the kender's pouches. Razmous clung grimly to one knee, while the other battered him about the ears in its throes. His companions rushed to his aid. While Snork and Commodore Brigg wrestled the free leg, the professor felt inside the top of the legs. The legs suddenly fell limp and lifeless. They clung to the legs a few more moments in anticipation of their bursting into frenzied motion once again, before finally rising to their feet, slapping off the dust, and laughing nervously. Razmous gingerly palpated the pointy tips of his well-pummeled ears.

The kender was about to say something clever when the turbaned gnome was suddenly among them, rudely shoving them out of the way as he knelt beside his armored legs and examined them for damage. "What did you do?" he angrily demanded of the professor. "You'd better not have broken anything."

"I simply flipped the kill switch," Professor Hap said, pointing to the device in question, only to have his hand slapped away. "It seemed the logical thing to do," he finished in hurt tones.

The turbaned gnome stood and, crossing his grease-smeared arms in front of his naked chest, frowned grimly. "Who are you? What are you doing here?" he asked, studiously glaring at the kender.

Commodore Brigg stepped forward. "We are searching for Sir Grumdish."

"Thou hast found us. What wouldst thou have of us?" the turbaned gnome asked.

"We are gnomes of Mount Nevermind," Commodore Brigg said. Razmous cleared his throat. "And a kender of impeccable reputation," the commodore added.

"Nevermind is home to the vile dragon Pyrothraxus and controlled by those evil Knights, is it not?" Sir Grumdish shrewdly observed. "My Life Quest is to slay just such a dragon. I am busy at my quest. If you are its servants, I warn thee to get thee hence lest I sheath my blade in thy black innards."

"Your Life Quest is to slay a dragon?" the kender interjected. "How interesting! Most gnomes' Life Quests are to build some useful device or other."

"Well, actually, it is a rather interesting story," Sir Grumdish said, flattered and brightening visibly. "My great-grandfather Jugdish, you see, was trying to build a flying machine to aid the Knights of Solamnia in the great War of the Lance. He dreamed of one day becoming a Knight himself, and hoped his invention would pave the way for his admittance. Since dragons are formidable aerialists—as even I, who am sworn to slay them, must admit—he decided to model his machine on dragons, with various improvements, of course."

"Of course," the three listeners agreed, nodding.

"Yes, but he needed a dragon in order to obtain his measurements and design his pattern. Dragons are notoriously unwilling volunteers, having a natural dislike of being boiled down to their bones for the sake of our technological curiosity. Therefore, Jugdish determined to slay one. It became his Life Quest. After he was burned to crisp, the Life Quest passed to my father, Lugdish, and after he was frozen into a solid block of ice, it passed to me."

"Sir Grumdish, we are all servants of the Life Quest of our race," Commodore Brigg answered fervently. "No evil has or ever shall corrupt our noble purposes, and if you come with us, you shall see that we are devoted to a quest of our own that will accrue to the further glory of the gnomish race. This I swear by the Cog and the Wheel, and the All-seeing Mobile Optical Scanning Device of Reorx, our god of old."

The gnome's faced hardened a bit below his turban. "Those are indeed grave oaths. But be that as it may, what would you have of me? By the devices on your uniform, you are a ship's captain."

"I am Commodore Brigg of the MNS *Indestructible*. This is Navigation Officer Snork, Cartographer and Chief Acquisitions Officer Razmous Pinchpocket, and Science Officer Professor Hap-Troggensbottle."

Sir Grumdish nodded to each in turn as he was introduced. Then he turned back to the commodore, his bushy white eyebrows raised in curiosity.

"*Indestructible* is a Class C Deepswimmer," Commodore Brigg said proudly.

"A submersible!" Sir Grumdish exclaimed.

"You've heard of them, then?"

Sir Grumdish nodded his turbaned head. "Deathtraps," he said.

"Yes, well . . ." the commodore hemmed and hawed. "Most likely, you are thinking of the Class A or Class B. We've added a number of safety features."

"Of course," Sir Grumdish said as he stooped and grabbed his armor legs by the belt. "Pardon me. I have work to do."

The gnomes parted to watch him struggle to drag his legs across the meadow to where the upper body armor still lay. Commodore Brigg followed after him. "And we've made the hull out of iron instead of bronze this time," he persisted

"That . . . should . . . help it . . . sink . . . much . . . faster," Sir Grumdish grunted as he tugged. Razmous and Snork each grabbed a foot and helped him carry his legs the rest of the way. With a sigh, they set the legs beside the body.

"Thanks, lads," Sir Grumdish said as he removed his turban and used it to mop his face.

"Our mission, if you must know, is to try to complete the voyage of the MNS *Polywog*," the commodore continued. "The *Polywog* actually completed the west-to-east leg of the journey, but it was lost during the return voyage. It is Navigator Snork's Life Quest to complete this journey."

"Good show. Best of luck," Sir Grumdish said to Snork. "It's getting dark. I'd better be a-looking for my warhorse. Thanks for stopping by and telling me about all this." He extended one grease-grimed hand. Razmous shook it vigorously.

"But we want *you* to come with us, to serve as security officer," Navigator Snork begged.

"We were hoping for a Knight, but of course a gnomish knight is much better," Commodore Brigg added. "After all you are the only one . . . that is, I mean, you are a sterling example."

"Of course! But I must confess I am not a true Knight of Solamnia," Sir Grumdish said as he retrieved his shield. "That's why I want to slay a dragon. If I can slay a dragon, the Knights of Solamnia have no more cause to deny my petition."

He lay the shield over his armored legs and paused, thoughtfully stroking his moustache. "It's funny, though. I have no interest in building a flying machine anymore, and the war's been over for many years. But I still want to become a Knight. That part of the Life Quest is still important to me." His face hardened once more as he turned back to the commodore. "In any case, I have no desire to be cooped up in a ship, or dragging drunken sailors out of portside taverns. Besides, there would be no room on your ship for my steed, Bright Dancer."

Commodore Brigg frowned and chewed his beard in frustration. Behind him, the sun lowered behind the nearby hills, casting long shadows over the meadow. Sir Grumdish dragged his lance over to his armor and shield, aided once again by Razmous. They placed it carefully on the ground.

Sir Grumdish straightened his back with a groan, then cleared his throat. "I'm sorry, Commodore," he said sincerely. "I'm sure you understand. I have my own Life Quest to pursue."

Professor Hap stepped forward and placed one hand on the commodore's gold epauletted shoulder. "Did we mention that we'll be diving dangerously close to the portal to the Abyss?"

"Is that so?" Sir Grumdish said, trying not to appear intrigued.

"Indeed!" the commodore said, brightening to this new persuasive tack. "As a matter of fact, will be diving right down *into* the abyssal chasm."

The gnomish knight raised a shaggy eyebrow, tugging thoughtfully at his beard. He then asked in a low, non-committal voice, "You don't suppose there will be any *dragons* there, do you?"

"It seems inevitable," Commodore Brigg answered.

CHAPTER

3

The pounding on the door woke him from a black dream, one in which spirits crowded round him, touching him with fingers fine as spiderwebs, drawing the breath from his lungs until he didn't even have the air to scream. He awoke from the dream already rolling out of bed, his hand fumbling at the dagger under his thin pillow. He sucked air through his clenched teeth and glared about the room.

As he gradually recognized where he was and the last tatters of his dream began to fade, he tossed the dagger on the small, filthy bed and stumbled to a small table beside the window. Atop it, a pewter ewer stood beside a battered pewter bowl. He lifted the ewer and poured a stream of brown water into the bowl, then dunked his shaved head into it. Through the water, he heard someone pound on the door again.

He lifted his head from the bowl and listened, water streaming down his long, narrow nose. "Who is it?" he asked.

"Messenger," came the answer from the hall outside his room. It was a woman's voice, muffled by the wooden door.

"Messenger?" he asked suspiciously, still stooped over the bowl. With a sigh, he leaned against the small table, its rickety legs creaking under his weight as though about to collapse. "One moment. Let me dress. I just woke up."

He glanced out the window, seeing that it was midday outside. He could almost feel the messenger's disgust at his apparent laziness, sleeping until the sun was high overhead. The city of Flotsam was a-bustle with business and trade at this hour, while he snored half the day away, dreaming of bodiless spirits. He shuddered slightly at the memory, and he could almost feel their feathery fingers upon him.

He picked a tattered gray robe from a pile on the floor and shoved his arms through the sleeves. Not even bothering to belt it around his waist, he walked to the door, but as he reached for the door handle, he paused. He returned to the bed and, lifting his dagger from the soiled linens, tucked it into his sleeve.

In former days, he might also have surrounded himself with a protective shell of magic strong enough to deflect almost any attack. The words of the spell came to his lips almost without thought, but they were bitter as bile, and powerless. The magic was a sluggish pool in him now, where once it had been a hot, raging river of power. The simplest spell drained him, where once he had commanded powerful magics in the service of his Dark Queen. He was a Knight of the Thorn, a gray-robed sorcerer in the armies of the once-Knights of Takhisis, now called the Knights of Neraka.

He was still a Knight, still serving the Order of the Thorn, but he had little enough magic to command these days. The Order still found him useful, though—as a knife, a hand to wield a dagger in places an army could not go. Unlike many of his fellow gray-robed Knights, he was no pasty, thin wastrel quivering under the weight of a spellbook. He might have been a warrior, a Knight of the Lily, had he applied himself, for he was very good with orders—this person to be murdered, that cargo of grain to be poisoned, a ship to be sabotaged, a noble blackmailed, a merchant kidnapped in order to bring his family into line. If the Knights of Neraka needed something done in territory not directly under their control, they always seemed to call upon him.

Because he got the job done. He didn't always do it the way they wanted it done, but in the end the job was done. Even the impossible jobs.

And it always began this way.

He opened the door a crack and peered out into the hall. A little light managed to penetrate the grimy window at the other end of the hall, dimly outlining the face of a young woman with close-cropped black hair. She wore tight riding breeches and boots on her shapely legs, with a loose yellow blouse of thin cotton providing numerous places to secret a dagger or poisoned dart. A plain canvas backpack was slung over one shoulder, and she stood with one hand on her hip as she glared at the door.

"Sir Tanar?" she asked incredulously. "Tanar Lobcrow?"

"Yeah. Who are you?" he asked through the crack. "You're not the usual messenger. Where's Rogar?"

"Dead," she answered.

"Figures. So you're the new messenger. Did they tell you what to say?"

"What do you mean?" she asked, suddenly suspicious.

"Good," he answered. "The password is that there isn't a password. I'll take that now." He reached for the backpack through the cracked doorway.

"I'm tired. I could use a bath."

Tanar laughed. "You are new," he said. "Don't you know where you are?"

"Flotsam," she answered angrily.

"And this inn is the Ogre's Tooth. You'll get no bath here. For a bribe, you can get a pitcher of dirty water and a flour sack to dry off with. But you're welcome to use mine," he said as he opened the door.

The woman entered cautiously, glancing quickly around the room at the meager furnishings. A sneer crossed her face as she paused in the doorway, then she flung the backpack at Sir Tanar. He dodged instinctively, catching the pack by one strap as it hurtled past his shoulder. The woman laughed, then crossed to the bowl and pitcher. Tanar shot her a black look and sat down on the bed.

"What's your name?" he asked as he undid the straps. His practiced fingers removed the intricate and secret knots in the leather cords binding the pack shut.

"Liv," she answered as she gazed in disgust at the brown water in the bowl.

"Live and let Liv," he said with a sneer. He searched under the flap without lifting it, finally finding the small metallic disk concealing the firetrap. His sensitive fingertips detected the trap's invisible tabs, and he pressed them in the correct order to deactivate it. "Do you think you will?"

"Will what?" she asked. She stirred the water in the bowl with her hand, testing its temperature.

"Live," he answered as he opened the flap and shook the contents out on the bed.

Shrugging, she leaned over the bowl and began to splash water on her face and the back of her neck.

From the upraised pack, a round silver plate tumbled out on the bed. As Tanar picked it up, he felt an electric jolt pass through his fingertips and up his arm. He almost cried out in surprise, but he managed to bite his tongue as he stared in wonder at it.

It seemed an ordinary enough thing—a piece of fine silver flatware from some noble lady's dowry—that is, until one noticed the runes engraved around its rim. And the aura of powerful magic that surrounded this thing was palpable. As he held it, he felt a delicious tingling numbness in all his limbs. He marveled that this woman could have had this thing in her possession for so long without feeling its power. He could almost smell it, like hot metal baking on the stove.

Then it occurred to him that she probably wasn't a magic-user. The powers that be would have chosen her to deliver it for that very reason. Any mage on Krynn would give his soul for an item such as this, for with it he could power spells. Artifacts from the time before Chaos could be used to power spells, but such items were rare as a red dragon's good will. He wondered what its powers were and who had sent it to him. More importantly, he wondered why.

Inside the backpack, he found a sealed letter. He examined the red wax seal, recognized its authenticity, and broke it open. He unfolded the note and spread it on the bed between himself and the woman. She had opened her blouse and was squeezing water over her shoulder with a rag. A muddy pool had begun to collect on the wooden boards at her feet.

The note read:

To Sir Tanar Lobcrow, Knight of the Thorn,

The object accompanying this letter is a communication device of great power. You are ordered to keep it near at hand, for I shall soon be contacting you through it. Do not, under any circumstances, attempt to contact me until after such time as I have initiated contact with you. At that time, you will receive instruction as to its uses and powers.

You are, however, granted permission to use it sparingly to power your own spells. I cannot stress enough that you are to use its magic sparingly, and only in the direst emergency.

   *You are further ordered to kill the messenger. If you fail, she
will take your place.*

—The Voice of the Night

Sir Tanar looked up from the letter to find the woman tow-
eling off with a flour sack. Her back was half turned, but
he took no chances. Reaching across the bed, he touched
the silver plate and began to chant the words to his protection spell. Magic, so long stagnant, surged through his
veins.

   At the weird sound of the chanted words, Liv turned,
her eyes widening in alarm.

CHAPTER

4

Normally, they would not have drawn much attention passing through the streets of the port city of Pax. Gnomes were a common sight here. They had their own shipyard, such as it was, though they didn't just build ships there. The shipyard was located at a safe distance from nearly everything else of importance in the city, including the dump. Once upon a time, the dump had been much closer to the shipyard, but a gnomish milk-freezing experiment gone horribly awry had set the dump on fire, and it burned for forty days. The citizens relocated the dump closer to their city's walls, while the gnomes spent the next eight years trying to perfect the garbage-burning steam-driven sugared milk freezer.

But it wasn't every day that the citizens of Pax witnessed four gnomes and a kender leading a beer wagon horse, astride which sat a Knight of Solamnia in full battle armor, bound upright in the saddle by an intricate web of ropes. The first real Knights of Solamnia they met upon entering the city tried to arrest them and free their captured "brother." Only when they sliced through the ropes and their restrained and heretofore silent fellow Knight

33

toppled in two pieces from the saddle did they believe the gnomes' protestations of innocence. Sir Grumdish was especially vociferous, demanding satisfaction with an immediate formal joust in a nearby rutabaga patch. Commodore Brigg and the others helped him set his armor back in the saddle while the offending "churls" rode away, scratching their heads.

"I told you we should have thrown a blanket over him," Razmous said as the street ahead grew thick with curious citizens. People hung out of the windows that crowded close along the narrow lanes. Whole taverns emptied into the street. Fishwives gawked and jeered noisily from the stalls in the market. Sir Grumdish gnawed his beard and eyed the crowd nervously, as if he might lay about him with his sword at any moment.

They were followed most of the way from the city gate to the gnomes' shipyard by a concerned contingent of grim-faced Knights of Solamnia. It was apparent they believed that Sir Grumdish's mechanical armor, though it contained no dead or captive brother Knight, was the ill-gotten booty of shady adventures, and they wondered if some law or other was being broken. That a kender was involved did not lighten their moods. Commodore Brigg's obvious military rank held them at bay—for the moment—until their lawyers and clerks could scour the Measure and the city laws for some rule by which they could clap the five diminutive miscreants in irons.

In any case, the gnomes and kender arrived at the shipyard without serious incident. Most of the curious citizens eventually dispersed. The Knights stopped at a safe distance, then posted a guard before returning to their duties. Meanwhile, Commodore Brigg and his companions paused on the overlooking bluff to take in the marvel and majesty of the scene spread below them.

The bluffs dropped steeply down into the water, providing Pax with its famous deepwater harbor that brought ships from all over Krynn during the balmy months when the seas allowed travel between Ansalon and Sancrist Isle. However, no foreign vessels crowded the quays of the gnomes' shipyard, as it was located across the bay from the city. Instead, each berth held its own peculiar addition to the Maritime Sciences. At one dock, several dozen gnomes were busily installing a giant six-bladed, steam-powered fan into the hull of what appeared to be a large, flat-bottomed ship. Commodore Brigg explained that this ship, the MNS *Blowfish*, was a Class A prototype of a self-powered ship that would create its own wind to fill the sails. The fan was being mounted onto a hydraulic elevating swivel base that would allow them to change the direction of its airflow, to take advantage of the wind for drying laundry and sea soaked cargoes, and other such menial tasks. They had been forced to invent hydraulics first, of course, before they built the hydraulic elevating swivel base, but this new technology promised all sorts of uses, like keeping doors from slamming shut or for crushing garbage into neat little easy-to-burn cubes.

"In fact," the commodore continued proudly, "hydraulics is also the primary technology behind our newest secret weapon, the Underwater Arrow of Epic Proportions—UAEP, for short. You can see one being loaded into the *Indestructible* now."

To the left of the *Blowfish* lay a vessel nearly twice its size, but of curious dimensions and features. It actually looked rather like two ships that had been placed deck to deck, like the two halves of a clam shell, hammered together, then covered from stem to stern and keel to keel with iron plating. Amidships, a conning tower had been built, and behind this a deck of sorts, where ropes, lines and anchors lay amongst piles of boxes and stacks of barrels. Two footrails leading forward from the deck allowed access to the bow of the ship, so that the sailors wouldn't have to navigate the sloping hull just to secure a bowline or the rigging that ran from the bow to the short mast around which the conning tower was built. From the top and bottom keels, just forward of the mast, projected two pairs of curious fan-shaped structures (not unlike fins), while at the stern, enclosed inside its D-shaped rudder, was a large six-bladed fan much like the one being installed in the belly of the *Blowfish*. Near the bow of the ship, below the craft's midline, there was a closed round door, shut like a great eye in sleep.

Presently, several dozen gnomes could be seen lowering, by way of an enormous, six-armed crane, a very large catapult arrow through the open hatch in the stern deck. Nearby, three other UAEPs stood in racks along the wharf, awaiting loading. One important-looking gnome wearing a white jumpsuit sat astraddle the upper keel fore of the mast, shouting directions into what appeared to be a large beer mug. Strangely enough, his voice was amplified many times by this curious device, loud enough to be heard by those standing at the top of the bluff. He directed operations with a large heavy wrench, wielding it like a conductor's baton.

"Be careful with that, you slack-jawed sons of a kender and a gully dwarf!" he shouted at the crane operators. There were six of them, one for each arm. "Numbers Two, Three, and Six, swing her a little more to starboard. Starboard, not larboard, you misbegotten spawn of an Aghar! Ahoy, beware below!" This to those gnomes employed in various tasks near the bow of the ship.

The UAEP began to swing crazily under the opposing directions of the crane's six arms, sweeping the stern deck clean of its barrels and crates and boxes. One wild gyration sent it careening through the workers at the bow, knocking more than a dozen from perches along the ship's sloping hull, which had been precarious to begin with. The remainder leaped for their lives into the sea.

"The one shouting directions is Chief Engineer Portlost," Commodore Brigg explained, pointing out the gnome with the mugraphone and the wrench. "He's our mishaps officer."

"How . . . um, how do they—meaning the UAEPs—work, exactly?" the professor asked while rubbing his bearded chin.

"It's quite ingenious, actually," the commodore said. "They were invented by the Plumbers Guild, which was trying to find a way to supply water to the upper levels of Mount Nevermind. The theory was based on the old water-in-the-cheeks trick, only many times amplified. Water is pumped into a tube until the interior pressure of the tube is sufficient to launch a column of water up the central shaft of the mountain, where it is caught by a cauldron swung out from the level requiring water. Different pressures are used to reach different levels. One day, a plumber sent to work on a leaking launch tube unknowingly placed a length of filling pipe inside another launch tube while he worked on the faulty tube, not knowing that the second tube was about to be used. When they launched the water column with the length of pipe inside it, the pipe acted like a stopper. So they continued to pump more water into the tube, trying the free the obstruction. Finally, it went off like a cork from a bottle of gigglehiccup. The pipe penetrated the bottom of the cauldron, which was accidentally (but fortuitously) swung out a moment too soon to catch the water, thus inventing the UAEP and the funnel at the same time."

"Its uses as a weapon were immediately obvious, especially where there is an abundance of water—like aboard a ship," Snork added. "That's why Chief Portlost included the UAEP in the design of *Indestructible*. It should come in handy for battling leviathans, giant squids, velorptamanglers and whatnot."

"That's more like it! I confess, I grow more enthusiastic with such weaponry aboard. How soon do we leave?" Sir Grumdish asked. "And what am I to do with my horse, Bright Dancer?" He stroked the massive beast lovingly on the knee.

"Er . . . I'm sure some useful occupation can be found for your loyal warhorse here in the shipyards," Commodore Brigg answered. "And as for leaving," he added quickly, noting Sir Grumdish's look of dismay, "we don't call it 'leaving' in the Maritime Sciences Guild. You can say 'embark' or 'set sail' or 'weigh anchor' or 'put to sea.' 'Leaving' is a lubberly verb you should break yourself of using. That goes for every and all lubbers. If you are going to be a sailor, you must learn to speak like one. Navigator Snork here will conduct remedial classes in shipboard etiquette and protocol once we are under sail."

Sir Grumdish chewed on that, while Professor Hap raised his hand, as though he were in school. "I have a question. I thought this was a submersible deepswimmer Class C, yet you keep talking about setting sail. How does one use a sail underwater?"

"One doesn't *use* a sail, one *sets* sail, and one doesn't set sail underwater at all. Unless . . ." the commodore's voice trailed off as his brain wheels begin to spin. "A tidal sail, employed underwater to catch the sea currents . . ." he muttered while fumbling at his pockets in search of a pencil.

Seeing his commander thus distracted, Navigator Snork completed his thoughts. "*Indestructible* is equipped with a normal step sail—you can see it there, rising from the conning tower—for use when 'running on top,' as we call it. We shan't always be traveling underwater. In fact, during the trip to the Blood Sea, we'll probably not submerge at all, except for drills. We'll sail on top for most of the way. Of course, Commodore Brigg has developed several improvements to the standard wind and sail design that should shorten the trip considerably."

Returning from his woolgathering, Commodore Brigg said, "So, no more questions? Good. Come. Let's go meet your fellow officers. Sir Grumdish, you can leave your armor with the crane for loading."

Sir Grumdish eyed the crane dubiously as they made their way down the bluffs. There, all manner of activity was underway. Hundreds of gnomes scurried to tasks more numerous and varied than could possibly be identified. Most seemed concerned with the loading and preparation of the *Indestructible*. In addition to the shipwrights, carpenters, and ironsmiths engaged in the building of the various ships, boats, and other fascinating devices of mysterious purpose, there were carters and craters, net weavers and sail hemmers, accountants and bookkeepers and counters of everything from beans to butter tubs. Crates, boxes, and barrels lined the docks awaiting loading by surly, foul-mouthed longshoregnomes. And for every gnome lifting, pushing, pulling, dragging, flinging, hoving-to, clicking-off, checking-out, battening-down and buttoning-up, there were two or three more watching, worrying, directing, misdirecting, or noting the labors of the others. Over, under, around, and on top of it all were the ever-present, watchful members of the Mishaps Guild with their clipboards and surveying equipment. Every movement, every nail hammered and cog oiled was carefully catalogued and recorded in case something unexpected happened, for better or for worse.

As Commodore Brigg led them through this hive of activity toward *Indestructible*'s dry dock, Sir Grumdish's mechanical armor attracted its share of speculative whispers and appreciative exclamations. Behind Sir Grumdish's horse, Professor Hap-Troggensbottle and Razmous

Pinchpocket compared observations, shouting so as to be heard over each other. Navigator Snork ticked off the things he still had left to do before the launch as he walked closely behind Razmous and removed the various interesting objects that unaccountably tumbled into the kender's pouches.

Busy as he was with his musings and kender thwarting, Snork barely noticed the tugging at his sleeve. Only when a brash voice said his name almost in his ear did he turn.

He found before him a younger gnome who was taller than he only by the shock of red hair standing up from the crown of his head. Red hair was most unusual in gnomes, the general rule being white hair or no hair at all, except for the obligatory beard. This one's beard was as red as his hair. The newcomer wore a leather apron and long white pullover with the emblem of the PuzzlesRiddlesEnigmas Etcetera Guild mysteriously affixed—meaning it was not sewn, stitched, embroidered, pinned, or even heat-transferred—over the right breast pocket. His gray eyes had a sort of philosophic inward stare that made him look shy, as though he were trying to avoid meeting the gaze of anyone else because he was busy solving some complex mathematical puzzle, such as trying to compute the volume of an open container. As Snork looked him over, the young gnome looked right back.

Suddenly, Snork slapped himself on the forehead. "Conundrum!" he shouted.

The younger gnome bowed. "Cousin Snork," he answered.

"The last time we met, you were entering your guild back at Mount Nevermind. I see you made it."

"I did," Conundrum answered proudly. "I am now an important member of the Guild of PuzzlesRiddlesEnigmasRebusLogogriphsMonogramsAnagramsAcrosticsCrosswordsMazesLabyrinthsParadoxesScrabbleFeminineLogicandPoliticians—otherwise known as P3 for short, though no one knows exactly why it is called P3 for short, unless it is that there are three words starting with P in it, in which case it might also be called L2, M2, or even A2 for short."

"Hmm, what are you doing here?" Snork asked.

"Didn't you receive my letter?" Conundrum asked.

"Letter? No, I don't recall a letter. How did you send it?"

"By the automated post," Conundrum said.

"Ah, of course, that would be the problem then. What did the letter say?"

"I asked if I could go with you," Conundrum said. His eyes twitched for a moment, and that brief flicker conveyed such an overwhelming flood of desperation that Snork took a step back in surprise. Then he stepped closer and took Conundrum by the elbow, leading him into a narrow alcove between stacks of crates.

When they were alone, Snork leaned close to his cousin and whispered, "What's the matter? Why do you want to go with me on this dangerous mission? Are you in some kind of trouble?"

With each question, Conundrum twitched as though struck with a ruler across the knuckles. He pulled his hands up close to his bearded face, knitting his fingers in an endless weave of nervous energy.

"It's my Life Quest," Conundrum said, "given to me by the Guild—to solve an unsolvable puzzle, to create the world's most unsolvable puzzle. It doesn't matter what kind of puzzle. It could be a puzzle or a maze or a riddle or whatever, the only stipulation being that it must be a true puzzle and not just a question without an answer. And it must be a puzzle with an answer, one which no one could ever possibly find out."

"But no one has invented the unsolvable puzzle yet!"

Snork exclaimed. "How are you supposed to solve it if it hasn't been invented?"

"Yes, I know. You see my conundrum," Conundrum answered.

Snork pondered this for a moment, then asked, "What does that have to do with the voyage of the *Indestructible*?"

"Nothing," Conundrum said.

"Then, why?"

Conundrum's gray eyes locked with those of his cousin. He breathed a sigh that seemed to come up from his shoes. "I have an office in the guild hall, an important office, with a secretary and an assistant. There aren't any books in my office, no maps, no diagrams, not even any paper or a pencil or a protractor. I sit in my office and wait to invent an insolvent puzzle. And I wait. And *wait*. I need to get out and see and do things. No more waiting."

Pity and understanding welled in Snork, and, without another word, he dashed away, dragging Conundrum behind him in pursuit of Commodore Brigg and the others.

Snork and Conundrum caught up with the commodore at the quays as Sir Grumdish's armor was being hoisted aloft by the six-armed crane. Sir Grumdish stood beside his mighty steed, nervously stroking the beast's knee while he watched his armor rise a hundred feet in the air and halt, dangling like a hanged man above the bay. His heart was in his throat, his face as gray as a sun-bleached board.

Commodore Brigg was just introducing everyone to Chief Engineer Portlost, the gnome directing the loading operation, and explaining the chief's Life Quest—to record and detail the most extraordinary mishap the world has ever seen, whenever that might occur.

"I am confident of just such an opportunity on this voyage," Chief Portlost was saying with a toothy grin as he shook hands with everyone. Like the commodore and the navigator, Chief Portlost wore the tarbrush-and-bilge-pump symbol of the Maritime Sciences Guild on his left breast pocket, but on his right breast pocket he wore the upside-down-burning-gnomeflinger emblem of the Mishaps Guild.

"Chief Portlost is our engineer *and* chief mishaps officer," Snork added solemnly.

"Tell them to be careful with my armor, Mr. Mishaps," Sir Grumdish croaked. "He'll come apart with all that jerking and bouncing."

"He will?" Chief Portlost exclaimed. "You mean there's someone inside that armor? Why doesn't anyone tell me these things?" He shouted into the beer mug—they called it a mugraphone—"Carefully, you lot of boot-scrapings! Gently, now! And someone alert the Mishaps Guild! Tell them to be ready!"

Commodore Brigg continued the introductions, "And this, Chief Portlost, is Professor Hap-Troggensbottle, our science officer."

The professor shook the chief's hand so vigorously that it made the zippers jingle on his white jumpsuit.

"Ah, Professor!" the chief greeted just as vigorously in return, rattling his fellow gnome's teeth. "I've heard a great deal about you—only favorably of course. We are glad you'll be coming along for this little jaunt."

"Jaunt? It seemed rather more like a dangerous voyage of weighty consequence, to me," the professor commented huffily.

"Dangerous? Who says so? This ship is sound enough to balance eggs on her deck in a high sea. Two kender and a trained gully dwarf could run her in their sleep—not that I'd let them! And no offense intended to our chief acquisitions officer," he finished with a nod to the kender.

"None taken," Razmous answered with a sly smile.

"Of course you know Navigator Snork and . . ." the commodore paused, looking Conundrum over with an appraising eye. "I'm sorry. Do I know you?"

"Conundrum," Snork said quickly. "You haven't met. Conundrum is my cousin, delegate from the Guild of PuzzlesRiddlesEnigmasEtcetera."

"Come to see us off, eh?" the commodore said as he shook hands with Conundrum. "Should be quite a show."

"Actually . . . that is . . . I, um . . . the guild was wondering if he couldn't sign on with us," Snork said. "It fits in with his Life Quest, you see."

"Really? You don't say," Commodore Brigg said excitedly. "Are you going to solve the riddle of the seven seas? I've been wondering about that appellation for years. I only count four—North Sirrion Sea, South Sirrion Sea, New Sea, and the Blood Sea of Istar."

"What about Courrain?" Razmous interjected.

"Courrain is an ocean, not a sea! Any idiot knows that," the commodore muttered with a fierce glance at the kender. "Besides, that would make only five, wouldn't it?"

"Actually, his Life Quest doesn't really have anything to with the sea," Snork interrupted tentatively.

"No?"

Clearing his throat, Conundrum glanced at those gathered around him—the grim-faced Sir Grumdish, the smiling Razmous, and his encouraging and nodding cousin Snork. Professor Hap-Troggensbottle removed a pair of concave/convex lenses from his breast pocket and perched them on the end of his long nose to scrutinize him, while Chief Engineer Portlost fingered his directing wrench as though preparing to tighten a nut at a moment's notice— or else clout someone over the head.

"So, do tell—what experience have you aboard ships?

What exactly is it that you plan to do, my good gnome?"
Commodore Brigg asked.

"I am very good at waiting," Conundrum answered
forthrightly.

"A waiter?" Razmous asked. "Oh, that will be convenient, having a waiter onboard, bringing us sandwiches and
whatnot."

"No, I wait," Conundrum repeated, interrupting the
kender with a dark look. "I wait until I am inspired," and
then, raising his voice slightly in what he hoped was an
impressive tone, he added, "until it is time to *do* something."

"Hmm, I see," the commodore mused as he stroked his
long white eyebrows. "All that and riddle-solving too. A
most unusual Life Quest. You could prove useful, for we
never know when 'the time' might come. And as luck
would have it, the ship is designed for twenty and we have
only nineteen. You seem more than qualified to fill that
empty seat. Welcome aboard, Ensign Conundrum! You will
be chief officer in charge of, hmmm . . . let's see. How about
seating? Chief Officer in Charge of Seating."

Everyone gathered around to give Conundrum many a
congratulatory smack on the back or tug of the beard,
while the commodore strode about beaming with pride and
trying to hitch his thumbs behind the suspenders he
wasn't wearing. He also checked his watch, then remembered he hadn't invented one yet. When everyone had finished pummeling the newest member of the crew, the
commodore turned to Chief Portlost. "Is everything ready?
How soon can we launch?"

"Not until all my instruments are aboard," a voice
answered him from the ship. Waddling down the gangplank came the owner of the voice—a short, enormously
fat gnome wearing a tight blue jumpsuit stretched over his
rolls and bulges. The gangplank creaked under his mass,

bending dangerously in the middle. "This ship doesn't sail
—or dive or whatever it does—until I, as medical officer,
say so."

"Doctor Bothy," the commodore explained, introducing
him with a gesture. There were nods and handshakes all
around. "His Life Quest is to discover a foolproof cure for
hiccups."

"Hiccoughs, sir! Hiccoughs! Hiccups are child's play.
Why, I could cure your hiccups with a snap of my fingers,"
the portly doctor said, demonstrating beneath the commodore's nose. "Hiccups are commonplace, while hiccoughs have been a mystery to the medical sciences for
generations. Why, if one could cure hiccoughs, one could
cure any number of involuntary spasms of the primary
musculature. Take yawns, for example. Or blinking. I esti-
mate that approximately thirteen hundred gnome hours
are wasted every year with blinking. Imagine the savings,
the increase in productivity, if we could but do away with
blinking!"

"But what about the drying of the orbital surfaces?" the
professor asked with the avidity of a fellow scientist.

"A simple device could be invented, not unlike your
spectacles, which periodically squirts soothing fluids into
the eyes. I should know. I've already invented it," Doctor
Bothy declared humbly.

"Sounds fascinating," the professor agreed.

"A squirting device?" Razmous asked. "Actually, I
think I have something here in pouches that is quite similar, if only . . ." he muttered as he began to rummage
through his pouches.

"Another time," the doctor said with a sharp glance.

"What medical equipment have you still to load?" the
commodore asked with rising impatience.

"Just my Peerupitscope. It is on its way from Mount
Nevermind, but they are having some trouble with the

mule train transportation system," Doctor Bothy said.

"Mules? How quaint! Why don't they use our newer, mechanical transportation systems?" Commodore Brigg asked.

"The Coastandroll is still down for repairs. They are having trouble with the braking system, which, if not resolved, may reclassify the steam-powered rail cars as a system for launching heavy projectiles. The Weapons Guild seems most interested in its applications. Besides, the Peerupitscope is too long to make the corners."

"Can't we get along without it?" the commodore asked. "I am anxious to set sail."

"Why take the risk? The Peerupitscope is an invaluable tool of the medical sciences. With it, we can look into matters previously hidden from our knowledge."

"Oh, very well," Commodore Brigg said as he turned and stalked up the gangplank. "Only remember, we have a schedule to keep. We sail in three days!"

CHAPTER 5

The morning of the launch of the MNS *Indestructible* dawned as bright and clear as anyone who dares the perils of the briny deeps could desire. Not a cloud marred the brilliant blue dome of the sky, and it seemed a fine day for putting out to sea.

Hundreds of gnomes gathered along the bluff overlooking the shipyard where the *Indestructible* waited in the quays. In their midst stood a smallish catapult, newly built for the occasion out of Sancrist yew wood and gnome-forged iron, gilt with silver images of gnomes in flight. The purpose of the machine remained something of a mystery even to those busily examining and commenting on its newest safety features and design improvements. Papers fluttered in the stiffening land breeze as several dozen gnomes attempted to sketch the catapult's more interesting safety devices.

The event had the party atmosphere of a technology fair, the gnomish national pastime. There were banners, flags, and standards of the various representative guilds snapping in the land breeze. The largest contingent was from the Maritime Sciences Guild, naturally enough, but almost as prevalent were the members of the Boilermakers Guild. Important personages from this guild had been wheeled out from the hospital for the occasion, their bandages decorated with ribbons and buttons of every color of the rainbow. The Caterers Guild drove their steam-powered serving trays through the crowd, proffering a variety of savories, prepared by automatic stoves towed behind them and shot out of dispenser tubes at random into the crowd, most of which were nabbed by the hundreds of seagulls swarming overhead.

There was, of course, a wagon of beer parked beneath a nearby tree. In the wagon's traces stood Bright Dancer, Sir Grumdish's doughty steed, who seemed happy enough in his new occupation, if fence posts can be happy. The beer, being the product of a gnomish brewery, packed quite a wallop, enough to satisfy gnomish sensibilities—despite the early hour, many having sensibly already begun—though dwarves might have found the recipe a bit lacking. Luckily, there were no dwarves around to complain.

Indeed there were dwarves watching, but from a safe distance across the bay, and they had their own beer, which they weren't inclined to share. They sat behind a row of tower shields, somewhat apart from the other citizens of the city who had gathered to witness the promised event.

The city of Pax treated the event as something of a spectacle. The citizens thronged the docks—at a respectful distance of course—to watch and wonder at the preposterousness of gnomes. "The ship is supposed to sink on purpose, which means that it won't," was the consensus among the onlookers. Still, the occasion promised to be fun, and wagers were being taken as to how fast the strange-looking vessel would sink, and when it did, how many of the twenty crew members would survive.

JEFF CROOK

A great cheer went up from the gnomish side of the harbor as Commodore Brigg and his crew took their places on the narrow aft deck of the *Indestructible*. Out from the top of the mast rippled the red banner of the Maritime Sciences Guild, crackling in the wind. The crew saluted it, while a band on shore hooted, honked, oom-pahed, and bellowed in a weird cacophony of sound that purported to be an anthem of some sort. It frightened away most of the gulls. The crew remained rigidly at attention throughout the song's ten-and-a-half-minute duration, while the band members, nearly invisible in a jungle of brass, tooted and blew until their faces were quite flushed. When the song wandered off to its broken and disjointed conclusion, it was discovered that three band members had succumbed to asphyxiation, still propped up inside their instruments, some of which required a team of horses to move.

Afterward, Commodore Brigg made a speech, little of which could be heard or even understood by those in the city across the bay—the common gnomish dialect being too compressed and rapidly-spoken for the human ear to comprehend. With much heroic gesturing, the commodore extolled the virtues of the *Indestructible*, from its sleek, shark-like body to its innovations in propulsion and weaponry. He promised that, before they put out to sea, everyone would witness a demonstration of the ship's most remarkable features. To that end, a decommissioned garbage scow had been towed into the center of the bay. They would circle the scow once, then submerge and sink her.

This brought an appreciative round of applause from the crowd of gnomes and indistinguishable noise from the other onlookers. At a shout from the commodore, the crew members scurried to their stations below decks, while Commodore Brigg and Navigator Snork climbed into the conning tower. Now the ship's single mast began to rise, growing taller and taller. When it shuddered to a stop at its full height, Commodore Brigg gave a nod and a wave to the crowd.

Suddenly, members of the Maritime Sciences swarmed around the curious small catapult at the top of the bluff. The dwarves across the bay perked up, smiles splitting their grim beards, while the betting grew hot and furious amongst the humans. Something was loaded into the basket of the catapult, and with a loud *huzzah!* fired at the *Indestructible*.

It missed, splashing in the bay a hundred yards aft. Another was loaded and fired. This missile struck the ship's taut rigging, bounced off with a *twang*, and clouted an onlooker in the forehead, knocking him senseless to the wharf. A pack of gully dwarves swarmed out from their hiding places beneath the pier and looted his body before anyone could say Jack Robinson. A third missile was loaded and fired. This one struck where it was supposed to, shattering against the bow of the ship and dousing its iron hull with a generous splash of golden foamy giggle-hiccup. Third time seemed to be the charm, indeed.

The band struck up a march as the ship slipped from its moorings into the bay. Someone in the crowd set off a volley of gnomish fireworks, which wreaked havoc among the crowd and frightened Bright Dancer from his stupor; he snorted once and galloped away with all the beer. As several gnomes leaped in pursuit, one of the representatives of the Boilermakers Guild, who unfortunately had not locked the brakes on his eight-wheeled chair, got bumped from behind and ended up in the bay.

Meanwhile, Commodore Brigg ordered the MNS *Indestructible* hard alee once clear of docks. She swung slowly round, her iron sides gleaming darkly, like some great whale come up to take a look at the city. Except it was a whale with a stepped mast, up which now rose the ship's sails. Two gnomes scurried to the bow along her footrails to secure the jib to inset stirrup belays—quite ingenious! —while four more raised the boom from the aftdeck and rigged the mainsail and main gaff topsail.

Actually, they didn't need all this sail to make a turn around the harbor, but Commodore Brigg wanted to show off the *Indestructible* under full sail. The fresh breeze carried them past the jetty and well out into the main fjord of Gunthar, and threatened to take them on out to sea, which would have been a public relations disaster. At least they hadn't sunk yet, which was making unhappy the lives of the oddsmakers on shore. The dwarves drank their beer and watched patiently.

They were almost out of sight of the city when Commodore Brigg, tearing at his beard in frustration, ordered all sails lowered. The *Indestructible* handled like a barrel under sail, and he couldn't get the ship turned in the narrow inlet for fear of running her aground. Finally, with all the sheets safely stowed below decks, he ordered the engines powered up and the main flowpellar engaged. The engines were, in fact, large springs, and to power them up one simply turned them by way of a crank until they were tight. Spring engines were found to be much safer underwater than steam engines, even if they did occasionally break their retaining bolts and unwind rather explosively and all at once.

The flowpellar was the large six-bladed fan fitted into the ship's stern. When spun, this ingenious device chopped up the water into a chaotic froth. Since it is a well-established fact—the Natural Philosophies Guild having proven it in their famous 213,000-page treatise on the subject—that Nature abhors chaos, when the flowpellar creates this chaotic froth, the water behind the ship rushes in to still it. At the same time, this wave of water pushes against the stern of the ship, thus imparting forward motion.

Thus the *Indestructible* moved back into the bay under her own power. The gnomes along the shore had recovered the beer wagon, and so they were cheering mightily at the ship's return. Not a few thought she had already completed the voyage for which she had been built. The townspeople of Pax also cheered, especially those who had money riding on a generous time spread before the *Indestructible* sank completely. The dwarves watched patiently.

Commodore Brigg ordered a stealthy assault on the garbage scow. They completed their circuit of the bay and hove-to before the gnomish shipyard, her bow pointed directly at the unsuspecting scow. The commodore ordered all hands below, UAEPs loaded, and Tube One flooded and pressurized. The mast was retracted, leaving only its top third above deck. Navigator Snork ushered the last sailor into the hatch before following himself, leaving the commodore above. With one final wave to the crowd on shore, the skipper stepped into the hatch, climbed down, and secured it behind him. The gnomish band broke into song.

The *Indestructible* lay still in the water, without a sign of life about her. Seagulls settled onto her mast and conning tower, while the waves lapped quietly at her darkly gleaming hull. The band finished its song and the cheering crowd quieted into bemused silence. The dwarves glanced at one another with a knowing glint in their eyes.

Suddenly, the gulls lifted off the *Indestructible*, squawking in irritation. The waters around her sides began to bubble as though she were floating in a pool of gigglehiccup. The ship commenced to sink, slowly and evenly, as if on purpose. As it sank, the flowpellar started spinning, propelling the ship toward its waiting victim. Her nose dipped beneath the surface, dark water rolled over her bow and she descended into the depths bit by bit. Now the pair of fins situated fore of the conning tower started to swim in the air. As the ship sank deeper and the water reached this strange apparatus, its purpose became apparent. The fins swirled in the mounting wave and the nose of the ship dipped even deeper, sending the *Indestructible* into a swift and graceful dive. The water mounted higher, swirling around and then over the conning tower, until all that remained above water was the mast. Suddenly, it, too, vanished beneath the waves, leaving behind hardly a ripple. A trail of bubbles continued toward the garbage scow for a few more seconds until the last bubbles appeared, popped, and were gone.

The crowd waited in breathless anticipation. It seemed improbable if not entirely impossible that the gnomes had actually built something that worked as it was supposed to work. Those who had bet heavily on its sinking gnawed their fingernails, while those who had wagered a copper or two on the ship actually performing as promised made quick mental calculations of the fortunes they stood to receive, and then began to sweat. The dwarves muttered into their beers.

Then a bald brown head appeared on the surface not far from where the *Indestructible* had slipped beneath the waves. It was joined by a second, and then a third, then a dozen, then a narrow, spritely head sporting a bedraggled topknot. For the next few minutes, more gnome heads bobbed up, until the crowd along the shore counted an even twenty. Those who had bet on all the crew surviving made quite a nice return on their wagers, as this had garnered the best odds next to the ship actually working.

Dozens of small fishing craft darted out from the city docks and in less than thirty minutes, the rescue was complete. The gnomes (and their kender companion) were treated to a sumptuous breakfast at the Ring and Feather, a reputable inn not far from the docks, for it was still quite early in the morning and most people were not quite ready to go home yet. The mayor stopped by to offer his condolences, which were graciously accepted by Commodore Brigg despite the fact that he already had a nasty sniffle. The dwarves finished their beers and returned to their forges.

In six weeks' time, the gnomes raised the *Indestructible* and pumped her dry. The problem had lain with the seal around the mast—there wasn't one. Never in gnomish shipbuilding had anyone ever needed to place a seal around a mast, and so they never even thought of installing one, obvious though it seemed upon post-sinking reflection.

So they pumped the vessel out, held an enormous fish fry with all the fish left floundering inside the ship, and replaced all her now-rusted gears, switches, levers, motors, and springs. A few rust spots had also appeared on the gleaming black hull, but these were deemed to give the ship character and were ignored. Members of the original crew who had fled, never to be seen again after the breakfast in the Ring and Feather that inauspicious morning of the *Indestructible*'s first—note: first—sinking, were replaced. Returning crew members were trained to operate the various improvements conceived, designed, created and installed since the ship sank to the bottom of the harbor six weeks before.

The morning of the relaunch of the MNS *Indestructible* dawned brighter and clearer than the first, and it seemed impossible that the sky could be any bluer. Despite the brilliance of the day, there were noticeably fewer attendees watching from the city. The gnomes were there in full regalia, of course, but there wasn't any band, and the catapult that had launched the *Indestructible* with a bottle of gigglehiccup had already been shipped to Mount Nevermind to be put to the use for which it was designed—launching loaves of bread from the Baker's Guild level up to the Dining Hall level. On the city side, the dwarves were noticeably absent, as were the bookmakers and gamblers, who couldn't get odds on the ship's success. A few bums, old salts, seadogs, rummies, and loungers idled around the docks, but the results of the launch seemed such a foregone conclusion that most of the citizens of Pax who desired distraction this fair morning were attending the unveiling of a new marble statue of Gunthar uth Wistan, former grandmaster of the Knights of Solamnia, dead some thirty years. The statue had been erected in the city center by the family of Lady Jessica of Isherwood, herself a Knight of some renown. Even as the *Indestructible* slipped out of the quays, the mayor of Pax was giving a speech honoring Lord Gunthar's achievements, as well as the generosity of Lady Jessica.

Commodore Brigg gave no speech. He wore a dark leather jacket and a leather cap pulled well down over his eyes, hiding the angry coals smoldering there. But the grim set of his white-bearded chin, and the harsh bark of his voice as he ordered the ship on a direct course for the garbage scow still anchored in the midst of the harbor, betrayed his disgust with humans and their fickle ways, as few had bothered to come to see them off.

As the *Indestructible* neared its rusting victim, the gnomes along the shore cheered with new enthusiasm, and their shouts brought something of a smile to Commodore Brigg's face. He ordered both UAEP tubes flooded and pressurized in preparation for firing. Deep inside the ship, things begin to clang and clamor busily. The commodore took aim on the scow, sighting along the lubber's line drawn on the forward rail of the conning tower. He lifted a small flexible tube, blew into it, and then shouted "Prepare to fire!" Something in the bowels of the ship rang out like a struck bell, sending vibrations throughout the ship.

Commodore Brigg placed the tube to his ear, listened for a moment, then put it to his mouth again. As he began to blow, his outpuffed cheeks were suddenly filled with seawater. He dashed the spewing hose from his mouth, coughing and gagging. The stern of the ship began to sink, lifting her bow out of the water. Commordore Brigg opened the hatch to see what was the matter, but this only hastened the ship's demise. Green seawater fountained forth from the opened hatch, bowling the commodore overboard while vomiting out much of the crew along with the water. The *Indestructible* slipped stern foremost beneath the waves, pausing only long enough to launch one of its UAEPs in a concussive explosion and spray of green seawater.

The giant arrow scribed a tremendous arc hundreds of feet in the air across the brilliant blue sky. The people along the docks (and the gnomes) suddenly realized, to their horror, that the projectile was bound to fall to earth somewhere within the confines of the city. Commodore Brigg cringed as he bobbed in the water.

The UAEP descended like a hive of bees, buzzing madly over the first row of warehouses, past streets of homes and businesses, onward and downward toward the city square. It streaked down an alley, slicing through clotheslines strung between the buildings like so many strings of a harp, before passing over the crowd gathered to listen to the mayor's dedication speech. It then struck off the head of the statue of Lord Gunthar, as neatly as an executioner's blade, just as the mayor and the sculptor were triumphantly pulling aside its covering sheet. The head leaped from Lord Gunthar's shoulders in nothing less than complete surprise and landed on the mayor's foot, breaking only his pinky toe, by some strange luck. The giant arrow careened off the statue, passed through the open second story bedroom window of the house of Nathan the Tailor, through the open bedroom door, down the hall, and out the open staircase window without touching a thing or waking any of the occupants of the house. From there, it skipped once off the shallowly-pitched roof of a chicken house, frightening its occupants out of three days' laying before coming to a quivering stop inside the slat wood fences of a pig sty owned by the dwarf Dernbannin—who was busy at his forge next door and heard the whole thing, he would loudly proclaim in the months that followed— and neatly skewering his prized and much-beloved pig, Humphrey. Afterwards, no one could say who squealed the louder: Humphrey, or the mayor with his broken pinky toe.

Meanwhile, out on the bay, twenty-one heads surfaced in the general vicinity of the sunken submersible, greatly defying the odds a second time. Of course, there were only twenty crew members on board at the time she sunk. The extra head belonged to a very angry oyster diver who had nearly been crushed under the *Indestructible* as she settled to the bottom of the harbor. He'd been working the oyster beds, completely unaware that the *Indestructible* was to launch that morning, else he'd have never come within a hundred leagues of the place, he would later declare in court.

* * *

Three weeks later—the gnomes having learned much about re-floating and re-outfitting sunken submersibles after the first time the *Indestructible* sank—Commodore Brigg stood in the conning tower and leaned against the rust-covered aft rail as his ship slipped for the third time from her moorings. *Indestructible*, fully provisioned and stocked with a handsome supply of fresh Humphrey sausages, pulled quietly away from the quay under its own spring-generated power. Its once-gleaming black iron hull was now a dull rust red. Across the bay, the city of Pax slept, for the most part blissfully unaware. Only the mayor and a few of his closest advisers huddled behind a newly-fortified observation post hastily constructed atop a nearby hill, to watch and make sure nothing else untoward happened. The garbage scow had been towed out to sea and sunk a few days before, to remove any last temptation for Commodore Brigg to try to prove the soundness of his clearly unsound submersible design.

But even if it hadn't, the commodore was having nothing to do with further tests or demonstrations. He counted himself lucky that the Knights of Neraka hadn't been around to give him trouble during all the sinkings, and he wasn't about to send for more money to scrape and paint the ship, much less refloat her after another mishap. The ship, such as it was, would have to do, come what may. Besides, he reasoned as only a gnome can reason, if the ship sank one more time, they'd likely have to call off the mission altogether as the ship would rust to bits. 'Twas better not to risk it.

He ordered the ship ahead three-quarters as she cleared the docks. Quietly, in the dead of night, they steered *Indestructible* out of the harbor and into the Fjord of Gunthar. Conundrum joined Commodore Brigg atop the conning tower. He watched the strange white moon of Krynn sink into the dark North Sirrion Sea.

"So that's the sea," Conundrum commented as he leaned against the rail beside the commodore.

"One of them," Commodore Brigg answered quietly.

CHAPTER
6

The *Indestructible* cruised northward with a following sea and a favorable wind for many days and nights. Mount Nevermind, the home of the gnomes, receded in the distance, its great summit the last portion of Sancrist Isle still visible by sunset of the third day of their voyage. Come morning, the gnomes and their kender companion found themselves sailing in the midst of the open ocean.

Many of the gnomes, including a few members of the Maritime Sciences Guild, had never been out of sight of land. They took turns, when duty permitted, coming up on deck and gazing in awe at the great gray rolling sea. Sir Grumdish took one look at the heaving waves and unbroken horizon and turned as yellow as a sheet parchment. Professor Hap-Troggensbottle had been many times to sea in his quest to discover the nature of the buoyancy of very large rocks, so the sights held little wonder for him. But he was often seen above decks collecting buckets of seawater, which he took below to continue his experiments in his cabin. Exactly what he was doing remained a mystery.

Razmous was literally all over the ship during these exciting first days, so much so that some of the crew began to speculate that there were actually three identical kender onboard. In the first days of the voyage, he fell overboard and had to be rescued so many times that he was ordered to wear a pair of large, inflated shark bladders under each arm and a fifty foot rope around his waist, which was fastened to the mast any time he was on deck, under threat of indefinite confinement in the bilge. The next time he fell overboard, they hauled him aboard without having to lower sails and stop the ship. He was wet and bedraggled but keen for another go.

Commodore Brigg and Navigator Snork spent most of their duty time in the conning tower, directing the ship's course, taking navigational readings from the sun and stars, and ordering the trimming of sails as circumstances and winds dictated. When off duty, they plotted (with Razmous's help) their future course beneath Ansalon. Conundrum was invited to attend these high-level sessions, as his training for the Guild of PuzzlesRiddlesEnigmasEtcetera included the study of labyrinthine documents. In these sessions he proved himself a valuable companion, as he was able to sort out the kender's unnumbered and unlabeled maps on more than one occasion.

Razmous's map, drawn by the navigator of the ill-fated MNS *Polywog*, was of hideous complexity—a many-headed hydra of tunnels, passages, dead ends, switchbacks, wells, and caverns, a three-dimensional nightmare that the navigator had rendered onto a series of two-dimensional pages, enough to fill a book. Though the landmarks were carefully noted to exacting standards, the navigator had failed to mark the *Polywog*'s actual course beneath the continent, which seemed to indicate that the map was but a copy of the original. It also meant that, if Snork and Conundrum couldn't unravel the two-hundred page map before they began the undersea leg of the journey, they'd be almost as lost as if they didn't have any map at all. So, as they crossed the North Sirrion Sea and came in sight of Northern Ergoth on the twelfth day, Conundrum, already having shown aptitude, was promoted from his position as chief officer in charge of seating to first assistant cartographer. He had an important task, and felt happy and contented. He moved his bunk into his cousin's cabin, and they stayed up many a night with the kender Razmous, poring blissfully over the tangle of maps by the light of a lamp swaying from an overhead steam pipe.

———◆●◆———

Far across the sea, in the city of Flotsam, in the middle of the common room of the Sailor's Rest, one of the better inns in the city, two men attacked each other with knives. The fight had just begun and people were still leaping over tables and crashing through chairs trying to get out of the way of the two flashing blades. The innkeeper was still in the kitchen, a ladle lifted to his lips to taste the soup, turning his head in surprise at the commotion beyond the door.

The city of Flotsam had been built on a cliff overlooking the Blood Sea of Istar, that great red ocean created when the fiery mountain struck Krynn, destroying the city of Istar and its Kingpriest who, in his pride, demanded of the gods what the hero Huma had received in humility. The city and all the land about it had been blasted into the earth by the anger of the gods, and the sea rushed in to fill the void, creating the Blood Sea. Once, a whirlpool had swirled at its center, a great maelstrom that sucked down any ship that sailed too near. Some said that at the bottom of the maelstrom lay the smashed temple of the Kingpriest and a bottomless chasm that opened directly into the Abyss. But the whirlpool had been quelled almost forty years ago, when the god Chaos was driven from Krynn, taking with him all the other gods.

Flotsam was built at the head of a deep bay of the Blood Sea, at a place where shipwrecks and anything else the maelstrom—or for that matter the rest of Krynn—vomited up, washed ashore. Once a free city, Flotsam now lay within the domains of the great red dragon Malystryx, the most powerful dragon in all of Krynn. Several years ago, she had destroyed the old city, burning much of it to the ground. What remained was but a ramshackle shadow of the former city, a slum of tacked-together shacks and shanties for the most part, with here and there a more permanent building rising from the refuse. The streets and alleys of Flotsam were filled with every sort of ne'er-do-well, brigand, pirate, and cutthroat that Krynn could produce. Mercenaries from Kern, ogres from Blöde, and Ergothian pirates sought work in the galleys and vessels that paid the proper bribes to the proper people and so were allowed to dock alongside the very merchant ships they would pillage and sink should they meet on the open sea. It was all a very nicely organized state of affairs, everything balanced on a knife's edge of fear.

Even so, being one of the more sturdily-built structures in the more respectable part of town, the Sailor's Rest rarely experienced these sorts of disturbances of the peace. This was an inn frequented by those made somewhat more respectable by wealth, no matter how ill-gotten their riches might be, people who subscribed to the pretense of civilized manners even though in practice they employed the selfsame cutthroat behaviors (and the selfsame cutthroats) so common in other parts of the city. A knife fight here among the salvaged and sea-tarnished silver and pirate-looted tableware was a rare occurrence indeed.

Still, most of the patrons of the inn showed an uncanny and unexpected agility in their flight from danger. Only one remained seated, his enjoyment of the excellent baked flounder seemingly undisturbed by the life-and-death struggle taking place mere feet from his table. The two men snarled and circled one another, shifting their knives from hand to hand, seeking some advantage, while he watched them as if watching some farce staged for his own personal amusement.

One of the knife wielders was a semi-successful exporter of cypress lumber, the other a waiter of some years' experience, with an impeccable reputation for discretion. The nature of their dispute was unknown, so suddenly had it erupted. One moment, the waiter was serving the exporter his steamed prawns, the next he was dumping the butter down the front of the man's shirt. It had escalated just as quickly to knives. The waiter's shirtsleeve was torn at the shoulder, the cypress merchant's coat was split neatly down the back from the collar to the hem, so that the two halves swung freely whenever he lunged or dodged, teeth bared.

The man at the table put down his fork and calmly sampled his wine. He wore gray robes decorated at the hem with hermetical symbols stitched in red and gold thread. Though seated, he was obviously a tall man, for his arms stuck well out from the sleeves of his robes as he rested his elbows on the table. His hair, black as pitch and cropped close, complemented the darkness of his eyes.

The two men continued to circle warily, thrusting and feinting, testing one another for an opening. Suddenly, the waiter stumbled into an overturned chair, dropping his defenses for a moment to catch himself against a table. The lumber merchant launched himself with a scream of victory, but the waiter's stumble was a cleverly concealed ploy, for he immediately sidestepped and prepared to catch the unwitting lumber merchant on the tip of his knife.

At that moment, the innkeeper intervened with a stout length of oak, cracking the waiter's knife from his hand with a swift blow to the wrist. He then turned on the merchant and swatted the man across the forehead with his club, felling him before he could recover from his flying leap. A third blow behind the knees swept the waiter from his feet even as he was stooping to recover his dropped blade. His head cracked against the wooden floor.

The man in the gray robes set his napkin on his plate and stood.

"My apologies, Sir Tanar," the innkeeper said in a curious accent. He flashed an oily smile from beneath a thin black moustache. "I am not knowing what has come over these two. They act like some kind of madness has gripped them."

"Don't worry about it," the gray-robed man said. "I would have intervened, but I did not wish to destroy the excellent furnishings of your dining area."

"I am thanking you," the innkeeper said. He motioned violently at the two men sprawled on the floor. Three waitresses and the cook rushed out and dragged them into the lobby. "Of course, this evening's meal shall be compliments of the house."

"I thank you," Sir Tanar said as he casually sucked his teeth.

"It is our pleasure, Master," the innkeeper acknowledged. Bowing once more, he hurried away to welcome and reassure those guests cautiously reentering the room. Waiters and other members of the staff scurried about, righting tables, clearing away spilled dishes, and refilling glasses with complimentary wine.

Sir Tanar made his way from the common room to the lobby and then up four flights of stairs before turning down a long hall decorated with red carpets and paintings of oceanside scenes. At the end of the hall, a window looked out over the docks below. To the left of the window was a door. As Sir Tanar approached the door, his footsteps slowed, for a tiny ringing sound beckoned to him from beyond the door.

His listened for a moment, his head cocked curiously. The bell rang again, insistently.

"Damn!" he swore as he sprinted for the door. He slid to a stop on the rug in front of the door, already fumbling in his pockets for the key. Frustrated, he placed his palm against the door, spoke a single arcane word, and burst the door from its frame, leaving it hanging by one twisted hinge.

He rushed into the room as the ringing grew louder and more urgent than before.

Fumbling at a dresser beside the ornate bed, he jerked open a drawer and removed a wide, flat wooden container like a jewelry box. He turned and dashed the cluttered contents from the top of his desk before setting the box gently on a leather mat, then pulled up a chair, sat on its edge, and opened the box.

Soft black felt covered the interior of the box's bottom and hinged lid. The felt glimmered like a night sky filled with stars, for sewn into the ebon cloth were numerous small clear crystal gems, red garnets, green peridots, and blue aquamarines. In the box's lid was set the magical silver plate he had received a month or so before. Since that time, he had not been yet been contacted as promised, although he had used the object's magic to better his situation in small ways.

Even as he gazed at the plate, the ghostly image of his reflection vanished and the last ringing tones faded. A black darkness appeared in the center of the upright plate, spreading slowly like oil. Nothing could be seen in that darkness, yet he felt something staring at him. He scowled and shifted uncomfortably.

"I have been waiting for you to answer my summons," said a voice that leaped fully formed in the air. Though deep as the roots of a mountain, the cadences, the rhythm, and the demanding tone of the voice was female. But it was strange, distorted, as though spoken over a great distance or from the depths of a deep well.

"Your forgiveness, Mistress," Sir Tanar said as he tilted his head slightly in a bow.

"You know how I dislike waiting," the Voice of the Night continued.

"I was not in my room, Mistress. I was taking some refreshments—" he began.

"You will dine in your room from now on," she interrupted. "I will not be kept waiting."

"Yes, Mistress," he acquiesced reluctantly.

"I am glad to see that you survived my messenger. I shall soon have need of you, Tanar," she continued.

"As you wish," he said.

"You are a Knight of Neraka, Tanar, yet you serve me. What is your loyalty to the Dark Queen?"

"The goddess Takhisis is no longer with this world, nor with us," the Thorn Knight answered. "I am loyal to myself."

The darkness in the platter seemed to grow even darker, if that were possible. Feeling the anger welling from it, Tanar added, "As well as those I have sworn to obey."

"Very good, Tanar," the Voice of the Night said. "You may yet please me in some small way. Still, you must obey the commands of your superiors. That is why I have contacted you. You will be receiving orders from your usual contacts in several days. I will contact you at that time. Meanwhile, I remind you not to abuse the powers of this magical communication device."

"Yes, Mistress," Tanar said, bowing as the darkness in the plate faded. In moments, he found himself looking once more at his own distorted image dimly reflected in the plate's shining surface.

CHAPTER

7

"We should have stopped in Palanthas," Doctor Bothy said. He stood beside Commodore Brigg in the conning tower in the last light of the day.

Fore and aft, gnomes were busy stowing the sheets and dropping anchor. *Indestructible* lay in a calm harbor several hundred yards from shore. Although at first glance it seemed an excellent safe haven for ships, this was but a disguise concealing a lurking danger. Little more than a dozen yards from the bow of the ship, jagged reefs and rocky shoals lay just beneath the placid surface. All around them stood the naked masts of ships that had sailed heedlessly into this place and found their doom. Perhaps they had come here seeking shelter from storms, or concealment from pirates, or perhaps they came in search of fresh water and game. From where the commodore and Dr. Bothy stood, they could count four wrecks, while dark shadows in the depths spoke of numerous others.

This particular stretch of the coastline was one of Ansalon's most desolate. On maps, it was called the Northern Wastes, a vast desert region lying within the domain of the blue dragon Khellendros, home to little more than rock vipers, lizards, and scorpions. Nearer the sea, the land was broken into hills, and here where the warm moist winds blew could be found a few green plants, creosote bushes, palms, and thorny willows clinging to the stubborn soil wherever a trickle of water appeared. Only wild goats, rabbits, and the leopards and desert eagles that stalked them managed to wring a meager existence from this place.

Into the harbor flowed a small river. Down from the surrounding hills it tumbled, white and frothing over the stones. Likely, it had been the sight of cool, fresh water that had drawn the ships into the bay, only to wreck themselves upon the shoals.

Doctor Bothy gazed out over the mirror-flat water at this stream and sighed with longing before continuing. "We are almost out of fresh water," he said.

"I am aware of that," the commodore answered. His attention was focused on the sky and the setting sun. He was waiting for darkness so he could take a star reading and enter their location in the ship's log before retiring for the evening. It had been another hard day of sailing, tacking against the prevailing winds in an effort to reach Thoradin Bay and the port city of Kalaman.

This leg of the journey had taken longer than the commodore had expected, for the winds were blowing more strongly out of the north than was usual for this time of the year. They had made good time for the most part, sailing without incident around the tip of Northern Ergoth, then crossing Zeboim's Deep to the peninsula known as Tanith. Much to everyone's dismay, especially Dr. Bothy, they did not then turn south and visit the fabulous port of Palanthas, City of Seven Circles, gleaming jewel of the old Solamnic Empire. Dr. Bothy had long looked forward to sampling the city's gastronomic offerings, while most everyone else on board simply wanted to get off the ship and visit the greatest city in all Ansalon, especially Razmous, who had passed through and been expelled from Palanthas more times than he could count. Conundrum had never been out of Mount Nevermind in his entire life, so this entire voyage was a wonder and a mystery to him. The world was far larger than he had ever imagined.

Instead, they had sailed due east, crossing the mouth of the Bay of Branchala in the early hours of the morning, while most of the crew crowded the deck, hoping for a glimpse of the city. But they passed the rocky headland an hour after sunrise without spotting even a twinkle of a lamp or glimmer of sunlight off a golden dome or marble tower. Palanthas slipped away, hidden behind the Vingaard Mountains marching up from the south.

Their course took them eastward until they reached the coast of the Northern Wastes. There, they had turned north, and their troubles and delays began. The wind was blowing hard out of the north, raising the seas in anger, and the ship climbed the swells and tacked back and forth across the face of the wind. Day after day they had fought their way along the coast, finding rest at night in bays and inlets and natural harbors, rather than dropping anchor in uncertain and wind-swept waters. Meanwhile, their supplies had dwindled.

"Of course, fresh water isn't too great a concern," Dr. Bothy commented. "After all, I still have plenty of my fresh water tablets." He reached into a pocket of his tight blue jumpsuit and removed a small brown bottle, inside which rattled several dozen tiny pills. "When I made these, I was trying to invent a pill to remove fresh water from seawater, leaving behind only the salt. With such pills, I could have cornered the salt market. However, they worked in the opposite manner, removing the salt instead, and leaving the water fresh and drinkable. We need only draw a barrel of sea water and drop one of these pills into it, and hey!" He rattled the bottle for emphasis. "Presto! Fresh water."

"Most ingenious," the commodore said with a bored little yawn. He'd been reminded of the doctor's invaluable fresh water pills at least a dozen times since leaving Sancrist. Bothy had an almost kenderish tendency to repeat his favorite stories, especially when he was the hero of said stories, but Commodore Brigg tolerated him because he was a doctor with remarkable deductive abilities and scientific acumen. Even if his Peerupitscope had proved too big to peer up much of anything.

"No, it isn't fresh water that concerns me," Doctor Bothy continued as he tucked away the bottle of pills. He leaned closer to the commodore and whispered. "It's the crew. Moralc is flagging."

Commodore Brigg snorted in derision and angrily stroked his white whiskers. "Ever have leaders been plagued by the bellyaching of those they lead!" he growled. "They'll cheer up once this north wind shifts."

The doctor shook his head. "If we had stopped in Palanthas, this wouldn't have happened, no matter how the wind blows. They've been sailing for weeks without a break in the monotony of their sailorly duties. Only this morning, I had to treat the cook for severe burns after he tried out a new stove that he has been designing—a strange device, but it has great possibilities once he discovers a way to contain the explosion. He calls it a flashcooker. But when he lit it, it blew the door off and flashcooked the cook rather than the flatbread he was trying to bake."

"So that's what that noise was," the commodore said. He had not paid much attention to the explosion, because explosions aboard gnomish vessels are fairly common and are generally ignored unless followed by something else, like a massive inrush of water.

"Yes. You see, Commodore, I fear . . ." He leaned closer still, so that his full, bearded lips tickled the commodore's ear. "I fear even the kender is becoming *bored!*"

Suddenly, the hatch at their feet flew open, and Professor Hap-Troggensbottle climbed out. He kicked the hatch shut with a clang and turned on the commodore. "Sir, you really must do something about Razmous!" he hissed so that the gnomes working above deck to prepare the ship for night watches wouldn't hear.

"See what I mean?" Doctor Bothy nodded, thumbing his bulbous nose.

Commodore Brigg frowned at the doctor, then turned to the professor and asked, "What has he done this time?"

With a deep sigh, Professor Hap groaned, "I found him in my cabin again, going through my things. He claimed to be trying to return my combination slide-rule-and-nose-hair-clippers, but he very nearly ruined a delicate experiment."

"I will say something sharp to him," the commodore said as he turned back to his skygazing.

"If you can get a word in edgewise," the doctor mumbled.

"You can talk until your beard grows to your belt, words will not dissuade a bored kender," the professor warned. "Of all the punishments devised by man, elf, dwarf, or ogre," he added, "few rival the sentence of being shut up in an enclosed space—for example, a deepswimmer submersible—with a bored kender."

"What do you suggest I do, my dear gentlegnomes?" Commodore Brigg turned and said. "There isn't another port until we come to Kalaman."

"Send a party ashore to explore and collect fresh water from yonder stream," Doctor Bothy suggested. "Give the others a day of relaxation. This is a fine place, the water is warm and still. They can swim, wash their linens and uniforms in the stream, and there are some wrecks. Perhaps they can explore those."

"I begrudge even a day's delay, for we are already

behind schedule," Commodore Brigg answered. "Besides, this is the worst possible place for swimming and exploring. Probably you haven't noticed, but these waters are filled with sharks. We can't approach yonder shore in this ship because of the reefs, and we don't have a dinghy or other vessel to go ashore in." Placing his arms round their shoulders, the commodore drew his two companions closer. "I have already taken all these matters into consideration," he whispered. "Trust my sage experience."

"My apologies," the professor said, bowing.

"S-sir . . ." Doctor Bothy stammered.

"Ahem, I appreciate your concern, but leave the sailing to the members of the Maritime Sciences Guild. The crew will have to grit their teeth and struggle onward. This is no place for a shore leave," the commodore finished.

"Indeed, I bow to your wisdom," Professor Hap offered in a docile tone, before raising one eyebrow and adding provocatively, "but after working all night, I have invented an option that is bound to intrigue even you, my captain."

"Commodore," Brigg corrected with a grunt, looking intrigued.

"I have been dying to try these underwater uniforms out," Professor Hap-Troggensbottle whispered to Doctor Bothy as they stood in the conning tower the next morning. The sun mounted the sky beyond the eastern hills from which the white stream flowed and tumbled. "I perfected them only last night, but I have been working on them, in secrecy, for several days."

The doctor nodded and leaned over the rail to observe the activities on the aft deck. The commodore had called an assembly of all hands, and now the deck was crowded with every member of the crew, not counting the doctor and the professor, who observed from above. Fifteen gnomes—most wearing the red jumpsuits of the Maritime Sciences Guild—and one green-vested kender jostled elbows and tried to arrange themselves into a line under the directions of Commodore Brigg, who strode the deck dressed in a tight-fitting suit of grim black with gold braids at the sleeves. He pointed and directed with a white cane carved from a whale's tooth, and his tall crested black hat with its red plume nodded as though in emphasis of each shouted command.

The twentieth member of the crew stood apart from the others, but not by choice. The original color of his uniform was indiscernible under the coating of black grease that seemed to cover every inch of his diminutive body, even his shaggy unkempt beard and long pointed nose. He was shorter than any of the other gnomes—even shorter than Conundrum, who stood closest to him and held his nose. The whites of his eyes blinked out of the greasy black of his face as he stared about him in awe or squinted at the rising sun. He was surrounded on all sides by at least five feet of empty deck, for he smelled abominably. Not even the wholesome odor of axle grease and gear oil could quite cover up the stench of gully dwarf.

"Who is that one?" the professor asked of the gully dwarf. "I haven't seen him before. Where has he been hiding?"

"Ensign Gob," Doctor Bothy answered. "He keeps the ship's gears properly oiled and greased. He is so small he fits nicely into the deepest workings of the ship. His bunk is in the bilge, and he's not allowed into the inhabited parts of the ship, usually. That's why you haven't seen him."

Finally, the crew was lined up to the commodore's satisfaction. He thumped his cane on the deck to get everyone's attention, then strode over and hopped atop a large, leather chest that had been brought on deck. Beside it lay a wooden case not unlike the kind used to store weapons for long sea voyages, and beside this an ordinary water barrel filled with ballast stones. All eyes turned to the commodore.

"I have called all of you on deck because I have decided to allow Professor Hap-Troggensbottle to conduct an experiment," Commodore Brigg announced. At these words, an excited whisper rolled down the line of crew members.

"As you can see, getting ashore is no easy matter. We have no side boat, nor can we risk taking the ship through those reefs. We might swim, but it is a long way to shore, and these waters are infested with sharks." Suddenly, all those eager smiles became thin with concern, and no one, except Razmous, would meet the commodore's gaze.

"Professor Hap-Troggensbottle has come up with a solution that should prove . . . interesting. Professor, if you wouldn't mind explaining?" the commodore prompted.

The professor nodded and climbed down from the conning tower. He approached the leather chest and threw back its lid. Despite their reservations, what with the talk of reefs and sharks and all, the gnomes leaned a little forward to better see what surprises were inside. Razmous, breaking with all naval discipline, stepped completely out of line and stood on his toes.

The professor removed from the opened chest several items and laid them out carefully on the deck. "Gather round," he said. "Everyone take a look."

First there was a large round glass fish bowl, but it didn't look like it would hold water as it had a long tube projecting from the bottom. Next came a tiny jumpsuit of some glossy black material. It looked far too small even for a gnome. After this, the professor removed a sort of backpack that contained a large, silvery fish's bladder. Last of all, grunting with exertion, he pulled out a pair of very large shoes, which thumped noisily as he dropped them to the deck.

During all this, he was assaulted by a barrage of questions. The shoes, the fish bowl, and tiny black jumpsuit excited everyone, but the hose sticking out of the top of the fish bowl drew the most attention, its purpose obscure to even the most imaginative theorists. Meanwhile, Razmous discovered that the chest contained several more identical objects.

As the hubbub died down and everyone returned his attention to the professor, he gathered up his unusual items. "I will explain the function of each in turn," he said. "If I might have a volunteer."

Razmous eagerly stepped forward, but the professor instead turned to Conundrum. "You are the smallest—er, the youngest," he said. "Might I trouble you?"

"Please," Conundrum acquiesced.

"First the suit," the professor said, handing Conundrum the tiny black jumpsuit.

Conundrum dubiously eyed the outfit as he took it from the professor. It appeared barely large enough for a small gnomish child. However, the material proved most unusual, springy and elastic to the touch, like the belly of a frog. Conundrum stripped out of his leather apron and white under-robe, then with the professor's assistance and guidance he stepped into the black suit, pulling it up from the legs, then over his back and shoulders, and working his arms into the sleeves. Amazingly, it fit, the material stretching to almost double its previous size to accommodate his gnomish physique, until only his hands and his bearded head were left uncovered. He looked like he had been dipped in dark chocolate and set out to harden into candy.

"This material will keep the body quite warm," the professor explained. "Though snug, it allows for full range of movement." Snug it was indeed, embarrassingly so. Conundrum was only glad there weren't any female gnomes aboard. Even so, Razmous could not stop giggling at his bulgy protuberances. Conundrum's face turned quite red, almost as red as his beard.

Next, Conundrum donned the backpack, which the professor called a bladderpack, and the professor set the fish bowl over his head. The hose stood straight up out of the top of the glass, falling down over his shoulder. Professor Hap took the hose and connected it to the fish bladder in the bladderpack. The bottom of the fish bowl was then sealed to the black jumpsuit with a ring of similar black material. A buckle allowed it to be tightened until no air could escape around his neck.

With each breath, the fish bladder on Conundrum's back inflated and deflated. Now, the other gnomes could see that as the bladder expanded, pleats along either side opened up, revealing a mesh of crimson material.

"How is that?" the professor asked. To Conundrum, his voice sounded strange and distant, as if he were speaking out of a cave.

"A little stuffy," Conundrum repeated. His own voice sounded as if he were speaking with his head inside a large bell, which was not very far from the truth. To those outside, his voice was muffled but hollow, as if he had fallen down a well.

"The bladder and the sealed fish bowl allow the wearer to breath underwater, by way of the pleats, which act like the gills of a fish, drawing in water and transforming it into breathable air," the professor said. "Of course, it has never been tested when fully immersed, but the theory is sound, so it should work."

The gnomes began to nod and talk. They now saw the full extent of the possibilities of this apparatus. Not only could it be used for undersea exploration, it could also prove advantageous anywhere there was an undesirable overabundance of water, such as inside a clogged sewer, flooded mineshaft, drowned wine cellar, or, for that matter, a sinking ship.

Last of all, the professor had Conundrum step into the large shoes. He called them duckfeet, and they did indeed look rather like the natural paddles of a large waterfowl. When Conundrum tried to move, he found his feet firmly planted to the deck. Only by tremendous effort was he able to lift even one foot.

"The duckfeet are lined with lead, to help you sink to the bottom," the professor explained. "That way you can walk wherever you need to go, without the bothersome need to swim."

Everyone clambered for an opportunity to try out the professor's invention. Although it had no moving parts —those would likely come later, as improvements were designed—the underwater uniform seemed a wonderful innovation. Everyone thought so, that is, except Chief Engineer Portlost, who found the entire thing rather fanciful. Actually, he was thoroughly jealous for never having come up with the idea himself.

All told, there were only six suits to go around. Commodore Brigg solved the problem by assigning the first party to go ashore. Because he was already suited, Conundrum would go, along with Sir Grumdish, in case they met any creatures of hostile intent. Unfortunately, Grumdish would have to go armorless; his knightly uniform wouldn't fit inside the "frogsuit"—the professor's name for the ingenious elastic-skinned underwater garb.

Much to his chagrin, Chief Portlost was chosen next. He acted as if he had no doubts that they would all drown the moment they stepped overboard. The commodore reminded him that his Life Quest was to record and detail the most extraordinary mishap the world has ever seen, to which the chief replied as the fish bowl was being placed over his head, "Yes, but I must live long enough to record it! And we have yet to invent the pen that can write underwater."

Next, surprisingly, the commodore chose Razmous Pinchpocket. Well, not surprisingly. The kender had been hopping on one foot trying to attract the commodore's attention the entire time, all the while pointing at himself and crying in a tiny voice, "Oh, pick me! Please pick me." He was out of his pouches, green vest, and leather leggings before the commodore could finish pronouncing his name and, even more astonishing, assigning him the command of the expedition.

"Me? Commander!" Razmous squeaked, almost forgetting for a moment his delight at being allowed to try on the frogsuit, the inside of which he described as being "all squooshy," accompanied by a sour expression that wrinkled up his nose and squinted his bright periwinkle eyes.

"You are chief acquisitions officer, are you not?" the commodore barked. "You are in charge of all supply expeditions. You didn't think you were coming along just for the fun, did you? This is the first land reconnaissance of the MNS *Indestructible*, the first use of Professor Hap-Troggensbottle's marvelous new invention, the frogsuit, and the first test of your leadership."

"Of course!" the kender said, as seriously dutiful as he could. Then, when the commodore turned to assign the last two members of the expedition, he whispered to the professor, "Still, it's gonna be fun."

To fill out the shore party, Commodore Brigg chose ensigns Merliguttal and Wigpillow, for they were the two largest gnomes on the ship, the strongest and the most capable of carrying the large barrel he was sending with them to collect fresh water. However, Ensign Merliguttal proved much too large to fit into the last frogsuit. In fact, the suit would hardly come up to his waist, and only then after it was stretched almost to splitting. The professor admitted that he had run out of material and so had to make a smaller suit.

In the end, the only member of the crew small enough to fit into this small suit was Ensign Gob, the gully dwarf, and he was none too keen about allowing the gnomes to stuff him into the slithery garb. Loudly and vehemently he proclaimed, "Stinks unnatural!" Clearly, he thought they were feeding him to some kind of small black creature that was all mouth, for he screamed and wailed, thrashed and bit, as only a cornered gully dwarf can. Luckily, Doctor Bothy had plenty of anti-infection ointment, as gully dwarf bites can sometimes prove lethal if not properly treated.

He seemed to calm somewhat once the fish bowl was placed over his head. Perhaps it was the closeness of his own body's odors crowding inside the glass helmet that made him think of his gully dwarf warren and took his mind off the strangeness of his predicament. Or perhaps it was the duckfeet keeping him firmly rooted to the deck, unable to run. In any case, something resembling a smile spread through the thick, greasy mat of his beard. Then he fainted. Professor Hap had tightened his neck seal a bit too much, probably on purpose. Once loosened, he awoke in a better humor. "Do again," he requested, pointing at his throat.

They lined up along the edge of the deck, six in a row, and a queerer, more outlandish lot had never before been witnessed on the face of Krynn. They looked like something from another world, with their tight black suits and glass helmets, and backs swelling and deflating with each breath.

"What about the sharks?" Sir Grumdish asked, his voice sounding tiny inside his helmet.

"Yes, what about the sharks?" Chief Portlost concurred.

"You haven't forgotten about the sharks, have you?"

"Of course not," Professor Hap said as he stooped and opened the small, flat weapons box. From it, he took a strange device that set every gnomish heart palpitating with excitement. Its conglomeration of hoses and tubes, and its dangerous pointy end, looked most promising indeed.

"What is that?" Razmous asked, intrigued.

"UANP," the professor answered. "Underwater Arrow of Normal Proportions. It works on the same principle of the UAEP, except it is considerably smaller. The arrow is loaded here—" he pointed to the dangerous end where a large steel arrowhead protruded. "Water is pumped in through the hoses using this hand pump," he demonstrated, cranking out one of the tubes and pressing it back into place. He handed the weapon to Sir Grumdish, who eyed the strange device with an appraising glance. He hefted it and aimed along the length of the tube at a shark-like shadow passing near the ship.

"The firing mechanism is here," the professor said, pointing at a large red button on the side. "Be careful, though. You have only one shot, and I've had time to build only three." So saying, he distributed the other two weapons to Chief Portlost and Ensign Wigpillow.

"Gentlegnomes and kender," Commodore Brigg intoned solemnly, addressing the members of the shore party. "Go with the blessings of Reorx, wherever he may be." He saluted, thumping himself on the forehead and chest, then tugging his beard. The others returned the salute to the best of their abilities, banging their fists against their glass helmets. With a muffled scream, Ensign Gob tumbled overboard and sank out of sight.

CHAPTER
8

Conundrum quickly—or as quickly as one can while wearing a thirty-pound shoe on each foot leaped overboard and followed Ensign Gob to the bottom. He feared that the gully dwarf might panic and try to tear off his glass helmet. But as he sank, he felt a similar terror building in his chest, which he struggled to control while at the same time feeling an almost overwhelming sense of marvel and wonder at seeing the mysterious depths of the sea. He had expected everything to be dim and murky, and indeed everything in the distance was lost in a gray-blue haze, but the things closest to him—the lacy fronds of coral, the billowy puffs of pale white jellyfish, the swirling clouds of tiny silver fish, and even the occasional grim-toothed shark cruising the reef's outer edges—appeared as distinct as though cut from paper and pasted to the outside of his helmet.

For the first twenty feet of his descent, he held his breath, half from fear, half from awe, until he noticed a trail of bubbles rising up from beneath him. Glancing down, he saw the gully dwarf spiraling away below, arms wagging above his head. From the gully dwarf's bladderpack, the cloud of bubbles was spreading upward. Conundrum passed through the bubble-cloud, experiencing for a moment a queer tingling sensation, as if he were submerged in a glass of tricarbonated water (one of Doctor Bothy's more recent attempts at a cure for hiccoughs). The fancy passed, and then he purposefully exhaled and created his own cloud of bubbles. He craned his head around inside the helmet to watch them ascend, and saw the duck-feet of his four companions not very far above his outstretched hands. The surface of the water, seen from below, glimmered like a pool of quicksilver, and the *Indestructible* hovered above them all, like a huge, dark whale pausing for a breath of air.

A thump from below caught Conundrum's attention. It was the gully dwarf, plumping down awkwardly in a puff of sand. Conundrum flapped his arms to keep from landing atop the gully dwarf. He settled to the bottom and quickly shuffled aside to make room for the others. Once submerged, his shoes didn't feel quite so heavy as they had on board the ship. He gave Gob a reassuring smile and reached out to pat him on the shoulder. Gob, his eyes bugged-out either in wonderment or fear, gave a tentative smile back.

The others floated down around him like so many strange birds in a dream, arms a-flutter to guide their descent. Their faces looked blue inside their helmets, and Razmous's topknot dangled in his face. The kender expedition leader puffed and blew and crossed his eyes, but to no avail; his hair insisted on tickling his nose.

"I wonder if I can get my hand up inside my fishbowl," the kender said as he squirmed and tried to withdraw one arm into his frogsuit. Strangely enough, everyone could hear him, even if it did sound as if he were talking through a pillow. When he spoke, his words were accompanied by an outrush of bubbles from his bladderpack.

"I wouldn't do that if I were you," Chief Portlost warned. The chief was more than a little green around the edges of his beard, and his eyes looked large and bulging with fear behind his glass helmet.

"Why not?"

"Let's just get to shore and stop the nonsense," Sir Grumdish snarled as he fingered his UANP and eyed a shark that had approached to investigate the strange new visitors to its territory.

"We can't go without—" Razmous began, but then a large barrel filled with ballast stones dropped on his foot. Only his heavy, lead-lined duckfeet shoes prevented broken toes.

Conundrum unhooked the rope used to lower the barrel from the ship, while Sir Grumdish and Ensign Wigpillow tipped it off the kender's foot. They rolled it over on its side and dumped out enough of the ballast stones to make it float, buoyed by its wooden slats. It hovered in the water before them, as though in a dream. Ensign Gob was assigned to push it.

They set out, climbing up a long winding valley between two towering coral reefs. A modest current pushed against them as they walked, and their heavy boots made for slow going. The seafloor here was of old gray coral, ground away by the steady current of the inflowing stream, while white sand filled all the reefs' hollows and crevasses. Wherever there was sand, there were small dark spiny urchins, like little pincushions dropped by some seamstress in her fright, and sometimes they came across an old bare bone, or part of a skull, sticking up out of the sand. Razmous found a bony finger with a glimmering golden ring still dangling from it, but he had no pouches in which to tuck it away for safe keeping.

To either side, long valleys lay between the reefs, stretching back into the blue haze like aisles in a darkened temple. In these, they came across the wrecks of ships. Some were ancient and wormeaten, half overgrown by the wild luxuriant coral. Others appeared newly sunk. Were it not for the jagged holes in their sides or bows, they might even now be running before the wind in some faraway sea. Seeing the dark gaping mortal wounds of these ships filled everyone except the kender with a strange loathing and horror, as if by looking too long they might glimpse the pale cold corpse of some doomed sailor peering out, his flesh pecked by fishes, his eyes still staring wide at some ancient peril. They hurried on as quickly as they could.

Still, there was many a marvel to behold, and despite the sharks, the greatest danger they faced was losing their leader to an aqueous version of wanderlust. Luckily, Razmous still had on his lead shoes, or he might have escaped them altogether and vanished down some dark coral cave where giant eels were waiting to devour him. Surely few other kender had ever seen anything quite so marvelous and lived to tell the tale.

Yet all found themselves filled with an almost kenderish childlike delight. They saw jellyfish that so resembled the underside of a Palanthian lady in her hoop skirts and frowsy pantaloons that Conundrum blushed to see them and nearly fogged up the inside of his helmet. In a deep coral grotto, Razmous pointed out a giant clam that could have easily swallowed him whole, and very nearly did. They saw corals and fish of every size, shape, and description, from huge man-swallowing anemones to finger-long shrimp that carried tiny hammers instead of claws. The shrimp beat these minute weapons against the stone with a startling crack whenever anyone approached too closely. Colors were strangely muted, but their eyes quickly adjusted and began picking up subtle variations in the grays and blues of corals that were almost as beautiful as if they had been vibrantly alive with every color of the rainbow.

What interested them most were the sharks. There were dozens of them, of every shape and kind. They saw the long, flat docile kind that were nearly invisible against the sand, and only spurted away when you were almost stepping on them. They saw the square-snouted toothy kind that circled them endlessly, perhaps wondering if frogsuited gnomes—and kender, but likely not gully dwarves—were good to eat. But mostly there were the small, thin ones than moved through the water like dragonflies in a lazy summer glade in the woods. These had white tips on the ends of their fins, and long curved tails like pirate swords. Once, they spotted a monstrously big shark, but it ignored them, swimming slowly over their heads with its toothless maw gaping wide as a beer barrel. It disappeared into the bluish haze of distance, headed out to the open sea on business of its own.

Nevertheless, and despite the distractions, they eventually reached shallower water. The light grew by stages brighter and less blue, and things about them began to take on color. The sand, they found, was not white but a peculiar shade of tan, like the hide of a lion. In the shallows they encountered numerous skates and huge dark rays like magical underwater flying carpets. There were also a good deal more of the square-nosed toothy sharks, and these were more aggressive or curious than their reef cousins. They swam closer, and one even bumped Sir Grumdish from behind. Perhaps it smelled his fish bladder breathing apparatus. Certainly the six divers did. They had all had their fill of its faint but nonetheless fishy odour, and were none too glad to unstrap their helmet seals and breathe fresh air again once they had come safely to the shore. They clambered out of the surf and collapsed on the beach, dragging their water barrel after them. Ensign Gob stumbled all over his duckfeet, fell facedown on the sand, and couldn't get back up. Conundrum tried to help the gully dwarf, only to have him slip through his fingers like melted butter and fall onto his back. The gully dwarf lay there, thrashing like an overturned turtle.

"What's the matter with Gob?" Razmous asked.

"He's like a wet bar of soap," Conundrum answered as he struggled to lift the gully dwarf to his feet. "I can't get hold of him. Help me."

Together, they managed it, but only by lifting Gob by his helmet. When wet, their frogsuits exuded some peculiar, odorless oil, probably to help the diver slip more easily through the water. But once dry, the suits returned to their normal—if it could be called normal—rubbery state. Conundrum and Razmous helped Gob out of his lead shoes.

Once they had all removed their helmets, duckfeet, and bladderpacks, the five intrepid explorers—and the gully dwarf—gathered around the upended barrel. Three hundred yards from shore, the *Indestructible* appeared as a dark hump in the water, crawling with activity. Inland, the silent hills rose up wave upon shingled wave. Where the stream cut through them, a wide band of greenery crowded either bank, softening the grim browns and stony grays. In the sand of the beach were the deep, cloven hoofprints of numerous goats, as well as what appeared to be the soft pugmarks of a prowling leopard.

"I say we get our water and be gone," Chief Engineer Portlost said warily, taking the initiative. "The stream is as fresh here as it is inland. No use hauling that barrel over hill and dale when water is close at hand." He had not been pleased at the sight of the leopard footprints, and besides, he didn't like land anyway. He was a seafaring gnome, and had spent the last half of his life walking the heaving decks of ships at sea. Being ashore made him nervous.

"Nay, we should explore a mite," Sir Grumdish said, "discover the lay of the land, and search for fresh meat. We've all the day before us, plenty of time to set some snares and try to catch a sheep or two. I know I'd not turn my nose up at a bite of broiled mutton, no offense to Cooky's skillet meat, may his burns heal swiftly."

Though he had brought neither sword nor dagger, the UANP weapon gave Sir Grumdish a comforting sense of security. He did not doubt the device's ability to skewer a beastie at a hundred paces, and he was simply dying to fire it at something, be it shark a-sea or leopard ashore. Or even a large and rather famous blue dragon, if it came to that. He had not forgotten that they were now within the domains of Khellendros.

"I agree," Conundrum said. "We do have all day."

Razmous smiled as he shrugged off the shoulder straps of his bladderpack. "Well, you know how *I* feel, and as Commodore Brigg placed *me* in command of this expedition, *I* say we have a look around. Agreed?"

Chief Portlost muttered some expletive about putting a kender in charge and flung off his bladderpack. The rest followed his example, except Ensign Gob, who had not even removed his glass helm, for he seemed to enjoy inhaling his own vapors. He left his helmet seal tightly cinched, baring his teeth at anyone who offered to help him out of his diving gear. The morning sun was already growing hot on their black frogsuits, and they gazed with longing at the cool shade promised by the gently swaying palms and tall hedges of thorny willow.

The stream leaped and tumbled over the hills' sun-bleached stones, gushing in torrents over small falls, or flowing deep and cold through still forests of tall reeds. Its water was icy cold, indicating that it probably emerged from some spring deep in the hills rising to the east. It entered the sea down a long ebullient fall of many steps, so that the sea's tides could not enter and make the water brackish. But farther inland, it paused in its journey to spread in a wide bean-shaped green pool bordered by papyrus reeds along its curving shore. On the side on which the five intrepid explorers—six, counting their gully dwarf—found themselves, the land sloped down swiftly through willow forests to the lake's deep shores.

Here, in a sheltered, sunlit cove, they discovered a sight that filled them with wonder and curiosity, if not a niggling twinge of fear. High in the forest where they hid, they could not be seen, and so they stood and watched it without fear of discovery. But still, it was such a horrid thing, they could not help but feel a quickening of the pulse and a tightening of the chest.

Except, of course, for Razmous. Kender are born without the self-preserving instinct of fear. A monstrosity such as this was nothing less than an opportunity for grand adventure. Even if it did have three large, egg-shaped eyes—the largest one in the middle of its forehead—and a single scythe-like horn sweeping back from the center of its skull. Even its skin was flaming red, and steam rose around its thighs where it stood almost hip deep in the lake. Still, for a kender that was no reason not to creep closer for a brief examination of the creature. Even if it was easily sixteen feet tall, with legs like tree trunks and biceps as big as the average dwarf, that was no reason to assume even more interesting details couldn't be spotted upon nearer inspection.

"Come on," Razmous whispered to his companions. "We'll be very stealthy."

He was creeping away on his tiptoes before anyone could object. The others followed with a great degree of trepidation. Sir Grumdish shook and chattered his teeth like a frightened child, all desire for testing the UANP vanished from his mind—upon reflection, the weapon appeared woefully inadequate. They edged far too close to those enormous bloodshot eyes (one of which was always scanning its surroundings), flapping ears, and piggish nostrils—and especially its prognathous out-thrust jaw with its goblinoid tusks dripping with saliva that hissed when it struck the water.

But the monster had not heard, scented, or seen them. Perhaps their black frogsuits blended with the shadows of the forest or covered their scent sufficiently, or perhaps the monster was too busy with its own activities to notice them. It seemed most intent on something in the water. It stood still as a stone, only its massive chest swelling with each breath, as it eyed something in the water.

Suddenly, it dove after some fish or other creature, chasing it round and round the pool with much noisy thrashing and angry snarling. So huge was the monster that its violence sent huge waves crashing half way up the bank to the explorers' hiding place. It smashed the water with its gigantic black-clawed hands, lunged this way and that, angrily snapped its jaws, and plunged beneath the surface, revealing a broad back studded with bony protrusions.

"What is that thing?" Conundrum whispered in awe.

"Probably a chaos beast," Razmous answered. "All sorts of strange monsters were born from the Chaos War. Probably, he's attracted to this area because of the shipwrecks. It's a fact that shipwrecks often—"

At that moment, the beast surfaced, its three eyes smoldering and its claws empty. It glared around at the surrounding forest, its flat, piggish nostrils testing the air currents. The gnomes held their breath, the gully dwarf cowering behind them. But the fearless kender crept another step closer.

Though Razmous made no sound, the monster suddenly crouched, all three eyes swiveling around to probe the dense underbrush where the gnomes hid.

"Who is there?" it howled in a voice that was somewhere between the rumble of a crocodile and the bellow of a charging bull. The smaller trees shook at the volume of its voice. Out on the *Indestructible*, everyone suddenly looked up in wonder at the strange noise.

"Who is there?" the monster demanded again. It took a step back and crouched low in the water. "You might as well show yourselves. You can't escape me. My three eyes are sharper than an eagle's, my nose more sensitive than a hound's. I can hear the heartbeat of a mouse at a hundred paces, or the water passing through a fish's gills at ten. There is no place to hide in this barren wilderness, no stone under which you can cower that I can't overturn. Come out and let me see you and tell me the nature of your ship and how many survived, for I have eaten many of your kind, farers of the salty sea, but—" Here it paused and tested the air with its flaring nostrils— "I cannot place your smell. What are you?"

"Nothing!" Razmous squeaked cleverly in his high kender voice. His words came out of the forest like an echo, scattered by the trunks of the trees so that it was difficult for the monster to determine its exact origin. However, his companions were beside themselves in fear and rage at his foolishness.

"Who is it who is nothing yet answers my questions?" the monster asked as it crouched a little lower in the water.

"Nobody," Razmous squawked again, suppressing a giggle. Conundrum clawed at his arm, trying to pull him down and shut him up, but the kender merely turned on him with a grin spreading from pointed ear to pointed ear, and stepped out from their covering screen of trees.

"Don't worry," he chided over his shoulder. "I read this in a book somewhere."

CHAPTER

9

"**Y**ou're mad!" Sir Grumdish howled. "You'll get us all killed."

"Don't worry," Razmous repeated confidently. Those accustomed to traveling with kender learn a number of words and phrases that, when spoken by non-kender, are not indicative of anything especially alarming, but when voiced by the merry adventurous race usually portend some disaster or otherwise unpleasant event. "Oh, look!" "Wow! I wonder if . . ." "You must have dropped it!" and the much dreaded "Did I ever tell you about the time . . ." are some of the more common cues to either flee without looking back, or grab the kender before he gets himself chopped. Yet few words ever spoken by kender conjure up such fear as "Don't worry." Except perhaps "Oops!"

Which is why Sir Grumdish launched himself from his slightly higher position and grabbed Razmous by the topknot. Not very gently he jerked the kender back to the cover of the trees. Razmous emitted a squeal of pain, great tears starting in his eyes.

With a loud, "Ah-ha!" the monster lurched forward, its arms spread wide. A huge wave of water rose before it and washed up the forested bank. Before the six adventurers could move, water surged around their legs and swept them from their feet. It carried them a short distance up the hillside, then swept them back, dragging them down through the trees toward the lake, where the creature waited with glaring eyes and champing, slavering jaws.

The gnomes scrabbled desperately at the branches, clinging to any twig or root within their grasp. First Razmous, then Conundrum, managed to catch themselves before they were swept completely away. Ensign Gob, being the smallest and the lightest, was thrown farthest up the bank by the surging wave and fortunately left high and dry out of harm's reach. Conundrum managed to grab Chief Portlost by the beard as he swept by, while Sir Grumdish snatched a handful of the kender's sopping-wet topknot and held on for dear life. But both gnomes lost their UANPs to the flood.

The unfortunate Ensign Wigpillow tried to hold on to his weapon, and as a result slipped away from the hands reaching out to catch him. As a last desperate act, he tried to fire his weapon at the chaos beast, only to have a powerful jet of water exit the rear of the UANP and propel him forward, down the last few feet of the bank. He slid and tumbled through the mud and leaves and vanished into the water at the monster's knees.

With a cry of delight, the chaos beast reached down and snatched him up in one massive, black-clawed hand and lifted the hapless gnome to its huge toothy maw. His companions on the bank turned away or hid their faces in their hands. Razmous peeked. As he neared those gaping jaws, however, the shrieking Ensign Wigpillow struggled against the monster's ironlike grip and *pop!* He squirted free like a watermelon seed.

Wigpillow scribed a long screaming arc across the desert sky. The monster craned its head round to watch in nothing less than slack-jawed surprise. Razmous simply said, "Wow!" and then had to be physically restrained to keep him from rushing down to the water and begging the monster to squirt him, too.

Ensign Wigpillow ended his flight with a thunderous splash a hundred or so yards upstream. The monster turned and surged off after him, a huge wake spreading out from its chest like the bow wave of a man-o-war under full sail.

"Come on!" Sir Grumdish roared as he pulled everyone to their feet. "Let's get out of here!"

"But Wigpillow!" Conundrum cried.

"He's creating a diversion, noble lad," Chief Portlost said. "To give us time to escape back to the ship."

Sir Grumdish had to push the others up the hill, shooting a quick glance over the ground in the faint hope that his UANP might not have been washed into the lake, but finding nothing.

"Hurry! Back to the ship!" he shouted, but no one needed his advice. Once again led by Razmous, they were already out of sight.

Despite his shorter legs, Ensign Gob was the first to reach the beach. Those observing from the *Indestructible* wondered at his haste. When it became apparent that he had no intention of stopping at the water's edge, they began to wave and shout, "No!"

But the gully dwarf ignored them, charged straight into the water, and fell flat on his glass-helmeted face. He thrashed his arms in the shallow surf, trying to swim, and throwing more sand than water. His companions, arriving immediately behind him, dragged him by his helmet back to the beach. Conundrum pointed at the gully dwarf's duckfeet, lying there in the sand next to the others, but Gob seemed not to understand, and so they demonstrated by frantically getting into their own helmets, bladderpacks, and duckfeet.

Chief Portlost was the first into his gear. He grabbed the gully dwarf and forced him into the duckfeet, then pushed him toward the water. Finally getting the idea, Gob started off, slowly dragging his heavy shoes through the sand. The chief followed, a little more quickly, and was himself followed more quickly still by Razmous. Next came Sir Grumdish and Conundrum, grunting with the water barrel between them, now filled with fresh water.

Out on the *Indestructible*, Commodore Brigg observed this flurry of activity with growing curiosity. "The shore party seems in an awful hurry, wouldn't you say?" he asked Snork, who had joined him on the bridge. A few crew members stood along the aft deck, pausing in their duties to watch. "And where is Pigwillow?"

"Wigpillow," Snork said, glancing up from his navigational log. "Aye, that they are."

Chief Portlost's head vanished under the water. Razmous paused when the water was up to his neck and waved something in a frantic manner, but neither the commodore nor Snork could tell what he meant by it. Dragging the heavy barrel filled with fresh water, Conundrum and Sir Grumdish had barely entered the water, while the gully dwarf was still several dozen feet from the shore.

"I don't see Pigwillow," the commodore repeated.

"Wigpillow, sir," Snork corrected again.

"Probably lollygagging," the commodore snorted.

Snork fished a glass of farseeing from his navigator's pouch, extended it to its six-foot length, and aimed it at the shore. "There's something coming through the forest. Maybe it's Ensign Wig . . . pi . . ." His voice trailed off, and his jaw dropped open.

"Well, is it him?" the commodore demanded. "Don't stand there like you've seen a naked mer . . ." His voice trailed off as well, for neither one of them needed the navigator's farseeing glass to see the gigantic monster bulling through the trees like a steam catapult broken loose from its moorings. With its clawed fists, the monster shattered into matchsticks huge thorn willows and towering palms, ripping them from the ground and tossing them aside like weeds. Sighting the gully dwarf still struggling toward the water, the fearsome creature loosed a thunderous bellow.

Chief Portlost and Razmous Pinchpocket were already safely underwater, their progress marked by two small surface eruptions of bubbles winding their way toward the boat, but Conundrum and Sir Grumdish were barely up to their knees. Ensign Gob clearly was doomed. The monster was bearing down upon him.

Commodore Brigg opened the hatch and shouted below, "All hands to battle stations! Bring the ship about!"

With bits of black frogsuit hanging in tatters from its champing tusks, the monster closed on its new quarry. As it ran, it scooped up a handful of sand in one massive paw and hurled it at the gully dwarf. The mass of wet sand was huge and struck Gob square in the back, knocking him out of his heavy shoes.

That was all the gully dwarf needed to set him free. In a flash, he was up, circling back away from the water and toward the forest. For a few moments, the beast paused in confusion, glancing first at the two gnomes struggling through waist deep water, then at the gully dwarf plunging into the forest. Quickly making up its mind, it leaped into the sea.

Glancing over his shoulder, Sir Grumdish yelled, "Forget the barrel, boy! Save yourself!" He plunged ahead, kicking out of his duckfeet and swimming with his arms.

Conundrum struggled through the surf, thrashing at

the water with both arms. His heavy shoes made even walking a chore, and he was already weary. Fear lent him strength, but hardly enough to escape the monster.

The chaos beast paused in its charge as it reached the water barrel. Half suspecting some kind of trap, it approached the barrel warily, sniffing suspiciously and reaching out one massive hand to touch it. Finding it filled only with water and ballast stones, it snatched it up and hurled it at Conundrum, missing the gnome by inches.

The barrel exploding nearby startled him briefly, and that was all the monster needed to catch up. Desperately, Conundrum dove beneath the waves, but a gigantic hand clapped down over him. Terrible, rending black claws dug into the sand around his feet, then squeezed like strangling tentacles around his legs and lifted him out of the water. He struggled and twisted, trying to squirt free as Ensign Wigpillow had done, but it did him little good. The sand kept him firmly in the monster's steely grip. Its jaws gaped wide, huge ivory tusks wreathed in gruesome tatters of gnomish flesh and frogsuit. Conundrum gagged as its stinking breath penetrated though his bladderpack and filled his glass helm with its reek. But this was nothing to the horror of being lifted ever closer to that slavering mouth and looking into those three monstrous eyeballs.

And then the creature paused, jaws agape, the gnome gripped in one fist. Its three bloodshot eyes swiveled around to focus on the *Indestructible*, now turned about, its bow pointing directly at the giant beast. The commodore crouched in the conning tower, sighting along the lubber's line with one eye closed and head cocked toward the open hatch at his feet.

"Fire!" he shouted.

The ship lurched backward and to starboard, while from the portside bow a cloud of bubbles exploded. Out from the cloud shot a projectile of enormous proportions.

Just beneath the surface of the water it coursed, like a great long silver-nosed barracuda, a perfect triangular wave spreading to either side, a trail of tiny bubbles following in its wake. The UAEP crossed the coral lagoon in three slow elephantine heartbeats. The monster watched as if hypnotized, saw it skim over the reefs, clipping stony projections without altering course or slowing. The monster stared at it until it arrived to bury itself in its bloated belly.

It continued to stare for three more agonizing heartbeats as its black blood spread in the water around the enormous arrow that had skewered it like a pig. Ever did its grip tighten on Conundrum's legs as it watched its life pour out into the sea. The little gnome bit his lips to stifle his own scream of crushed pain.

And then the monster staggered, screaming as though the doors of the Abyss itself had been opened. It convulsed, every muscle tightening like steel cords, including those of its hands. Conundrum felt every joint of his legs wrenching from its socket, every muscle fiber tearing, every tendon fraying like old rope, ready to snap, and then, like an arrow plucked by the archer, he was free. Free and sailing high in the air. He opened his eyes in relief, and then wished he hadn't.

It was with something between horror and curiosity that he watched the *Indestructible* pass below him. Down below his feet, the whole bay spread like an illustrated map in a cartographer's shop. He saw the chaos beast clutching at the giant arrow sprouting from its belly, then fall backward in the water. Elsewhere, the dark shadows of numerous sharks diverted from their course toward Sir Grumdish, still swimming with strong strokes toward the *Indestructible*, and honed in on the bleeding corpse of the beast. Conundrum also saw his other two remaining companions, two tiny figures peacefully walking along the bottom of the bay between mountainous reefs of coral. He saw the dozens of ships that had wrecked here, lying in various states of decay on the ocean floor.

In fact, one in particular caught his attention. It lay almost at the mouth of the harbor, and he was plummeting toward it.

Despite the tremendous squeezing he had received, he still wore one duckfoot. It was this leaden weight that kept him upright upon entry. Still, his splashdown drove every particle of air from his lungs, and seemed to drive his knees into his bowels. The impact nearly ripped his helmet off his head, and as it was, he cracked his nose against the interior of the helmet and blood streamed into his beard. The splash thundered in his ears, stunning him, and as he swiftly sank the bladderpack tried to slip from his shoulders. With his last particle of strength, he fought to keep hold of it, knowing that it meant his life. Dark spots swam in his vision, and for a moment he thought he was going to faint.

The spots grew larger, and it was then that he realized they were sharks, swimming toward his bubble trail down through the deep blue water. His downward progress slowed as he lost momentum. His one duckfoot was barely heavy enough to counteract the buoyancy of his bladderpack. He was glad about one thing—his bloody nose wasn't leaking into the water. Slowly now he sank toward the deck of the sunken ship while the sharks circled above.

Finally, with a soft bump he came to rest on the wooden deck. The ship, some sort of caravel, lay on its keel, its deck nearly level. The entire deck was littered with broken swords and cloven shields, and hundreds of spent arrows stood everywhere, eerily balanced on their steel points. The wave created by his landing, soft as it was, sent several dozen dancing away from him in all directions, gently skittering across the deck like frightened faeries of the deep. A few leaped the ship's rail and vanished over the sides.

In addition to weapons, all sorts of other common items lay scattered in profusion, everything from a small silver hand mirror that might have belonged in some lady's bedchamber, to a huge copper kettle used to boil water for the laundry. Part of the deck appeared to have been scored by fire, but of the ship's former occupants and crew there was no sign.

In the center of the deck, a large dark opening into the cargo hold gaped wide, its heavy doors swung open to either side as if, as the ship sank, its crew or those who sunk it had tried to loot its cargo. It filled him with loathing just looking at this dark hole, for it made him think of those who might have been trapped below. Perhaps their bodies were still there, but Conundrum had no desire to see them. He turned away and looked up for some sign of the *Indestructible*.

At last he found it, hardly visible at all in the distance, a dark shadow against the darker blue of the sea. Almost he thought he could discern a tiny shadow slowly rising toward it, and he imagined that this was Razmous or the chief being hauled aboard. He hoped that Sir Grumdish too had made it safely to the ship, despite the danger of the sharks.

This made him think of his own sharks, and looking up he confirmed that they were still there, slowly circling overhead like vultures in a stormy sky. Even if those onboard the *Indestructible* had noted where he splashed down, and even if they managed to lower him a rope, he doubted he would survive the ascent. He would be like a worm on a fishing line, an irresistible lure to all those hungry sharks as he rose slowly up toward the ship. They'd tear him to ribbons.

For a moment, he had a vision of a cleanly picked skeleton being pulled aboard the *Indestructible*, one skeletal hand grimly clinging to the rope.

Despite it all, Conundrum chuckled. This was no time to despair, he reminded himself. This was but another kind of puzzle to solve, one with higher stakes—much higher indeed. But a puzzle just the same.

Now that he had had time to take in his surroundings, Conundrum realized that the sunken ship lay on somewhat of a slope. The bow was clearly several feet higher than the stern. The closer he was to the surface, even by a few feet, he reasoned, the greater his chances of being rescued, and so he tried to make his way toward the bow of the sunken ship.

This was no easy task. Because of his unusual bouyancy, he was forced to adopt a hopping gait, not unlike the arrows when disturbed, gently bouncing along in a slow dream, his one lead shoe bump, bump, bumping with each protracted leap.

Perhaps it was this noise that awakened the creature sleeping in the ship's hold. It had grown fat over the last few weeks feeding on those who had gone down with this ship that it now called home, and so it was sluggish and sleepy. It slithered slowly toward the open cargo doors, pulling itself along with its long black tentacles. First one, then another sucker-covered appendage writhed up out of the hold, grasping the doors to either side and heaving its huge bulk up to the light.

Of course, Conundrum was completely unaware of his imminent danger. The ladder up to the ship's forecastle had been consumed in the fire; only the top three rungs remained, and these were far out of his reach. It occurred to him that he might use the copper kettle as a boost, and so he hop, hop, hopped toward it. If he could move the kettle over to the sterncastle's damaged ladder, he might be able to reach the lowest rung.

He was just stooping to grab the handle of the upturned kettle when he heard a noise like a rusty nail being pulled out of a board. While clambering out of the cargo hold, the monster shoved open one of the doors.

Conundrum froze, his mouth gaping and eyes popping inside his helmet. His heart thundered in his chest, and his nose started to bleed again. His breast heaved in panic, he gulped the stale filtered air through lips suddenly dry as old parchment, a storm of bubbles erupted from his bladder-pack, and then he turned and saw the horror creeping from the ship's hold. Lifting the side of the heavy copper caul-dron, Conundrum crawled beneath it. It dropped down over him, shutting him in total darkness. His blood roared in his ears.

Unfortunately for the gnome, the giant octopus was used to prying clams from their shells. Before it took up eating sailors, it had dined many a time on oysters pulled from their rocky beds. Slowly, silently, it crawled across the deck of the ship. It sent one tentacle probing toward the cauldron, feeling under its edge for a grip so it could flip it over and reveal the juicy meat inside.

Conundrum screamed inside his fishbowl helmet when he saw a black tentacle lift the edge of the cauldron and writhe toward him. It was a high-pitched scream, a true blood-curdling yell, the scream of the rabbit in the wolf's jaws, the scream of the condemned mutineer as the point of a saber prods him off the end of the plank and into the shark-filled waters below. It nearly burst his eardrums. Conundrum jerked his foot out of his heavy iron shoe and used it as a weapon, smashing the intruding tentacle against the boards. The octopus jerked it back, leaving the tip of its tentacle stuck to the deck between Conundrum's knees.

Slowly now, the entire cauldron began to rise as though lifted from above. Conundrum dropped the shoe, and sud-denly buoyant, found himself pressed against its underside of the cauldron. To his wonder, he found that an air pocket had formed here, and with each exhalation of bubbles it grew larger and the cauldron rose higher. It was only a few inches off the deck as yet, but continuing to rise.

Dimly sensing this, the giant octopus paused. The cauldron was now a foot above the deck, now two feet, now a yard, and steadily rising. The monster lunged forward, grasping at the empty deck with all eight of its tentacles, searching for the juicy meat that it knew was hiding there. Its suckers gripped the deck and tore loose the boards, searching for its victim, ignoring for the moment the cauldron rising above it as it would ignore the discarded shell of a hermit crab.

Conundrum watched this violence occurring mere feet from the end of his nose. His instinct was to hold his breath, but when he did that, the cauldron began to slow in its ascent. With each breath, a cloud of bubbles erupted from his bladderpack, and it was the growing pocket of air that these created inside the upturned kettle that caused it to rise. As Conundrum clung desperately to the inside of the kettle, he realized that his only hope was to panic, perhaps even hyperventilate. He set himself to the task of breathing as rapidly as he could, and slowly, but ever more quickly, he rose above the deck of the ship inside the overturned cauldron.

Higher and higher he climbed, until the entire length of the ship was visible below him. The giant octopus squeezed its massive bulk through the newly-torn hole in the deck. Still searching for the gnome, it vanished into the ship's dark hold.

The light grew brighter by stages, the water less murky. Shafts and beams of sunlight lanced downward, dancing as the waves rippled overhead. A shark, long and steely gray, slid by beneath him, unaware, perhaps thinking him some weird new jellyfish.

Suddenly, his ascent stopped as though he had struck a wall. For one panicked moment, he thought something had caught him at last, and then he heard waves lapping against the outside of the cauldron. He had reached the surface.

One problem remained—how to get out. There were still the sharks to consider, and *Indestructible* was probably hundreds of yards away from him. It might even have sailed away, thinking him lost forever, another victim of remorseless Chance (ever the greatest enemy of the gnomish people). It might even be sailing past him now, completely unaware that their crewmate floated beneath that curious copper kettle. If so, his only hope was that the kender had survived and was on deck to beg the commodore to stop and investigate a strange buoy bobbing on the surface.

And then a new danger presented itself. The waves increased in size, and as they lapped against the kettle, it commenced rocking back and forth. If the waves grew any larger, the cauldron might tip over. Its bubble of air would then escape, and it would sink, leaving the gnome stranded on the surface, food for sharks. Conundrum pressed the palms of his hands against the inside of the kettle, trying to help keep its balance in the rising sea.

Just as he was getting comfortable with the ever-shifting balance, something clanged against the kettle, almost upending him. He yelled, for he knew that the kettle had collided with the *Indestructible*. He could hear the commodore shouting curses at the helm. The cauldron, with Conundrum inside it, bumped down the length of the ship. Conundrum tried to call for help, but his voice inside his helmet inside the cauldron was so muffled that he doubted anyone could hear him.

A pair of hooks suddenly splashed into the water beside him. They sank a moment, flashing in the water, and then jerked upward, snagging the lip of the cauldron and lifting it streaming from the sea.

"You've got her!" Commodore Brigg shouted to the boom hand. "Swing her aboard now!"

While one gnome cranked the winch that lifted the cauldron, another swung the boom round and deposited it upright on the aft deck, all done so quickly that there was still seawater sloshing inside it.

"Good show!" the commodore shouted, then turned to Razmous, who stood at his side, still wearing his frogsuit and wringing water from his topknot. "You were right. It's a fine cauldron. Should come in handy."

The kender nodded, shaking water from his ears.

Then Conundrum stood up inside the cauldron, spilling water onto the deck. Razmous gaped proudly, and the boom operator screamed once, high and sharp, then fainted, certain he had seen a ghost.

CHAPTER
10

After another fortnight's sailing, the *Indestructible* made port in Kalaman, the halfway point of their journey. There, the crew purchased nine more large copper cauldrons to convert into Conundrum's ascending-kettles, as he named his invention, for these held much promise as escape devices useful for vacating a permanently submerged submersible. Commodore Brigg granted everyone three days' shore leave, most of which was spent visiting relatives among the city's resident population of gnomes and inspecting their rather quaint and antiquated collection of catapults. Really, they were rather behind the times, but that was to be expected with anyone living so far from Mount Nevermind. The kender spent the larger part of his time in the city jail, also visiting relatives.

When the ship was stocked and provisioned for the journey to Flotsam, they bailed Razmous out, and the *Indestructible* set sail with a diminished crew of eighteen. A makeshift plaque honored Ensign Wigpillow as a fallen hero, while Gob was officially listed as missing in action. No one knew his fate for certain; they had waited a full day and seen no sight of him, even though the chaos beast was dead with the *Indestructible*'s UAEP in its belly. Conundrum, now the smallest member of the crew, was promoted yet again, this time to chief officer in charge of oilage.

Now, in addition to his duties as first assistant cartographer, Conundrum had also to make sure the ship's gears were properly oiled. This had been the meat of Gob's job, and it was a nasty and uncomfortable job indeed, fit only for gully dwarves and their ilk.

Still, the maze of gears, pipes and conduits lurking behind the *Indestructible*'s walls, beneath her floors, or sprawled across her ceilings did whet his professional curiosity to a certain extent. Everything, simply everything had to be oiled and greased to the nth degree—this fact being drubbed into his head by Chief Portlost—from the largest spring engine to the tiniest screw valve. The ship's schematics were nearly as complicated as Razmous's map of the sub-Ansalonian passage. Luckily, he had a few weeks in which to master his new business. They still had to sail round Nordmaar, the last northern cape of the continent of Ansalon, before turning south and making for the Blood Sea. If all went well, they wouldn't have to submerge until then, and they hoped not at all before they reached Flotsam.

Although the exterior of the ship was plated with heavy iron, the interior compartments were not unlike their below-deck counterparts on normal wooden sailing vessels. The officer's cabins—located forward of the bridge on the main level—though not large, were comfortable and accommodating, paneled in rich browns and warm tans. Open fire was ever a danger aboard any ship, but the *Indestructible* was outfitted with several redundant fire-suppression systems, so for light they burned candles or small pottery lamps of whale oil. Here also was the mess and the kitchen, the fabrication shop for creating new devices and improvements—that work *never* stopped, and Doctor Bothy's sick bay.

The rest of the crew occupied community quarters beneath the bridge on the engineering level. There they slung their hammocks wherever there was a free space, among the machinery and stores that powered the ship and its crew. They also shared their chambers with the *Indestructible*'s main drive springs, as well as her ascending and descending spring, and the two UAEP tubes that ran the length of the ship. In the forward compartments on this level were the chambers where sails were stored. Aft was the engine control room and mechanism that diverted energy from the springs to the pumps to pressurize the UAEP tubes.

Beneath this level was the bilge, where Ensign Gob had had his quarters before his untimely . . . whatever-it-was that happened to him. For the most part, Conundrum avoided the bilge, as there was little here requiring his attention other than the bilge-pump valves, which required oiling only every three days. Fore and aft of the bilge were the fore and aft ballast tanks. These were more important, their valves requiring oiling every day. When fully flooded, they began the ship on its descent beneath the waves.

The days waxed longer as they sailed farther and farther north—longer and considerably warmer, until most everyone was wearing little more than a loincloth wound about their hips. At night, when duties allowed, they worked on the aft deck by lamplight, stripped down to their skivvies to take advantage of every breeze. These were the most pleasant hours of the voyage as far as Conundrum was concerned, these days spent lazing through tropical waters, watching dolphins play by moonlight, and eating as many deep-fried flying fish as they could catch with their butterfly nets.

A tiny tinkling noise wakened Sir Tanar Lobcrow from his reverie. He sat in the open window of his room at the Sailor's Rest in Flotsam, thoughtfully sucking on a lime. The night was warm; silver-lined gray clouds raced across the setting moon. He wore only his undertrousers, letting the breeze play over his naked chest, and stretching his toes against the windowsill of his fourth-floor window. The sea gently lapped at the nearby shore, the slightly stale scent of Flotsam Bay competing with the rank odors rising from the alley below his window.

At the noise, he started, realizing he had been hearing it for some time without noticing it. He looked round his bedchamber, still a little groggy from the balmy night and his woolgathering journey. A figure moved impatiently beneath the sheets of his bed, rolling over in annoyance at the disturbance of the ringing bell. Sir Tanar smiled at the figure, not lovingly, his teeth gleaming in the darkened room. Then he moved to his desk and removed the small box from its drawer. He opened the box as its last bell-like tones faded.

"Good of you to answer my summons, Tanar," the gruff feminine voice purred from the magical communication device.

The figure on the bed rolled over again, crying out in her sleep, "Wha . . . ? Sweetest, did you say something?"

"It's nothing. Go back to sleep," the Thorn Knight muttered. The figure murmured something sleepily and rolled back to face the wall.

"A woman, Tanar?" the Voice of the Night softly inquired.

"It is not forbidden," he said, turning his head to the side and blinking at the moonlight shining in through his window.

"No, but revealing the secret of our communications most certainly is," the Voice said in a dangerously calm voice. The steadiness of her tone spoke of her underlying anger.

The Thorn Knight swallowed. A sudden lump of fear had risen in his throat. "She is sufficiently . . . subdued," he said tersely.

"And how did you manage that?" the Voice roared.

Before he could answer, the woman sat up in the bed, clutching the sheets to her breast in terror. Her eyes rolled in her head as she stared round the room, confused, bewildered. "What? H-how . . ." she stammered. Her gaze fell on Tanar.

"Who are you?" she cried, crawling to the head of the bed and pulling the sheets close to hide her nakedness. "How did I get here?" Her eyes darted in panicked confusion around the room, noting the open window, the closed door, the half-naked man, the small box on the desk.

The Voice laughed mirthlessly from the magical device. Tanar stepped in front of the woman, trying to hide the box from her gaze, but she had already seen it.

"What is that? Who is that?" she gurgled in terror as the sound of the bodiless voice.

Suddenly, the laughter ceased, as though cut off with a knife. "Silence her, Tanar. Silence her now."

Without hesitation, he leaped across the bed, grabbed the woman by the arm, and dragged her to the floor. She lashed out with her free hand, clawing the Thorn Knight across the face, while at the same time sinking her teeth into the root of his thumb.

Tanar snarled in pain and cuffed her with the back on his fist, stilling her protests for a moment. She fell limp at his feet, moaning.

"She mustn't be allowed to tell what she has seen," the Voice urged.

With a sigh, Tanar lifted her from the floor by her dark disheveled hair. She clutched weakly at the fingers knotted in her hair as he dragged her naked heels across the wooden floor. He set her in the windowsill with a thump. Still dazed by his blow and blinking stupidly, she tried to steady herself against the window frame. Tanar stooped, lifted her feet, and dumped her like a wheelbarrow out the window. She struck the filthy cobbles sixty feet below before she could think to open her mouth to scream.

Tanar turned back to the magical communication device. His sheets lay stretched from the bed to the window, a long white accusing finger pointing the way to his crime. He balled them up and tossed them on the bed before returning to his seat at the desk.

"It is done," Tanar sighed, as he slid into the chair. "The woman will not speak."

"Well done, Tanar," the Voice purred. "I hope her death does not interfere with your duties."

Tanar stiffened. "The proper authorities will be consulted. There is nothing to worry about. I know how to do my job."

"I sometimes wonder. You were warned not to abuse the power of this artifact, yet here I find you using it to subdue your . . . evening's entertainment."

"A simple spell," he answered. "I could have cast it without the magic of the device."

"Remember that when you are at the bottom of the sea."

Tanar started, genuinely surprised.

"You are ordered," the Voice of the Night continued, "to accompany a ship of gnomes on their journey to find the sub-Ansalonian passage, and to report back everything that they find. Should they attempt to return to a Solamnic port, or find themselves in danger of capture by Solamnics or any other power, you will destroy the crew and scuttle the ship. Do you accept this assignment, even though it may mean your own death?"

"I'll do it," Tanar answered darkly.

"Of course, you know that Lord Targonne has ordered you on this journey, even though he has no confidence that these gnomes will succeed on their mission, and that he fully expects you may die with the gnomes in their ship. He would be rid of you, but without directly offending the Order of the Thorn. You, Sir Tanar, are a Thorn in his side. He fears you as he fears me."

"Then why do you concur with his orders?" Tanar ventured to ask.

"Because I have confidence," the Voice continued. "Confidence the gnomes will succeed in their curious task. Portents and auguries indicate a high probability of success. These gnomes are not yet aware that they are also working for me, to further my power, but you shall teach them this—and other lessons on my behalf. Besides, I do not wish to openly oppose Lord Targonne."

"How shall I proceed, then?" Tanar asked petulantly. He despised politics and didn't really care who he was working for or why, as long as he was paid according to agreement.

"You shall sail this submersible of theirs with them to the bottom of the Blood Sea and there discover the crack that leads to the Abyss. If you can find the way for me, Tanar, we shall enter the Abyss together."

Tanar's face darkened. "The Abyss?" he growled suspiciously. "What do you seek there? Takhisis is no longer there. She doesn't answer our prayers. She fled with the other gods from Allfather Chaos."

"It's the Abyss, Tanar. Why do I need to explain every little detail to you? Think! If a magical artifact such as the communication device can grant a little power, how much more power is there in even one stone of the Abyss? The

Abyss served once as the home of a goddess, Tanar. Its power must be infinite. And so shall be ours, if you succeed. Will you do it?"

"I said I would," he answered shortly. "Don't I always do what I say?"

"Eventually," she answered. "In your own time. But you must not dally this time. You must be of the most serious mind. You must not fail. Barring any unforeseen accidents, the gnomes should be in Flotsam before winter arrives. Be ready for them."

"I will," he said, glancing around and rehearsing his story of the poor woman's suicide, as the Voice of the Night faded.

CHAPTER

11

Even in Snork's glass of farseeing, the boat was tiny, cutting its way through the green northern sea with two great sails of red and white stripes pushing it through the waves. A black flag, unadorned, rippled from the top of its single mast. They saw the white waves curling away from its sharp prow like parings before the planer blade.

Snork passed the glass to Commodore Brigg. He sucked his teeth as he put his eye to it. "There's no doubt," he muttered. "She's already seen us."

They had just rounded the northern tip of Nordmaar. Off the starboard bow lay a land sparsely populated—poor, terrorized by the ceaseless raids of buccanners, and unfriendly to strangers. To port stretched the endless leagues of the Northern Courrain Ocean, which no ship had ever navigated and returned to tell the tale.

Commodore Brigg passed the glass to Razmous, who sighed as he put the wonderful device to his eye. "I've never met a real live minotaur before," he said. "Much less a pirate."

"It is to be hoped that continues," the commodore said sternly.

But Razmous went on. "It must be very interesting to have big cow horns sticking out of your head. Awfully convenient, I should imagine, for hanging things like umbrellas on them, when it is raining and you don't have enough hands." He lowered the glass and gazed out over the ocean at the tiny dot barely visible on the horizon.

"Hey! Give me that!" Sir Grumdish snapped, indicating the glass of farseeing that was sliding into the kender's pouch.

"This? I thought you were through with it," Razmous protested.

"I haven't even looked through it yet!" Sir Grumdish barked as he yanked the glass from the kender's grasp.

"Well, you should have said something!" retorted the kender in hurt tones.

With a frown, Sir Grumdish lifted it to his eye and peered through. He harrumphed, then gnawed his lower lip. "What do you suppose is her crew complement?" he asked, lowering the glass and passing it to Conundrum.

"Forty at least, not counting officers," Snork said.

Conundrum lifted the glass to his eye. The minotaur galley had drawn closer as they talked, near enough now to see tiny figures scurrying around on her decks. A steely blade flashed in the sunlight.

"More than enough for the likes of us," Sir Grumdish commented. "Well, someone will have to help me get my armor up here on deck."

"Nay, we cannot fend off a boarding," the commodore said. "We're a ship of exploration, not war."

"Well, it's come to war, no matter what your intentions," Sir Grumdish argued.

"She's lowering her sails!" Conundrum cried. "Perhaps she hasn't seen us after all!"

Commodore Brigg snatched the glass from Conundrum's eye and put it to his own, a fierce grin splitting his white beard. After a few moments, the grin faded, and he passed the glass back to Snork. "She's seen us all right. She's putting out oars. They need oars to ram us and board us."

"Well, if we aren't going to fight, what are we going to do?" Sir Grumdish asked.

The commodore thought for a moment, some inner struggle revealed in the anguish of his expression. His hands gripped the rusty rail of the conning tower until his knuckles turned white. Then, sighing, he released his grip and plunged his hands into the pockets of his red jumpsuit. "We'll submerge and wait her out."

"But you said—" Sir Grumdish began.

"What would you have of me?" the commodore interrupted. "We cannot outrun her, and we dare not fight her, not even with UAEPs. Even if we sunk her, her crew would simply board us to save themselves. What good would that do us? We'd still be dead, and our Life Quests would remain incomplete."

"This ship is a submersible," Snork chimed in cheerfully. "I think it's high time we submersed."

"Aye!" the others agreed, even Sir Grumdish, albeit reluctantly.

"Chief Conundrum, are you prepared to maintain proper oilage levels?" the commodore asked.

"I think so, sir," Conundrum answered.

"Then man your station, sir," Brigg ordered.

"All hands! All hands!" Snork bellowed through the open hatch. "Prepare to submerge the ship!"

Conundrum made his way into the ship while several gnomes rushed topside to lower the reefed sails and stow them in the forward compartments. Meanwhile, he threaded a path through the chaos of activity on the bridge until he reached the hatch leading down from the crew quarters to main engine room. Chief Portlost was in a tizzy, dashing in three directions at once and shouting orders at anyone who stopped to listen.

"Conundrum!" he shouted when he saw the red-bearded oilage officer pressing through crew quarters, climbing over those busily stowing personal items and loose cargo beneath every available tube and pipe. "Conundrum, get over here! The main drive spring is in sorry shape!"

"I just oiled it this morning!" Conundrum answered.

"Well, it needs more oil, boy. Every gear and spring must be oiled. Never forget that."

"I know," Conundrum shouted from the center of the crew quarters, where a large half-tube rose up from the floor and passed through the bulkhead above. "But first I have to grease the mast-lowering apparatus. We're about to dive!" He dipped a large, hairy brush into a bucket and slopped black grease onto his shoes. He then began to paint the interior of the half-tube.

"I already knew that, didn't I?" the chief oilage officer shouted in reply as he adjusted a bank of large, important-looking levers, pulling some down, and pushing others up. A gnome rushed into the engine room with an armload of torches. He replaced the old ones with fresh new torches burning with bright merry flames, then rushed to the next room to do the same.

"But what are we diving for?" the red-bearded chief shouted as he wound a few extra turns into the main drive spring and checked the torque meters for the diving and ascending flowpellars. "That's what I want to know. And without a bit of warning!"

"Minotaur pirates!" Conundrum shouted. Suddenly, the thick round wooden mast descended from above, nearly catching the bristles of his brush between it and the bracing-guidetube that he was greasing.

"Minotaur pirates?" the chief cried, pausing in his frantic labors for a moment. "Save us!"

Snork's voice floated down from the bridge above. "Stand by to flood the forward ballast tank and engage the descending flowpellar!"

Conundrum dropped his brush and bucket of grease, and, snatching up a small glass bottle with a long skinny neck that was filled with olive oil, he rushed forward to where a tangled nest of tubes and pipes protruded from the bulkhead. From the shadowy midst of the pipes peered the beady red eyes of a rat. "Out of the way, Onslow!" Conundrum shouted. "There's work to do!" The rat he had nicknamed thusly scurried out and vanished beneath a sack of buckwheat flour.

"Standing by to flood the forward ballast tank!" Conundrum shouted at almost the same time that Chief Portlost bellowed, "Standing by to engage the descending flowpellar!"

A loud clang sounded from above, followed by a metallic grinding noise. "Secure all hatches!" Commodore Brigg ordered.

"All hatches secured."

"Prepare to dive."

Four gnomes descended the ladder from the bridge, landing with four thumps on the deck of the crew quarters one right after another. Two hurried forward, one each to man the spring crank of the descending and ascending flowpellars, and the other two to man the crank of the main spring engine. If these were engaged, Conundrum would have to rush about keeping them oiled, but for the moment his main duty lay with the forward ballast tank valve, making sure it didn't stick closed, or even worse, open.

Snork's voice floated down from above, "Flood the forward ballast tank!"

In the engine room, Chief Portlost shouted, "Flooding the forward ballast tank, aye!" He dropped a large, heavy switch, and Conundrum heard water gurgling behind the bulkhead beside which he crouched. Satisfied that the valve was working properly, he ran aft, his bottle of oil sloshing in his fist. He ducked into the engine room, avoiding the two burly gnomes, stripped to the waist and already sweating profusely as they madly cranked the main drive spring. Conundrum took his place beside the aft ballast tank valve. He set the bottle of oil on the ground and noticed that its contents were not level. Instead, they tilted toward the front of the ship. The watertight door leading into the engine room slammed shut. Chief Portlost hurried to open and secure it.

"Flood the aft ballast tank," Snork shouted from the bridge, "and engage the descending flowpellar!"

"Flooding the aft ballast tank, aye!" Chief Portlost responded, dropping another large, heavy switch into place. "Cross your fingers, lads," he muttered under his breath.

Presently, they heard the sound of gurgling water, but more important was what they didn't see—water spewing in around the bulkheads.

Conundrum watched the oil in his bottle slowly level out. Chief Portlost sighed.

"Engaging the descending flowpellar, aye!" Portlost shouted triumphantly.

A cheer went up from the bridge—it had been during this phase of the dive that the *Indestructible* sank on its second trial run. Chief Portlost reached above his head and pulled a string that ran forward through the engine room bulkhead. With a whirling noise, the *Indestructible* began to descend into the blue depths of the sea.

As they sank, they noticed how the air began to change. Sound was dampened, yet at the same time they became acutely aware of new and unusual sounds. There was no longer the gentle slap and slosh of the sea against the hull, a noise they had become so used to hearing that they only noticed it now by its absence. The air became close, compressed, and more difficult to see through because of a growing haze. On the bridge, people began to cough, softly at first, then more harshly. The hull commenced to pop and creak most alarmingly, as if there were a company of dwarves outside beating it with hammers and prying at the seams with crowbars.

The gnomes found that they could hear things outside the ship quite well. They heard all sorts of clicks, whirs, chitters, squeaks, pops, whoops, and warbles, as though they were in some kind of jungle aviary and not beneath the bright briny sea. They also heard the dip and splash of the oars of the approaching minotaur galley. Almost it seemed already on top of them, but after a time, they realized that this was but a trick of hearing.

When they had descended a sufficient distance below the surface, Commodore Brigg ordered, between coughs and gasps for air, the flowpellars disengaged. The ship gradually slowed, but it never really seemed to stop. Even when lying motionless in the water, it seemed to those aboard that it was still sinking slowly. This was not the case, Commodore Brigg assured the crew that had begun to gather near the bridge. It was but a trick of the mind, like the sensation of flying one feels for days after being flung by a gnomeflinger for the first time. Everyone on the upper deck was coughing most uproariously now, as though the whole ship were trying desperately to get someone's attention, with Conundrum and the chief alone as yet unafflicted by this strange new malady. Finally Chief Portlost noticed this oddity and raised his bushy eyebrows in consternation, pondering aloud, "Undersea sickness?"

And so, in a silence broken by waves of hacking and wheezing, they waited and listened to the approaching pirate ship. It seemed to take much longer than any of them could have imagined. In fact, it took so long that many of the crew began to drop down the ladder by ones and twos, then in mass, even the officers from the bridge, all hacking out their lungs.

"The ship is filling up with smoke," Snork gasped as Conundrum helped him to a hammock.

"Is it a fire?" Chief Portlost cried.

"No," Sir Grumdish wheezed. "It's the torches. They're smoldering.

"It's like a cave-in in a tunnel," Conundrum cursed. "We're sealed inside the ship, and we're using up all the air! The torches need plenty of air to breath and burn properly. All they do is smoke."

"What we need is a vent, a tube to the surface, to let the smoke out," Snork said. "Something that we can extend and retract . . ." He slapped weakly at his pockets, feeling for a pencil. "I'd draw up the design if I could only see!" he exclaimed. "My eyes are on fire."

"And I can barely breathe," someone else said.

"Well, we're safe here for a while, at least," the commodore said. "Extinguish all the torches on this level."

Commodore Brigg had recovered sufficiently to begin nervously pacing the crew quarters with his hands folded behind his back. Snork lay in his hammock while Conundrum held a cool cloth to his cousin's eyes. Doctor Bothy sat in a small chair with his flab hanging over the sides, looking rather uncomfortable and put-out, like a child made to sit in a corner. Occasionally, a cough shook his bulk like a tub of jelly. Sir Grumdish lay half-dead of asphyxiation atop a pile of grain bags. The professor leaned against the forward bulkhead, eyeing Razmous the kender, who was following the commodore like a shadow of apprehension, his topknot bouncing with each step. Sometimes he was forced to duck a pipe or brace or strung hammock, which the commodore passed under with ease, so great was the difference in their height.

"What *are* we waiting for?" Conundrum complained as Commodore Brigg and the kender passed him for the umpteenth time, stepping over his outstretched legs.

"Nightfall," the commodore answered curtly.

"I'm bored," Razmous sighed. If there was one thing that frightened seasoned travelers more than a kender's assurance of "Don't worry," or the always portentous, "Oops!" it was the restless sigh of a bored kender. The commodore froze, and everyone turned his gaze on the kender. Even Sir Grumdish stirred uneasily in his sleep.

Razmous looked up and found himself the center of attention, six faces staring at him gravely through the gloom. "What?" he asked innocently. He ran a hand down the length of his topknot. "Have I got something in my hair?"

Everyone returned to whatever nervous habits in which they had been indulging. Razmous peered around at everyone suspiciously, as if he suspected they were playing a joke on him. It was then that he noticed how dark it had become on the bridge, as though everyone's dark mood had filled up the very air itself.

"It's getting dark in here," he commented. "What's happening to the light?"

As if cued by his words, the last torch flickered and went out. Darkness blacker than any goblin cave descended upon them all. The air seemed to be getting thinner by the moment, and what air they did manage to gasp into their lungs was tinged with the sharp sweaty scent of fear and burned-hair reek of torchsmoke.

Into this came the sound of the oars once again splashing around just above them. Commodore Brigg called for quiet, and gradually the interior of the ship grew as noiseless as it was dark; only the occasional muffled cough broke the stillness. Everyone waited, staring up with bulging eyes, ears straining to hear.

The oars splashed nearer and nearer until they seemed just above the ship. Then, at a muffled and unintelligible cry, they stopped. There followed a series of fumbling echoing thumps. Snork whispered—though he couldn't have said why he was whispering—"They're shipping oars."

They heard a loud splash, followed several seconds later by an even louder clang against the hull of the ship. "They've found us! They're attacking!" Conundrum cried out in fear.

"No! No! Be quiet!" Commodore Brigg shouted, silencing everyone. "It's only the anchor. Their anchor has struck the hull," he hissed into the darkness.

"They *must* know we are here," Razmous whispered excitedly. "How could they not?"

"What will they do? Will they attack?" Conundrum asked, voicing the question on everyone's mind.

"It was almost nightfall when we submerged," the commodore said. "They probably think we're a normal ship that has sunk, scuttled rather than be taken by pirates. It wouldn't be the first time."

"Ah, yes! Yes, I see," several members of the crew exclaimed in the darkness, patting each other reassuringly. "The commodore will save us yet," many whispered. "He is very wise."

Commodore Brigg continued, bolstered by this support. "Likely, they plan to wait until morning, then send divers to see what can be salvaged. But we'll already be gone. My plan is that we'll wait a bit, then engage the flowpellars and slip quietly away."

Now a babble of excited voices greeted him as the crew

members began to break up, returning to their stations. But the officers on the bridge were not yet easy in their hearts, despite the evident ingeniousness of the commodore's plan. What about the air? It was still thin, and growing thinner with each breath.

Professor Hap-Troggensbottle was the first to see the problem with this strategy. In fact, it came upon him so suddenly that he slapped himself on the forehead. "Air!" he cried. "If the torches can't burn, we can't breath. If we stay here much longer, there'll be no one alive to engage any flowpellars."

"And even if we do slip away unnoticed, how will we know in which direction to go?" Conundrum asked. "We can't see where we are going if there is no light."

"Right!" the professor barked. "We don't want to go the wrong way and beach the ship, or worse, surface within sight of the minotaurs. Excuse me commodore, but how did you plan to see what was on the surface once you submerged the ship?"

No answer was immediately forthcoming. A curious, brooding silence greeted his question.

Then Conundrum spoke up. "We might try Doctor Bothy's Peerupitscope."

CHAPTER

12

And so it was that, after inserting Doctor Bothy's Peer-upitscope through the mast's seal—and hastily plugging, with thirty-nine pairs of socks, the resulting leak caused by the scope's inexact fit—Commodore Brigg was able to navigate a silent course away from the minotaur galley. Once out of sight of the pirates, the gnomes, and one kender, surfaced and ventilated the ship. The commodore agreed that an unscheduled stop was needed in order to permanently install Doctor Bothy's Peerupitscope and Navigator Snork's torch chimney, which Conundrum named the Snorkel after its inventor.

According to Snork's charts, the nearest port was a small village called Jachim. Actually, the nearest port was a place called Unger, but Jachim was known for its wools, and so promised a ready supply of desperately needed socks. Unger was known more for its pirates than its footwear. Furthermore, Jachim offered better facilities for shipboard modification and repairs, what with its deep harbor and nearby forest providing a plentiful source of lumber. In addition, Razmous's copy of *A Wandering Kender's Almanac and Pocket Guide to Krynn* identified

Jachim as the place to go for first-class haggis, which none of the crew had ever tasted, or even heard of, but whose fame was noted in the kender guide. Razmous was desperate to try the famous haggis, and by the time they reached Jachim, he had convinced most of the crew that they needed to try it as well. Doctor Bothy wondered if it might not prove to be a cure for hiccoughs. As it turned out, haggis was a cure for something, if not hiccoughs.

"A cure for hunger," the doctor was heard to declare after his first mouthful of the mealy, grease-laden dish of offal. "One taste of this and you'll never want to eat again." Nevertheless, he didn't let his go to waste.

They sat round the tables of the Wet Weskit, Jachim's best inn and source of its famous haggis. Everyone except the kender was turning green but trying very hard to be polite; the innkeeper was a kindly host.

"This is the best haggis I've ever had," Razmous declared to the innkeeper. His cheeks were stuffed like a chipmunk's with half-chewed haggis, for he was unwilling to swallow, considering the taste.

"It's too bad Ensign Gob isn't here," Conundrum lamented earnestly when the innkeeper had gone. "Just when you need a gully dwarf begging at the table, there isn't one handy. I think I actually miss the little guy."

In the end, it was decided that, for the sake of diplomacy, everyone would stuff their haggis into their pants —and especially Razmous's pockets—for later disposal.

Because he had convinced everyone of the marvels of haggis, and because he was chief of supply, it was given to Razmous Pinchpocket the duty of hauling their combined dinners out into the woods and burying them at the first opportunity. They dared not dump the haggis into the harbor, for fear of attracting sharks, nor of transporting it out to sea for disposal, lest it breed some plague. And nobody wants plague, not even gully dwarves.

A warm northern night covered Jachim, the stars glimmering in a sea of velvet blackness. Many of the citizens of this village lay atop their sheets, trying without much success to fall asleep to the whining of the mosquitoes and the sway and splash of the Northern Courrain Ocean lapping gently against the shore. The village's many inns and taverns burned like jewels in the night, yellow torchlight streaming out of doors and windows to illuminate squares and rectangles of the nighttime streets. Sometimes a dark silhouette appeared, a fan or doffed straw hat waving, bedewed tankard in hand, to gaze at the stars and wonder at the sultriness of the night. The sounds of muted lutes hung like sweet fog in the air. People moved beds out of doors into alleys or yards or atop roofs, anywhere they could find a breeze, however warmed the wind was by the northern current.

Down by the waterfront, various small craft belonging to local fishermen lay pulled up along the beach. Their moonshadows darkened the silver sand, here and there sheltering some fisherman snoring with his head couched in the crook of his arm, a jug of sweet brown liquor lying empty beside him.

Through these shadows, 'twixt fishing vessels leaning together with step masts crossed in X's against the star-dappled sky, stole four darkly-clad figures. The tallest led the way, his topknot bouncing with each tip-toeing step. Across his back was slung a large lumpy sack, from which exuded an appalling odor that kept his three shorter companions at a distance of ten paces behind him. They made their way across the beach and up the main street of the village, keeping well within the shadows and avoiding the more well-lighted taverns.

Once beyond the last house, the street tapered off into

a well-worn footpath, which entered a thick forest whose blossom-laden bows were stirred by the warm wind off the sea. The four conspirators crept beneath the dark eaves of the forest and paused, looking back along the way they had come to see if anyone was following.

"I don't think anyone saw us," the stoop-shouldered kender whispered as he unslung his pack and set it on the leaf-strewn ground. He straightened to his full four-foot height with a sigh, digging his knuckles into the small of his back.

"Ooooh," Doctor Bothy groaned, clutching at his belly. "I shouldn't have eaten so much haggis." He had been ordered on this mission because he had asked for seconds at the inn.

"Let's bury it here and get back to the ship," Sir Grumdish muttered. He glared around the woods leaning over them with their dark, spreading branches. As chief security officer, it was his unfortunate duty to accompany the others on this nocturnal excursion. "I don't like the feel of this forest. What do they call it?"

"The Black Fairy Wood," Conundrum answered.

"I don't know. I think they meant the Blackberry Wood," Razmous said. "I think I smell some blackberries."

"How can you smell anything except haggis?" Sir Grumdish snapped as he clapped a hand over his own nose and mouth.

"Oh, please don't say haggis," Doctor Bothy groaned.

"Let's go a little deeper into the woods, at least," the kender said with a wry grin and a sparkle in his periwinkle eyes. "So the villagers don't see us. We wouldn't want to offend them." Picking up his sack and slinging it with a sickening squish over his shoulder, he crept deeper into the woods, leaving the light and noise of the sleepy village behind. His companions followed reluctantly.

When they had gone about a bowshot further into the

woods, Sir Grumdish called them once more to a halt. "This is far enough," he said as he pulled a shovel out of his pack and tossed it to the kender. A sliver of moonlight penetrated the canopy overhead, illuminating a small patch of leafy soil at their feet. A number of curious mushrooms or toadstools poked their speckled caps up through the mold.

"Let's dig!" Sir Grumdish almost shouted as he produced a second shovel and jabbed it into the ground. He began flinging scoopfuls of dirt over his shoulder like some sort of demented badger burrowing into the hillside.

Dropping the sack full of haggis to the ground, Razmous then stood to the side, gripping the shovel in his nimble brown hands. "I don't know," he sighed. "Maybe haggis is what they call an acquired taste and we should give it another try."

"Give me that," Doctor Bothy muttered angrily as he took the kender's shovel. "I'll dig. Maybe it will get my mind off my poor belly. When I get back to the ship, I'm going to invent milk of amnesia. That's a taste I would dearly love to acquire right now."

"What will milk of . . . milk of . . . what will it do?" Conundrum asked as the doctor joined Sir Grumdish in his labors.

"Make you forget you are sick," Doctor Bothy grunted in answer. "But a glass of regular old cold cow's milk would do me just fine—or better yet, a bowl of vanilla-flavored frozen-sugar-cream." He smacked his lips, then continued to dig.

Soon, the two gnomes had excavated a sizeable hole in the loamy forest floor. They towed the wet, heavy bag of haggis into it, and within another turn of the glass were tamping down a small mound of freshly turned black earth with the flats of their shovels. Sir Grumdish stood up, his old gnomish joints cracking with the effort. He stowed the two shovels in his pack, then looked to the kender.

But Razmous and Conundrum were busy staring at something off through the trees. "What is that?" Sir Grumdish whispered, stepping closer and peering over Conundrum's shoulder.

"It just appeared," Conundrum breathed in awe.

"It looks like a cottage," the kender said. "A cottage made of—"

"Vanilla-flavored frozen-sugar-cream!" Doctor Bothy finished for him.

"Looks more like custard to me," Conundrum offered.

"I was going to say butter," Razmous said.

Doctor Bothy laughed and ran past his companions. "Don't be ridiculous! Who ever heard of a cottage made of butter?" he cried, his last words fading away even as he disappeared into the darkness.

Despite his girth, the doctor displayed an unexpected agility and speed. No one could keep up with him, not even the nimble-footed kender. They raced after him as best they could while being careful not to brain themselves against some tree in the dark. But Doctor Bothy leaped and darted through wood and glen like some fey creature out of a dream.

He reached the cottage before any of the others, and they found him already eating his way through one of the walls. A strange, yellow light emanated from the interior of the cottage, setting it aglow in the midst of the woods. Doctor Bothy turned at Razmous's shout, creamy goo dripping from his beard and the tip of his nose, and coating his arms up to the elbows.

"It ith fanitha-flaforeth frothenthugarcreamth!" he shouted with his cheeks bulging full of frozen dessert.

"Truly?" Razmous cried with delight. He dearly loved vanilla-flavored frozen-sugar-cream, even more than the greediest gnome.

"Un-hungh!" the doctor moaned in ecstasy.

Razmous started forward, but Sir Grumdish pulled him back by the shoulder of his green vest. "Not so fast, kender!" he snarled, pushing Razmous into Conundrum's arms. "Here, hold onto him and don't let him go. I'm going after Doctor Bothy before anything happens. Something uncanny is afoot here."

With that, he stomped off toward the doctor, who was even then teetering on his toes in an effort to sink his teeth into the fudge drooping from the eaves of the cottage.

Suddenly, Doctor Bothy gripped his ears, squeezed his head in his hands, and staggered back with a cry. Sir Grumdish rushed forward and steadied him, crying, "What's the matter? Are you injured? Poisoned? Magicked?"

The doctor shook his head and tried to push Sir Grumdish away. "It's nothing. A frozen-sugar-cream headache is all."

Before Sir Grumdish could give voice to his annoyance with the doctor, a queer tittering giggle echoed through the forest. The doctor looked up in surprise. Sir Grumdish looked down. Conundrum heard it right in front of his face, so near that he fell backward over a log. But Razmous spun around, peering into the forest behind them. He heard the giggling everywhere.

Then, with a pop like a cork from a bottle of gigglehiccup, the magical house disappeared. Two more loud pops followed in succession, one for Doctor Bothy, and the second for Sir Grumdish, who vanished even as he was turning in surprise at the sudden and noisy disappearance of the good doctor. Razmous and Conundrum stared in horror for a moment at the now empty forest clearing, then turned, and without any clear purpose or direction, fled screaming into the night.

That is to say, Conundrum fled screaming. Razmous, being a kender, wasn't exactly frightened. Instead, he was mightily concerned, and he ran calling, "Doctor Bothy! Sir Grumdish!" in his loud ringing kender voice. No one answered, and he didn't wait around to listen. It was all he could do to keep up with his gnome companion.

Conundrum knew not in which direction he fled, whether toward Jachim or away from it. Neither was he particularly frightened, yet he felt almost as if some extra-terrestial power had taken over his body and was hurling him as fast as his legs could carry him through a dark and fearsome forest.

Suddenly—and rather painfully—he caught his toe against a old gnarled root splaying across the path, and down he went. He threw out his hands to catch his fall and felt them sink up to his armpits in the soft leafy mold. But it didn't stop there. Down, down he fell, leaves and twigs and a spatter of loosened soil pouring down around him, and it was some moments before he realized he was slid-ing on his belly down a long stony slide that led deep underground.

Of course, what Razmous saw was Conundrum fall headfirst into nothingness, disappearing without even an accompanying pop. Instinctively, the kender leaped up and caught hold of a low-hanging limb. Looking down between his kicking feet, he found himself dangling over an ever-widening hole, a forest trap door with a honest-to-goodness stone slide leading downward to who knew what awful kind of awful doom.

So, naturally, he had to explore further. Obviously, Conundrum had gone that way, and if the doom was par-ticularly awful, the little gnome would need help. With a shrill squeal of delight, the kender let go of the branch and fell with a thud down the hole.

As he slid down the sloping tunnel on his rear end, Razmous noticed a blue light glowing somewhere below, and moments later a dark squat figure lurking in the middle of the slide. He slid smack into Conundrum, who, being lighter and falling from a lesser height, had less momentum to carry him all the way to the slide's bottom. The scale and construction of the trap bespoke of a design for much larger creatures and not light-boned peoples like gnomes or kender. Conundrum had slid to a stop many feet yet from the slide's end—wherever it was that it ended— but now Razmous, being a little bigger and with the added momentum of plunging from the higher height of the tree, swept into him with a loud *oof!* Down the two continued, Conundrum on top, Razmous below, rubbing to the thickness of a few threads the seat of the latter's breeches against the stones.

Slowly, they ground to a halt a few feet from the end of the slide. Razmous pushed Conundrum out of his lap and leaped up, swatting at his behind and hopping around on one foot. Spotting a trickle of water running down one of the walls, he backed against the wall and stood there sighing, his eyelids fluttering.

Meanwhile, Conundrum investigated their surroundings. The slide came to an end at the edge of a deep, dank pit, from the sides of which protruded numerous old rusty sword blades and spear heads, all set into the stone at a downward angle as though to prevent those falling into the pit from climbing out. The strange blue glow they had noticed earlier had turned red as blood, but even as Conundrum looked round and Razmous cooled his stone-chafed hindquarters, it began to change to a cool dim violet. The glow originated from a multitude of tiny worms feeding on moss growing on the walls and stony roof overhead. Each worm glowed with blue or red phosphorescence, but as Conundrum examined them, more and more of the red ones turned blue.

Razmous joined him in peering at the curious little worms, then very gently allowed several to crawl onto his outstretched fingers. He giggled at the feel of the tiny creatures nosing about the creases of his palm.

"I wonder what happened to Sir Grumdish and Doctor Bothy," he whispered, glancing around and dropping the worms into one of his pouches, "And I wonder what this place is."

Conundrum stood at the edge of the slide, looking up. He shrugged. "A trap of some kind," he answered.

Razmous peered over the side and into the pit. "Yes, but who built it, and for what? You don't suppose there is anything down there in that dark, fearsome-looking hole, do you?"

"I don't know, and I don't want to find out," Conundrum declared.

"But what if it is some sort of horrible monster that fell in long ages ago and has been down there ever since, languishing in the dark, unable to escape, with hunger ever gnawing at its reason? Poor blighter. I almost feel sorry for it, don't you?"

"Not particularly! I'd rather go back to the ship and get help," Conundrum said. "We've got to rescue Sir Grumdish and Doctor Bothy somehow—assuming they need rescuing."

Searching the floor and walls of the slide for cracks and fingerholds, Conundrum started up the slide. With a sigh of disappointment, Razmous followed.

The stones were mossgrown and slimy, and the slope steep and treacherous. Before they had gone very far, even the nimble kender found himself unable to progress farther without climbing aids of some sort, and without the glow of the worms, the passage was dark as a goblin den. He brushed back a few loose topknot hairs with one begrimed hand, then stepped back and glanced up the slope. High above, at what distance he could not begin to guess, he thought he saw a light like a star winking. He blinked, but then it was gone.

"We're stuck," Razmous sighed. "There's no way out, not unless you can invent something."

"What do you mean?" Conundrum asked.

Razmous shrugged. "You're the gnome! I thought you might invent some machine to get us out of here."

"I can't make machines out of air. I can't even see in this . . ." his words trailed off, then he muttered, "Machines made of air? Hmmm."

"Shhh!" the kender hissed like a broken steam pipe. "I hear voices!"

"What are they telling you to do?" Conundrum asked, suddenly filled with concern.

The kender slapped him in the dark. "Not that kind! *Real* voices. Listen!"

They held their breaths and listened with straining ears. Conundrum pressed his ear to the wall. At first, there was nothing, but then he heard, muffled at first by unguessable thicknesses of stone and earth, now growing more distinct as they approached closer, two voices as alike as the chirping of two crickets. Or it might have been one voice carrying on a conversation with itself.

"I tell you I heard a noise, and the beetlespriggins reported that the hole has opened and the glowworms were red," said one. "That can only mean something is in the trap."

"Beetlespriggins! I'd sooner trust our own mother than trust beetlespriggins. You're dreaming!" the other admonished. "Let's go back and watch them torture the prisoners."

Conundrum's breath caught in his throat. Razmous clapped a hand over his mouth.

Suddenly, a tiny door appeared in the wall almost between Conundrum's feet. Out popped a creature about the size of a beaver, only it was covered from head to head with short bristling spines, like a hedgehog. Razmous checked again. It was true—covered *head to head* with spines. The creature had an identical spine-bristled head at either end, so that he couldn't tell if it was coming or going. A warm yellow glow spilled around it, apparently from some tiny torch or glowglobe hidden within the secret passage.

It crept out between Conundrum's legs, seemingly without noticing them, and peered with its leading head down the pit.

"There. It's like I said. The worms are blue. There's nothing in the pit, or if it is, then it's dead!" the first head cackled.

"Good! I'm hungry," the rearward head said.

"Nar! It'll wait. I wants to watch the interrogation. Back us up, now."

"But what if it's a troll?" the second head argued. "Hole won't hold trolls."

" 'Tweren't no troll," the first head said. "You'd of known if it was a troll. Here, if you won't back us up, turn round and let me go first, then."

"I can do it. You're always wanting to go first. I get tired of being backwards." Without turning, the creature started back into the hole.

Suddenly, the now-rearward head—formerly the leading head—hissed, "Don't look now, Bern, but it *is* something."

The creature stopped, half in and half out of its hole.

"What is it, Stang?" the forward head asked with a trembling voice.

"Some kind of . . . of . . . dwarf! And a long-haired elf, I think," the rearward head answered. Its voice then sank to a whisper. "And what's more, the dwarf is standing right above us!"

"I'm not an elf, I'm a kender," Razmous declared, extending his small, slime-smeared hand. "And this is a gnome!"

"Run, Bern!" the rearward head screeched, its tiny rat-like eyes opening wide in fear at the kender's reaching paw.

"You run, too, Stang!" the forward head shouted, while all four of its tiny legs began to spin, claws scrabbling on the slick stones.

"There's no need to run. I won't hurt you," Razmous said, reaching down and catching the creature by one of its legs before it could get away, "very much."

He lifted it off the ground, but the strange little creature responded by rolling itself up into a small, spiky ball. The spines dug painfully into Razmous's knuckles, and he dropped it.

The creature bounced once, twice, three times and then it was gone, rolling away at a tremendous speed toward the gaping, sword-rimmed pit. Conundrum made a grab to try to save it, but got a jab in the meaty part of his thumb for his efforts, and nearly lost his balance. Razmous caught him by the collar to steady him, then went back to sucking his own throbbing, stinging fingers. They heard a sharp double cry, followed by a small, muffled thud.

They looked down at the small door, which still stood open, spilling out a small trapezoid of yellow light. Razmous knelt and peered into it.

"Do you think . . . ?" Conundrum asked.

Nodding, Razmous said, "Doctor Bothy is much too fat to make this squeeze. So we'll have to find another way out, once we rescue them."

CHAPTER

13

Several dozen small stinging flies buzzed round Doctor Bothy's head, laughing at him with their tiny, buzzing voices. He blinked awake, squinting into a bright light. After a few moments he realized that the light was only a candle, but it was blinding compared to the darkness of the previous hour.

However, the candle was quite plainly hanging upside down from the ceiling, its flame pointed straight at the ground in blatant defiance of every law of nature. He blinked again, trying to shake the hair out of his face, then he remembered he was bald. The hair was his beard. With that realization, the full horror of his situation rushed at him like a starved gully dwarf, yellow teeth flashing.

It was he who was upside down, bound with hundreds of blackberry vines and dangling by a rope looped over a particularly thick tree root in the ceiling. Dancing round him in the air were several dozen small, naked, fantastically-painted and gossamer-winged beings that seemed right out of a child's picture album, except that many wore hideous masks carved out of acorn caps and the half-shells of walnuts and pecans. Others brandished tiny, needle-tipped spears from which depended a variety of shrew skulls, hummingbird feathers, dusty gray mouse scalps, and other diminutive-yet-no-less-horrific trophies. Every once in a while, one of the fierce little creatures would fly closer and prod him with the butt of its spear, an action which reminded him all too vividly of a cook testing the doneness of his roast. He glanced up—no, he reminded himself, down—and to his relief saw not a cooking fire smoldering beneath him, but a single yellow candle affixed to the floor in its own pool of hardened wax.

Then again, maybe these tiny creatures were used to cooking their meals over the flame of a candle, he thought with a shudder. He wondered how long it would take him to cook by candle.

"Stop that!" someone shouted.

Doctor Bothy craned his head round and discovered that Sir Grumdish hung nearby, similarly trussed and dangling over a single green candle. He angrily spat his beard from his mouth. This seemed to amuse the creatures to no end. They buzzed merrily around the small, stuffy underground chamber, squeaking, "Monkey talk! Monkey talk! Listen monkey talk!"

"I am not a monkey!' Sir Grumdish spat. Every time he opened his mouth, his beard fell into it.

One of the creatures swooped close and hovered a few inches from the tip of Sir Grumdish's nose, its wings a blur. It gathered up a fistful of the gnome's white beard. "Hair . . . face . . . monkey!" it cried with glee, then gave Sir Grumdish's beard a sharp tug. Sir Grumdish bellowed in pain and tried to twist his head away, which only set him to swinging in crazy circles.

"Why are you doing this?" Doctor Bothy asked.

"This is your fault, Bothy!" Sir Grumdish howled. "I hold you to be responsible. I should have let you eat that whole cottage."

"Please be quiet, Grumdish!" the doctor shouted. "I am trying to establish polite communication."

"How do you propose to accomplish this miracle?" Sir Grumdish mocked.

The tiny creatures now concentrated on the doctor, buzzing all around his head. They took turns thwacking him on the thighs and belly with their small spear-staves, giggling uproariously at the way the blows rippled across the expanse of his dangling portliness, like waves in a pond. "Cry fat monkey! Fat monkey cry!"

"This is intolerable!" the doctor wailed.

Suddenly, the tiny creatures let off and flew away to the corners of the chamber to hide amongst the roots dangling from the roof or sprouting from the walls. Doctor Bothy tried to turn his head to see what had startled them. Grumdish slowly twirled at the end of his entangling vines, first one way, then the other.

The only thing unusual they saw was a small door in the center of one wall. It was set into an arched frame of rough unmorticed stones. Through the cracks in this door, they noticed a bright white light shining, but a shadow came before it, walking with a slow, purposeful gait toward the door. They also noticed a peculiar scrape-thumping noise, repeated at regular intervals, like a shutter tossed against the side of a house in a storm. As the shadow behind the door grew larger, the odd noise grew louder, until it seemed to be just outside the room. Then, ominously, it stopped. A nervous titter rippled through the room's occupants, gnomish and otherwise.

The door creaked open, spilling the light brightly across the floor. A cold gust of wind snuffed out the two candles, casting the chamber into startling contrasts of light and shadow. The roots hanging down from the roof took on a horrific aspect, as though they might writhe suddenly to life and reach out to grip and choke the helpless gnomes. The two gnomes cried out in terror, their eyes starting from their heads at the thing that lurked in the open doorway.

Its shadow stretched across the length of the floor and loomed up the further wall. Most like a bear it seemed, standing on its hind legs, but it had a tiny head sunk down between its shoulders, and no neck at all. What was more, it had only one leg. The other was a wooden peg.

As it entered the chamber stump-clumping on its wooden leg, it seemed to diminish in size, if not fearsomeness. They perceived that it was not a bear but a largish badger, but this failed to bring them much comfort, for what difference is it whether a bear or a badger enters your room stumping along on a wooden peg? It seemed to walk with something of a swagger, exaggerated by its false leg, and it carried a small, twisted twig or stick tucked military-fashion under one arm—or foreleg—like a riding crop. It was from the nether tip of this curious wand that the brilliant white light emanated.

The badger strode a few paces into the chamber before stopping and gazing up with hate-filled eyes at the two dangling gnomes. The door, seemingly of its own accord, swung shut and thudded in its frame. The badger then flipped the stick—which was a wand—out from under its arm and stood it on the floor before him, like a staff of office, his small, clawed fists gripping it fiercely. The glow at its tip softened and dimmed until it was no brighter than the flame of a single candle.

"Who are these miserable creatures?" the badger snarled.

"My name is Doctor Bothy," the doctor gasped after he had got over his astonishment. "And this is Sir Grumdish, a knight of renown."

The badger thumped his staff/wand on the ground three times, which had the effect of starting a spume of sparks from its glowing end. The sparks fell about him like a shower, and where they settled, they seemed to cling together in a discernible shape or pattern. In moments, they had formed a large chair or throne, which continued to glow and throb with its own light. The badger eased his furry bulk into this amazing piece of furniture.

"Say, you wouldn't mind lending me your wand, once this is cleared up and we are released?" Bothy said. "I know some folks who'd like to study it for a day or so."

The badger shouted, "Silence!"

His small but powerful voice tolled like a bell, resounding through the small underground chamber, and Doctor Bothy found that his tongue was suddenly stuck to the roof of his mouth, as though he had been eating hot marshmallows.

"What did we do to deserve this?" Sir Grumdish asked angrily.

"You did criminally bury your nasty haggis in my forest," the badger said.

"Your forest?"

"*My* forest!" the one-legged badger growled. "I am Grim Alderwand, king of this place. This very night by light of the ugly new moon, you fouled my forest with your nasty sheepses' stomachs. What vine did you hope to sprout from such a seed?"

Before either astonished gnome could answer, the creature continued, speaking now to no one, or perhaps to everyone. He lifted his small black eyes to the roof and raised his hands as though invoking heaven. "These nasty monkeys is always stinking up my forest with their rubbishes. We are the burrowers, the diggers under the roots. We finds all these things that they be trying to be hiding here, their garbages and their fish heads and their nasty sheepses' offals. They are worse than trolls, for trolls eat everthings: bones, scales, prickles and all. But these mens, these humans . . ."

"But we are not humans. We are gnomes!" Sir Grumdish argued.

"And a kender," Doctor Bothy mumbled, finally freeing his tongue from its magical confines.

"Did you not this very night dig holes in our forest for to hide your nasty haggises?" the badger king asked.

"It was horrible! We couldn't eat it, or at least some of us couldn't," Sir Grumdish said, glancing sharply at the doctor. "We had no other choice!"

"Yes, we didn't wish to be impolite to our hosts, and we certainly couldn't keep the haggis onboard our ship," Doctor Bothy said. "We have a long sea voyage ahead of us, and we don't want to attract sharks."

"Yet you are impolite to us, most impolite indeed, I must say," the king said, looking round. The shadows in the corners shifted and hummed with the winged creatures hiding there. "You does not want to take the sheepses offals into your houses, so you come here and bury it in ours."

"But we didn't know you were here," Sir Grumdish said.

"That is because monkeys, so high up their trees, never looks down to see whose head it is upon which they are peeing," the king said, waving his wand over his head like a director's baton. "When you monkeys come round our homes burying your haggises and fish heads, you do not think of these trolls that your nasty things attract. And when these trolls come rooting round our houses for sheep stomachses that you are burying, which they can smell from miles away I can tell you by golly, they do not care if they accidentally eat themselves a hedgehog or a badger or whatnot!"

"We meant no offense," Doctor Bothy said.

"Yet offense you have given," the king countered.

"How can we make amends?" the doctor asked. "Truly,

for we gnomes are sympathetic to your plight. You call us monkeys and confuse us with humans, but we are smaller than humans and are ever their subjects."

"Even now, humans rule our home mountain in the name of an evil dragon," Sir Grumdish added.

"They do not take us very seriously," Doctor Bothy continued, "and then only when something goes wrong or explodes."

"That all sounds very terrible," the king sympathized. "Very terrible indeed. Yet it does not excuse you to come burying your haggis in our roofs to attract these trolls hereabouts to come and eat us up. If these things that you are telling me are true, then you should have been even more thoughtful than these other monkeys who live in the villages."

"What are you going to do with us?" Sir Grumdish asked worriedly.

"We will take you up to the forest again," the king said.

Sir Grumdish sighed in relief. Doctor Bothy said, "Good. Because I didn't want to complain, but all the blood has gone to my head, hanging upside down this way."

"Yes, you will be taken to the forest," the badger king continued, smiling in a snarly sort of way, baring his short but wicked fangs, "and there you will be hung from the tree under which you buried your nasty haggis. Then, when the trolls come sniffing round, they can eat *you*, rather than our small burrowing selveses."

"I told you we went the wrong way," Conundrum said. He and Razmous stood at the mouth of a dark forest cave, looking out at the stars peeping through treetops.

"I went down," Razmous said as he stood there scratching his head. "Everybody knows that when you are in a dungeon, you go down to find its secret chambers, not up. Up is for haunted castles and ruined towers. Down is for dungeons."

"Well, down brought us to the entrance, seemingly," Conundrum said. "Or perhaps it is an exit. I don't see any guards."

"There's only one thing to be done. We must go back," Razmous said, with not a little enthusiasm. "Sometimes getting lost isn't such a bad thing, you know. I've been lost many times, and I've often had a better time than when I knew where I was going."

He turned and led the way back into the dark depths of the cave. They felt their way along the wall until they found the small entrance through which they'd come. The kender ducked down to enter it, then froze, a hiss whistling through his teeth.

"That's torn it!" Razmous whispered. "There's a light! Someone's coming. We can't get in this way now."

"Let's hide. Maybe they'll pass." By the light shining from the passageway, they made their way to a crack in the far wall and squeezed themselves into it to hide. Razmous had to turn his pouches sideways just to make it inside the crack before the light emerged into the cave.

"This crack must lead somewhere," the kender whispered. "I feel a draft."

"I should say you do," Conundrum answered with a barely-suppressed snicker. "You've finished tearing out the seat of your breeches."

But they had no more time to discuss cave exploration or the superiority of various fabrics. From the small passage appeared as strange a procession as even the kender was ever likely to see in his long and adventurous life. A dozen or more badgers and hedgehogs, some with one head, some with two, and some with as many as four, strode into the cavern. They walked upright with a curious

waddling gait and carried in their tiny paws a comparatively tall pole. From the end of the pole depended a small
glass globe glowing with a wan blue light. Conundrum realized with a start that the globes were glowing because they
were filled with the tiny glowworms they had seen earlier
in the trap. In quick whispers, he described to Razmous
what he, being wedged in front, saw.

"Ah, yes! How ingenious!" the kender replied also in a
whisper. "We could use those onboard the boat when we
dive!"

Next to emerge from the passageway was a pair of badgers crawling along on all fours. These looked more primitive and stupid—and vicious—than their upright,
multi-headed fellows, and each wore a type of muzzle
made of woven grapevine. The badgers were bound together by a sort of harness, to which was attached a squat,
two-wheeled cart. Atop the cart, secured with numerous
ropes and blackberry vines, lay the enormous bulk of their
friend and shipmate, the good doctor Bothy. Another pair
of muzzled badgers appeared behind the cart, towing Sir
Grumdish similarly trussed. Last came a second company
of badgers and hedgehogs, some carrying coils of rope,
others with tiny silver crossbows held at the ready. With
ponderous ceremony they crossed the floor of the cavern
and vanished into the nighttime forest.

Conundrum slipped out of their hiding place and scampered silently to the cave's mouth. Razmous followed, and
the two of them peered out of the cave into the night-dark
woods. It was as though the motley group had vanished
from the face of Krynn. The two crept out, listening, staring into the deep shadows for any sign of their friends.
Finally, they spotted a gleam of blue light, like a will-o-wisp
floating up the hillside through the trees. They set off after
the light, moving as quietly and quickly as possible in the
unfamiliar woods.

Before they reached the hilltop, they came upon the returning party of badgers and hedgehogs. Razmous scampered like a squirrel up a tree, while Conundrum hid behind a large black boulder overgrown with gray lichens and straggling vines of blackberry laden with unripe red fruit. The badgers passed first, pulling their now-empty carts, followed closely by the hedgehogs. When they had gone, vanished with hardly a sound down the hill, Conundrum stole out from his hiding place.

The kender swung down from his branch and landed with a crunching thump in the leaves. "What do you suppose they've done with them?" the kender asked.

A scream of terror, echoing through the woods, seemed to answer his question. They paused a moment, their faces turning gray as they looked at one another, then Razmous was off like a shot, quickly leaving Conundrum struggling up the hillside as fast as his legs could carry him. Soon, he was utterly alone in the vast dark wood, too frightened to call out, with only the steady blue glow at the hilltop to guide him.

As Conundrum neared the light, he slowed and crept forward cautiously. Another scream rent the night, followed closely by a long rumbling laugh, like a boulder rolling down the hillside. A screen of matted vines hid from him the source of the light, which was now red—he guessed its cause—and the laughter. He tried to find a way through the vines, but finding them thorny and tangled, he chose to search for a path around. He started off to his right, only to stumble into a hole of some sort. He almost cried out in surprise, but something caught him and kept him from falling. At the same moment, a small hand clapped over his mouth. He struggled a moment, then grew still at the sound of Razmous's voice whispering in his ear.

"Be very, very quiet, unless you want to get eaten," the kender said as he removed his hand from Conundrum's mouth and set him back on his feet.

"Why? What's wrong?" Conundrum asked.

In answer, the kender pointed through a gap in the vines. Conundrum closed one eye and peered through.

In the clearing beyond stood a troll, its massive fists resting on its narrow hips, and its long gangly neck craned back to stare up into the trees at the two gnomes dangling just out of its long-armed reach. The badgers and hedgehogs had left a half dozen of their glowworm globes lying about on the ground, apparently either to attract the troll or to allow the gnomes to see their doom. The globes glowed with a deep crimson light as the gnomes above struggled and wept. The troll stood below them, contemplating a way to get at the juicy, vine-wrapped morsels.

Doctor Bothy, being the fatter of the two, especially attracted the troll's attention. The creature gazed at him with its black eyes and smacked its leathery lips in anticipation.

"A troll!" Conundrum gasped. He had heard of such monsters, but it was the first he had ever seen. It was nearly as tall as the chaos beast that had nearly eaten him a few weeks ago, and it was tremendously strong, as it proved when it strode over to the towering oak from which the gnomes dangled, grabbed its massive trunk in its claws, and shook the tree vigorously. Doctor Bothy and Sir Grumdish tossed and jangled at the end of their ropes, but they did not fall. The troll growled in annoyance and stared up at them.

"Isn't this the same place where—" Conundrum began.

"Where we buried the haggis, yes," Razmous finished for him.

"Well, that's awfully convenient. It makes things much easier."

"Easier? How?" Razmous asked.

"Don't worry. I've got a idea!" Conundrum said, scrunching up his eyes in a huge grin. Razmous leaned close as Conundrum explained his plan. The kender only smiled more broadly as he heard it. He clapped a hand over his mouth to suppress a giggle.

"Can you do it?" Conundrum asked.

"Certainly!" Razmous bragged. "No problem."

"After you do your part, I'll skinny up the tree and cut them down," Conundrum said.

"Then you'll need this," Razmous said as he dug through his pouches. He removed something and pressed it into the gnome's hand. Conundrum opened his fingers and looked at it.

"What's this?" he asked.

"Commodore Brigg's remarkable all-purpose-thousand-in-one-uses-folding-knife. He must have dropped it while we weren't eating our haggis, and I forgot to give it back to him," Razmous explained. "When I give the signal, you can start."

With that, he dashed away as silently as a cat

"Signal? But what's the signal?" Conundrum asked, but Razmous had already gone, vanished, as quiet as quiet can. He had left his pouches, which meant he meant business. Conundrum chewed his lip and peered back through the gap in the vines, waiting and listening.

"I don't think I can skinny up anything," he muttered, having second thoughts. "Oh, well. I'll solve that puzzle when I come to it."

The troll apparently had a new idea for getting at the gnomes. In one huge long, knobby hand it held a largish stone, about the size of mush melon, and it was at the moment searching the ground for another. Conundrum had no doubt that, once it had dug up a similarly-sized boulder, it would fling them at his friends, like a child trying to knock a beloved toy from the crook of a tree. Conundrum gripped Commodore Brigg's wonderful all-purpose knife and waited. He wondered for a moment

JEFF CROOK

whether it had a tool that might prove of use against trolls. He knew it had one for clipping nose hairs, but he didn't know if trolls had nose hairs, nor did he much care to get close enough to find out. But they did have jolly big noses, of that he was sure.

Then he heard the kender's voice on the other side of the clearing. Razmous was shouting in a mocking sing-song voice, "I say, you'll never get them down that way. What you need is a ladder or longer arms. But I don't suppose you have thought of that, have you, your being a troll and all?"

The troll stopped and glared around, its piggy black eyes prying into every shadow. Conundrum felt sure he would be seen, despite the screen of the vines. He crouched down and gripped the all-purpose knife more tightly.

Meanwhile, Razmous continued. "I heard once that trolls reproduce by budding, but I don't believe it. They say that when you want to have a family, you just rip off various body parts and throw them on the ground to grow new versions of yourself. That must be why you are all so butt-ugly. But of course, that can't be true, because everyone knows that trolls are so ugly when they're born the doctor slaps the mother."

The troll dropped his boulders and growled. His long warty nose tested the air.

"And their noses are so long because that's what the doctor steps on when he pulls out your tails," Razmous taunted. His voice seemed to come from various places within the forest, first here and now there, so that the troll was making itself dizzy turning round and round.

"Of course, when he pulls out your tail, most of your brain comes with it, the troll butt being the scientifically proven location of the troll brain. Or, I should say, what's left of the troll brain. When you sit down, aren't you afraid you will smother yourself?"

With a howl of rage, the troll tore off into the forest. Razmous's voice floated back, pitched high to carry over the troll's infuriated thrashing through the forest.

"Now, Conundrum!"

Conundrum scurried from his hiding place into the clearing and ran over to the trunk of the tree where Doctor Bothy and Sir Grumdish hung, their mouths open wide in surprise. Searching all around the tremendous bole of the tree, Conundrum found no way to ascend and rescue his companions. He was as stuck as the troll, even more so. He stood beneath his friends, looking up at them helplessly.

"You need a ladder," Sir Grumdish said. "I don't suppose there is time to hurry back to the village. That troll won't chase him long. There hasn't been a troll born that could catch a kender in a wood."

"But I don't have a ladder," Conundrum cried. "What can I do?"

"It's a shame Commodore Brigg isn't here," Doctor Bothy sighed. "He'd have a an idea. Born leader, the commodore is."

"Oh, please, Bothy! Be reasonable. The lad feels bad enough as it is. No use comparing him to the good commodore. He's a great gnome, but he certainly doesn't go about with ladders in his pockets."

"Oh, but he does!" the doctor protested. "He has the most wonderful knife, invented by the master of the weapons guild in Mount Nevermind."

"I have it here!" Conundrum exclaimed. He showed it to them, holding it up on the palm of his hand.

"That's it! Glory and salvation, Conundrum, how did you come by it?" the doctor asked.

"Razmous!"

"I might have guessed," Sir Grumdish said. "Are you trying to tell us, Bothy, that thing has a ladder in it?"

"Yes!" Doctor Bothy said. "A mini-extension ladder. See if you can find it, Conundrum."

"I'll try." He began flipping out the knife's various tools and apparatuses. There was a curly-cue wire useful for removing corks from bottles of medicine and whatnot, a thin, flat shim such as a burglar might use to slip open the latch on a window, a tiny pair of scissors not useful for much of anything, a larger pair of scissors useful for trimming hedges or the beards of dwarves, a backscratcher, a small plow, a bronze birdbath with a sundial in the middle, a spoon, a fork, even a tiny plate and frying pan. Conundrum wondered if he might not soon come across the stove, and the dinner, too! Before long, he looked as if he had the entire contents of a kender's bedtable drawer clutched in his hands.

Suddenly, out of the commodore's pocket apparatus sprang a thirty-foot ladder with rubber safety pads on the feet to keep it from slipping. Conundrum nearly fell over in surprise, which would have been disastrous, as he would likely have been skinned, filed, polished, trimmed, julienned, and uncorked all at the same time.

"Good show!" Sir Grumdish shouted. "Now climb up here and cut us down."

"Um . . ." Conundrum hesitated, still flipping through tools.

"What is it?" Doctor Bothy hissed. "Hurry, before the troll comes back!"

"Um, there doesn't seem to be . . . um, a knife," Conundrum said as he looked up in dismay. Then he spun round, for something was coming through the woods toward them.

———◆———

Razmous Pinchpocket ran for his life, as only a kender can run when a troll is hot on his heels. He could almost feel its hot, reeking breath on his neck as his topknot cracked like a flag in the wind of his speed. The dark forest flashed by, and he dodged, dipped, ducked, and leaped like a whirling dervish, avoiding low-hanging branches that would have brained him, groping roots that would have tripped him, and looming trunks that would have pulverized him had he run into them head on.

And he wouldn't have had it any other way.

There is nothing that makes a kender feel quite so alive as the hot breath of doom blowing down his shorts. Perhaps it is the nearness of death that makes the creatures so enjoy life, like the condemned prisoner who treasures every moment, every glimmer of the sun off the spiderwebs in his cell, the taste of the earth in the stale bread and rank water that is his last meal. The kender race is without fear, a trait that gives them their power and indeed their very nature, their spirit, their reason for living, and at the same time usually leads to their demise. For it is lack of fear that makes them such intrepid travelers, and it is lack of fear that provides the only real check on their population. The kender are too peaceful and good-natured to involve themselves in war, too clever with their hands in other peoples pockets to ever starve, and too mobile to be threatened by plague. The normal limiting factors that keep most civilizations from destroying themselves utterly or so theorize the gnomes of the Philosophers' Guild, are completely absent from the kender race because of their very nature. So the gods made them fearless, to keep them from ruling the world.

But Razmous wasn't thinking of all this as he fled from the troll. He was thinking of his leap. He must time the leap perfectly, or else end up on top of an angry troll at the bottom of a very deep, sword-lined hole.

Of course, it had come to him as he sat in the briars looking at the troll stalking round his dangling friends, that the badgers and hedgehogs had built their trap to catch trolls, among other things. Nothing else could explain the trap's gargantuan scale, its huge stones, and wide, deep, sword-lined pit. And he thought, if I can get the troll to chase me to the pit, maybe I can get him to fall into it, too. Of course, there is always the danger that the limb will break, or that I will miss it in the dark, or that I won't be able to leap the hole. . . .

Really, he reminded himself, he had been around gnomes for far too long. He was almost beginning to think like a gnome, more concerned with a thousand possibilities and designing against what might go wrong than concentrating on making it go right—or at least trying to make it go right. The trying was the important part, he reminded himself, as he slapped aside a sapling and hurtled a fallen log. After this voyage, he planned to find some kender and go on a real adventure for a change.

Then he saw it, or thought he saw it. He saw something that certainly looked like it—a darker spot against the near-blackness of the forest floor, and a tree looming over it. The troll was almost on his heels, and there were twenty yards to go, twenty open yards in which the troll's longer legs could gain the advantage. Razmous wondered if he would soon feel the troll's hot breath upon his neck, like in the stories told by bards. Ten yards now, and he felt something tug briefly at his topknot. It might have been the troll clutching at the rippling pennant of hair streaming out behind the kender, or it might have been only a bit of underbrush becoming momentarily entangled in his top-knot. In any case, it gave Razmous the brief surge of encouragement—he liked to call it—to cover the last few yards and leap for the tree's overhanging limb.

He caught it, swung up almost vertical, and reversed his grip like a trapeze artist so that on the down swing he'd be facing the way he had come. He swung down to find the troll teetering on the edge of the trap, its long arms swinging wildly, trying to maintain its balance. Seeing the kender within easy reach, it shot out one clawed hand and grabbed him by the legs, and this, oddly enough, proved its downfall.

Razmous, caught in the troll's deadly grasp, tried to pull free, which was just enough to overbalance the troll and drag it into the pit. Of course, now Razmous was dangling from a tree limb, and the troll was dangling from him. The kender cried out in agony as he felt his arms being wrenched from their sockets, while the troll's cruel nails dug into the flesh of his legs. The troll thrashed and kicked, trying to find some purchase with its long black toes against the sides of the trap's stony walls, and it roared in fury and fear. Only by the most heroic effort did Razmous manage to hang onto the tree limb as long as he did.

He felt his fingers slipping, slipping . . . the skin of his palms tearing against the cruel bark of the tree . . .

But it wasn't his skin or even his joints that gave way first. It was his breeches. Worn to a frazzle from sliding down chutes and crawling through stone cracks and bramble patches, the last few threads now tore with a small ripping noise. The troll seemed to hang in the air a moment, staring in amazement at the sun-bleached yellow rags clutched in its fist, before it vanishing with a cry down the hole—a cry that, seconds later, was suddenly cut short.

Razmous looked down the hole and heaved a pained sigh before pulling himself up into the tree. He sat balanced on the tree limb for a moment, contemplating his next move. The sea breeze felt cool as it stirred the fine downy hair covering his much-paler legs.

"It's a good thing this is the balmy north," he groaned as he scrambled to his feet on the branch and teetered there like a high-wire artist that he had seen in Palanthas once, "and there are no ladies about."

Conundrum faced the creature thrashing through the woods toward them, the ball of convenient tools clutched protectively before him. He hoped it would make him look more dangerous somehow.

"It's only me!" said a high, thin voice from the deep shadows beneath the trees.

"Razmous?" Conundrum asked.

"I see him!" Doctor Bothy said from his vantage point dangling high up in the tree. "I see his topknot!"

"Razmous, come help me!" Conundrum shouted. "There isn't a knife in Commodore Brigg's wonderful all-purpose knife."

"First I have to put some pants on," Razmous answered.

"What's happened to your pants?" Conundrum asked.

"More importantly, what happened to the troll?" Sir Grumdish demanded.

"Both fell in the trap," Razmous said as he stepped into the clearing, a large sheet of rotting bark held modestly before him. With every step, it rotted and crumbled just a little more.

Conundrum explained the trap to his companions while Razmous crossed the clearing and retrieved his pouches. From them, he pulled a freshly-washed pair of homespun trousers and a new set of bright yellow leggings. Behind the screen of the vines, he slipped them on, then settled his pouches over his shoulders and around his waist. When he returned to the clearing, he felt like a new kender.

"That's better," he announced.

"Do you always carry an extra set of clothes in your pouches?" Sir Grumdish said from the treetops. "I don't suppose you've got a knife or a dagger or anything actually useful for our current situation?"

Presently, Razmous produced one of Doctor Bothy's scalpels—one that had been missing for some weeks.

"It's a good thing for you that I found it!" the kender chirped as he sawed at the doctor's ropes.

But even with the ladder and the scalpel, there was little to prevent them from falling on their heads and breaking their necks once cut free. So cleverly had they been trussed that the cutting of a single strand would unravel the whole bunch and send them both plummeting headfirst to the ground. Conundrum managed to scrape together a smallish pile of dead leaves to cushion their fall somewhat, while Razmous advised them to try to fall as softly as possible.

"How, pray tell, shall I do that?" Sir Grumdish snarled as he watched the sharp blade slice into the final bit of rope from which he dangled.

"I don't know," Razmous answered crossly. "Pretend you are a feather!"

CHAPTER
14

In two weeks' time, the *Indestructible* looked quite a different ship than the one that had sailed from Sancrist.
For a solid fortnight after the adventure of the haggis burial
party, Commodore Brigg had worked the crew relentlessly,
re-outfitting the ship with various improvements and
changes necessary for the last unsubmerged leg of the journey. For one thing, the mast and sails were gone, replaced
by Doctor Bothy's Peerupitscope. Commodore Brigg declared that they would either be a sailing vessel, or a
spring-powered vessel, but they couldn't be both any
longer. Besides, they were now within a few days of beginning the underwater portion of their journey, at which
time they wouldn't need the mast and sails any longer. The
mast was removed and sold to a Palanthian timber merchant, and the sails were cut up and made into new hammocks for the crew. The forward sail compartment was
converted into an oil storage space and private cabin for
Chief Oilage Officer Conundrum. He had his own small
hammock stretched over several dozen large amphora jars
filled with various local oils, and a locker for his extra pair
of clean new woolen socks. The oils were for oiling the

gears and springs—something that would require all his attention now that they were using only the spring engines to power the ship.

Aft of the Peerupitscope, they installed the Snorkel. A network of pipes and tubes running all through the rafters of the *Indestructible* were connected to this Snorkel, which was in turn connected to a large bellows. The bellows were meant to pump the smoke out of the ship once the torches were lit and the ship submerged. This was a sound principle, though it hadn't been tested yet.

However, the haggis burial party's discovery of the glowwormglobes had made the Snorkel prematurely obsolete. In the two weeks it took to re-outfit the *Indestructible* with the Peerupitscope, Snork, Conundrum, and Razmous spent their days building a small, compact glowworm farm in the dark hold of the bilge. Fed on a rich supply of moss, the worms multiplied quickly enough to fill several dozen small glass globes in just two weeks. These were placed strategically throughout the ship—the bridge, the engine room, the kitchen, and the head—with an ensign assigned to conduct regular feedings at least twice each day. Razmous helped Conundrum collect enough moss to make sure they could feed their ever-growing population of tiny light sources.

They were sailing south by southeast, steering for the island of Saifhum. They had no intention of stopping there, but Saifhum guarded the entrance into the Blood Sea of Istar. By the time they sighted its shores after ten days of steady going, Conundrum was nearly worn out. The ship's spring engine provided plenty of power to push them along at a good clip, but it needed constant oiling. Finally, Commodore Brigg realized the enormity of his duties and reduced an exhausted Conundrum to the sole duty of first assistant cartographer, while his oilage assignments were passed on to Chief Portlost for distribution among the idlest members of the crew. Conundrum moved his meager possessions back to his cousin's quarters and slept for three solid days.

When he awoke, Saifhum was far behind, and the dirty crimson expanse of the Blood Sea lay all around, below, and above them. *Indestructible* had submerged.

The disappearance of the Maelstrom that once swirled at the Blood Sea's center didn't change the fact that the area was a dangerous place. It was still home to innumerable hazards—especially minotaur pirates, for their islands defined the eastern edge of the Blood Sea. It was also the abode of countless dragon turtles, leviathans, kraken, and all manner of dangerous sea beasts, not to mention ghost ships, will-o-the-seas, and other evil spirits who made a habit of leading ships to their watery graves on shallow rocks and dangerous shoals.

Therefore, the *Indestructible* was running submerged in order to avoid the worst of these dangers. There was still nothing to keep some sleepy leviathan from mistaking the ship for a large fish and swallowing it whole.

Even submerged, they had two close calls with pirate ships, one Ergothian and the other the same minotaur galley—or one very much like it—they had avoided off the coasts of Nordmaar not so very long ago. The minotaur ship nearly surprised them in the dark off the southern coast of Saifhum, but their encounter with the Ergothian pirates was an accident as a result of heavy fog. Without Doctor Bothy's Peerupitscope, they would have come to grief for certain.

In any case, Commodore Brigg asserted they could not continue to avoid these hazards much longer, as their luck was quickly running out. Therefore, he declared that should they reach Flotsam intact, they would re-outfit the ship once more, this time adding an extendable/retractable, iron-shafted ram. He and Chief Portlost sequestered themselves in the commodore's cabin for several nights drawing up the designs, which would require cutting the ship in half and opening it like a clam.

Eight days south of Saifhum, they passed over the ruins of ancient Istar, many hundreds of feet below the surface of the bloody sea. For a time, they discussed going down to at least have a look round and maybe draw up some maps so that they could better plan their course, but Commodore Brigg and Chief Portlost were anxious to get started on their ram and wouldn't abide a delay.

It was during these conversations that Conundrum asked, innocently enough and perhaps a bit naively, how exactly did they intend to have a look around and draw maps of the ruins, once they were down there? The *Indestructible* had no windows. This ended all further discussion about diving to the site, and the commodore and Chief Portlost spent several more sequestered evenings drawing up plans for installing portholes.

Soon they were but a day away from Flotsam, and Commodore Brigg had finished his designs. Chief Acquisitions Officer Razmous and Chief Engineer Portlost were below compiling a list of the supplies and materials they would need to effect the improvements. Doctor Bothy and Sir Grumdish were in the galley along with the rest of the crew eating the last of the ships' store of beans and salt meat. All that was left was hardtack and crackers, and everyone was glad to be nearing their destination, if for no other reason than they were dead tired of beans and salt pork. Professor Hap was in his quarters, heating very small rocks in the tiny oven he had designed according to the principles first enunciated by the cook's flashcooker (which still wasn't working properly; the cook was in sick bay at the moment,

soaking in a barrel of pickle juice to ease his burns).
Conundrum was on the bridge discussing the course of the
sub-Ansalonian passage with his cousin Snork, while the commodore kept a close eye on things through the Peerupitscope.

It was the end of a long and wearisome day, and even
the commodore was glad that they'd be arriving in Flotsam
on the morrow. The city was quite old and had a dark
reputation. Thieves, cutthroats, pirates, and ne'er-do-wells
of every evil sort found their way there, for Flotsam was a
bustling port, the largest human city on the eastern coast
of Ansalon, and the pickings were better there than anywhere else for many hundreds of miles around.

Still, they weren't likely to find any better place. Flotsam had decent dry dock facilities, plenty of supplies, and
good food and entertainment of the seedier sort. If one
knew where to look, and Razmous's *A Wandering Kender's
Almanac and Pocket Guide To Krynn* was a good place to
find out, one could find places where the host didn't water
the beer.

As Commodore Brigg stood with his eye pasted to the
Peerupitscope, he ran through all the things needing doing
once they reached Flotsam. The first order of business was
to arrange dry dock facilities. Next, he'd send Razmous in
search of a glazier capable of producing porthole windows
several inches thick, and also a good ramming beam,
preferable something made of aged ash or even ironwood,
to which they could then bolt a layer of iron. Not only
would the ram serve them well in an attack, they could also
use it to widen passages of the undersea caverns they'd be
exploring.

Next, they'd need to restock the ship with provisions.
Once they departed Flotsam on this final leg of the journey,
their supplies would have to last until they reached the
other side of the continent—if they made it.

Also, he reminded himself, they urgently needed to locate this Knight, this Tanar Lobcrow, although Commodore Brigg hoped that they'd not be able to find him. He didn't want a human aboard his vessel, especially not a Knight of the Thorn, for they were sorcerers, and like most of his race, Commodore Brigg had a fascination with magic, but no real use for it. And he distrusted Thorn Knights. Like most humans, they didn't take gnomes seriously, but Thorn Knights were especially bad because such sorcerers were generally distrustful of technology, and to be quite frank, jealous of it. Every gnome knew this by the time he learned to spell his name, a feat which usually takes years to master. (Commodore Brigg's name, for example, told the story of his entire family, from the time of the Graygem to the present, and took three days to pronounce.)

The commodore harbored no illusions about the real reason why the Knights of Neraka wanted to place one of their own aboard his ship. Just as Professor Hap-Troggensbottle was fond of saying, scientists had ever been the pawns of the military. With a fleet of deepswimmer submersibles, the Knights of Neraka could rule the seas. They could strangle any Solamnic port on the face of Krynn, or extort heavy "protection" fees from honest merchants. Commodore Brigg didn't trust this Tanar. He suspected him of being a warmonger and a spy, added to his trappings of sorcery.

Brigg hoped they'd not find the Thorn Knight, but, unfortunately, he knew exactly where to look for him. He had explicit directions from Sir Wolhelm, and indeed carried orders for Sir Tanar. He'd read these, of course, steaming the wax seal loose from the scroll and perusing its contents before they'd even left Sancrist. It was filled with the usual inane dribble, ordering Sir Tanar to observe and report any findings. As if they needed an official observer during this voyage! Everything would be duly recorded in triplicate and notarized by a notorious republican from the Useless Functionaries Guild. The Knights could glean from it all that they needed. Certainly, gnomes were better suited to the rigorous recording of minutiae than some infernal gray-robed human.

Sir Tanar Lobcrow took his meals in his room these days, as a general rule. The maids of the Sailor's Rest took turns changing his bedding—ever an unnerving undertaking, for the Thorn Knight often sat in a darkened corner of the room and watched them with glowering eyes. Rumors connected him to a mysterious suicide, and other rumors circulated that he was performing monstrous experiments and conversing with creatures that he summoned with his magic. The voices sometimes heard from behind his door seemed to prove this last point especially. He rarely bathed, shaved, or cut his hair, and his room, which he never seemed to leave any more, smelled abominably. Not even a small fire in the inn's kitchen provoked him to exit his chambers, even though the rest of the inn was evacuated.

And so it was that Sir Tanar failed to hear of the strange craft that appeared almost at the city's doorstep, rising up leviathan-like from the murky waters of the harbor at dusk the day before. Nor did the cries of the crowd that quickly gathered to view the curious ship and its even more curious crew reach his ears. While the citizens of Flotsam gathered to marvel at the new arrival, empty bottles of dwarf spirits continued to pile up outside Sir Tanar's door. As he had done most days, and as was his habit when not occupied with a job for the Knighthood, he drank all night long and into the late hours of the next morning, watching the sunrise but blind to its beauty. After wetting his parched lips with the last drop of dwarf spirits from his last bottle, he crawled under the bed to sleep.

It was in this state that Razmous and Conundrum found Sir Tanar, after pounding on the door failed to rouse him from his exhausted stupor. Conundrum had wanted to go for the innkeeper, but Razmous thought it better not to bother him, as it was such a simple lock on the door. It took him only seconds to open, and they entered cautiously, whispering the Thorn Knight's name.

At first they thought he'd stepped out for a moment, gone to enjoy the beautiful day despite the tale told by the innkeeper about Sir Tanar's drunken cloistering. They found the bed, rumpled and reeking of sweat, pushed into the far corner away from the window like some sort of barricade. A single wooden chair sat beside it. On the seat of the chair was a crust of stale bread on a gray pewter plate, and beside it an empty battered pewter flagon.

Razmous peeled back the sheets and recoiled at the sight of the vermin scurrying away from the morning light. Meanwhile, Conundrum lifted the edge of a blanket that had fallen off the end of the bed, and he discovered a foot in a worn gray slipper. The foot, which twitched in its sleep, was attached to the Thorn Knight. He lay on the floor under the bed on his side, curled into a ball, with a wooden box clutched to his chest. His thin lips were pulled back from his teeth in a hideous grin, his breath wheezed through his teeth as he slept, and his eyes rolled wildly beneath closed lids.

"Why is he sleeping under the bed, I wonder?" Conundrum pondered aloud.

"It's probably cleaner than the bed. Ugh!" Razmous shivered.

"Shall I wake him?" Conundrum asked.

"Let's have a look around first, and make sure nothing's been stolen while he slept. If it has, he'll be bound to accuse us. Wizards always do," the kender said sagely.

Razmous made a further search of the bed, but there were no treasures hidden beneath the pillows or the mattress. Conundrum sloshed the chamber pot with the toe of his shoe, one hand clapped firmly over his nose, while the kender hung half out the window and examined the exterior of the inn and the alley below. Next they overturned the table and the other chair to make sure nothing had been secreted on the underside. Finally, the desk beside the wall failed to yield anything of interest.

"How do you like that?" Razmous huffed. "This is some wizard. Not a ring or magic wand in sight. Just that box he's clutching like death. I wonder what's in it."

"Soap, I hope!" Conundrum said, pinching his nose. "He smells worse than a gully dwarf. I wonder what's wrong with him."

"Nothing some of Doctor Bothy's tonic won't cure," Razmous chuckled as he clambered under the bed. "I've seen cases like this before. Dwarf spirits will do this to a man. That box is probably full of bottles of liquor. The first thing to do it take it away from him and chuck it out the window."

"Do you think so?" Conundrum asked uncertainly.

" 'Sgotta be done. Can't cure him until the poison is removed," Razmous said with a grunt. "But he's holding . . . onto . . . it . . . awfully . . . tight."

Suddenly, the entire mattress and springs leaped from the bed frame. At the same moment, the kender cried, "Ow!" and the box came sliding out from under the bed. It bumped to a stop against Conundrum's shoe.

"Thieeeeeeeffff!" Sir Tanar howled as he crawled from beneath the bed. His long yellow fingernails clawed at the floor. "Thief! Stop, thief!"

"Hurry, Conundrum!" Razmous cried. "Throw it out the window!"

The gnome picked up the box and turned toward the open window, swinging the box back, preparing to hurl it like a mechanical discus thrower at the Mount Nevermind Games. Sir Tanar scrambled to his knees and pointed one clawlike finger at the gnome. "Stop! I command you!"

Conundrum felt as if his limbs had been turned to stone. He froze in place, his feet rooted to the floor, unable to even move an eyelid. Sir Tanar drew a dagger from his gray robes.

"Oh, that's impressive!" the kender said with a gasp. "Some kind of spell, I bet. I guess you've recovered from the dwarf spirits."

"Dwarf spirits?" the Thorn Knight snarled, spinning on his heel to face the startled kender. The man crouched like an animal, back hunched, fingers curled into claws around the hilt of his dagger, unkept black hair hanging in lank strands across his face. "Who said anything about dwarf spirits, you thief?"

"Thief! Well, I never . . ." Razmous stammered, unable to continue as he choked in rage at this undeserved insult.

Tanar turned once more to Conundrum, who had not moved. He stepped closer and pried the box from the gnome's iron grasp. "This box contains rare and priceless magics," he grunted, tearing the box free.

"Oh, so that's why Conundrum is frozen," the kender said, forgetting for a moment his offended dignity. "Neat trick. Can you undo it?"

A strangled cry escaped the gnome's clenched lips. "Ro roar. Ro roar, rease!"

"Who are you?" Sir Tanar growled, his eyes narrowing as he warily circled around the kender until he reached the desk. He set his box carefully on it, while never taking his eyes off the two.

"Razmous Pinchpocket," the kender said, proffering his small brown hand. The Thorn Knight ignored it. "I am chief acquisitions officer aboard the MNS *Indestructible*, sailing out of Pax on Sancrist Isle. This is First Assistant Cartographer Conundrum, of Mount Nevermind."

"Huh? What? The MNS *Indestructible*?" asked Sir Tanar, his speech slowing. "But you're a . . . a . . . kender!"

"Yes!" Razmous beamed.

"So," said Sir Tanar, licking his lips slightly, "you made it after all." He turned and waved his hand absent-mindedly at the still-frozen gnome. Conundrum, suddenly free of the spell, finished his throw empty-handed, nearly pitching himself out the window. Razmous caught him and dragged the terrified gnome back into the room.

"Naturally! Was there ever any doubt?" Razmous said.

CHAPTER
15

For over two months the gnomes stayed in Flotsam completing their modifications to the *Indestructible*. The ship had to be cut in half and the automatic retractable ram built into its superstructure. The three-inch-thick glass for the portholes had to be specially made, and the glazier's kiln was not large enough to accommodate the gnomes' needs, so a new one had to be designed. A large dwarven forge was converted, much to the dismay of the gnomes, who wanted to build the new kiln from scratch and incorporate into it their latest theories on the generation of high temperature by burning compressed garbage pellets.

Most of their work was conducted under a shroud of the strictest security. Before ever a rivet was popped or a nail pulled, Commodore Brigg posted guards at checkpoints along the quay approaching their dry dock. He issued identification badges to the crew and to a few carefully-screened contractors, like the glazier and the man who delivered the beer. He armed the guards with crossbows from the ship's weapons locker, for Flotsam was a seedy, disreputable town, and he feared the townspeople

—pirates and thieves, every one—might steal even the barnacles from the ship's hull.

Having recovered from his bout of dwarf spirits, Sir Tanar prowled Flotsam's scant libraries and poorly-stocked bookstores collecting information on Istar, the Cataclysm that sank it beneath the waves, and the chasm at the heart of the Blood Sea that supposedly led to the Abyss. He gathered from his discussions with Conundrum and Chief Navigator Snork that the entrance to the fabled sub-Ansalonian passage was within this chasm. He had to make plans of his own, and at night he visited graveyards to cast spells of divination. Unfortunately, these offered little useful information. Even with the power he drained from the device, his spells seemed most often to go awry.

At long last, the day of departure finally arrived. It was a still autumn morning, with a bite of frost in the air. The Blood Bay lay like a mirror to the horizon. On the quays, the gnomes prepared to cast off. Commodore Brigg was anxious to get started. With Snork at his side, the commodore leaned against the rusty red rail of the conning tower and impatiently chewed his beard.

The *Indestructible* rode low in the water, laden with enough food, fresh water, glowworm moss, clean socks, and lubricating oil to carry them through to the other side. The automatic adjustable self-extending ram lay just below the waterline, as did many of the ship's smaller portholes. The largest porthole was installed in the forward face of the conning tower, which made it possible for those on the bridge to see where they were going while submerged. Another large porthole was placed in the bow of the ship just above the ram, which meant it was smack in the middle of the wall in Conundrum's former quarters—what had been the sail room and was now the quarters of Sir Tanar Lobcrow.

The ram itself was a marvel of gnomish engineering. It could be extended and retracted and even used as a hammer to drill through walls or widen narrow underwater passages. It operated under the same principle as the UAEP, with water pressure forcing it into its forward locked position in the blink of an eye. To draw the ram back, one simply then drained the pressure tube and used a crank to return it to its retracted position.

The nose of the ram was fashioned of steel in the shape of a giant squid. The gnomes affectionately dubbed it the Automatic Adjustable Self-Extending Ram, or the Two-A-SER, which became the To-aser, the Toaser, and eventually the Toaster. Its only drawback was that it often took a few moments to pop out once engaged, and then only when one had begun to think it was stuck for good, which was quite startling the first three-dozen or so times they tested it.

Commodore Brigg and Navigator Snork saw three figures approaching along the docks. The shortest and the leading figure was Conundrum, dressed in a clean white robe and leather vest. Behind him bobbed Razmous, his pouches flapping about his thighs and chest as he hopped and skipped behind the gnome. Last of all strode a figure dressed in gray robes so long they dragged on the ground, hiding his feet. With the hood pulled up to hide his face and his hands folded into the sleeves, this last figure seemed to glide rather than walk.

"That'll be Sir Tanar," Snork commented as the three approached the ship and stopped at the end of the gangplank.

Commodore Brigg smoothed back the ruffled hair over his balding head, then grasped the lower hem of his dress uniform and gave it a sharp tug to smooth out the wrinkles. He had been looking forward to a glimpse of the Thorn Knight, who had steered clear of the submersible until now. All he had to go on was the somewhat fantastical reports relayed by the kender.

"Very good, Mister Snork," the commodore said gruffly. "Invite our guest aboard." His voice lingered sarcastically over the word "guest," hissing the "s" as though to further emphasize his dislike of the circumstances.

The commodore passed his small, curious whistle to his first officer. Snork placed it to his lips and puffed out his cheeks. An eerie, three-note squeal erupted upon the air, setting every dog within a mile to howling balefully. It seemed an ill omen to the superstitious sailors who had gathered along the docks to watch the strange proceedings. They made signs to ward away evil.

Conundrum strutted up the gangplank, followed by Razmous. As Sir Tanar stepped aboard, Commodore Brigg and Navigator Snork snapped to attention, their beards quivering with the effort. Commodore Brigg saluted grim-facedly. Sir Tanar looked up at the two standing on the conning deck. He scanned the aft deck of the ship, then glanced at the hatch leading into the conning tower. He looked up again, then grudgingly returned the gnome's salute. The commodore's hand snapped back to his side.

Snork quickly descended the ladder to the aft deck, then snapped to attention once more. "Commodore Brigg welcomes you aboard the MNS *Indestructible!*" Snork said in a sharp military bark. "Your quarters are in the forward sail compartment, now the forward viewing station. If you'll follow me . . ."

CHAPTER
16

Sir Tanar quickly discovered the interior of the *Inde-structible* was more cramped than he had imagined, and his room was as cold as the dark depths of the sea, which he knew to be dark because of the large glass port-hole in the wall. It seemed to glare at him like an accusing eye. Seeing fish and other slimy creatures swimming past his window made him feel like he was already drowning, and perhaps for the first time in his life, he experienced acute claustrophobia. He determined to spend every moment he could above deck, and before the ship ever cast off its lines, he was already dreading the days, weeks, months they'd spend submerged unless he could take over the ship, find the Abyss, and return to give his report. This hope was the only thing that kept him from diving through the porthole and taking his chances with the sharks.

So it was that, as the *Indestructible* made its way out of the Flotsam harbor and across the Blood Bay, Sir Tanar Lobcrow stood beside Commodore Brigg in the conning tower, crowding Snork from his usual place. The com-modore was much perturbed by the nearness of the Thorn

Knight, but he said nothing for the moment. Once at sea, he determined to put this "passenger" in his place.

Meanwhile, the *Indestructible* churned a steady course east by northeast. The rugged, black mountains of Malys's Desolation rose to their right, crawling like a line of angry clouds along the horizon. The ship plowed through the dark, rust-colored waters, while the commodore ordered the ship through its paces, raising and lowering the Peerupitscope, extending and retracting the Toaster, and checking the portholes and seams for leaks.

Sir Grumdish stood on the aft deck and eyed the Thorn Knight suspiciously as Professor Hap and Doctor Bothy directed the filling of numerous glass and pottery bottles with air. Once again making use of the technology of the UAEP, the professor had come up with an ingenious plan to carry along spare air, just in case they ran out. A large bronze bilge pump that he had converted for this purpose was used to compress the air into the bottles, which were then sealed by two gnomes armed with sledgehammers and a supply of corks. The corks were then bound into place with bottleneck cages of strong steel wire, and the bottles loaded into padded racks (they tended to explode even when gently tapped) in the fore and aft storage compartments. Professor Hap had dubbed the pump an airstuffer, for obvious reasons.

Conundrum and Razmous were in Snork's cabin making the final adjustments to the ship's planned course beneath the continent of Ansalon. Chief Portlost was busy ordering fresh oil splashed on every spring, pulley, wheel, gear and lever in the ship. The cook was testing the latest improvements to his flashcooker on the commodore's dinner of mutton and spiced potatoes. Snork ordered the pilot to maintain his course, then, taking his navigator's bag with its sextant and glass of farseeing, made his way to the aft deck to take a sighting for the ship's log.

Snork settled himself crosslegged on the deck and laid the logbook on his lap. With his sextant, he took a reading on the westering sun. A wind rising out of the east blew a fine spray over the bow of the ship and dampened his beard as he made his notes in the log. The commodore ordered the pilot to steer the *Indestructible* more into the wind. Snork adjusted his position and scanned the southern horizon with his glass of farseeing until he found the headland he was seeking. He took another reading off the sun and marked their position on the sea chart. Then he examined the headland again.

The distant hills looked tiny even in his glass, but he could tell they were desolate. The mountains beyond looked rugged and inhospitable, as broken and haphazard as newly-turned earth, and the air seemed thick with haze or smoke so that the farthest peaks were like the ghosts of mountains, and the sky above them as gray and weak as old dishwater.

From one of the distant, spectral peaks he saw a speck rise. It looked like a bird, but he knew that from this distance his glass of farseeing couldn't pick up any bird known to gnome or man. There was only one native of the skies of Krynn large enough to be seen from this far away: A dragon.

Snork leaped up, the logbook falling in a disordered heap at his feet and his sextant clanging noisily to the deck. The crew members, still busy filling bottles with air, stared at him in astonishment. He smiled wanly, not wanting to needlessly alarm the crew, and gathered up his things before hurrying forward and climbing up to the conning tower.

When he reached the top, he shoved his way between Commodore Brigg and the Thorn Knight. Sir Tanar swore and tugged the hem of his robes from beneath the navigator's feet, but Snork ignored him and pressed his glass of farseeing into the commodore's hand.

"Due south, sir," he said in a low voice so that the crew would not overhear.

Commodore Brigg took one look at the dour grimace on his navigator's face and snapped the glass to his eye. He slowly scanned the mountainous horizon as waves broke across the bow of the ship. "I don't see anything," he muttered into the wind.

"*Above* the mountains, sir," Snork urged.

At these words, Sir Tanar's head snapped round. The mountains were too far away to see anything other than a broken black wall stretching across the southern horizon, but the commodore's breath hissing through his teeth told him all he needed to know. His face turned gray beneath his hood.

"It's a red dragon," the commodore said under his breath.

"I couldn't tell the color before," Snork said. "It must be headed this way."

"What are its intentions?" the commodore pondered aloud as he lowered the glass. His brown forehead furrowed into a thousand worried wrinkles.

"You never can tell with red dragons, sir," Snork said.

The commodore nodded, then raised the glass to his eye once more. "It's a big dragon, bigger even than Pyrothraxus, and that's saying a lot." Pyrothraxus was the dragon who taken up residence in Mount Nevermind some thirty or so years earlier. "Yes, it's definitely headed this way," he finished after a moment. He handed the glass to Snork. "We'd better get below."

"The dragon is still too far away to see us," Sir Tanar said. "I don't think we should"—he gulped and finished with a whisper—"submerge." The palms of his hands felt all cold and sweaty.

Commodore Brigg spun on him, teeth clenching and veins popping out on his bulbous brown forehead. "What do you know of dragons? We've lived with a dragon in our very home for the last thirty years. It's no accident that dragon is coming toward us. It means us no good, so I'm ordering this ship submerged." He turned and shouted to the crew on the aft deck to gather up their bottles and get below, as they were diving immediately.

"But my airstuffer!" Professor Hap-Troggensbottle exclaimed.

"Leave it!" the commodore barked. "There's no time. A dragon is headed this way."

Only Sir Grumdish perked up at these dire words, for to kill a dragon was his Life Quest. But a dragon was far beyond their power to battle, and the commodore knew it. While Doctor Bothy squeezed his enormous bulk through the hatch, Sir Grumdish and the professor quickly gathered up as many air bottles as they could carry and hurried below. They were followed by their assistants, but even so, numerous bottles remained above decks.

"Here, you're not getting a free ride!" Commodore Brigg shouted at the gray-robed wizard. "Go help them move those bottles below."

Sir Tanar remained rooted to the deck, his sweaty palms gripping the rusted rail of the conning tower. Someone tugged on the sleeve of his robe, and looking down, he saw Snork gazing up at him with worried eyes. "Come along," the gnome said. "Help us get the bottles below. We may need them all!"

Slowly, Tanar followed the navigator down from the conning tower. As he crossed the deck, Commodore Brigg stood up with a tremendous load of air bottles stacked into his short arms. There still remained a loose pile of several dozen, more than he and Snork combined could carry, yet seawater was already washing over the aft deck as the *Indestructible* commenced to submerge. One wave lifted a bottle and carried it overboard. Sir Tanar watched it bob in the wake of the ship.

"Good idea," he said as he started picking up bottles. "I'll help." In a few moments, he arms were full, but still he stooped to grab a few more. He wanted all the air that he could carry inside that ship when it submerged. He was certain there wasn't enough for all of them as it was.

"You go on," Snork said. "I can get the rest of these."

Tanar nodded and hurried away as Snork stacked the last dozen bottles in the crook of his arm. Snork glanced around and, satisfied that he had not missed any, waded to the hatch and climbed inside the ship. The door clanged shut behind him, and two crew members hurriedly sealed it.

"Where's Sir Tanar?" the commodore asked as Snork stood dripping on the deck of the bridge.

"He went ahead of me with an armload," Snork answered. Conundrum and Razmous took their own loads and disappeared with them below decks.

"Shame he wasn't washed overboard," Commodore Brigg muttered as he raised the Peerupitscope. He pasted his eyes to it, then his whole body went rigid. "We got below just in time," he hissed.

A muffled roar echoed against the hull of the ship. The dim, murky water outside the forward bridge porthole suddenly burst into brilliant red light and began to boil. Commodore Brigg recoiled from the Peerupitscope, the skin around his eyes scorched by the heat.

"It's a good thing I designed it to Peer Up dragons, too," Doctor Bothy commented. "The metal and lenses should even withstand that blast of dragonfire."

Glaring at the doctor, Commodore Brigg turned and shouted below, "Engage descending flowpellar!"

"Engaging descending flowpellar, aye."

"Come about due north, Mr. Snork."

"Coming about due north, aye."

"Secure stations."

"Hull integrity secure. Peerupitscope undamaged."

"Portholes holding, sir!"

Above them, the dragon roared again in frustration and anger.

CHAPTER
17

The Blood Sea of Istar seemed a different place entirely than what they had crossed but two months earlier. With the first hint of autumn came the season of stormy weather. Squalls were frequent on the sea now, rising up black on the horizon and catching the ship before they knew what was happening. *Indestructible* was not designed to weather such weather, and those on board suffered cruelly during their passage north, especially Conundrum, Sir Grumdish, and the Thorn Knight, who were not sailors by trade. They might have submerged and run beneath the waves, but the commodore wanted to reserve their strength for the real work of subnavigating the continent. It wouldn't do them any good at all to use up all their air bottles before they began the last stage of their journey. They dove only when the weather gave them no other choice, like when they encountered a typhoon on the fifth day out.

In any case, they still had to surface from time to time so that Snork could take readings and plot their course. The Blood Sea was a vast and featureless place, with no islands in its midst to guide a sailor. Not many sailors ever sought out the middle of the Blood Sea. Most who sailed these waters were searching either for the nearest port or a fat, lumbering merchant ship. Now that the Maelstrom had disappeared, few knew or even cared to know exactly where it had once been. Most maps drawn before the Chaos War failed to pinpoint the center of the Blood Sea at all. The old cartographers left this area blank, or drew in a large whirlpool and surrounded it with dire warnings. The main problem was that the location of the Maelstrom varied by as much as a hundred leagues, depending on which map one consulted. Of all the maps of the Blood Sea that the gnomes had borrowed or purchased, only the kender's map of the subnavigational course of the MNS *Polywog* purported to show where it once lay.

It was to this place that Snork attempted to navigate the *Indestructible*, and this was no easy task. The weather played havoc with his calculations, both in the way the wind drove them helter-skelter across the sea whenever they ran "on top"—as they called it when the ship sailed on the surface—but also in how the clouds hid the sun for days on end. He navigated primarily by calculating the position of the sun above the horizon. He compared these readings with the time of the day and the date on various charts and arrays compiled by his family over many generations at sea, and from these he was able to determine their position anywhere on Krynn to within a league or two. He hoped.

The only good thing about the weather was that it kept the pirates away.

Professor Hap-Troggensbottle spent these last days sequestered in his quarters, perfecting some experiment or other. In those rare moments when he emerged to visit the galley or the head, he spoke to no one and no one spoke to him, for he had rather a crazed look in his eye.

That is, no one spoke to him—except Razmous. The

kender seemed to regard the professor's silence as something of a personal challenge to his kenderhood. He lurked in wait many an hour outside the professor's quarters just to catch a glimpse of the inside of the room whenever he emerged, and to engage him in conversation about his experiments or anything else that came to mind. One time, he even followed the poor professor into the head and prattled on about the peculiar antics of his uncle, Morgrify Pinchpocket, before the commodore dragged him out and gave the kender a good dressing-down.

Occasionally, when he wasn't feeling as though his stomach was about to perform a ballet, Conundrum was able to draw Razmous away to discuss the map of the subcontinental passages. At other times, Conundrum spent his hours locked away in the cabin he shared with his cousin, poring over Snork's books on navigation and the sea. The activities and operations of the ship were of little interest to him. He'd had his fill of seamanship during his stint as chief officer in charge of oilage. But navigation was another matter entirely. As a member of the guild of puzzles, mazes, and that sort of thing, the study of charting courses on the open sea fascinated him.

The least sailorly of them all, Sir Tanar, spent most of his time curled into a ball of misery in his cabin, his face as green as the kender's vest. He marked the time by the ensign who entered his cabin every twelve hours to feed the glowworms in his berth's glowwormglobe. He almost imagined he could hear the tiny worms munching on their breakfasts and dinners of moss, and this made him all the more ill. But he was too weak to protest.

His cabin was ridiculously small, located as it was in the bow of the ship above the Toaster. There almost wasn't room for him to stretch his hammock, and before he'd succumbed to seasickness, every time he stood up, he smacked his head on some beam or pipe. Sometimes, when the ship was being tossed about particularly violently by some storm, he imagined that he was dead and buried in a gnomish spring-driven coffin. The porthole caused him the most grief. Through it, he had a front seat to the worst heavings of the sea when they surfaced. When submerged, he witnessed the bounty of the sea in all its loathsome varieties, from grim-toothed sharks grinning through the shreds of their latest meal to stomach-churning jellyfish splattered and oozing across the porthole's glass. It was enough to give the most seasoned of assassins the heaves.

After three days and nights, the *Indestructible* finally managed to crawl out from beneath the typhoon, and at dawn the commodore ordered the ship surfaced and aired out. Those who had suffered the most from seasickness received a few hours of much-needed rest, as did the ship's springs and gears, for they had worked without pause for most of those three long days and nights. Lines and poles were brought out and rigged along the aft deck so that the galley staff could catch fresh fish for supper. A keg of beer was broached, and for the first time in many days, the professor, never one to miss out on beer, emerged from his cabin. Sir Grumdish practiced his swordplay, even teaching the commodore a few tricks with the cutlass.

Meanwhile, Navigator Snork stood in the conning tower and took fresh bearings on the newly risen sun. He then consulted his navigational charts and maps, and after checking the position of the sun once more, announced loudly that they had arrived. He estimated that the ruins of Istar lay somewhere directly below them. A great cheer went up from the ship, and in the galley Sir Tanar, drinking tarbean tea—the first thing he'd been able to keep down in days—wondered at the commotion.

"We've made it, sir!" the cook said as he poured the Thorn Knight another cup.

"Made what?" Sir Tanar asked.

"Istar, sir! Bless me. The commodore says we'll dive tomorrow!"

At these words, Sir Tanar's eyes narrowed, and the words to a charm spell sprang to mind, but the magic felt sluggish and unwieldy in his veins. "I'd like a word with the commodore in my cabin," he said. "Will you tell him?"

"Aye," the cook said, running his bandaged hand lovingly over the battered pewter pot in which he had brewed tarbean tea for over forty years now.

"Dive to the bottom of the chasm?" the commodore snorted. "You're mad. Everyone knows it's bottomless."

"But it might not be," Sir Tanar said in oily tones. "It might lead somewhere interesting."

"Where?" The commodore laughed. "The Abyss?"

"Aren't you the least bit curious?" the Thorn Knight asked.

"*I* am!" Razmous shouted from behind the closed door.

"No! I'll listen to no more talk of the Abyss," the commodore barked. "This ship is subnavigating the continent, and that's that. If you don't like it, we can put you off here and now. My orders are to take you along, and there's nothing in there about listening to your ideas. If you give me any more trouble, you'll be feeding the sharks before you can snap your fingers."

The words of a defensive spell came to Tanar's mind, but he held them. His magical communications device was stored in its box inside a crate across the room, and without it, his spell had little chance of success.

"Keep that in mind," Commodore Brigg finished as he opened the door.

Razmous tumbled into the room. The commodore stepped over the red-faced kender and strode away.

Conundrum entered immediately after the commodore was gone and helped Razmous to his feet. Without a word, Razmous bowed and hurried after the commodore. Conundrum started to follow, but Sir Tanar clutched at his sleeve.

Ever since that day at the Sailor's Rest, when the Thorn Knight had enspelled him with a single word, Conundrum had felt uncomfortable around Sir Tanar. The wizard was the first human with whom he'd had any regular dealings, and he found he didn't much care for their ways. He thought humans dull and stupid because they spoke so slowly, yet they were cunning—as the snake is cunning. He stared at the tops of his shoes.

The Thorn Knight eyed the gnome with a mixture of curiosity and disgust. Over the last few days, he'd learned more about gnomes that he had ever wanted. Yet just when he thought he had them pegged, they went and did something unexpected. That made them wily opponents. The safest bet, and his plan all along, had been to catch them sleeping and, after subduing the leaders with his magic, either force the others to do his bidding or kill them outright and take over the ship himself—after they reached the chasm to the Abyss, of course. But he had abandoned this plan at about the same time he became seasick, for two reasons. First, he was beginning to believe that gnomes never slept. Second, it became painfully obvious that he would never be able to operate the ship on his own. He needed the gnomes' help, but he wasn't quite sure how to convince them to do what he wanted. He certainly couldn't charm them all with his magic.

But it occurred to him that a mutiny might serve his purposes. If he could begin to sow dissension among the crew, doubts about their voyage, he might be able to wrest command from the commodore and take the ship where he wanted. A little magical intervention would help his cause along. Every mutiny started with one member of the crew. Just one.

"Please stay a moment, Conundrum," Tanar begged in a sincere tone as he clutched the gnome's sleeve. "I've wanted a word with you these many days since we put to sea, but there hasn't been a chance to speak. Close the door, if you would."

Reluctantly, Conundrum did as the Thorn Knight bade. As he closed the door, he felt the Knight's eyes boring into his back. He turned and placed his back to the door.

"Come now, Conundrum, I know you do not trust me," Sir Tanar cajoled. "Can we not forget that little incident in my room when I cast that spell on you? You were about to throw a priceless treasure out the window. I had to stop you. Will you not accept my apology?"

"I forgive you," Conundrum answered quickly, but without raising his eyes.

"That's right. It was all a misunderstanding," the Thorn Knight said, a toothy smile spreading across his face, "and I want you to know that I'm not here to cause trouble—or try to steal your secrets, either. You do believe me, don't you?"

Conundrum didn't reply. He tried to think of some-where else he needed to be so that he could leave without offending or angering the Thorn Knight. He was sure it wouldn't be a good idea to anger Sir Tanar.

"I am a wizard, you see," Sir Tanar continued. "I seek knowledge, like yourself. Gnomes and wizards are not so different. Yes, we are very much alike, you and I. We could be friends. Don't you think we could be friends?"

Conundrum shrugged.

"I want you to understand how sincere I am," the Thorn Knight said. Suddenly, the wizard's powerful hand clutched Conundrum under the chin. The gnome started in surprise and banged his head against the door. The room swam, and from the center of it the Thorn Knight's dark eyes started out like two lamps through a fog. Conundrum rubbed his bruised pate and tried to shake the cobwebs from his mind, but Sir Tanar's eyes held him.

"You do understand that I want to be your friend," Sir Tanar said.

Slowly, Conundrum assented. He felt it impossible to refuse. His suspicions of the wizard dropped away, and now when he thought about them, he wondered how he could have been so silly. He and the wizard were very much alike, both passengers on this ship, both seeking to fulfill a Life Quest. He smiled.

"That's better," Sir Tanar said as sweetly as he could manage. "You'd better let Doctor Bothy take a look at your head. Say nothing to him about our meeting. It is better if the others did not know of our friendship. They might not understand."

Conundrum agreed and opened the door. He ran into his cousin, who was coming to look for him. A strange expression crossed Snork's face, seeing Conundrum exit the Thorn Knight's chambers, but he quickly let it pass. He hurried forward, reaching out to clutch Conundrum by the arms.

"What is it?" Sir Tanar asked as he emerged behind Conundrum, hearing a commotion break out in the galley down the hall. Sailors and officers alike rushed out, hurriedly downing mugs of tarbean tea or stuffing the last bites of pie into their mouths as they rushed to their stations.

"A pirate galley!" Snork exclaimed. "Minotaurs!"

"Not—" Conundrum began.

"Yes! It's the same one!"

CHAPTER

18

A thunderous blow rattled the ship, nearly knocking the gnomes off their feet. Sir Tanar toppled backward into his cabin and fell over his hammock, hitting the deck with a thud. Conundrum and Snork clutched one another and stared about in fright.

"Have we been rammed?" Doctor Bothy cried as he staggered out of sick bay.

"I don't think so," Snork said.

At that moment, the commodore's commanding voice shouted down from the conning tower, "Prepare to dive! All hands, prepare to dive!"

Another blow resounded off the iron hull, staggering the *Indestructible*'s occupants. Snork and Conundrum rushed to the bridge, where they found the commodore sealing the hatch. "Ahead full! Hard to starboard!" he shouted.

As the commodore's commands were answered and the ship lurched forward in the water, they turned and looked through the forward porthole.

Still some distance away, but near enough to see its monstrous crew scurrying about on its decks, the pirate galley cut a swath through the waves. Its two great sails of red and white stripes bellied full with the wind. There was no way the *Indestructible* could outrun it. Their only hope was to dive.

Sir Grumdish stood beside the helm as Snork took over from the pilot. Sir Grumdish held a dagger in his fist, his knuckles whitening around the hilt as he stared out through the porthole at the approaching ship. Even as he watched, a large catapult on the bow of the minotaur ship loosed a large boulder.

"Flood the forward ballast tanks and engage the descending flowpellars!" Snork shouted. The ship immediately began to nose under the waves. The boulder careened off the conning tower, jarring everyone to his teeth. Sir Grumdish loosed a string of curses and shook his daggered fist at the pirates.

Indestructible continued her descent even as the minotaur vessel drew closer. Water lapped against the porthole, and the gnomes felt and heard the sudden quiet of the deep close round them. Commodore Brigg ordered the Peerupitscope raised. He placed his eye to the eyepiece, then swiveled round until he found what he was looking for.

He started back in surprise. "Lower the Peerupitscope! Quickly!" he shouted. The long metal tube slid down. "Brace for impact!"

"What's wrong?" Snork asked.

His answer came in the form of a long painful wail of metal against metal, of copper keel scraping against iron hull. The *Indestructible* lurched violently to starboard, nearly capsizing and sending the crew and everything else that wasn't tied down flying off walls, pipes, and each other. Suddenly, the ship righted, tossing everyone about once more.

Through it all, Commodore Brigg managed to keep his hold on the Peerupitscope. As the rest of the crew members crawled back to their posts, he shouted for it to be raised again. After a few moments, it shot up, and he peered through it, his mouth set in a grim line.

"Sir Grumdish," he said.

"Aye, Commodore?"

"Load the UAEPs."

"Aye, Commodore!" Sir Grumdish exclaimed with obvious relish.

"Navigator, come about on my mark," the commodore shouted. "Chief Portlost, prepare for a crash ascent, and give me everything you've got. We're going to sink that ship, if it's the last thing we do."

As the crew prepared for battle, the glowworms in the glowwormglobes hanging from the overhead pipes reacted to the excitement, changing from their normal cool blue light to an angry blood red. Professor Hap-Troggensbottle stumbled onto the bridge, the edges of his beard black and smoking.

"What happened to you?" the commodore asked as he maneuvered the *Indestructible* into attack position.

"Small mishap. Nothing to worry about. What's going on? Are we under attack?" the professor said.

"We were. Now we're the ones doing the attacking!" Sir Grumdish answered fiercely.

"Stand by the Toaster!" the commodore shouted. "Prepare to ascend. When we reach the surface, we'll give 'em both UAEPs, and if that doesn't work, we'll stave a hole below her waterline she won't likely forget!"

"Aye, Commodore!" Sir Grumdish cheered.

Conundrum joined Snork at the wheel now, and together they peered out the porthole at the murky water of the Blood Sea of Istar. Snork made small adjustments to their course according to the directions of the commodore, who kept his eye glued to the Peerupitscope. The *Indestructible* grew quiet as, with everything ready, the crew members waited at their stations.

Sir Tanar crept from his chamber and down the corridor to the bridge. The sudden silence, after so much commotion, filled him with foreboding. He found the gnomes standing dutifully at their posts, washed by the eerie red glow of the glowwormglobes, only their goggling eyes and quivering beards showing any outward sign of their excitement.

"Commodore Brigg," he said. "Have we begun our descent?"

The commodore ignored him, and instead stepped back with a broad smile on his face. "Lower the Peerupitscope," he said softly. The long gleaming tube of metal sank into the floor.

"Commodore Brigg," Sir Tanar said insistently, clearing his throat for emphasis.

Again, the commodore ignored him. Turning to Snork, he said calmly, as though telling the cook what to prepare for tonight's mess, "Navigator, surface the ship."

"Aye, sir!" Snork assented with a red gleam in his eye. He turned to Sir Grumdish.

"Emergency ascent!" he shouted. "Blow the ballast tanks! Engage the ascending flowpellar!"

Sir Grumdish shouted down the ladder to engineering, "Emergency ascent, aye! Engineer, blow the ballast tanks! Engage the ascending flowpellars!"

They heard the chief shouting, "Blow the ballast tanks, aye! Engage the ascending flowpellars, aye!" His voice quickly became lost in the whir and shriek of spinning gears and clattering spring cranks.

Responding to the controls, *Indestructible* leaped upward. The crew staggered and held on as the bow of the ship tilted upward and the engines drove her through the water. The brownish light shining through the porthole quickly brightened and shaded to a deep red, then a pale pink. Suddenly, it vanished, replaced by fingers of foam running down the surface of the glass. The bow of the ship rose up out of the water like a breaching whale, then came down with a heavy surge, huge waves lashing out to either side.

"Fire the UAEPs!" the commodore shouted.

"Fire the UAEPs!" Sir Grumdish repeated. "Aye!"

Just as the ship began to settle back into the water, it lurched backward. Twin forty-foot-long sprays of glistening water erupted from the bow, and from them shot two enormous arrows, directly at the minotaur vessel.

The pirates spun round in surprise at the sudden appearance of the *Indestructible* less than a hundred yards off their starboard rail. Half panicked by the sight, their crew tried to swing their catapult around and bring it to bear on the gnomes' submersible, but their efforts were wasted. One UAEP swept through them, scattering them across the decks and knocking not a few overboard. The other UAEP struck home in the mast, thudding into the hard timber and splitting it from base to wind-bellied topsail.

The minotaur captain, seeing the steel-headed ram jutting out from the bow of the *Indestructible*, recognized the hopelessness of the situation. Already, the mainmast of the pirate galley was cracking under the weight of the sails and push of the wind. He swept out his scimitar and roared in a bestial voice, "She's gonna ram us! Prepare to board and take 'em, lads!"

Indestructible closed on her helpless prey. The crew cheered as the galley's mainmast split asunder, spilling its sheets and lines in a chaotic heap upon her decks and burying many of her crew. But they saw numerous other pirates, steel in hand, gathering at her starboard rail, the red gleam of murder in their eyes.

The commodore held on. "Full speed!" he shouted. "Brace for impact!"

Indestructible struck the waves, spray flying before its bow. The galley loomed closer, larger, filling up the port-hole with its stout timbers. And then, with a rending shriek of metal and cracking of wood, the *Indestructible* lurched to a sudden stop. Everything not tied down or braced flew forward, smashing against walls and bulk-heads.

Conundrum climbed to his feet and pressed his face against the bridge porthole. "That's done her!" he screamed joyously, pointing at the sea rushing into the pirate galley around the bow of the *Indestructible*, which was firmly lodged into a hole in the galley's side large enough to swallow a small whale. The others crowded closer to witness the destruction.

Suddenly, a dark shape dropped before them, its hideous bestial face filling up the window, red eyes blazing, forward swept horns rising from its head. It had a dagger clamped firmly in its mouth, and a scimitar in one sledge-like fist, swept back to strike. The bitter edge of the blade pinged against the glass of the porthole, inflicting no damage but causing everyone to leap back in fear. Other shapes dropped around it, and soon they were pounding on the hatch with their blades.

"Let's hope they don't have hammers!" the commodore said, laughing nervously. He turned and shouted down the ladder, "Withdraw the ram!"

"It's stuck!" Chief Portlost answered as he climbed up to the bridge. He stood before the commodore, wringing his beard in frustration.

"Well, back us up. They're boarding us," the com-modore said.

"We can't, sir!" the chief wailed in dismay. "We don't have a reverse."

"Is it broken?"

"No, sir. We never designed the ship to go in reverse," the chief answered.

"Well, that's torn it," the commodore said, placing his fists on his hips and stomping his foot.

"Commodore," Snork said. "The galley's sinking." Already, the sea covered half the porthole. The pounding on the hatch had an air of desperation to it, and the minotaur outside the porthole had dropped his scimitar and was trying his dagger against the hatch's seals.

"She's sinking," the commodore repeated, "and taking us with her."

CHAPTER
19

"**W**ell, Chief, this may complete your Life Quest," Commodore Brigg said. "This is a wondrously bad mishap by any definition. I hope you're recording it."

Chief Portlost's head appeared at the top of the ladder. "Thanks for reminding me! Let me get my notebook." He disappeared below decks.

Now, seawater completely filled the view from the porthole. They saw a pair of large booted feet kicking madly and rising slowly upward. A stream of bubbles poured out of the gaping hole in the galley's side and vanished upward as well. The sunlight shining through the water grew steadily dimmer and browner.

"How deep do you suppose it is here, Navigator?" the commodore asked, almost as if he were asking for the time of day.

Snork shook his head and shrugged, unable to find words, then turned back to the porthole. Gradually, it grew darker and darker, until it was like a large black eye peering back at them. And still they sank, the two ships twirling round and round each other. Commodore Brigg didn't voice his greatest concern—that they'd come to rest on the sea floor upside down, or worse, beneath the galley. That's why he didn't order the ballast tanks flooded, for he hoped the *Indestructible*'s buoyancy might keep them on top, if not pull them free entirely.

As the two ships sank deeper and deeper into the Blood Sea, the hull of the *Indestructible* began to pop and groan in a most alarming fashion. The deck beneath their feet buckled, bowing up a good three inches during the course of their descent. Here and there, where the hull was exposed, they noticed water droplets forming around the ship's seams, and the air grew noticeably cooler. Every once in a while, the entire ship shuddered from stem to stern, rattling their teeth and everything else not bolted to the deck. Outside the ship, the sea slowly grew as black as a dark elf's heart.

Suddenly, there was a groan, and a shudder more violent than any they had yet experienced passed through the length of the ship. They felt the ship slow, settle, and come to rest with a bump on the bottom of the Blood Sea. Commodore Brigg looked around at his officers and crew that had gathered in the forward corridor and around the ladder leading below. He thrust out his chin, his beard bristling defiantly, and tugged at the bottom of his jacket. "Well," he said. "Here we are."

Razmous stood before the porthole, his jaw hanging open like a broken gate, his eyes glazed. Conundrum touched his arm, and slowly the kender's head swiveled round to look down at him.

"Isn't it fantastic?" the kender asked dreamily.

"I can't take this any more," Sir Tanar said in a voice tinged with hysteria. His claustrophobia seemed to be getting the better of him at last. He ran toward the ladder leading up to the hatch. "My magic will save me," he snarled. "To the Abyss with the rest of you!"

Sir Grumdish caught the Thorn Knight around the legs

and dragged him to the deck before he could reach the ladder. He and the professor sat on Sir Tanar's back to keep him from rising. The wizard clawed at the floor, spitting curses and threatening to kill them all. Doctor Bothy hurried from sick bay and administered a sedative to the base of the Thorn Knight's skull. Sir Tanar went limp at the blow, though he continued to moan and gibber incoherently. The doctor passed his reflex hammer to Conundrum in case the Thorn Knight needed another dose of sedative, then directed Sir Grumdish and the professor to carry the Knight to his cabin.

The two gnomes heaved Sir Tanar's limp bones between them and staggered forward, the doctor and Conundrum following. They entered Sir Tanar's chambers and tossed him into his hammock. Sir Grumdish staggered back, blowing heavily and digging his knuckles into the small of his back. In the blue light of the glowwormglobes, his white beard looked grayer and older than before, and there were dark circles under his eyes.

"Why, oh why did I ever come on this voyage?" he moaned. "I should be questing after dragons, not dragging hysterical wizards back to their cabins. I miss the smell of fewmets, the crackle of a fire at night, the sound of a sword unsheathing. A pox on the maritime sciences!"

"Now, now," Doctor Bothy said. "I've got something that will cure you. Come to sick bay and I'll give you a little nip." The two departed.

Sir Tanar lay in his hammock, twitching feebly, his eyelids fluttering. Conundrum stood at his side, filled with an unreasoning concern. He didn't quite understand why he should be worried about this human, but he couldn't help the way he felt. Even as he stroked the Thorn Knight's brow and tried to comfort him, deep down inside he felt repulsed by the sight of the ungainly, sprawling, paleskinned human. It was quite mystifying.

To take his mind off his conflicting emotions, Conundrum watched the professor, who was at that moment standing before the bow porthole, a blue glowwormglobe resting in the palm of his outstretched hand. At first, Conundrum wasn't sure what the professor was looking at, but as he gazed closer, his eyes met with a startling, fascinating, and thoroughly gruesome sight.

They were inside the galley.

When the *Indestructible* rammed the galley, her iron-shod bow had punched completely through the galley's wooden hull and become lodged in the hole. Sir Tanar's cabin was located in the bow of the *Indestructible*, so the light from the professor's glowwormglobe shining through the forward porthole actually illuminated the interior of the pirate ship's hold. The murky water, filled now with freshly-stirred mud from the sea floor, seemed nearly as thick and opaque as tarbean tea, and things floated in it, things difficult to identify because they were hovering, without gravity pressing them down into their accustomed shapes. What appeared at first to be a shred of fog proved in fact to be a bolt of diaphanous silk, partially unrolled, stolen from the-gods-only-knew-where. Personal items littered the scene—brushes, curry combs, leather flasks crushed flat by the weight of the water, a cracked mirror, a hunk of half-eaten meat with teeth marks plainly visible.

But what filled Conundrum with horror were the bodies, six at least. They were all minotaurs, but a sickening feeling washed over Conundrum when he looked at their bestial faces. In each case, the mouth hung open, and the tongue, mottled gray, dangled out the side. The eyes, too, were open, and seemed to be staring at something very far away. Their ears, their big bovine ears, struck him as the most pathetic. Soft, keen, intelligent, they swayed in the gentle currents and eddies still swirling through the hold, as though they yet listened for the order to abandon ship.

Conundrum turned away, trying to blank the vision from his mind. He ground his teeth and clawed at his curly red beard in frustration. All he ever wanted to do was solve puzzles. He wasn't a warrior or a sailor. The sight of the drowned pirates filled him with cold loathing, and disgust, and pity—yes, pity—even for an enemy, even for a monster like a minotaur.

Doctor Bothy stuck his head into the room. "How's the patient?" he asked.

Conundrum composed himself and looked at Sir Tanar. The Thorn Knight had regained consciousness. He sat up and glared about, feeling the back of his head and counting the lumps.

"Feeling better?" the doctor asked with a smile. Behind him stood Sir Grumdish, cheeks flushed and beaming happily. "I could give you another shot if you are still nervous."

"No!" Sir Tanar shouted, then winced. "That won't be necessary," he finished in muted tones, but his eyes flashed with hate.

"Good. the commodore wants everyone on the bridge."

The officers and crew of the MNS *Indestructible* drew together around the commodore. Their trembling white beards and drawn faces turned to him in the dim blue light. He'd ordered all but one glowwormglobe covered in order to darken the bridge. This allowed them to see, through the bridge porthole, the professor's light shining from the bow porthole inside the sunken galley. It revealed to them the true gravity of their situation.

They were strangely silent—quiet as no gnome should be. Usually, given a situation calling for ingenuity and daring, they would have all been talking at once as rapidly as their tongues could wag, proposing, discussing, arguing, counter-arguing, counter-proposing, revising, and discarding a dozen ideas and theories all at the same time. But they needed to be able to get their hands on the problem, so to speak, and this was something quite beyond anyone's grasp. For the problem literally lay outside their ship, and that was the one place none of them could go, not even wearing the professor's diving suit. The steel head of the ram could not be withdrawn from the heavy beam into which it had embedded itself. The *Indestructible* and the pirate galley were bound together, irreversibly it seemed.

The commodore had called them all together to discuss their options, but when it seemed no one had anything to say, no theories to offer or experiments to try, he turned to Chief Portlost. "Chief," he said, "how long would it take to reverse the engine?"

"Well, if we were in dry dock and I had a full crew of engineers," he pondered, tapping his front teeth with a pencil, "I should say a month at least. Of course, it would require dismantling the ship."

"That doesn't sound practical, given our present situation," the commodore said.

"Yes, I agree," the chief replied. "You must admit, this is certainly a remarkable and unforeseen occurrence. You would have thought we would have included a reverse gear in the design from the beginning, wouldn't you? This will require months, simply months of investigation. There'll be interviews, and committees, and commissions, and possibly even a task force. We'll produce a study of the events, with speculation and conclusions. It should run at least ten thousand pages. That is, if we live, of course."

"The good thing is," Snork offered, "we'll know better with the next ship design."

Everyone agreed that this was indeed an excellent point. "Should we call the next prototype the Class D?" the commodore asked.

"That would be the logical progression," Chief Portlost answered. The mood among the crew began to lighten somewhat, now that they had something positive to think about—the design of the next ship. Several spontaneous discussions broke out, and one argument.

But Sir Tanar silenced all debates when he cried, still a little hysterically, "There isn't going to be another ship, you . . . you . . . you . . . *gnomes!* You're all going to die here. We're trapped! Trapped like rats!"

He glared wildly around at the small, brown faces turned toward him, then stepped back when he saw Doctor Bothy edging toward him, reflex hammer in hand.

"Speak for yourself." The commodore pshawed. "You don't understand, do you? Humans never do. You humans look at us, and you see a funny little people, a race of preposterous inventors. Sometimes you find our inventions useful, like the gnomeflinger, and sometimes they seem ridiculous, like the gnomeflinger. You're always ready to take our successes and profit by them, but you are also always ready to disparage our mishaps, not knowing that the mishap is at least as important as the success, if not more so. For only from the mishap do we learn." He turned back to the crew. "Now," he said, his lips setting into a grim line. "We know what can't be done. Tell me what *can* be done."

"We can escape in the ascending kettles," Conundrum offered, reminding them of his invention.

"Possibly, and I had already thought of that," the commodore said. "But I am not yet ready to abandon the *Indestructible*. She's not a perfect ship, but she is mine. And besides, even if we did escape, that would only leave us lost in the middle of the Blood Sea."

"What about the ascending and descending flowpellars?" Chief Portlost asked. "We might use them to wiggle free."

"They're pinned in the retracted position by the galley's hull," Snork answered.

"But we might still wiggle free," Chief Portlost countered, "by repeatedly flooding and emptying the aft ballast tank."

"Now that's an idea," the commodore said.

"What we really need is some rearward thrust," Conundrum said. "If we could put a pole out and push against the galley somehow. Perhaps through the Peerupitscope?"

"The UAEPs!" Professor Hap-Troggensbottle exclaimed.

"What about them?" the commodore asked. "There isn't room to fire them. The arrow probably wouldn't even make it all the way out of the pressure tube, and what good would that do us?"

"You've all felt the way the ship lurches back when they are fired," the professor said excitedly. "The outward force of the released pressurized water generates a momentary reverse force on the ship."

"He's right," the chief agreed.

"If we fire the tubes without the UAEPs inside, I calculate we could generate approximately twice the normal force," the professor continued. "That, in combination with the positive and negative buoyancy induced by the repeated flooding and evacuating of the aft ballast tank, might be enough to break us free."

"By Reorx, I think you've got something, Professor!" the commodore applauded. "All right, gnomes, let's make it so. Sir Tanar! Come here, if you would, sir."

The Thorn Knight approached, warily eyeing Doctor

Bothy, who still stood by with his anesthetic hammer ready. The rest of the crew scurried to their tasks, except for Conundrum and Razmous, who stood close by, listening. Conundrum hoped the commodore wouldn't offend the Thorn Knight.

"See here, you're a wizard, right?" the commodore asked.

Sir Tanar's eyes narrowed, and he straightened himself almost to his full height, but carefully, so as not to bump his skull on the pipes overhead. "I am," he answered guardedly.

"Well, we could use some light out there, to see how we are progressing. I've always heard wizards could make lights appear with a snap of the fingers. Is it true?"

"The light spell is one of our simpler forms of magic," Tanar said with caution.

"Well, do you think you could cast one for us?" the commodore said. "I'd think better of you, if you did."

"But what shall I cast the spell upon?" Sir Tanar snapped. "I must have a target."

The commodore glanced around for a moment, considering. His eyes finally came to rest on the Peerupitscope. "There!" he said, pointing at the place where the scope passed through the hull of the ship. "Cast your spell there, and then we'll raise it up until the light is outside the ship."

Sir Tanar allowed that this was rather a good idea. He slowly approached the Peerupitscope, ducking his head to avoid a pipe, all the while eyeing its cool, gleaming metal cylinder. Where it passed through the hull of the ship, a black, flexible seal prevented the seawater from rushing in around it. Even so, he noticed a few droplets of moisture gathered around the seal, and he thought about all that dark weight of water pressing down on top of them. This settled him to the task at hand.

He closed his eyes, stilling the wild angry beating of his

heart, concentrating on the magic flowing sluggishly through his veins. A few years ago, he might have cast this simple spell with hardly a thought. Now, he knew it would cost him.

He opened his eyes, lifted one arm and pointed a claw-like finger at the top of the Peerupitscope. A brilliant white light flared into being, starkly illuminating the bridge of the *Indestructible* and casting harsh shadows in its corners and recesses. Conundrum squinted in the sudden light, but Razmous blinked at it in open-mouthed wonder.

Sir Tanar staggered, feeling drained. The spell had exhausted the last of his powers. "Conundrum," he said weakly. The gnome rushed to his side, but Razmous was too busy staring in awe at the magical light to notice, and the commodore was shouting down to engineering to be ready at the ballast tanks.

"Help me to my cabin. I am . . . too weak." Tanar sighed as he sagged against Conundrum, carefully, so as not to overburden him. The two staggered forward, forgotten by everyone in their excitement.

CHAPTER 20

Commodore Brigg stepped back and shouted, "Raise the Peerupitscope!"

The shaft of metal slowly and silently slid upward, and almost immediately the interior of the bridge was plunged once more into near-total darkness, with only the dim light of a single glowwormglobe hanging from a overhead pipe. Yet through the porthole there now shone a strong reddish glow. In it, the hull of the sunken pirate ship was plainly visible, as was a school of small silvery fish that flashed briefly into view.

"Stop!" the commodore said. "Hold the Peerupitscope right there."

Snork climbed up from engineering and took his place at the helm. Sir Grumdish hurried from his quarters, from which he had retrieved his Solamnic sword. It now clanked at his side, much too large for him to carry. The professor joined him at the fire control station. Doctor Bothy leaned in the hatchway leading forward to the officers' quarters, almost filling it with his enormous bulk.

The commodore looked round at his officers and the seventeen remaining members of his crew—Conundrum had not yet returned from helping Sir Tanar to his cabin. A deep sense of pride brought a fierce smile to his wrinkled brown face. He buttoned his jacket up to his neck, then tugged his leather cap tighter down over his eyes. He glanced down the ladder and saw Chief Portlost looking up at him. The chief gave a thumbs-up, then tugged his beard for luck.

"All right," the commodore said, clearing his throat. "Flood the aft ballast tank."

His order was answered a moment later by a deep gurgling noise. The *Indestructible* slowly sank, settling onto the muddy bottom of the Blood Sea. Swirls of silt filled the view through the porthole, but they saw that the hole in the side of the galley seemed to widen a bit, and a few loose timbers broke free and floated out of sight.

They waited a moment, listening, hearing the creaking of wood, and far off, a mournful sound—the song of a whale.

"Blow the aft ballast tank," the commodore ordered.

A hissing, rushing noise now sounded from the pipes crisscrossing the roof and running beneath the deck. The *Indestructible* rose upward, loosening a few more timbers, but before she completed her short ascent, Commodore Brigg turned to Sir Grumdish and said in a low, controlled voice, "Fire both tubes."

An explosive rush shook the ship. Wood howled against rusty iron as the *Indestructible* lurched backward a half-dozen feet before grinding once more to a halt, firmly wedged in place once again.

The crew cheered, but the commodore silenced them with a glare. "Once more," he said. "Pressurize both UAEP tubes. This time, stand by to flood the forward ballast tank as well."

"Aye, sir!" Chief Portlost shouted up from below.

"Flood the aft ballast tank," the commodore ordered.

Again, a gurgling noise sounded from behind the bulkheads, and the *Indestructible* slowly sank, pivoting around her bow wedged in the pirate ship. This time, before it settled on the bottom, the commodore spun and shouted to Sir Grumdish, "Now, fire the port tube!" Then, "Navigator, rudder hard to starboard!"

A rush from the tube and the ship lurched sideways in the hole, tearing out more timbers.

"Flood the forward ballast tank now!" he shouted as he raised one fist and shook it at the galley. Water gurgled forward. The ship teetered.

"Hard to port, Navigator!" Brigg shrieked. "Hard to port! Fire the starboard tube!"

A rush of water, a groan of metal, and suddenly they were free, the dark hull of the galley receding slowly before them, vanishing into the gloom of the deep sea as the *Indestructible* floated away. They looked down upon her, lying below them on the uniform mud of the sea floor, the hole amidships, the deck littered with wreckage, and here and there a form, a body, tangled in the rigging or trapped beneath a spar.

They did not cheer.

After a time, Commodore Brigg cleared his throat. "Very well, Navigator. You may engage the engines. Well done. Well done, all of you."

"Thank you, sir," Snork said with sudden and sincere emotion. He turned, and with a trembling voice shouted, "Engage the main!"

"Engaging the main, aye!" Chief Portlost answered from below.

The *Indestructible* slowed in its rearward spiraling ascent as the main flowpellars swirled into action. As she glided to a stop and then started forward, Snork steered her into a course dead ahead. The galley disappeared below them. Before them lay a vast and featureless expanse of mud. Beyond it there seemed to be a darker area, a place where the rusty mud gave way to something blacker, perhaps the top of some submerged mountain.

Commodore Brigg walked forward and stood beside the kender. Together they peered into the gloom illuminated by the magical light still burning atop the Peerupitscope.

"Where in the Abyss are we?" the commodore whispered.

"Not the Abyss, sir," Snork said with a sigh.

As they drew nearer, the dark shape began to resolve into a recognizable outline—a vast, dark crater. As the ship passed over the crater's edge and nosed downward, they saw in its midst recognizable shapes—walls, roofs, towers, all shattered, broken, and covered with hanging growths. As they sank down among once-stately avenues, their paving stones buried under three hundred years of sediment, mighty trees that once lined them reduced to wasted, mud-red stumps, black windows gazed back at them from the ruined edifices that lined the ways.

"It's Istar!" Razmous gasped.

Conundrum gazed in awe at the ruins of Istar visible through the porthole in Sir Tanar's cabin.

At the heart of Istar had stood the Temple of Paladine, the most magnificent of all the temples of the city—of the world—from which the Kingpriest ruled his empire with a hand guided by wisdom and piety. Yet like his city and his empire, deluded by his own grandeur, the Kingpriest sought glory for himself rather than for Paladine. In his arrogance, he called upon the gods to grant him the same powers that had been bestowed upon the hero Huma in humility. In their rage, the gods cast a fiery mountain upon the temple of the Kingpriest, destroying it and the city and the lands about, and plunging the world into a darkness of despair that lasted for over two hundred years.

It was through this ancient city, ravaged by fire and earthquake, wracked by the anger of the gods, drowned by the sea, its glory lost forever, and now a ruin covered by a blanket of rust red mud, that the *Indestructible* picked her way. Guided by the sure hand of Navigator Snork, they soared over vast fields of rubble and down boulevards between buildings broken as though the entire city had been lifted up a hundred feet in the air and then dropped. Occasionally they came upon some house or shop or temple that had somehow escaped the Cataclysm, only to be consumed by the sea. Everywhere lay the wrecks of ships, countless ships, that had been sucked down to their doom by the great Maelstrom that once swirled here.

Yet even here, this place most forsaken by the gods, there was life. Much of it was small and hard to find. Pensive and shy, it hid in cracks and in the dark interiors of buildings, or beneath the rubble, or buried in three hundred years worth of silt, with only its spines or the bulges of its eyes showing above. They saw shadows—some small and compact, others long and snaky, and still others broad and flat like flying carpets or cloaks lifted by in the wind—dart away at their approach or as they coursed overhead.

Of other types of sea life there was plenty. Small, transparent krill and queer prawns striped like bumblebees swarmed around the magical light shining from their half-raised Peerupitscope. The broken avenues were dotted with small black creatures covered entirely in long spines, like some kind of sea porcupine. These left long serpentine trails in the mud that could be followed for hundreds of yards. Many of the walls that survived the Cataclysm were covered with large bulbous growths, out of which darted (in a most startling fashion) the hollow tops of long, red worms with white frills like coxcombs or trailing white beards. These seemed mostly to hunt the prawns and smaller fish, though they saw growing on the side of one large ruin a fantastically bearded and frilled worm that could have easily swallowed the ship whole. Conundrum was glad to see that Snork was steering a course well around it, though he could hear the kender shrilly crying for a closer look.

For the most part, the ship followed the crisscrossing avenues when they were visible. Conundrum had spent many an hour in Flotsam looking over old maps of the city of Istar, and so he knew that the larger streets led to the center of the city, where they expected to find the chasm that led to the Abyss.

Sir Tanar had studied many of the same maps, and longer. With his practiced eye, long used to searching ancient tomes for hints to magical secrets, he could easily pick out the landmarks of the city, ruined though they were. There lay the outline of the Temple of Mishakal, and beyond it, the mighty pillars of the Stonemason's Guild, toppled and forlorn, their marble flutings pitted and scarred by the relentless teeth of the all-devouring sea that dissolved everything—wood, iron, steel, marble, even a man's bones. Only gold and precious gems were immune. Reminded of this, the Thorn Knight's eyes searched greedily for any glint or sparkle among the rubble, but the sea elves and the evil creatures that once haunted this accursed place had long ago picked Istar's bones clean of her last treasures. There was nothing left on the surface but muddy, wasted ruins and a dim memory of the city's vanished glory.

Even as he searched, knowing such searching to be vain, ever did Sir Tanar probe the dim distance for some sign of the chasm, the pit down which the temple of the Kingpriest was said to have fallen when struck by the fiery mountain—fallen down to the Abyss itself. More than any gold or jewels, he longed to find the lost gate leading to the realm of his former goddess, Takhisis, Queen of Darkness. She was no longer there, he knew. She had fled with the other gods, fled from the awful face of Chaos.

Tanar knew where it must lay. The chasm must be at the heart of the city, and so he turned his eyes thither. The *Indestructible* continued along her course, and it seemed to Sir Tanar and Conundrum both that the nearer they came to the center of Istar, the greater the destruction they saw. Now, they saw few standing structures of any sort, and the ground was a broken and jumbled mass of stone and mud. No longer could they discern the streets and avenues of this once great city. All was tumbled together—column, doorpost, and cobblestone. Only the navigator's peerless sense of direction held them on the true course.

Soon they were rewarded. Sir Tanar's breath caught in his throat when he saw it—a gaping rent in the earth that led to a pit as black as any nightmare hell.

"There it is, Conundrum," Tanar said in a voice trembling with excitement, "the door to glory."

Conundrum, misunderstanding the wizard, nodded in agreement and continued to stare open-mouthed through the porthole. Their breath had begun to fog the glass, so he wiped it with his sleeve, but this only served to smear it and further ruin his view—it had been some days since he last washed his robe. He turned to search for a clean rag and found Sir Tanar pulling a crate up to the edge of his hammock.

On top of the crate lay the curious box Conundrum had almost tossed out the window that morning at the Sailor's Rest when he and Sir Tanar first met. As soon as the Thorn Knight had moved the crate into position, he seated himself carefully in the hammock and opened the box.

Unable to contain his curiosity, Conundrum edged closer to see what rare and magical treasures lay inside it, but Sir Tanar turned quickly, as if sensing the gnome's approach, and said, "Make sure the door is closed securely, Conundrum. The others would not understand, were they to see what I am about to show you."

Conundrum hurried to do as he was bade. A strange loathing overcame him as he tested the latch—a soiled feeling, as if he were betraying his friends. Yet at the same time, he felt superior to them, as if they weren't his friends at all or didn't deserve to share in the wizard's secrets. A voice inside him was screaming for rescue, but it never found its way past his teeth.

Assured that the door, which had no lock, would not suddenly fly open, Conundrum moved to the wizard's side. With a predatory smile on his narrow face, Sir Tanar turned the box slightly so that the gnome could better see what lay within. Conundrum leaned closer, his eyes growing wide in his wrinkled brown face. But then a frown creased his red beard. It was only a silver plate set into the lid of the box. He had expected at the very least to behold some bejeweled rod of great power and mysterious purpose, or a tome filled with vile spells, the mere sight of which would drive the uninitiated to madness and death. But it was only a silver plate. He could not hide his disappointment.

Despite himself, Sir Tanar couldn't help but feel a little disappointed. He had hoped at least to elicit a gasp of awe from his ensorcelled companion. But then again, how was a simple gnome supposed to grasp the import of what he beheld? A gnome could not feel the magic that radiated from this artifact of power, nor was he likely to divine its purpose and uses. Conundrum's mind was geared to understanding gears and levers and redundant safety systems, not the nuances and subtleties of magical paraphernalia.

Tanar had his reasons for exposing his secret to the gnome. The time had come for him to dominate Conundrum completely, to bind him to his will. Using the power of the magical communications device, he could cast a spell that would create such a powerful bond that only death could break it. Once enslaved, the gnome would do anything he asked of him, even murder his companions.

To prepare Conundrum for the spell, Tanar started by creating as friendly and companiable an atmosphere as possible. The sharing of a secret would open the gnome to suggestion, so Tanar began to explain to Conundrum how the magical plate was used to communicate across great distances.

"There are actually two of these plates, each one made of silver polished to a mirror sheen, as you can see," he said. "This one is but half of a matched pair. When the proper incantation is spoken, its twin, wherever it is in the world or outside it, even in the Abyss, will ring like a bell. These two mirrors then become like a single window. Whoever sits before this mirror can be seen in the reflection of the other mirror, and whoever sits before the other mirror can be seen here."

"Are you going to make it work now?" Conundrum asked. "Who are you going to contact? You . . ."

His voice trailed off as the plate chimed of its own accord.

"Did you do that?" Conundrum asked.

"Silence!" Sir Tanar snapped. The plate chimed again, insistently. Suddenly, his reflection on its surface vanished, replaced by the now-familiar spot of oily darkness. Conundrum's breath caught in his throat at the sight of it, but he said nothing.

"It is good to see that you are still alive, Tanar," the Voice said from the darkness.

"I am, and I have news," Tanar answered, unable to suppress the excitement in his voice. "We are here. Even as we speak, the ruins of ancient Istar surround us. In moments, we will begin our descent into the Abyss."

As the *Indestructible* drew ever closer to the gaping black chasm in the center of the ruin of Istar, those on the bridge gathered near the porthole to gape in awe and wonder. Even the normally unflappable commodore joined the others in pressing his nose against the cold glass. Professor Hap-Troggensbottle was quite beside himself, and Sir Grumdish accused him of acting like a kender. Both Razmous and the professor felt insulted, but they were in too good a humor to complain. It seemed the final and most important—and probably the most difficult, though no one thought so at the moment—leg of their journey lay before them.

Snork maneuvered them into position above the pit. The ruins of Istar were a barely-visible collection of darker shadows hovering around the chasm's rim. The gnomes grew quiet, one would almost say respectful, thinking of those who died here in the Cataclysm.

After a time, the commodore shook free of the shadow that had descended upon them. Addressing the crew, he said, "We begin now on the last stage of our journey. I ask you to remember your duty. Let us not forget that we are scientists."

"Aye, Commodore," Chief Portlost acknowledged first, "that we are, and we shan't forget it!" With these words, he leaped to the ladder and descended it in a flash.

Sir Grumdish took his position at the firing station, joined now by the professor. Doctor Bothy returned to the sick bay. Snork gripped the wheel, and the commodore took up a post beside the half-raised Peerupitscope. He glanced once more round the bridge, as if settling himself, and let out a long, satisfied sigh.

"Navigator, engage the descending flowpellars," he said.

"Engage the descending flowpellars, aye," Snork confirmed. He turned and shouted down the ladder to engineering, "Engage the descending flowpellars!"

The *Indestructible* began to sink.

Down she went, and the walls of the pit rose up to surround them, as if it were not them but the sea floor that had begun to move. The lip of the chasm passed, shutting off their view of the ruined city. Now, they dropped past a dark face of rock pocked with caves and fissures.

"Which cave is it, Snork?" the commodore asked. "It's not one of these, is it?"

"No sir," Snork said as they continued their descent. "These caves lead to flooded passages beneath the ruined city. Once, these housed all manner of vile and evil creatures, attracted here by the nearness of their Dark Queen. Conundrum and I discovered a small travel guide written by a kender over a hundred years ago that spoke of a particularly evil being called the King of Darkness that was supposed to dwell here."

"You've, ah . . ." the commodore stammered as he gazed through the porthole at a darkness that had suddenly become quite ominous. "You've never mentioned this, ah . . . before. Do you think it is possible this king might still be around?"

"The *Polywog* seemed to have no trouble with him or any of the other sea creatures," Snork answered. "I imagine this king and his minions departed with their Dark Queen. Without the Maelstrom to suck hapless sailors down to their doom, there probably hasn't been much around here to keep evil creatures occupied."

"I see," the commodore said without conviction.

Descending flowpellars a-whirl, the *Indestructible* sank deeper into the black pit to the accompaniment of an ever more alarming series of groans, pops, and creaks from the hull and bulkheads. Guided downward by Snork's sure hand on the helm, they glided harmlessly past protrusions of black stone that would have dashed them to pieces. At first, the walls of the pit were pockmarked with dark cave-like openings, but soon the stone planed away to a glassy black smoothness polished by the incessant swirling of the Maelstrom.

With his hands folded behind his back, Commodore Brigg watched the stone walls slide past. Doctor Bothy reappeared on the bridge and stood quietly beside him, his fingers drumming one of the large brass buttons decorating the breast of his blue uniform. Professor Hap-Troggensbottle paced before the porthole, turning with each pass to gaze out into the eerie darkness of the deep sea. He paused occasionally to peer at some peculiar creature of the briny deeps never before recorded or observed by science. These floated in all their alien strangeness into and out of their view quickly, like people passing in the street. The gnomes had an uneasy feeling that they, inside their iron, spring-powered bubble, were the curiosities on display, and that these creatures with their long, wavering antennae, streaming swimmers, phosphorescent bodies, and bulging white eyes were popping by for a quick peek at these interlopers into their dark, mysterious domain. Some resembled creatures often seen in shallower and friendlier waters—

lobsters, shrimp, jellyfish, rays, and eels—only horribly transformed into creatures out of nightmare. Others were clearly quite beyond the wildest imaginings of even the kender, as evidenced by his open-mouthed speechlessness. Some of these seemed almost not to be natural creatures at all, but the mad creations of some demented gnome inventor. Others flashed and quivered with life, their internal parts visible through bodies as translucent as polished glass.

It was Sir Grumdish who spoke first. "Shouldn't we arm, Commodore? These things might just be the babies. I'd hate the meet that one's mother." He pointed to a particularly fearsome fish, ghostly white, with more teeth than three sharks put together and one large, pink eye that gazed back at them with an unsettling spark of intelligence. "Besides, I imagine we are getting close to the Abyss now. There'll probably be dragons attacking us at any moment." He sounded almost gleeful.

The commodore nodded.

Sir Grumdish shouted below, "Extend the Toaster!"

They heard Chief Portlost scramble to follow the order, all the while complaining that the drive springs needed more oil. The ram slid out from the bow of the *Indestructible* and snapped into place with a satisfying shudder.

Suddenly, the walls of the pit fell away to either side, opening into a huge dark cavern, the mouth of which was wider than the view through the porthole allowed them to see.

"Disengage descending flowpellars!" Snork shouted.

The whirling of the motors wound to a stop, and the ship hung like a rusty carrot before the gaping black maw of the continent of Ansalon.

"We're here," Snork said with a broad, toothy smile.

The gnomes huddled in excitement around the porthole, while Razmous leaped like a terrier trying to see over or around the massed group of wrinkled brown pates crowding the view. As word spread quickly throughout the ship, crew members gathered on the bridge and spoke together in a raucous babble. There was much shaking of hands, slapping of backs, and tugging of beards. Even Chief Portlost poked his curious face up from below, though he did not entirely abandon his post—his feet were still below the bridge deck. The cook staggered out, wrapped like a mummy from his latest trial of the flashcooker, to peer via eyeslits through the thick glass at the dark sea cavern opening before them.

It was about this time that Commodore Brigg noticed that they were floating into the cave, even though the engines had been disengaged. "There must be a current," he noted with some concern. "The ship will be difficult to pilot with a following sea."

"But that also means that there is a way out!" Snork said excitedly. "All we have to do is follow the current and it should bring us out the other side!"

"Are we prepared to enter upon this last stage of the journey? All stations report green or not green," the commodore commanded.

"Propulsion systems green," Chief Portlost shouted as he ducked back down the ladder.

"Weapons systems green," Sir Grumdish confirmed.

"Medical bay is ready," Doctor Bothy said.

"Please confirm with green or not green," the commodore admonished.

"Medical bay green," Doctor Bothy answered with a scowl.

"Sciences are green," the professor said.

"Navigation green," Snork confirmed.

"What about cartography?" Commodore Brigg growled

when the kender failed to speak up.

"Oh, you mean me?" Razmous asked. "I'd forgotten. Um, cartography not green. I don't have my *Polywog* maps."

"Where are they?" the commodore asked.

"In my cabin," Snork said. "I'll get them."

"And find the first assistant cartographer, Conundrum."

"Aye, Commodore," Snork said as he rushed forward.

With the majority of the crew on the bridge and the engines disengaged, the forward parts of the ship were eerily quiet. Even the popping and creaking of the hull had ceased now that the ship had stopped its descent. Snork made his way along the corridor until he reached his cabin. Darting inside, he scooped up the loose pages of the kender's maps as well as the copies they had made to try to trace their future course. But Conundrum was nowhere to be seen.

Tucking the papers up under his bearded chin, he began to shut the cabin door, but a burst of evil laughter from the bow of the ship sent the maps spilling across the deck as his jaw dropped open. He spun, half-expecting to see the ghost of a minotaur pirate floating down the passage toward him, ready to freeze his blood and turn his bones to water, as the bards and storytellers liked to say.

But the corridor was empty, bluely illuminated by a couple of glowwormglobes hung at regular intervals along its length. At the end of the corridor was the small, round door leading to the wizard's quarters. From behind this, Snork thought he heard voices. One obviously belonged to the wizard, but the other was new to him. It sounded deep and sinister, but tiny and remote, like a giant shouting from a mountaintop. It certainly wasn't the voice of a gnome, of that much he was certain.

Leaving his maps where they had fallen, he crept

toward the door. The voices behind the door grew in volume until, still a few feet away, he could hear quite plainly what they were saying.

"So the gnomes' ship actually works?" a deep, feminine voice chuckled. "Amazing!"

Snork felt a flush of pride, even as he wondered at the source of the voice. Could it be some stowaway that the Thorn Knight had slipped onboard? It seemed impossible. Then again, he was a wizard, and with wizards many things were possible.

The feminine voice continued, "Even now you descend to the Abyss."

"We've stopped," said a third voice. To his amazement, Snork recognized it as his cousin's voice. Now deeply concerned, he placed one hand on the latch to open the door.

"Yes, it seems we have stopped," Tanar confirmed, glancing out the forward porthole at the huge cavern yawning before the bow of the ship. "Even now, the gnomes are preparing to enter the cavern and continue on their preposterous quest to find a passage beneath the continent."

Gently, so as to make as little noise as possible, Snork lifted the latch and pushed the door open a crack. Inside, he saw Sir Tanar sitting in his hammock facing the door, but with his eyes lowered to the box before him, he failed to notice Snork's intrusion. Behind him, the porthole was filled with the awful seascape of the submerged cave, toward which the *Indestructible* floated. Of the source of the female voice, he saw no sign.

Fearful of being discovered by the wizard, Snork began to close the door, pausing only a moment to glance quickly around the cabin for Conundrum. He spotted his cousin standing among some barrels, an admiring expression on his red-bearded face as he gazed at the Thorn Knight.

"You had better act now, Tanar," the voice urged from the open box. "You must take over the ship and continue to the bottom of the chasm."

Snork started, the door still half open. *Take over the ship?*

"Mutiny!" he gasped.

CHAPTER

22

Before he could move, Sir Tanar spoke a single word in a voice that made Snork's beard crawl. An irresistible force grabbed the gnome by the front of his uniform and lifted him into the air. Suddenly, he was flying across the cabin, only to come to a crashing halt against the forward porthole. His teeth, broken and bloody, scraped across the cold, thick glass as he slid to the floor.

With a wave of the Thorn Knight's hand, the cabin door slammed shut, and a word of magic sealed it against intrusion. Drawing a dagger from the sleeve of his robe, he turned toward Snork, who was rising groggily to his feet. "It's not mutiny if you don't tell anyone," he laughed as he stepped over a coil of rope.

Still dazed, Snork blinked up at him. But a cry of anger brought the wizard up short. Spinning, he found Conundrum stumbling toward him, fists clenched, tears streaming into his beard.

Sir Tanar chuckled and reached into a pouch on his belt. With a wave of his hand, he flung sand into the advancing gnome's face, at the same time speaking words of magic, *"Ast tasark sinuralan krynaw.* Go to sleep, little one. I'll deal with you momentarily."

Conundrum blinked, stumbled, and—already snoring—
fell face first onto a pile of canvas. Smiling, the Thorn
Knight turned back to Snork, only to find him gone. He
spun, spitting a curse that turned into a howl of pain as the
ship's navigator brought a heavy belaying pin cracking
down across the wizard's wrist. The dagger fell from his
numbed fingers, and he staggered back, spittle flying from
his lips.

"Mutiny!" Snork accused through broken teeth and
bloodied lips. "Dirty, rotten, stinking mutiny!" He raised
the pin for another blow.

"Shinarr shonthes alaharandan betriabal ast avantar!"
the wizard said as he extended one clawlike hand at the
gnome. Snork froze, the pin dropped on the floor, and he
rose slowly into the air. His breath rattled in his throat, and
his eyes bulged from their sockets. His feet, free of the
floor, kicked spasmodically.

The wizard's outstretched hand closed into a clenched
fist, and at the same moment, with a sickening crack,
Snork's bearded head spun round on his shoulders. His
twitching stopped and his head fell limply and unnaturally
to one side, like a hanged man. Where he lay on the canvas,
Conundrum groaned and stirred but did not wake.

Sir Tanar released his magical hold, and the body of the
navigator fell with a thump to the floor. A moment later,
someone began hammering on the door. Tanar staggered to
the hammock and clutched at its ropes to hold himself up.
The spell had taken more out of him than he had expected.
In fact, he hadn't meant to cast that spell at all. But in his
rage and his pain, the words had formed upon his lips
almost before he knew what he was saying.

He gathered himself and straightened his robes. Outside, the pounding on the door grew more insistent.
Nearby lay the body of the navigator, his head turned back

to stare with sightless eyes over his shoulder. Conundrum still snored atop the pile of canvas. Sir Tanar smiled ruefully at him, then closed his eyes, gathering and focusing a portion of his remaining power. Stooping over the sleeping gnome, he gently shook him by the shoulders. "Awake, little one," he whispered. "Awake. There has been a terrible accident."

Conundrum stirred, his mind fighting through layers of sleep. His eyelids fluttered, revealing the whites of his eyes beneath. "Conundrum," Sir Tanar whispered. *"Tan-tago, musalah.* Your cousin has been killed. He tripped over my hammock and has broken his neck."

Still half asleep, tears started out from Conundrum's eyes and rolled down his cheeks to be lost in the red curls of his beard. "Snork?" he cried, struggling feebly to awaken.

"Yes," Sir Tanar continued, "and you must tell the others what you have seen. You must tell them how you saw Snork trip over the hammock."

"Tell the others?" Conundrum asked, his eyes finally coming to rest on the wizard's face. Instinctively, he recoiled, yet nodded his assent.

"You must report to the commodore exactly what you have seen," Sir Tanar said.

"Snork!" Conundrum cried as he lurched to his feet. He leaped over the coil of rope and collapsed beside his fallen cousin, tears of grief wracking his small body.

Sir Tanar smiled and turned to the door, then settled his features into a proper expression of shock and dismay. With a wave of his hand, the door flew open.

The hall beyond was filled with gnomes arguing over the proper way to employ the stuck-door-opener, a large contraption that resembled a mechanical spider. As the door opened, they leaped back in surprise, those in the rear collapsing in a heap of flailing arms and shocking curses.

Commodore Brigg, who was nearest the door, stepped quickly inside. "What's going on here?" he demanded. Then, his eyes coming to rest on the body of his navigator, he froze in horror. "Snork!" he gasped.

Conundrum looked up, tears streaming down his face. "He . . . he . . . t-t-t-tripped!" he sobbed. "O-over the hammock."

The commodore ran back to the door and shouted, "Doctor Bothy! Doctor Bothy! Get up here immediately! Make way for the doctor."

Those crowding the door stepped back to allow the portly doctor to pass. He struggled through them, huffing and blowing under the burden of his medical kit, a black bag the size of a sea chest. He pushed it before him into the cabin and let it fall to the floor. The corners of his mouth fell as he gazed upon the body of the navigator, and he heaved a mighty sigh, shaking his head and clucking his tongue.

. Commodore Brigg pulled Conundrum away to make room for the doctor. Groaning with the effort, Doctor Bothy kneeled beside Snork and examined his twisted neck. Then he lifted one limp hand and let it fall to the floor. Finally, he pressed his ear to the navigator's chest and listened for a moment. Clucking his tongue again, he sat back and shoved his legs straight out before him. He looked up at the commodore.

"He's dead, sir," the doctor pronounced sadly.

Conundrum wailed at the news.

Commodore Brigg shook the weeping gnome to get his attention. "Be quiet!" he shouted. "Remember, we are scientists. Tell me exactly what happened. And," he snapped, turning to Sir Tanar, "I want you to keep your mouth shut! If I want your opinions, I'll ask for them."

The Thorn Knight bowed in acceptance, smiling inwardly all the while.

Conundrum tried to calm himself. He wiped his nose on the flap of his brown vest and pushed the tears from his cheeks with the heels of his hands. He closed his eyes and tried to bring to mind the last moments when his cousin tripped and fell, but he couldn't envision the scene. He knew what had happened, but he couldn't see it. Perhaps it had been too horrible. Perhaps the vision had erased itself from his mind, leaving him only the cold facts that he must now, in the interest of science if not justice, repeat.

"He tripped over this hammock," Conundrum said. "He must have fallen. I . . . I think I tried to catch him. I am sure I would have tried to catch him."

"You did all you could," the commodore reassured him with a gentle pat on the shoulder. Conundrum nodded and snuffled.

Professor Hap-Troggensbottle and the kender pulled a blanket up over the navigator's body. Then, while the professor helped Doctor Bothy to his feet, Razmous stooped beside a bag of flour and lifted Snork's belaying pin from where it had rolled during the fight.

"Perhaps he stepped on this," he offered, displaying the pin.

"That's probably what happened," the commodore said as he gazed around. "This cabin is a mess, things lying everywhere. This was an unfortunate mishap. Chief Portlost will record it, and we will move on. This has always been our way in the Maritime Sciences Guild. We do not allow these tragedies to distract us from our goal. The attempt to subnavigate the continent of Ansalon was Snork's Life Quest. As his closest available relative, it falls upon Conundrum to attempt to complete his Life Quest."

He turned to address the other members of the crew still crowded into the hallway. "As a member of the PuzzlesRiddlesEnigmasEtcetera Guild, Conundrum is qualified to navigate us during the remainder of this voyage. He is familiar with the maps and Navigator Snork's intended course. Therefore, I name Conundrum the ship's navigator. I shall take over the piloting duties myself."

Conundrum swallowed nervously, but saw by the nodding of heads that the crew thought the commodore's choice a good one.

"What . . . um, what will we do with the . . . um, body?" the professor asked.

The commodore thought for a moment, his eyes straying to the porthole. "We'll bury him at sea at the first opportunity," he said quickly. "But for now, look alive! We've drifted into the cavern! Conundrum, I'll need you on the bridge now."

The crew hurried back to their stations and Conundrum followed Razmous back to Snork's cabin to retrieve the maps. "I'll help you," the kender piped. "I'm quite good with maps."

In moments, the commodore and Sir Tanar were alone in the cabin, facing each other over the body of the navigator. "You aren't going to just leave him in here, are you?" the Thorn Knight asked.

"This is as good a place as any," the commodore growled. The glint in his eye said that he wasn't entirely convinced of the sequence of events that led to the navigator's death. "Gather up your things. Bunk in my cabin, where I can keep an eye on you."

CHAPTER
23

In the days following Snork's death their journey should still have been relatively easy to chart on the map. Conundrum and Snork had already traced out most of the course before they left Flotsam. However, it was difficult to reconcile the map to the murkiness they saw through the ship's portholes. Even with the map, they often had the option of a dozen different passages without being sure which was the correct one, or was even if it a passage at all. Oftentimes, the submersible was forced to back out of dead ends and blind alleys—a feat made possible through repeated empty firings of the UAEPs. The twin jets of high-velocity water fired from the bow of the ship proved a reliable if cumbersome reverse gear, a tool without which they would have long before come to a disastrous end, since the *Indestructible*'s main flowpellars provided only forward thrust. The chief's only concern was that the UAEPs were not designed to be fired so often. If they should fail catastrophically through over-use, the ship could become hopelessly stuck in some crevasse.

For this reason, they had begun to take special care in their navigating. Using the weak current as a navigation tool had proved utterly unreliable, for once in the caverns, its pull was hardly detectable at all, and the deeper they went the less they noticed its effect. Still, on more than one occasion, they had been forced to rely entirely on its influence to identify the correct way ahead, and these instances caused delays of several days as they waited for the *Indestructible* to float toward one passage or another.

Now, however, they had come to the one portion of the map that neither Conundrum nor Snork had been able to fit together. Conundrum suspected that there was a missing portion, something that Razmous vehemently denied, as he had copied the map himself and so knew that there couldn't have been any mistakes. Though dubious of the kender's claims, Conundrum allowed that the error might belong to the *Polywog*'s original maps.

Their situation was made worse by the lessening of Sir Tanar's light spells. Oftentimes, because of the silt and sediment stirred up by their flowpellars, they were unable to spot a passage or turning before they were almost upon it. How the navigator of the *Polywog* had managed to make such extensive and accurate maps of the first voyage, Conundrum could not begin to hazard a guess. The *Polywog* had been primarily a ship of exploration and was equipped with a number of feelers, claws, pinchers, grabbers, rules, and prods used for feeling its way through night-dark caverns, but certainly their underwater light source must have been more efficient than the wizard's spells.

Sir Tanar was concerned that they would run out of air before light, and Conundrum had begun to share the Thorn Knight's fears.

At the moment, he was busy puzzling over a series of interlinking passages that the *Polywog* had mapped but that didn't seem to fit together in any way he could discern. He and his cousin Snork had studied this section for many weeks during the first leg of their voyage.

"You haven't gotten us lost, have you?" Razmous whispered in Conundrum's ear. The gnome squatted over his maps, which were spread over every available inch of the deck of the bridge.

"Maybe it goes together like this," the kender offered, taking two portions of the confusing map and fitting them together.

"No, no, I've already tried that," Conundrum said with some annoyance. "See, these passages here don't link up properly." He took the sheets from the kender and tossed them on the floor. Razmous sighed and picked up a handful of maps to study them, several of which unaccountably found their way into his pouches.

Presently, the ship lay motionless in a huge submerged cavern. Careful exploration had revealed at least two dozen possible exits. They might spend days—weeks—trying each one and still not find a way out.

As Conundrum stood before the porthole trying to penetrate the obscuring veils of sediment, Sir Tanar's light spell suddenly winked out, casting the cavern once more into utter darkness. Sir Grumdish, who had been polishing the helm of his Solamnic armor, threw it to the floor in disgust.

"This is pointless," he grumped, half to himself. "We'll never find the way."

Commodore Brigg sighed. "Somebody fetch the wizard and tell him he needs to renew his spell again."

"I'll do it," Razmous offered, quickly skipping from the room.

Professor Hap-Troggensbottle watched him go, then said, "Sir Grumdish is correct, I think. This Life Quest is a dead end. The caverns go on forever, I'm afraid, and there doesn't seem to be an underside to them. *And* I'm beginning to think that very large hot rocks don't float at all, that the islands and continents are but the tops of mountains growing out of the ocean floor."

"And I haven't come across one case of hiccoughs since we left Sancrist," Doctor Bothy added.

"Nor any dragons," Sir Grumdish finished. "Maybe we should have taken the Thorn Knight's suggestion and looked for the entrance to the Abyss. At least there we might find some dragons."

"An excellent idea," Sir Tanar said as he entered the room. He smiled, pleased that his spells—and the carefully-phrased words of dissent that he had instructed Conundrum to spread secretly and privately among the crew— were having their desired effect. "Indeed we've wasted enough time on this fruitless quest."

"We are not looking for the entrance to the Abyss!" Commodore Brigg snapped, his white beard quivering with anger. "The Life Quest of this ship is to find the east-west sub-Ansalonian passage and discover the fate of the *Polywog* and her crew."

"I respectfully submit that our chances of accomplishing either are undeniably poor, considering our present difficulty," the professor said. "The wizard's spells grow weaker with each casting. Our food, fresh water, and bottled air are running low, and Conundrum seems no closer to finding a way out of this maze than when we first entered it."

"Technically, this is not a maze," Conundrum corrected. "There is a missing page from the maps—that is all."

"Hey, what's that?" Razmous asked softly. But everyone ignored him, as they often did.

"Blast it all!" Sir Grumdish snapped. "We should go back while we still can, before our air runs out. We can at least refill our air bottles in that cavern where we buried Snork."

At this reminder of their fallen navigator, the crew grew silent. Sir Tanar shuffled nervously. Remembering Snork might inspire them to continue with their quest, just when they were on the verge of turning back. Days of suggestive comments to Conundrum had served well to demoralize most of the command crew.

"Oh, wow!" Razmous gasped, pressing his face to the porthole.

"What do you think, Navigator?" the commodore asked, still taking no notice of the kender. "Can you find us a way through or not?"

"I could," Conundrum answered hesitantly, glancing at Sir Tanar. The wizard nodded. "Given enough time, and provided the maps are accurate, I could. But I am inclined to doubt it, considering that the *Polywog* apparently came to ruin following these same maps. So perhaps we should turn back."

"And abandon your cousin's Life Quest?" Commodore Brigg asked.

Conundrum swallowed the sudden lump in his throat, hung his head, and sighed, "Yes."

"There's a light outside the ship!" Razmous cried. "Maybe it's the *Polywog*!"

"What's that?" Commodore Brigg exclaimed, pushing the excited kender aside and staring through the porthole. Outside the ship, there was indeed a number of shifting beams of reddish light shining through the murky water off the starboard bow. The other members of the crew, even Sir Tanar, crowded nearer for a look at the amazing sight. Here, unnumbered leagues beneath the Khalkist Mountains, there was another light, perhaps signifying another group of intrepid travelers, perhaps even, as Razmous had suggested, it was the ill-fated *Polywog* herself! It had become visible only because Sir Tanar's spell had expired, casting the cavern into total darkness long enough for their eyes to adjust well enough to see the dim glow.

"Maybe it's lava," Sir Tanar offered without much conviction.

"Nay, we'd feel its heat. The water would be boiling," the professor answered. "I should know. I've made extensive study of lava and other forms of heated rock."

"Maybe it's a dragon!" Sir Grumdish exclaimed.

"With hiccoughs," Doctor Bothy added.

"Fellow scientists and engineers, I propose that the only way to find out is to observe and record," the commodore said while stroking his curly white beard.

Sir Tanar ground his teeth in frustration.

"Chief Portlost, engage the flowpellars," Commodore Brigg ordered. "Crew to your stations."

The *Indestructible* lurched forward. While the commodore steered toward the light, Conundrum leaned close to Sir Grumdish and whispered, "You don't think it's really a dragon, do you?"

The usually sour-faced gnome grinned and shrugged.

CHAPTER

24

They followed the light to its source through one of the passages that they had not yet tried, a narrow crack barely wide enough to allow the *Indestructible* to pass. But Commodore Brigg's firm hand on the controls guided them safely between two vicious angles of rock that could have torn the ship in two. Soon, it opened out into a much larger chamber that was filled with similar light. The water here was a clear green, lit from above by a flickering red glow. Everywhere they looked, bubbles rose up in unceasing streams to a glimmering silvery surface, proving that the cavern was not entirely flooded. Glad for a chance at some fresh air—the interior of the ship had begun to ripen with the smells of gear oil, gnome sweat, and flashcooked beans—the commodore quickly ordered the ballast tanks blown and the ship surfaced.

A cloud of bubbles swarmed up around the ship as his orders were carried out, and the *Indestructible* slowly rose to the top. With their last glimpse before breaking the surface, Conundrum noticed several underwater passages leading off from this cavern. Quickly, he turned to his maps to note the exits, only to find that most of the maps had unaccountably disappeared. He grabbed the kender and began rifling through his pouches.

"Hey! You were walking all over them!" Razmous protested. "I didn't want them to get damaged."

The large, half-flooded chamber was lit by lurid flames dancing along the surface of the water. Sometimes the flames were like foxfire, thin shimmering veils floating dreamily along the surface. Sometimes they were bright roaring jets of blue-white fire that could have melted through the hull of the ship in seconds. But the danger of their situation was nothing compared to their wonder and amazement. Heedless of the fires leaping around them, Commodore Brigg steered the *Indestructible* toward a broken stalagmite protruding above the surface of the water near the center of the lake. The large stalagmite was a flat plateau large enough to put on a respectable circus— an island. A number of smaller stalagmites rising from the water around it promised a safe place to moor the ship.

At the center of the island lay a mound or heap, like an old mud hut thatched with golden straw. It was difficult to tell at this distance whether it was a construction or an accident of the light. The cavern itself stretched away into hazy darkness in either direction, a natural cathedral the dimensions of which could only be guessed at. With the ship fully surfaced, the hatches were opened and most of the crew members poured out onto the aft deck to marvel at their discovery. Commodore Brigg steered the ship nearer the island, guiding it between two stalagmites jutting like teeth from the flaming water. Crew members cast ropes over these and moored the ship fast, tying it off to the portside fore and aft recessed cleats. The island itself lay within easy reach of the *Indestructible*'s gangplank. Razmous was all for going immediately ashore, but most of the crew was more interested in the flaming waters that lay all about them.

Professor Hap-Troggensbottle was the first to put forth a theory. "If many such caverns exist, then the hot air trapped within them might provide sufficient buoyancy to make the islands and continents float," he said.

"Imagine the engine such a cavern could drive!" Chief Portlost said, beginning his own conjectures. "Hot air rising up through chambers drilled in the roof above could drive fans to wind enormous springs. Those could then be used to power the moving stairs I have always wanted to build to replace the gnomeflinger system currently employed in Mount Nevermind for travel between levels."

"Moving stairs?" Razmous asked. "I thought you were Maritime Sciences."

Smiling, the chief removed his jacket and turned it inside out, revealing a gray tweed with the emblem of the Intramountain Transportation Guild sewn over the right breast pocket.

"But what about the island?" Sir Tanar groused, wiping his brow with the sleeve of his gray robe. The air in the cavern was sweltering, but the gleaming mound at its center had attracted his attention. "Isn't someone going ashore to explore?"

"I'll go!" Razmous offered.

The commodore eyed Sir Tanar suspiciously. "Very well," he said. "Sir Tanar, since it was your idea, you may go ashore with Razmous, Conundrum, and Sir Grumdish. Report back immediately if you find anything. There may be creatures here that it would be wiser not to trifle with."

"Shall I get my armor, then?" Sir Grumdish asked hopefully.

"There's no time," the commodore answered. "I've no intention of remaining surfaced longer than it takes to fill our air bottles. This cavern is too large. There may be unfriendly eyes watching us even now. Go quickly and return."

Crestfallen, Sir Grumdish waited with the others while the gangplank was run out. He led the way ashore, followed by the kender and the Thorn Knight, with Conundrum bringing up the rear.

As they neared the center of island where the mound or hut stood, the flames from the water provided only a pale illumination. The walking proved more difficult than they expected. What had from a distance appeared to be a broad, smooth surface turned out to be pitted and blackened as though some intense flame had blasted it. The cracked edges of the stone were sharp as barbed knives, continually snagging the hem of the wizard's robe and tearing it to shreds. Once, Conundrum stumbled and fell, slicing the palms of his hands into ribbons. They almost turned back then, but Razmous had gone ahead a bit, and as Sir Grumdish helped Conundrum to his feet, the kender called out, "I believe it's gold."

"Gold?" Sir Tanar asked.

Using his hoopak staff, the kender vaulted over a particularly large crack, then knelt and peered ahead through the gloom at the glittering mound at the island's gloomy center. "Yes," he said almost matter-of-factly. "It's a large pile of gold."

"He's insane," Sir Grumdish muttered, using the universal gesture of a finger circling the ear to emphasize his meaning.

"And jewels, too!" the kender exclaimed shrilly, as though to prove the gnome's point. "And some really big swords and stuff, and . . ." He had nearly disappeared from their sight, his travel-worn clothes blending into the hazy dun background. "Oh!"

"Oh?" Sir Tanar shouted. *"Oh?* Oh, what?"

"A dragon's egg! Sir Grumdish, you were right. This really is a dragon's lair!"

———————◆◆◆———————

Bottles littered the aft deck of the *Indestructible*. Professor Hap-Troggensbottle had designed a new air compression device after his original one was lost overboard when they were forced to crash dive after leaving Flotsam. The new pump was, like the first one, a converted bilge pump, but to this he had devised several improvements, including a self-capping mechanism that exploded only one out of every three bottles. It required twice as many operators as the previous model just to monitor the safety features. It also could be used as a sausage grinder, had they any spare meat in need of grinding.

As the professor directed the filling of the bottles, several members of the crew busied themselves stowing the filled bottles below while others brought the remaining empty ones topside. Doctor Bothy was busy belowdecks concocting yet another cure for indigestion to counteract the cook's newest recipes, which Chief Portlost had kindly agreed to test. Commodore Brigg stood in the conning tower, keeping one eye out for anything approaching over or under the water, while with the other he followed the progress of his landing party until it were no longer visible in the darkness. Even so, he continued to listen to team members' voices, though he had difficulty discerning their words over the banging and clanging of the air compression system.

It had been several minutes since last he heard the kender's shrill voice, and he was on the verge of growing concerned. The island was not large, but it was large enough for them to wander out of earshot or become lost. He wondered if they hadn't fallen down some hole or been overcome by fumes, or, more likely, been done in by the treacherous wizard. He shaded his eyes with one hand as he peered into the darkness, not because shading his eyes helped him see better, but because it was a habit long ingrained by gazing out over the featureless gray sea. He could still see the yellow blob that hinted at a hut thatched with straw, but of his party there was no sign.

Lifting a tube from its hook within the conning tower, Commodore Brigg placed it to his lips and blew. Then he shouted into it, "Chief Portlost!" He pressed the end of the tube to his ear.

"Aye, sir?" came the tiny response through the tube.

The commodore shouted into the tube, "Take two of your command and search for the landing party."

"Aye, sir," the chief responded.

Before Commodore Brigg had finished returning the tube to its hanger, the chief and two gnomes in red jumpsuits were clambering out of the forward hatch and leaping to shore. They rushed off into the darkness, the chief bringing up a puffing and wheezing rear. He was not the gnome he used to be, having put on a few pounds in recent decades.

They had only been gone a few moments when it began—a curious whirring noise. It started low, almost at the edge of hearing, so that it was some time before the commodore realized he was hearing it. Then the low whirring grew into a whine, increasing in volume and pitch until it sounded like the voice of a banshee crying across the moors.

The crew members on the deck looked around in wonder, dropping what they were doing to stare at their commander. The commodore shouted down to the professor, "What's that noise?"

"Hoopak!" the professor answered, demonstrating by twirling an imaginary kender weapon above his head. "Generally used to scare off intruders, or as a warning."

"A warning?" the commodore shouted in alarm. "Get everyone below deck! Hurry!"

The whirring sound died abruptly. The commodore turned and stared into the darkness. Still, he saw nothing, unless it was a vague swirling in the hazy shadows at the far end of the cavern. He heard confused shouting, curses, the kender's shrill cries, yet nothing clear enough to discern the nature of the trouble.

Chief Portlost appeared from the darkness. He swerved aside to make use of the gangplank, and in moments was aboard.

"What's wrong?" the commodore shouted.

"I don't know," the chief gasped, pausing for a moment before the open hatch. "Someone said run, so I did."

"Where is your command?"

"Sir Grumdish ordered them into some kind of defensive line. They haven't any proper weapons—no catapults or anything."

"Damn his eyes, I told him . . . Get below!"

Chief Portlost saluted by tugging his beard, then dove through the hatch and disappeared. Commodore Brigg turned his gaze back to the center of the island. Now, the darkness there was complete, as though no light had ever been. He wondered if perhaps Sir Tanar had cast some kind of defensive spell to shield the party's retreat, but before he had time to form any other theories, all mundane thoughts were driven from his mind, replaced by a sickening, unreasoning fear. Out from the depths of the cave rolled a hollow roar of such rage and hatred that he felt his knees go weak beneath him. It struck him like a storm wave, and he was forced to clutch the rusty rail of the conning tower to keep from being blown overboard. And where there had once been impenetrable darkness, there was now brilliant light—fire, red and golden, liquid fire pouring down upon what, for the briefest of instances, appeared to be three diminutive figures throwing up their hands to fend off destruction. They quickly vanished in the white-hot inferno, perhaps leaving behind three tiny piles of oily ash.

It was a dragon, red as murder, soaring on leathern wings, pouring down its fiery breath on the tiny figures fleeing back toward the ship. In that one brief flare of light, Commodore Brigg saw them and despaired. But even as he was overcome with horror, he gaped in awe at the majesty and beauty of the evil wyrm as it passed within arm's length over the top of his bald brown head. As it passed over, he heard it give a small cry of surprise at the sight of him, and then it howled in fury. Its great wings pummeled the air, lifting it into the gigantic heights of the cavern. The wave of dragonfear that passed over him turned his bones to water and his blood to ice, just like the storytellers always said.

As the dragon soared overhead, banking round and peering over its outstretched wing at the ship, out from the darkness stumbled Razmous, helping Conundrum, who had fallen and skinned his shins. Sir Tanar was right behind them, the bottom of his robes a mass of flapping tatters. Commodore Brigg took heart and found new courage at the sight of them, as he had believed them dead already. Not that he was overjoyed to see the wizard, but even an unreliable and untrustworthy evil wizard might prove useful against a dragon.

"Thank Reorx!" he cried. "Hurry and get below. Where's Grumdish?"

"Coming! Coming!" a hoarse voice shouted from the shadows. Moments later, Sir Grumdish staggered onto the gangplank, his clothes reduced to a few tattered, smoking threads, and his Solamnic mustaches scorched down to a gray stubble. His skin was blackened and wet. He looked like a coal miner escaped from a cave-in.

"The others?" the commodore asked.

His jaw quivering with anger, Sir Grumdish shook his

head. "They were guarding our retreat. I took cover beneath a magical shield in the beast's treasure hoard."

"Get below," the commodore ordered, turning round to glance up at the dragon. Even as he did so, the gigantic beast was swooping toward the ship, its jaws agape. He dove through the hatch and slammed it shut behind him.

"Flood fore and aft ballast and engage descending flow-pellars!" he shouted as he cranked the watertight seal into place. The ship commenced to bubble and sink, waves lapping against the hull.

All of a sudden the *Indestructible* jerked to a stop, tumbling the commodore from the ladder leading down from the conning tower to the bridge. The ship rolled to starboard. "What's wrong?" Brigg cried as he grasped the Peer-upitscope and pulled himself to his feet.

"We're still moored!" Conundrum answered, pointing through the porthole at the forward mooring line, pulled taut and quivering. The ship continued to list heavily to starboard, so much that it was in danger of capsizing. Not even Chief Portlost knew what would happen if the *Inde-structible* capsized. They heard him shouting below to secure some barrels threatening to break loose.

"Purge the ballast tanks," the commodore ordered. "Purge them before they sink us!"

"But the dragon, sir!" Conundrum exclaimed, pulling away from Doctor Bothy, who was trying to drag him to the medical bay.

"We'll have to fight," Commodore Brigg stated.

"A-ha! That's more like it!" Sir Grumdish howled with glee.

The ship righted itself, flinging everyone to starboard. Then it began to tilt slowly backward, water streaming down the hull and against the porthole. The bow of the ship rose up from the water, while the iron hull screamed at the stresses for which it had never been designed. Rivets began to pop, and they heard the rending of wood. Despite the efforts of Chief Portlost, a dozen barrels of grain broke loose and tumbled aft with a noise like thunder, in the midst of which they heard a hideous scream suddenly cut short.

But more than anything else, what they saw through the forward bridge porthole filled them with such terror as few of them had ever known. The dragon had its claws wrapped around the bow of the *Indestructible* and was lifting her in the air. It was a normal red dragon of Krynn—if such monsters can be called normal—not one of the gargantuan new dragons like Pyrothraxus and Malystryx that had come after the Chaos War. But this dragon was also protecting its egg, and the hells hath no fury like a mother hen distraught over her brood.

The dragon continued to lift the bow of the ship out of the water. Meanwhile its powerful claws ripped gaping holes in the iron hull, even tearing through the wooden under-hull. Its glaring red eyes burned with a mixture of curiosity and hatred as it twisted the ship this way and that to examine its terrified contents through the portholes, perhaps searching for a way to shake out the juicy bits inside. At the same time she snapped the mooring lines that had threatened the *Indestructible*'s demise.

Finally gathering his wits, Commodore Brigg realized the full measure of their danger. Any moment now, the dragon would tear the ship apart or incinerate them with its fiery breath. Lunging up the sloping deck of the bridge, he grasped the lever that released the attacking ram, pulling against it with all his strength.

The steel point of the ram shot out, shuddering to its full length mere inches from the breast scales of the dragon. The monster started back in surprise, nearly dropping the *Indestructible*. But then its red eyes narrowed and its wings spread out to either side of its body, quivering in anticipation as it sucked air in through gleaming ivory fangs, stoking the fires in its belly to a thrumming roar.

"Sir Grumdish!" the commodore shouted at the fire-blackened gnome warrior. "The UAEPs! Fire!"

Sir Grumdish stared for a moment longer in fascinated horror. Then, reaching above his head, he thrust home two large red buttons. The dragon opened its jaws to breathe crimson death over the ship, and the *Indestructible* seemed to recoil in fear.

Then, with a hollow rush, twin jets of water spouted from the bow of the ship, sousing the dragon thoroughly, pouring several hundred gallons of seawater into its gaping maw. It tumbled over backward with the force of the spray. As it fell, the dragon tossed the *Indestructible* aside, and the ship fell with a thunderous crash into the fire-licked water.

Immediately, she began to sink.

CHAPTER
25

Green water streamed in through *Indestructible*'s numerous wounds. The crew picked itself up and hurriedly dragged out various leak-plugging and bulkhead-bracing devices invented over the years by the Maritime Sciences guild. One after another, these inventions failed spectacularly. One leak-plugger swelled so quickly that it split the wood it was supposed to repair, sending a tremendous gush of water into the galley. Chief Portlost and Doctor Bothy were washed into the corridor, but the cook, still wearing his bandages, managed to catch the edge of the watertight door. He slammed it shut and sealed himself inside, thus dooming himself and possibly saving the *Indestructible* from a watery grave. Watertight doors on the *Indestructible* could be sealed only from the inside, an unfortunate design flaw that nearly proved the ship's undoing.

Despite the cook's heroism in stopping the largest of the leaks, there were still enough holes in the ship's hull to sink her faster than they could hope to effect repairs. Commodore Brigg stared round at his drenched crew, despair creeping into his heart. "We can't abandon ship in this dragon's lair," he said.

"If you'd listened to me and gone to the Abyss, we wouldn't be in this situation," Sir Tanar said.

"Before we surfaced, I noticed some passages leading out," Conundrum offered.

"We don't have much time," Commodore Brigg said. "Point the way. We'll try it. Chief Portlost, we'll need everything she's got. If we can get into another cave, we might be able to escape through Conundrum's ascending kettles. We're not dead yet."

He strode to the con and firmly gripped the controls. Conundrum wiped the porthole with the sleeve of his white robe, then peered through the glass into the lurid green water.

"There, sir," he said, pointing. "That one looks large enough."

"We'll have only one chance. I hope your luck holds. Chief Portlost?"

"Ready, sir!" came the answer from below. Glancing down the ladder, Sir Grumdish saw the lower deck swimming with loose barrels and broken crates. A crew member wearing a red jumpsuit—his name was Faldarten—floated past, facedown, bumping against the ladder before swirling aft, a trail of blood following him through the water. Sir Grumdish turned away.

Indestructible lurched ahead drunkenly. Commodore Brigg fought the wheel, trying to keep her on course, but with hundred of gallons of water sloshing about her lower decks, and with gaping tears in her hull, she handled little better than a log raft riding a storm-swollen river. First one way, then the other, then back again, the ship swung, her escape passage growing nearer by the second but seemingly never in line with the bow of the ship. The bridge crew clutched at anything sturdy, bracing for an impact with the wall.

At the last possible moment, the exit passage lurched into view. The commodore swore like a dwarf, and then they were through with only one bump—the Peerupit-scope. It snapped off against the overhead rock. A fresh blast of water shot from the viewpiece and struck Sir Tanar full in the chest, bowling him head over heels back to his cabin.

Now began as hair-raising a journey as any of them had ever adventured. *Indestructible*, still at full speed, zoomed through dark winding passages, round hairpin turns, narrowly avoiding the stalactites and stalagmites that crowded this submerged tunnel. In the distance, they saw another shimmering red light, dimmer than the cavern they had just fled but visible nonetheless.

"Not another dragon's lair!" Sir Grumdish shouted.

"I thought you wanted to slay dragons," the commodore snarled as he battled the wheel.

Two more tight turns, the last of which they did not escape without first suffering a scrape that set their teeth on edge, and they were into another cavern. This one, like the last, was lit from above by a red glow, and it also proved to be partially submerged. They shot out from the passage and were immediately confronted by a dark sloping wall.

Commodore Brigg threw the wheel hard to port, at the same moment screaming, "Allstopengageascendingflow-pellarsemergencyblow!"

But it was too late. The bow struck a thundering blow that lifted the ship so suddenly and violently that it was a wonder she didn't break in half. *Indestructible* ground to a shuddering halt, thrown up on a steep shore of black sand, her crew tossed about like Abanasinian popping corn in a pan.

Doctor Bothy awoke with the certain knowledge that he was dead. He was a doctor, after all, so he should know.

JEFF CROOK

He discounted his continued breathing as an unimportant temporary state. It would be only a matter of time, he was sure. A body could not hurt like this and not be dead. The mortal frame was not designed to withstand such punishment. He assessed his current state of health as very grave without meaningful hope of recovery. He was suffering from numerous contusions and lacerations about the head, shoulders, ribs, arms, legs, and feet. Even his toes hurt, having stubbed them all at the same time against the base of his examination table when the ship underwent its most spectacular misadventure. He found that he had been struck blind—or else the lights had all gone out, and there was an annoying whining in his ears. What was more, every so often he was subjected to an acute spasm of the muscles of the upper abdominal cavity, which resulted in a sharp, painful inhalation of breath. Soon, this recurring malady proved so uncomfortable that, despite his better medical judgment, he was forced to adjust his prone position.

This shifting of weight revealed a number of things. First, he learned that the light had indeed gone out, or to be more precise, spilled. Most of the ship's glowworm-globes had fallen during the crash, scattering their glowing contents. The decks were littered with tiny blue worms milling aimlessly about in search of food. The whining noise proved to be the kender, atop whom Doctor Bothy had come to rest, and who, once released, loudly complained of nearly being suffocated just when things were getting interesting.

Finally, it dawned on the doctor that the annoying spasms of his abdominal musculature were in fact symptomatic of a full-blown case of the hiccoughs. This realization caused him to shout, "Eureka!" for reasons quite beyond his comprehension. Nevertheless, he was quite pleased with the turn of events, even if it had nearly killed him. He set about collecting enough glowworms to light his desk so that he could begin recording the particulars of his malady.

Meanwhile, the other members of the crew took stock of their situation. A head count showed that ten of the original crew of twenty remained alive, not including Sir Tanar, who survived the collision bruised and battered but no more surly than usual.

The *Indestructible* had come to rest half out of the water, thrown up on a sandy beach at the edge of the small cavern. Most of the ship's glowwormglobes were broken in the crash. The ship listed about twenty degrees to port and lay at a rather severe angle to fore. The water she had taken on after the dragon attack had all rushed to the stern, completely flooding the engine room.

Chief Portlost, wet and bedraggled, clambered up from below. A little reddish light, shining in patches through the muck-caked bridge porthole, illuminated his wan features as he squeezed water from his beard and shivered.

"It's no use, Commodore," he reported. "Engine room is filled to the door with mud and water. We need to pump her out and patch her up before we can hope to float her again, provided we can unbeach ourselves. Meanwhile, there's no telling what's happened to the engines. Driveshaft probably bent; flowpellar blades snapped. And we haven't enough scrap iron on board to make even minimal repairs."

"I see," the commodore said, thoughtfully stroking his own wet beard. "How long, do you think?"

"With plenty of iron and a full crew, I'd say a week," the chief answered after a few moments' consideration.

"Then you'll need at least two weeks, provided we can find you the iron. Our first order of business is to see to our provisions. I heard cargo break loose, and I imagine most of our stores are waterlogged and useless. We'll need to load

JEFF CROOK

the UAEPs—with arrows this time," he said with a wry smile, "and make everything ready should the dragon appear. Once that is done, we can set to pumping out the ship, repairing what we can, and prospecting for some iron in the cave. The Khalkist Mountains are supposed to be filled with ore—or so say the dwarves. In any case, I suggest we take a look around. If we are still in the dragon's lair, we'll need to find someplace safe to hide. Sir Grumdish, bring out your armor."

"Yes, sir!" Sir Grumdish responded happily.

"And open the weapons locker. Daggers and crossbows all around."

CHAPTER

26

With the aid of Conundrum, Razmous, and the professor, Sir Grumdish dragged his mechanical Solamnic armor out of the ship. Upon their exit from the *Indestructible*, the gnomes were at first awestruck by what they saw. The cavern was enormous. The beach upon which they had landed was but one lonely spot at the edge of a vast and magnificent ruin.

As they assembled Sir Grumdish's armor on the sandy shore, they stared in awe at the towering ruins of a great city, one lost to time. It was built on a gargantuan scale, many times larger than dwarf or human cities. Columns twice the girth of the *Indestructible* marched right down to the water's edge, and edifices of epic proportions and ancient style had been cut out of the rock walls of the caves. Broad avenues of cracked paving stones stretched into the distance, lined along either side by bubbling pits of boiling mud, scalding geysers, and crackling pools of lava—the source of the dim red light filling the cavern like a dawning sun.

But the place was hollow and empty, dead, with only the hiss and pop of the steaming mud to break the silence of the deep earth. It seemed many years since anyone lived here, for the place was undoubtedly a ruin, the civilization that built it long ago fallen into forgetful barbarism before finally succumbing altogether to its fate. The gnomes did not care to speculate on who the original builders were, whether human or sea elves or creatures unguessed at, forgotten by time. The solidity of the construction hinted at the skill of dwarf masons, but if this city were an ancient realm of the dwarves, they were a race with a sense of grandeur unmatched by any dwarves of the modern days.

"Why do you suppose they needed such big doors?" Razmous asked while staring around in wonder, no longer even pretending to help the others assemble Sir Grumdish's armor.

"There's no accounting for dwarves," the professor commented as he cupped his hands to accept Sir Grumdish's foot. Together, he and Conundrum lifted the gnome into the legs of his mechanical armor. Once he was settled safely inside, they hoisted his top half and set it down over his head. They heard him ratcheting home the retaining bolts.

While they were doing this, the remainder of the crew disembarked and spread out along the sandy shore, staring in fear and wonder at the monumental architecture stretching off into the red haze of distance. Even Doctor Bothy had been dragged away from his research. He staggered down the sagging gangplank, his expansive, blue jumpsuited midriff convulsing with regular spasms, each one of which he dutifully recorded in a handy pocket medical diary that he continually misplaced between hiccoughs. Sir Tanar stood on the shore, staring at the *Indestructible* lying in the sand with her stern in the water.

Chief Portlost came down the gangplank last, bearing the keys to the ship—a massive bronze crank, nearly as tall as himself, which was used to wind the main drive spring.

He had retrieved it from the flooded engine room, nearly drowning in the effort.

With a few preliminary rattles, pings, and clangs, Sir Grumdish's armor whirred to life. Conundrum handed him his broad sword, which his mechanical gauntlet gripped clumsily. Lifting it aloft, he shouted, his voice muffled by his armor, "Follow me!"

The shining steel blade, which like his armor he kept immaculately polished, glinted in the scarlet glow of a nearby lava pool. The others looked at him and shook their heads in disbelief. They were stifling in the heat of the cavern, so Sir Grumdish must surely have been baking in his armor.

But he did not complain. Instead, he led off in a clank-ing stride, sword still held high over his head like a stan-dard. Commodore Brigg tucked a dagger into his belt and then followed, the others falling in behind him, each checking his weapon. The professor carried his last UANP —Underwater Arrow of Normal Proportions—over one shoulder, while Razmous tested the willowy flex of his hoopak. Satisfied of its soundness, the kender pulled from one his pouches Commodore Brigg's remarkable all-purpose-thousand-in-one-uses-folding-knife, which he still hadn't given back after the adventure of the haggis burial party, and continued his search through its many useful tools for an actual knife blade. Sir Tanar glared hungrily about, per-haps imagining the untold riches that might still lie buried in some hidden vault, forgotten by time.

Conundrum hefted the crossbow given him by Chief Portlost. He had, of course, fired a crossbow before. The crossbow was as much the birthright of every gnome as the long bow was for the elves. The crossbow, in all its vari-eties, was the one truly mechanical weapon, an ingenious design invented by *dwarves,* much to the shame of gnomes everywhere. Sure, over the centuries, the gnomes had introduced numerous improvements, like the crossbow that fired a weighted net rather than a normal bolt, and the self-propelled all-terrain crossbow and recreational vehicle. The one in Conundrum's hands was one of the light crossbow variety, with the standard issue apple peeler and vegetable juicer ingeniously stowed in the wooden stock of the weapon.

Conundrum settled his weapon into the crook of his arm and plodded after the others. Unlike his fellows, this cavernous place filled him with foreboding. Not the unreasoning terror he had experienced when the dragon soared over and glared down at him with its hateful red eyes. Instead, he seemed to feel eyes watching him. In his fancy he imagined that the spirits of the builders of this place were staring down at them as they crawled like ants along the broad and broken avenues. This place reeked of some ancient tragedy, as well as more recent violence. Here and there, he saw fire-blackened walls and piles of charred bones, pillars of stone with huge sword gashes marring their stark marble beauty, gigantic doors of granite, each large enough to serve as the banquet table of kings, thrown down and shattered like cheap crockery. At one point, the avenue was blocked by a massive pillar that had fallen from the façade of a nearby building. In several places, it had broken apart, and it was through one of these gaps, as tall and wide as the grandest hall of Mount Nevermind, that they passed, every one of them nearly overcome with awe.

After what seemed like miles, Sir Grumdish came to a halt at the edge of a vast, stone-paved plaza surrounded on all sides by buildings that towered into the darkness overhead. At the far side of the plaza, they saw a fountain as large as the lake filling the crater peak of Mount Nevermind. In its midst, a column of shimmering golden water rose a hundred feet in the air before splashing down with a noise like a mighty waterfall.

Sir Grumdish said within his armor, "I don't think the dragon is here. We'd have been attacked by now." He clumsily sheathed his broad sword, then opened a little hatch in the belly of the armor and took a gasp of warm, moist outside air. "We might shelter in one of these buildings."

"I'll not spungh—" Doctor Bothy hiccoughed— "spend a single night any where nnnungh—near here. I couldn't sleep in ungh—anything so huge."

"Maybe there are smaller buildings off one of the side avenues," Conundrum suggested.

"Let's not split up just yet. First let's check out that fountain. We need fresh water badly, especially if we are to spend much time here," the commodore said, mopping his sweating brow with a handkerchief. "Our supplies were ruined in the crash."

Closing the belly hatch of his armor, Sir Grumdish started ahead. He led them across the broad paved plaza, over stone littered with broken piles of rubble and large, fire-blackened boulders. The golden color of the fountain's water came from four flames, each burning from the top of a slender stalagmite that rose from the pool's depths. From the center of the pool, the water shot in a thick stream high into the air, filling the area around it with a fine cool spray that proved a welcome relief to the heat. At the first hint of such blessed coolness, the crew threw caution to the wind and hurried ahead, passing Sir Grumdish and leaving him clanking along in a stiff-legged stagger.

The water in the fountain proved to be as cool and sweet as elven wine compared to the stale stuff out of their ship's stores. Some of the more reckless crew members dove headfirst into the waters, the most vocal and frolicking among them being, of course, Razmous Pinchpocket. With a shrill scream of delight, he leaped in, performing a perfect catapult stone splash while still wearing his pouches. The others knelt on the low stone curb and splashed the refreshing stuff in their faces and over their heads, cupping their hands to drink deeply or lying with their beards streaming in the water. Sir Tanar leaned over the curb and plunged his whole head into the water.

Sir Grumdish arrived last and latest, his top half already swaying as he loosened the restraining bolts. Razmous, floating on his back near the fountain's curb, playfully sent a thin stream of water arcing from his pursed lips high into the air. "Look at me," he laughed. "I'm a fountain."

"I'll fountain you!" Sir Grumdish howled. "Help me out of here, somebody!"

"Shhh!" Razmous cautioned, sitting up. His wet top-knot hung over his eyes like a pony's mane. "Be quiet."

The others, having learned long ago of the kender's extraordinary hearing, paused in their cavorting, straining their ears to hear over the roaring of the fountain.

A horrible metallic grinding noise, like an old rusty gate, three hundred feet tall and weighing a couple thousand tons, swinging open, set their teeth on edge. The ground shook with heavy footsteps. As they watched in horror, a huge green crab, half as big as the *Indestructible*, lurched from the entrance of a nearby building and scuttled toward them, pinchers clanging together like shields. It crossed the distance to the fountain in three rapid heartbeats, closing on the nearest of the crew—Sir Grumdish, madly retightening the restraining bolts of his armor—before the others could react.

The thing scrabbled to a stop within pinching distance of the hapless armored warrior, then rose up threateningly on its two rearmost legs, performed a not-too-ungraceful pirouette, and fell over on its back with a resounding clang, its legs and pinchers waving helplessly in the air.

CHAPTER
27

Gradually, the thrashing legs grew weaker and weaker until at last they were still, with only an occasional twitch to warn the gnomes from approaching too closely. Not that any of them would have approached too closely—not at first anyway. But Doctor Bothy and Professor Hap-Troggensbottle had to sit on Razmous to keep him away from the huge, black creature.

"It looks dead!" he wailed. "What's the danger in just a little peek?"

"That's what you said about the dragon's egg, and look what happened there!" Sir Grumdish barked from inside his armor.

"I said I was sorry, didn't I?"

Meanwhile, with dagger drawn, Commodore Brigg crept near enough to touch the beast's shell with his out-stretched hand. He brushed his fingertips over the rough, pitted surface of one of the creature's legs, then leaped away, but the beast remained as still as the dead. "It doesn't feel like a crab shell," he whispered as he examined the tips of his fingers. "Hello! Is this rust?"

As if in answer, a door in the upturned belly of the

beast clanged open, and out from it crawled a bedraggled figure dressed in rags. Long, unkept strands of white hair sprouted in a halo around his enormous bald brown head, and a long, thick, filthy beard dangled to his knees. Taking no notice of the astonished crew of the *Indestructible*, he began to curse and stomp around on the crab's belly, waving a wrench at the still-twitching legs.

With a little cry of surprised joy, Commodore Brigg leaped onto the crab's belly. The diminutive figure stopped waving his wrench and eyed the commodore warily. The two stared eye to eye for a few moments. As the light of recognition slowly kindled in the wretched creature's eyes, his bearded lip trembled, and he dropped his wrench with a clink.

Then the two were in each other's arm, weeping and roaring like drunken dwarves who just won some money, pummeling each other on the back and madly tugging at their beards.

"Hawser, you old sea dog!" the commodore cried.

"Brigg, you old barnacle scraper!" the bedraggled gnome answered.

Slowly, the others gathered nearer, still cautious of the strange crab-creature, but their curiosity of it and its peculiar owner gradually got the better of them. Tanar rose up from the water and stared at the crab in surprise. Razmous stood knee-deep in the pool and wrung out his topknot, a bemused smile on his wrinkled brown face. Sir Grumdish opened his belly visor and stared out suspiciously. Doctor Bothy shook with hiccoughs and chewed the ends of his beard.

Conundrum approached the crab and examined its rusty surface. Spying something beneath the green patina covering its surface, he began to rub at it with the no longer white sleeve of his robe. After a few moments, he had removed enough of the thin verdigris to reveal letters painted in bright red: MNS POLY.

"The *Polywog*!" he gasped.

"What is left of it," the bedraggled gnome croaked. "Forgive me. It has been some time since I last spoke. My voice is a little raw."

"Then you are—" the professor began.

"Captain Hawser of the MNS *Polywog*," the commodore said.

"Last survivor of that ill-fated expedition," Hawser added.

"And my brother!" Commodore Brigg finished, fresh tears rolling down his bearded cheeks. "It was my Life Quest to find him."

Captain Hawser turned and gripped his long-lost sibling by the shoulders. "So how *did* you find me?" he cried.

The commodore then described their journey from Sancrist, leaving out few details and commending with undisguised pride the bravery and resourcefulness of his crew. His narrative was helped along by various supportive exclamations, clarifications, and corrections by the kender and other members of the crew. When the commodore came to their indecision in the cavern as a result of some confusion over the maps, Captain Hawser nodded his head in appreciation of their predicament.

"Aye, we had the same trouble, and that's how we ended up here, if you know what I mean, which I am sure you do. It seems we misplaced that portion of the map before ever we reached Winston's Tower, and therefore your cartographer must have made a copy of the incomplete copy of the incomplete original that we left there, if you know what I mean."

Nodding, the commodore finished his narrative, telling of the encounter with the dragon, and their crash landing on the beach here. Once again, Captain Hawser sympathized. "Lucky you had them iron plates on your hull," he said. "*Polywog* was covered in bronze and stood nary a chance against the claws of the dragon. We followed the same light as you did, being lost like yourselves, and the dragon was waiting for us, seemingly. She tore the ship to shreds, half my crew drowned, dead, or eaten. The survivors escaped to here."

"How?" the commodore asked. "Surely you didn't make that swim through the flooded passages."

"Nay, no gnome could do such a thing without some kind of underwater breathing apparatus like that one invented by your professor there," Hawser said, acknowledging Professor Hap-Troggensbottle. "But you forget we had a dwarf with us—old Brambull. He found a passage linking the city of the giants with Charynsanth's lair. Of course, the giants had blocked it up to keep the dragon out of their city, but we managed to squeeze through the cracks."

At these words, Sir Tanar perked up. Noticing his interest, Conundrum edged closer to the Thorn Knight but said nothing to him as yet.

"Giants?" the professor said in alarm. "You mean there are giants living here?"

"Well, only just a few, if you know what I mean. Charynsanth got most of them before they blocked up that passage I told you about," Captain Hawser explained.

"Who is Charynsanth?" Sir Tanar asked.

Captain Hawser's eyes narrowed as he glared at the Thorn Knight. He shot a glance at his brother, as though seeking his approval before speaking. Commodore Brigg nodded, albeit reluctantly.

"Charynsanth is the red dragon," Hawser explained. "That's her name, or at least that's what the giants call her. I don't know what her real name is, as I haven't bothered to ask."

"How do you know what the giants call her?" the Thorn Knight pressed.

"Because I overheard them. It's not been easy living here these—how long is it, two years?—without overhearing their conversations from time to time. They do holler so. You'd think they were stone deaf, if you know what I mean."

"Go on," the commodore urged while glaring at the Thorn Knight.

"So we escaped here, like I said, only it wasn't much better here than in the dragon's lair, what with the giants and all snatching up my crew and whopping them over the head with their big clubs and eating me pretty much out of the last of my command. Before I knew what was happening or how to hide from them, I was the last survivor. That's when I found that little beach. It was littered with wreckage from the *Polywog*. You may not have noticed, but there is a deep hole in the bottom of that pool. Bottomless I reckon it is, and the water from the dragon's lair flows through that passage that you navigated before swirling down that hole. The current carried bits and pieces of the *Polywog* along and threw them up on the shore. I gathered what I could and built this crab. When it was watertight, I planned to use it to escape down the hole. I don't know where it leads, but anything is better than trying to get past Charynsanth. I think you noticed how sensitive she is about folks wandering around in her lair."

"But what if the hole doesn't lead anywhere?" Conundrum asked.

"It's got to go *somewhere*," Captain Hawser said. "Where is the water going to? What's drawing that current from the dragon's lair? I ask you. Personally, I think it leads all the way through to the other side of Krynn."

"Maybe it leads to the Abyss," Razmous speculated. "Hey! Maybe that's what happened to the Maelstrom!

Maybe it didn't just disappear. Maybe it moved here."

Sir Tanar snorted in derision, then grew thoughtful. He clasped his hands behind his back and began to wander away, brows knit and lost in thought. Conundrum followed him.

"Hey! I wouldn't go too far," Captain Hawser said. "Unless you want to meet a giant or two, if you know what I mean. As a matter of fact, we'd best get underground before they show up."

"I thought we were already underground," Razmous said.

"We are, but there are burrows beneath the city that are too small for the giants to enter. It seems they had giant-sized rats, too, what made the burrows. Some of you help me flip this crazy machine over," Captain Hawser said as he jumped down.

Working together, the crew of the *Indestructible* managed to right the crab and set it on its spindly iron legs. These seemed constructed of bits and pieces of the *Polywog*'s driveshafts welded together—along with various other bars and tubes that did not bear the mark of Mount Nevermind forges. As Captain Hawser climbed up inside his machine, Chief Portlost asked, "Where did you get these other iron parts, and how did you manage to weld them without a forge?"

After ascending into the crab's mechanical belly, the captain hung his bearded head out to answer him. "As for the welding, there are lava pits everywhere, and the iron can be got if you're willing to scrounge for it. This is—or was—a city of giants. Their old, rusty, castoff weapons are everywhere. But if you'd like to see more, climb inside. I'll show you around."

"May I?" the chief asked delightedly.

"Please," Hawser said. "And Commodore, have your crew follow me to a place of safety. You have to hide around here when the geysers start venting. They'll be perking up any moment now. Mostly, that's when the giants come out. Mostly. They like the heat, and the steam hides them."

———————◆◆◆———————

Inside his clanking, creaking, mechanical crab, Captain Hawser led them by a circuitous route down broad alleys and through wide courtyards. Confusing though their course seemed, Conundrum realized that the captain was leading them back to the beach where the *Indestructible* lay wrecked on the shore. When he mentioned this, the captain said that the giants did not often patrol near the beach because of the water. The giants, he explained with his head hanging out of the bottom of the crab—Chief Portlost was, to his everlasting delight, now driving the contraption—had an intense dislike, almost a fear, of water in any form other than scalding steam.

"And the giants are at war with the dragon?" Conundrum asked.

"Aye, son, that they are. Though nowadays they are content to keep the passages between their two lairs blocked. Though they are strong and have the advantage of numbers, Charynsanth is too powerful for them."

The captain's knowledge of the subterranean city proved invaluable. They might have wandered for months before discovering some of the forgotten byways through which he led them, and as he had promised, here they found titanic weapons of forged iron lying everywhere, many of them reduced by the steamy atmosphere to huge piles of rust. What was more, as he had predicted, geysers throughout the city began to erupt during their journey, filling the streets and alleys with a warm, dense fog that obscured sight to within just a few feet—fog thick enough to hide even a giant.

Finally, they turned into a building no different than the hundreds they had already passed. The interior of the building was expansive and echoing but dark as a minotaur's heart. Captain Hawser steered his mechanical crab into a far corner of the chamber. The belly hatch popped open and he swung out, followed by Chief Portlost. Loosing a rope from a small boulder, he dropped a gigantic tapestry over the machine, then turned and pushed a flat slab of stone aside, revealing the dark mouth of a tunnel burrowed straight down into the floor.

"What's this?" the commodore asked, peering down into the rank darkness.

"Home," Captain Hawser answered. "Giants can't find us here, so this is home. But only for a little while, now that you're here."

CHAPTER
28

There are few things in this or any world that so cut against the kender grain as work when there is fun to be had. Razmous had spent three interminable weeks fulfilling his duties as chief acquisitions officer, leading expeditions through the ruins in search of iron to repair the *Indestructible*. As interesting as exploring a ruined city might sound at first, after thirty or so collection "missions," he was ready to put his head in a UAEP tube and explode. Once he got over the really, really big architecture and saw his two thousandth forest of stone columns, there wasn't much to it.

To really put the beard on the dwarf, Commodore Brigg had absolutely and irrevocably forbidden him, under any circumstances, unto perpetuity, to search for the giants' lair. It wasn't that he wanted to see a giant, in particular. He just wanted to do *something*.

The others were all cheerfully busy at their individual tasks. Doctor Bothy continued to search for a cure to his hiccoughs, which had not abated in three weeks. Conundrum and Commodore Brigg were helping the professor modify one of the ascending kettles so that it could be lowered by means of a wench attached to the stern of the *Indestructible*, down through the hole at the bottom of the flooded portion of the cavern. They wanted to see if it really was bottomless, or a way to the Abyss, or to the other side of Krynn, or a possible way out. They had renamed the ascending kettle for this purpose, calling it a diving bell. This interested the kender for a while, until Commodore Brigg refused to allow him to be the first to go down in the bell. As the most qualified scientist, the professor was going to hazard the journey himself.

Sir Tanar was busy doing whatever it was that wizards did. This seemed to consist of standing around looking surly and aloof, or else poking around in dark places when he thought he wasn't being followed, searching for secret passages leading to fabulous treasures, of which there apparently were none. Captain Hawser and Chief Portlost were busy with the mechanical crab, stripping its hull for parts for the *Indestructible* or effecting repairs to the ship. By the end of the three weeks, the crab was little more than a naked skeleton, though it still contained most of its mechanical components and could be operated as usual.

This left only Sir Grumdish to provide a measure of amusement for the kender, but he spent most of his days holed up inside his armor, sulking because the mechanical crab was so much more spectacular than his own humble mechanical armor. It had quite taken the joy out of his attempt to become a Knight. Razmous had spent the better part of a day begging him to go on a long explore, but to no avail. The next day, Sir Grumdish dismantled his armor and flung the pieces in a corner. He spent the remainder of the third week sitting atop the base of a fallen marble column, staring at a blank cracked wall.

After three weeks, Commodore Brigg finally released Razmous from his duties. They had all the iron they needed to complete their repairs, the *Indestructible* was once more afloat—with the addition of the boom and wench and the diving bell hanging from its end. With the gnomes no longer shouting, "Razmous, more iron! Razmous, find something a little bigger next time!" every two turns of the glass, the kender was finally able to slip away alone for a little private investigation. He had seen some promising ruins during his iron-mongering expeditions. One thing that Captain Hawser said in their first encounter stuck in his mind, rolling round and round like a pebble in a barrel, endlessly repeating until it had become a little chant, the first verse in a kender traveling song. *A passage linking the city with Charynsanth's lair.*

It called to the kender like the smell of honey to a bear.

The perfect time to search for the passage was, of course, while the geysers were venting. All the gnomes would be hiding underground, and he could slip away unnoticed. He might even run into a giant by accident in the fog, and he was pretty certain it wasn't breaking the rules if you just happened across a giant.

As he crept down a deserted, fog-shrouded street, he paused at a corner to consult a map by the light of a nearby lava pool. Warm sweat dripped from his forehead down his pointed nose and onto the parchment covered with his own cartographical scrawls. During his search for iron parts to repair the *Indestructible*, he had made careful observations of his surroundings and committed them to maps. Marked in red on these maps were those places he most wanted to explore, in green those places he sort of wanted to explore, and in blue those places Sir Tanar had already explored (with Razmous secretly following him), but which still contained interesting nooks and crannies that the wizard had probably overlooked.

It was toward one of these places in blue ink that he was heading, since it was nearest the ship. It was a pile of

JEFF CROOK

rubble cast up against the dressed stone wall of the cavern. Sir Tanar had poked around in it for a while, probably hoping to find dead bodies or some other nasty thing to use in his spells. Razmous didn't believe that it contained anything of that sort, though if it did, it certainly would be interesting. Instead, he believed it might cover an entrance or possibly even an exit.

Satisfied that he was on the right track, Razmous continued on his way, arriving a few minutes later at the site. It appeared to be nothing more than a pile of rubble extending more than halfway across the broad avenue, heaped up to a height of forty or fifty feet against the wall.

He avoided the loose piles of stone at the edges and went straight for the larger boulders nearer the wall. By turning sidewise and rearranging his pouches, he was able to slip between a promising pair and found himself, after a tight squeeze and a scramble over some loose gravel, in a long, tube-shaped cavern bearded with long pointed stalactites and prickled with short, stumpy stalagmites. The nearest of these looked to have been worn down to little more than a nub of its former self, and it appeared to have been blackened by fire. The far end of the tunnel, though hazy with smoke, was lit by a flickering blood-red glow.

Smiling, Razmous strode forward, and painfully stubbed his toes against the skull of some gigantic, ugly humanoid. Its heavy brow thrust out over a flattened, crooked nose and large, misshapen mouth filled with a hideous snarl of yellow teeth, some of which had fallen out. The skull was nearly as large as the kender and twice as heavy. Nearby lay a rib cage large enough to hold a bear. Razmous crawled inside, sat down, removed his boot, and massaged his bruised piggies. A reddish gleam near the wall caught his eye, and brushing aside some ancient cobwebs, he removed a large, dry, dusty crimson scale. He examined it for a moment before dropping it into one of his pouches, slipping his foot into his boot, and continuing on his way.

The cavern was much longer than he'd imagined. By the time he reached the farther end, Razmous was dusty, bedraggled, and thoroughly exhausted. His topknot hung like a limp rag over his nose, stray strands of hair clinging to his parched lips and the gummy corners of his eyes.

Yet he didn't mind, not at all. The trip had been worth every scraped shinbone, crushed toe, and skinned knuckle, for below him, at the base of a long broad slope, lay the red dragon.

Reorx's Black Boots! What a dragon. Razmous had to bite his tongue to keep from shouting, "How do you do?" He'd seen the dragon for only a few moments three weeks ago when it attacked them: once as it breathed fire on two of his companions—that had been interesting, though very sad—and once as it peered through the portholes of the ship. Of course, in both cases, he'd only caught a glimpse. Now, the dragon lay stretched out on a bed of gold and steel coins, snoozing like a cat before a warm hearth.

Even farther below lay the lake of fire, and in its midst was the island where the dragon's egg still lay atop its comparatively smaller pile of treasure. The dragon's lair was high up near the cavern's roof, where it could keep watch over its egg. Razmous noted the cleverness of this plan, nodding in appreciation of how exposed and vulnerable they had been when approaching the egg.

His eyes flickered back to the dragon and drank in the sight, burning it into his memory so that he could sit before a fire some day and tell others of what he had seen. Razmous was rather young for a kender, only being twenty years or so into his wanderlust—the peculiar urge to see the world firsthand that most kender begin to feel in their early twenties. Being so young, he had little memory of how things were before the coming of the great dragons and the subsequent Dragon Purge. He could count on two fingers the dragons he had seen before this one—Malys, whom he had glimpsed only from a distance, and Pyrothraxus, whom he had seen up close and personal during his visits to Mount Nevermind. But even Pyrothraxus, who was much smaller than Malys, dwarfed this dragon by many wingspans. This dragon was a house cat to Pyrothraxus's tiger. Nevertheless, Razmous could not help but be overcome by the majesty and beauty of the red creature. Even though it was evil. Very evil.

The unimaginable wealth that lay all about the dragon caught his eye. He could not suppress a sigh, fingering the gold in his mind, already seeming to feel the weight of it dragging at the straps of his pouches. It wasn't some kind of dwarven greediness that he felt, kindled by the sight of all that wealth. It was the desire to be able to slap down a coin on a bar, hitch his thumbs behind his suspenders —he'd have to start wearing suspenders first—and tell everyone that the coin came from a dragon's lair.

It wasn't like he was going to steal it from the dragon, Razmous reasoned. He'd return it someday. Now that he knew where he could find a dragon, he imagined he'd come back many times just to look at it. He could return the coins then, after he was finished telling everyone who would listen about the time he borrowed a pouch full of coins from a dragon. Yes, that was it! That was it perfectly. There couldn't be a better plan. He'd just slip down there, he thought as he started down the slope, moving as quietly as only a kender can move. Slip down there and . . .

Of course, this white-hot pain shooting through his back wasn't part of the plan, nor his knees betraying him and going off in different directions. He fell heavily on his rump, then toppled over on his face. Some of the precious things in his pouches spilled out on the stone floor, and the rounder objects—a silver salt shaker from the Sailor's Rest in Flotsam (how had that got in there?), a small steel coin with a hole punched through the middle for a string, a spool of green thread—rolled down the slope, picking up speed and noise as they neared the dragon.

Slowly, one of the dragon's great heavy eyelids lifted and stared at the three tiny round intruders as they rolled to a stop at the edge of its treasure bed.

Meanwhile, Razmous was struggling with his rudely uncooperative arms. His head was grinding his nose into the stone floor, but he could not lift himself off it. His arms lay spread to either side, as lifeless as sausage. Finally, he managed to roll himself over, and, strangely, found Sir Tanar standing over him.

"Oh, Shir Tanner," he said drunkenly. "Clad you arth 'ere. I canned seemb to move by armbs. Whathz thad in your hanth? A dagger?"

<hr>

Charynsanth lurched up on her bed of treasure upon hearing the commotion and spying the gray-robed mage. Seeing the writhing creature at his feet and the bloody dagger in the wizard's hand, she stayed her first impulse— to blast them both with dragonfire. But she did not spare the Thorn Knight the full onslaught of her dragonfear. It rolled out in waves, lashing his spirit, and he staggered back under the assault, but gamely he held his ground.

"What do you want here, human?" she asked, half in admiration of his bravado.

"I have slain the thief come to rob you of your treasures," Sir Tanar answered. He was thankful that his voice did not tremble, for in the face of this dragon, he dared not show fear.

"Thief?" Razmous said weakly. He blinked up at the

Thorn Knight. "Oh, good zhob. Now where wuz I?" His eyes closed again, and his face grew paler as the pool of blood grew wider around his outstretched body.

The Thorn Knight continued, "We serve the same mistress, you and I."

"Takhisis is gone!" the dragon roared. "I serve no one but myself."

"Be that as it may, I have been in contact with my Mistress, and it was she who suggested I make an alliance with you," Sir Tanar ventured. "She knows you of old. She was, in fact, surprised that you are still alive. She has not heard your name spoken for many a year, not since the Dragon Purge began."

Charynsanth's eyes narrowed, but she said nothing. She had fled here at the beginning of the Purge, after her mate was slain by the green dragon Beryl.

"We can help each other, you and I," Tanar continued, feeling more confident. "I've killed this thief, and I know of your war with the giants. I can tell you of a way to get into the giant's city, O mighty Charynsanth."

"You were with those miserable little interlopers before," she hissed. "I saw you go onboard their little ship after I roasted those two. They were small, barely more than a mouthful after I finished cooking them."

"There are enough left over to satisfy even your appetite," Sir Tanar said.

She purred, chuckling, the fires in her belly spouting from her nostrils. "And I after I kill them, what do you get?" Charynsanth asked.

"Their ship," he answered. "Nothing more. Just their ship, and a few members of the crew to operate it. The city, the giants, and their treasure I leave to you."

He did not mention that he needed the ship and her crew to find the entrance to the Abyss, nor that he planned to escape in the ship while Charynsanth was busy with the giants. Still, something in her eyes told him that she suspected as much.

"How very wise of you," the dragon said, but her tone was sarcastic, as if she divined his motives.

"I'll come tomorrow to tell you the way," Sir Tanar said, his voice shaking, "and I'll bring a morsel to whet your appetite." With these words, he turned and strode away, swallowing the ball of steel wool that had formed in his throat.

Charynsanth pulled herself up the slope to watch him go, her massive ivory claws digging into the stone. She paused over the outstretched form of the kender, sniffing at him hungrily. He was barely enough even to take the trouble to swallow, but at least he was warm and juicy, not burned to a crisp.

As she hovered over him, Razmous's eyes opened a slit. "Oh, hello," he whispered. "My name izh Razhmouf Pingepogget. Are you going to defour me?"

"I thought I might," the dragon answered with begrudging admiration, almost pity for this miserable wretch who had been treacherously stabbed in the back by what was probably his companion, if not his friend. That wizard would be one to watch, she thought. He might try the same with me.

"Oh, good," Razmous sighed sleepily. "Do hurry, 'fore I fall azleeb. I doan wanna mizh thizh."

Conundrum's ascending kettle had been fully converted into what they had decided to call a diving bell. Inside the large copper kettle, they had built a shelf to sit on and a rack to hold bottles of compressed air, and they had placed a small porthole on one side to allow the occupant to see his surroundings. The whole thing was wrapped in a large cargo net and doubly secured at the top to make sure the bell wouldn't tip over and let out all the air. It dangled by a rope that ran through a pulley, which was suspended by a boom attached to the stern of the *Indestructible*. From the pulley, the rope led down through a hatch into the engine room of the ship, where it wound round a wheel attached to the main drive spring—which, for this experiment, was connected both to the flowpellars and the wench, with power transferable between the two devices by way of an ingenious box of gears called a "dyno." (Short for "how do I know?" As in, "What does that thing do?" "How do I know?") Of course, the *Indestructible* had miles and miles of rope, because gnomes never went anywhere without miles and miles of rope, not if they could help it. One simply never knew when one might need to build, say, a suspension bridge, or for that matter, lower a diving bell to the other side of Krynn.

Maritime Sciences Guild motto: *Be overly prepared*.

The ship's remaining red-jumpsuited ensigns were placed in charge of operating the wench, while Conundrum and the commodore stood by the boom. Conundrum found himself once more in charge of oilage, this time of the pulley. Doctor Bothy stood by with his medical trunk, hiccoughing softly. Captain Hawser and Chief Portlost were ready inside the crab in case of emergencies—like a sudden attack by giants. Normally, Sir Grumdish would have handled the security details, but he was strangely absent, as were Razmous and Sir Tanar. Commodore Brigg not-so-secretly hoped that Sir Tanar had gotten lost in the city. In his opinion, the wizard was up to no good in his secretive exploration of the ruins. "Maybe," the commodore whispered in a prayer to Reorx, "he's been eaten by giants." He also crossed his fingers behind his back and tied a lucky knot in his beard, just for good measure.

For this experiment, they needed every bit of luck they could get, for this exploratory dive into the seemingly bottomless chasm at the bottom of the flooded cavern was fraught with danger. A million things could go wrong, and even the gnomes were willing to admit that, with them, things that could go wrong usually did. The rope could break, the diving bell could settle on a ledge and tip over, it could catch on a stony projection and be hung there forever, the wench could jam or break, or the water at the depths to which he was diving might be steaming hot and cook him like a lobster in a pot.

Yet Professor Hap believed that the scientific benefits of the dive would far outweigh its risks. It was possible, as Razmous had suggested, that the chasm led down to the Abyss, or as Captain Hawser suspected, to the other side of Krynn. But the professor had his own theory, one that he most hoped to prove and, in doing so, complete his Life Quest. He believed that the chasm led to the underside of the continent of Ansalon.

When everything was ready, Professor Hap-Troggensbottle emerged from below. In one hand, he carried a blue glow-wormglobe suspended, like the diving bell itself, in a net sling so that he could hang it from a hook inside the bell. He wore the last of his skin-tight black diving suits, including bladderpack, fishbowl, and duckfeet, just in case he ran out of air or the diving bell filled up with water. In his heavy shoes, he thumped slowly across the aft deck.

Commodore Brigg ordered the bell lowered to the deck. The professor paused to allow Conundrum to tighten the neck seal around his fishbowl and secure the hose to the bladder pack. He then gave the commodore a folded scrap of paper and said, his voice muted by the glass, "This is a code that I have prepared so that we will be able to communicate a little more elaborately than the old one-pull-two-pull system usually employed in umbilical diving of this sort. The diving bell, as you can see, acts as a sort of resonating chamber." He demonstrated by rapping it with his knuckle, producing a single metallic note. At the same time, the note was echoed by a small ringer attached to the pulley from which the diving bell depended.

"The vibrations travel up the rope to the ringer, and by tapping on the boom with a hammer, you can send messages down to me as well," the professor finished.

Commodore Brigg studied the piece of paper for a moment before handing it to Conundrum. "Looks confusing to me. Conundrum is better at these sorts of puzzles. He will be communications officer for this expedition," he said.

While the professor and the commodore wished each other good luck, Conundrum examined the code. It was a simple system of dashes and dots representing the three hundred sixty-four characters in the Gnomish alphabets. They had seven alphabets, each used for different circumstances, like technical documents, politico-religious treatises, warning labels, and so on. The code seemed simple enough to him, so he tucked it away in a pocket of his vest.

With a final wave, the professor climbed inside the diving bell, his bladderpack bumping awkwardly against the edge. Finally, his heavy duck feet vanished up into the overturned kettle. They saw the light of his glowworm-globe shining faintly through the bell's tiny porthole. A few moments later, the diving bell rang in a rapid series of thirty-six taps. Commodore Brigg turned to Conundrum, who was counting them out on his fingers and whispering to himself. After a moment's thought, he said, "The professor says to lower away."

The commodore turned and shouted down through the aft deck hatch, "Raise the bell."

With ropes creaking and pulleys squeaking, the diving bell rose from the deck of the *Indestructible*. Conundrum swung the boom out to a point where the bell hung directly over a dark chasm visible through the green water in the floor of the cavern.

"Lower away!" the commodore shouted. "Slowly!"

The diving bell began to drop. As it touched the water, the ringer in the pulley began to tap out a message. "Stop!" the commodore shouted. The wench ground to a halt. He turned to Conundrum.

"He says, 'See you on the other side,' " Conundrum translated with a snicker and a grin.

The commodore laughed. "Go ahead. Lower him down," he ordered.

The wench shuddered to life again, and the diving bell slipped into the water. Conundrum stood at the stern and watched it sink slowly down through the gaping black chasm at the bottom of the flooded cavern. The rope, stiff

as a pole, continued to slip down into the darkness, and the
pulley creaked for want of lubrication. He grabbed a bottle
of oil and climbed up onto the boom. It struck him as
remarkable that, less than a year ago, he would have been
terrified to climb out over the water on so narrow a beam.
Now he scampered aloft like the nimblest of sailors without even a second thought.

When he had the pulley turning as silent as a whisper,
Conundrum slipped back down to the deck. Commodore
Brigg stood at the stern, staring down into the water and
absently stroking his beard. He nodded to Conundrum,
then began pacing the deck with his hands clasped behind
his back. After a couple dozen circuits, he paused at the aft
deck hatch to watch the endless coils of rope unspool and
go quivering up and over the pulley and quietly down into
the water. While he watched, a member of the crew
attached another coil with a square sailor's hitch.

"How many does that make, ensign?" he asked.

"Number ten, sir," the gnome sailor answered, saluting.

"Ten!" the commodore exclaimed. "At a hundred foot
apiece, that's nearing a thousand feet." He turned to
Conundrum.

"Heard anything from below?" he asked.

"Nothing yet," Conundrum answered. He leaned out,
resting his hand on the boom to steady himself. "And the
rope's still going straight down."

"Better make contact," the commodore ordered.

Conundrum picked up a hammer and tapped out a
quick message on the boom. An answer came back almost
immediately.

"I think he says, 'Nothing unusual yet,' " Conundrum
translated after a few moments.

"What do you mean, you *think* he says?" the commodore asked.

"The message was a bit strange" Conundrum said.

"Actually, it said, 'Noth_ng unsususual yet_y.' "

"Could it have been garbled in transmission?"

"Not like that."

The commodore called for Doctor Bothy. The portly ship's physician hurried (as best he could) to the aft deck, where Conundrum repeated the professor's message with its strange spelling.

"Ask him how he feels," the doctor said, a worried frown on his face. Conundrum tapped out the query. The answer came back in disjointed segments. . . . *feel fyn²* . . .

"What did he say?" the commodore asked.

"I think he says he feels fine," Conundrum answered.

Another tapped message arrived, startling them. *W__base I__beautiful.*

"What does that mean?" Doctor Bothy asked.

Conundrum shrugged, already concentrating on another message ringing out on the pulley. "Thousand liquid yellow glowing submersibles, faces like moons."

"Tell him this has gone too far!" the commodore shouted. "Tell him we are pulling him back up."

Conundrum nodded and dutifully tapped out the message.

It came back, *Not.*

"You tell him I am ordering the wench reversed," the commodore said, then turned and shouted to the crew in the engine room. "Prepare to detach the wench and re-attach in reversed position! Stand by the dyno!"

"What's wrong?" Chief Portlost shouted from shore. He stood atop the crab, inside of which Captain Hawser sat, fingering the controls nervously.

"He's having hallucinatory distractions of the optical nerve," Doctor Bothy answered. "The commodore is pulling him back."

To which the chief responded, "Well, hurry up. Captain Hawser says that the geysers are starting to vent and it's getting foggy awfully quick, if you know what he means."

Conundrum said, "The professor just tapped, 'Wait. Feel better.' "

Commodore Brigg tore at his beard in frustration. He knew that if he ended this mission, the professor would only insist on going again. Or worse, Razmous would want to go. And where was that dratted kender, anyway? What about Sir Grumdish? And Sir Tanar?

The ringer on the pulley rattled out a short burst. The commodore broke off his musings to listen to Conundrum's translation, but the gnome seemed reluctant to speak.

"What is it? What does he say?" Brigg demanded.

"He says, 'Ahhh!' " Conundrum answered sheepishly.

"Ahhh?"

"Ay-aitch-aitch-aitch-exclamation point," Conundrum confirmed. He pulled out the sheet of paper with the professor's code and showed it to the commodore. "See here? Three dots and five dashes is an exclamation point."

"But what does it mean?" the commodore asked.

"Perhaps it is a sigh of surprise and delight?" the doctor offered.

Commodore Brigg shot him a black look, then turned to the open aft deck hatch. "Reverse the—" he began.

The ringer was tapping again, insistently. Conundrum listened for a moment, then shouted, "Stop the wench! Stop! He's found something."

Turning back to the boom, he cupped one hand to his ear and began to translate even before the tapping stopped. "He says, 'Remarkable! A great roof of rock as far as the eye can see. The rock ap-appears to be porous and filled with air holes like a sponge. I think this is the underside of the continent. Below me, there is a vast darkness swimming with lights. There are millions of tiny glowing shrimp, all swimming up from below and bumping their heads against the underside of the continent. In sufficient numbers, such creatures could exert enough upward force to make the continent float, whether the stone is hot or not.'"

"Yes, but is he still hallucinating, or has he truly found the underside of Ansalon?" the commodore asked with barely suppressed excitement, most of his doubts and fears erased.

"His spelling isn't muddled any longer," Conundrum answered, one ear turned to the boom to listen to the continued tapping. "He says that he is taking readings and sampling the water. The water is very cold, he says, but it is normal salt water. And . . . and . . ." Conundrum's face bent into a frown, the red curls of his beard bristling.

Suddenly, Commodore Brigg grabbed him by the shoulders and threw him through the open aft deck hatch. Conundrum tumbled down the ladder and fell at the feet of the startled crew members. At the same moment, something large and heavy slammed into the boom, bending it almost double. The force broke the wench loose from its mooring bolts. It skittered across the floor, careened across Conundrum's stomach (knocking the breath from his lungs), and began bumping up the ladder. It hung on the third rung, rope screaming as it stripped off. The metal rung began to bend.

"Close the hatch!" Conundrum gasped.

One crew member was already vaulting up the ladder. He grabbed the hatch and pulled it shut just as the wench bent the ladder rung double and broke free. The slamming hatch caught the wench as it was rattling through the opening, pinning it between the seal and the heavy weight of the door. Even so, it was all the poor gnome could do to hold it. His three fellows scrambled up and quickly tied it down.

Conundrum staggered to his feet and stared up at the jury-rigged affair. Even as he looked, he could hear the rope crackling under the strain. At that moment, another tremendous blow struck, this time smashing into the side of the ship, knocking everyone off their feet. He heard Commodore Brigg shouting above deck, and in the distance, a roaring like a tornado come down into the very bowels of the earth.

CHAPTER
30

Sir Grumdish flipped open the belly visor on his suit of mechanical armor and peered out at the massive heap of rubble piled up against the wall of the cavern. He glanced at Sir Tanar, who stood nearby, calmly waiting with his hands folded into the sleeves of his long gray robes. The wizard's narrow, craggy face was unreadable, as if it had been carved from marble. Growling in frustration, Sir Grumdish focused his gaze on the pile of rubble once more.

"You say that's the way to the dragon?" he asked with obvious suspicion.

"No doubt about it," Sir Tanar answered. "Of course, if you are afraid . . ."

"Balderdash!" Sir Grumdish snorted. "I was just wondering what the point was of bringing me here. The entrance is sealed."

"Yes, but your armor is more powerful than a human knight, correct?" the Thorn Knight prodded, his face still inscrutable.

"As strong as three men," the gnome bragged.

"Well, there is a crevice between two of those boulders

on the left there. I crawled through it yesterday. A couple of strong men might move those boulders enough for a knight in armor to pass. Anyway, that's what I thought," Sir Tanar said noncommittally.

"And did you see this dragon in its lair?" Sir Grumdish shrewdly guessed, catching the Thorn Knight off guard. Sir Tanar was still in the habit of thinking gnomes silly tinkerers. For a moment, his careful mask cracked, and he stared at the gnome in undisguised loathing. Sir Grumdish laughed.

"Well, so long as we really understand each other," the gnome said. "You want me to slay this dragon so you can grab the choicest items of treasure. If I happen to be slain in the process, all the better for you."

Sir Tanar smiled and said in a conciliatory voice, "I see I cannot fool you."

"I do not begrudge you," Sir Grumdish said as he snapped shut his visor. "It is no less than I expected of you. I just didn't know that you were aware of my Life Quest. If I could only slay a dragon, the Knights of Solamnia could no longer refuse my application. Well, let's take a look at this crevice anyway. Probably you are only wasting my time."

He strode clankingly toward the rubble pile. Sir Tanar dropped in behind, an evil twinkle shining in his black eyes.

After walking up and down before the heap of stones for several minutes, Sir Grumdish stopped and placed his gauntleted fists on his armored hips. The belly visor swung open once more.

"It has possibilities," he said. "One need only look at it as an architectural puzzle, and one sees that the structure of the pile has several fundamental instabilities. The giants who built it obviously knew little of masonry, while I know quite a bit about the craft, it being in the family, so to say. My mother and sisters are all members of the

Masons and Stonecutters Guild back in Mount Nevermind. With a proper fulcrum, a strong enough lever, and
several proper steam engines, this pile could be brought
down entirely." He clanked a few steps closer and leaned
back to get a better look at the entire problem. "Of course,
we don't want to bring down the entire pile. That might let
the dragon out. We just need a large enough space for me
to fit through."

Saying this, he approached a large boulder lying near
the crevice and set his gauntleted hands against it. Machinery began to whine complainingly deep within Sir Grumdish's mechanical armor, but the boulder did not budge.
Metal creaked and groaned under the stress. A thin stream
of smoke coiled from the left ear hole of his polished helm,
and a smell of hot steel permeated the air. The whining had
grown to a full-throated scream of stripping gears and
bending rods when, without warning, there was a crack of
stone from high above.

Sir Tanar leaped back and turned to run, shielding his
head with his arms, as the entire pile of rubble came roaring down in an unstoppable landslide. Choking dust filled
the air, and stones crashed around him, pelting his back
and legs. Dodging into the dark doorway of a nearby building, he narrowly avoided being crushed by a boulder three
times his size. Here he hid, cowering in the dark, until the
last echoes of the slide faded into nothingness. Then he
crept out to survey the damage.

"Damn gnomes!" he swore, mouth agape.

Sir Grumdish was nowhere to be seen. A pile of rubble
now covered the place where he had been pushing against
the boulder. Sir Tanar did not pause to mourn, unless it
was to curse his own luck. With gnomes, nothing seemed
to work as planned. Sir Grumdish was only supposed to
open a way large enough for him to pass in armor. Instead,
the entrance to Charynsanth's lair now lay wide open, and

his offering to the dragon was now dead underneath a dozen tons of stone. His plans had all gone to rot.

Not that it really mattered. He would just have to find a way to placate the dragon without the sacrifice of Sir Grumdish. In fact, this might even be better. He had intended to tell Charynsanth of the underwater passage that the *Indestructible* had used to escape her. Now he could keep that little bolt hole a secret. He might need it, once she had helped him gain control of the *Indestructible*. Yes, once he thought about it, this was infinitely better. He had one less gnome to deal with. If he did things right, he might not need the dragon after all.

But of course, by the time he realized this, it was too late. Charynsanth was coming. The ground began to tremble beneath his feet, and the last loose stones, released by the shaking, rattled down the face of the landslide. He had two choices now, and neither of them seemed exactly safe. Red dragons were notoriously unpredictable. She might rush out and, seeing him, flame him without a second thought. But if he hid and revealed himself only after she emerged from the tunnel, he might surprise her, and then she might flame him without a second thought.

Finally, he decided that the wisest course would be to stand his ground and show no fear. It had worked at their first meeting. He mustn't show weakness now, he concluded, so he folded his hands into the sleeves of his robes and waited.

This was not so simple a task as it might sound. To stand before an open tunnel from which an angry red dragon was about to emerge was a trial of the spirit. He trembled, sweated, and changed his mind a dozen times, even before the dragonfear struck him like a hammer blow to the chest. Then he heard the roar of Charynsanth, nearly blowing his robes off. Sir Tanar's light gray wizard's robes began to darken with moisture.

Finally, she appeared, her long serpentine neck writhing cautiously from the shadows. "Well, wizard, I see you were as good as your word. Except for the promised morsel. Where is it? Your kender only whetted my appetite."

"Unfortunately, he was buried while opening your door," the Thorn Knight answered, but this time his voice quavered with fear. He swore under his breath and tried to get a rein on his emotions.

"A shame," the dragon purred. "I do so want to trust you, but until then . . ." her voice trailed off in a bubbling snarl.

Sir Tanar staggered and stumbled over a rock, then scrambled to his feet, yawning uncontrollably. He shook the cobwebs from his mind, fighting off a sudden and powerful urge to sleep. His wizardly instincts screamed *sleep spell!* She was trying to ensorcell him.

Casting aside all his plans and schemes, Sir Tanar turned and fled down the rubble-strewn avenue. He had no power to fight this dragon, not even with the aid of the magical communication device—not out in the open anyway, where she could breathe her fire on him and use her natural armaments of claw and tooth, tail and wing. He needed cover from which to cast his spells.

Long used to athletic endeavors, Sir Tanar's long legs served him well, as did the fear pumping through his veins. He dashed down the avenue, hurtling stones and dodging boulders like a Palanthian steeplechase runner. Seeing what appeared to be a dark alley—although in this place of monumental construction it was probably nothing more than a space between two buildings—he skittered to a stop and dove inside without looking back to see if the dragon was following.

He ran to the end of the alley without coming upon any crossways. The alley itself was far too small for the dragon to enter, so for the moment he felt safe. Dragging out the small flat box, he set it on the ground, then knelt before it and opened it. He lifted the magical silver plate from its place, feeling its magic surge through him, giving him new strength and confidence. The words to a protection spell came to mind, and he opened his mouth to speak them.

But he never finished his incantation. A pillar of flame descended upon him from above, burning away robe, flesh, bone, wishes, desires, and regrets in one white hot instant. The flames splashed against the walls of the surrounding buildings, melting stone like candle wax. It flowed down the sides of the buildings and pooled in the alley, a little flame leaping up as it consumed the box. The silver plate, being magical, withstood the heat, but the molten stone flowed round it, encased it, then cooled and hardened.

But by that time, Charynsanth had already gone, knowing now where the gnome ship lay. There was only one place it could be. The little pool at the low end of the city.

CHAPTER
31

Conundrum rushed across the ship's bridge and shot up the ladder into the conning tower, climbing through the hatch just as another blow rocked the *Indestructible*. A splinter of rock stung his cheek, drawing a trickle of blood.

Below him on the afterdeck, Commodore Brigg danced an angry jig around the shattered boom, hurling curses as he tried to shore up the rigging while under fire from shore. Doctor Bothy lay flat out on his back on the deck, a queer smile on his pale chubby face. Conundrum leaped down beside him.

"What's happening?" Conundrum asked as he knelt beside the prone doctor.

"What are you doing here? I pushed you below!" Commodore Brigg swore. "I need you in the engine room. We're under attack!"

"By what?"

"That!" the commodore shouted, pointing to shore where Chief Portlost and Captain Hawser surged back and forth across the sand, engaged in mortal combat with a black-skinned giant. The creature was at least fourteen feet tall, broad-shouldered and powerfully built, with a shock of hair and a patchy beard the color of fire. Its low, backward-sloping forehead and heavy outthrust jaw gave it a primitive, bestial profile, but a cunning light burned in its deep-set black eyes. In one hand, it wielded a broken-off stalactite as a club, using it to fend off the snapping claws of Captain Hawser's mechanical crab. The two opponents circled one another, the crab darting in to snatch at the giant's legs, the giant bashing back the crab with mighty blows of its heavy club, neither gaining an advantage.

Suddenly, the giant lunged forward, smashing down with its club. Captain Hawser jerked back on the controls, sending the crab skittering a dozen yards down the narrow beach. In that moment, the giant stooped and, lifting a boulder in one fist, hurled it at the *Indestructible*. It sailed through the air with uncanny accuracy.

Commodore Brigg pulled Conundrum down behind the prone doctor, using his portly bulk to shield them. The huge, heavy projectile bounced off the aft deck, rattling the ship to its timbers. But before the giant could follow up with another boulder, the crab scuttled back up the beach and renewed its own attack, driving the giant up toward the edge of the ruins whence it had appeared, suddenly and without warning, from the steamy fog a few moments before.

Watching this in horrified amazement, Conundrum asked, "What happened to Doctor Bothy?"

Frowning, the commodore answered, "When the first boulder hit us, it scared him to death, I think. He clutched his chest, smiled, and toppled to the deck, just as you see him. He looked at me and said one word—'Cured!'—before he breathed his last."

The mechanical crab and the giant circled one another warily. Conundrum and the commodore crawled over to the wrecked boom. It lay half in the water, all but one of its bolts ripped from the deck by the giant's boulder. "It's hopeless," the commodore said. "We've got to help Hawser and Portlost battle that thing, and to do that, we've got to be able to maneuver."

"But that means . . ." Conundrum began, his voice trailing off in horror.

"We've got to cut him loose," Commodore Brigg finished for him.

"We can't!" Conundrum cried. "He'll die."

"If we can't maneuver to help Hawser fight that giant," the commodore said, "the professor will die anyway. This is something that has to be done. I don't like it, but there's no other way."

Seeing Conundrum hesitating, the commodore patted him on the shoulder. "Send him the message and my heartfelt thanks," he said. "The professor will understand. While you do that, I'll find an axe." He crawled away.

With his heart in his shoes, Conundrum found a hammer and began tapping out the commodore's message. *Under attack. Boom wrecked, and wench broken free. Commodore commends . . .* He was unable to finish. His new friends were dropping around him like drunken gully dwarves.

A moment later, a response came back, saving him the trouble of breaking the bad news to the professor. *Cut me loose. Nearly out of air, anyway. Life Quest complete, as long as someone survives to record results. Will you?*

Conundrum brushed away his tears and answered, *Yes. Sorry. Commodore commends your bravery and sacrifice.*

Cut me loose. Happy. No regrets. Thank you. See you on the other side.

Conundrum nodded to the commodore when he returned, dragging a small hand axe behind him. The commodore's bearded chin quivered as he hefted the axe above his head. With one quick chop, the blade sliced through the thick rope, and it slithered away through the pulley at the end of the broken boom and into the water. Glancing over the side, they saw the frayed end swirl for a moment in the green depths before slipping silently into the darkness below.

Commodore Brigg stood up and shook his fist defiantly at the shore. "Hap-Troggensbottle, you shall not have died in vain!" he cried.

But the giant and the crab were no longer visible. A thick fog had descended from the city above, enveloping the beach in a warm white cloak through which little could be seen. For a moment longer, they heard the hue and cry of battle, the ring of stone club on metal shell, angry snarl and clatter of bronze claw. And then silence.

The steamy fog continued to roll down from the city's numerous geysers and mudpits, eventually swirling across the surface of the water and enveloping the *Indestructible*. In this white dripping blindness, the commodore and Conundrum moved forward until they found the conning tower. They climbed up and found themselves above the mist, but only by a head.

Commodore Brigg picked up the comm tube, blew into it, then said into it, softly, "Switch power from the dyno to the flowpellars. Minimum speed. Secure aft deck hatch." The four crew members in the engine room obeyed, and the *Indestructible* slipped silently forward, turning to starboard under the commodore's hand.

"All stop," he whispered once they were in position. "Prepare to flood aft ballast tanks." The ship drifted to a stop, water lapping softly against her sides.

Through the fog, they occasionally heard a grunted oath or the scrape of an iron claw over wet stone. What the fog would reveal when it lifted, neither cared to guess. Conundrum stood beside the commodore and gripped the rail until his knuckles were as white as the fog. Water dripped from the rusting metal and the stone overhead.

Then the fog began to thin as though blown away by a freshening breeze. They felt the hair of their beards stir, and it brought with it a smell of brimstone. Commodore Brigg leaned over the rail to try to peer through the obscuring mist. One hand shot back and pulled Conundrum after him.

Conundrum caught at the rail to steady himself, at the same time feeling the commodore's hand trembling. He squinted, staring ahead, seeing the fog parting like many layers of snowy veils, opening, shredding, revealing once more the beach and what stood on it, facing one another.

To the left, the crab crouched low with its rear angled up in the air, pinchers extended and open before it. Captain Hawser and Chief Portlost were visible through the gaps in its armor shell. To the right, the giant stood, back bent, stone club held defensively before it, snarling, eyes darting from the crab—

—to the dragon.

Conundrum gasped at the sight of it. Commodore Brigg began whispering urgent orders into the comm tube.

Charynsanth crouched catlike between the crab and the giant, her great reptilian head twitching to glance first at the giant, now at the mechanical crab, her sulfurous breath hissing through bared fangs. Her wings fanned the fog nervously, helping to drive away the last tatters of the mist. She was by far the most powerful of the three opponents now facing each other, but in the blindness of the fog, she had placed herself directly between them, with the water blocking her escape in front, and her natural weaknesses of mobility on the ground preventing a rearward retreat. She knew she could easily dispatch either opponent with her breath weapon or a spell, but in doing so, she opened herself to attack by the other.

The giant, though it looked a brute, was smart enough to know it stood no chance against the dragon alone. Its only hope was that she attacked the crab first. Then it could wade in with its club and crush her skull. Of course, Captain Hawser and Chief Portlost knew the same was true for them. If the dragon attacked the giant first, they might rush in and grapple her with the crab's mechanical claws, but if she directed her attack toward them first, they stood little chance of surviving a blast of her fiery breath.

And so all three waited. Captain Hawser twitched the controls, adjusting the crab's stance in minute increments, trying to line his machine up for the best angle of attack should the dragon turn toward the giant. The giant shifted restlessly, black eyes darting, its huge boots grinding the sand underfoot, knuckles cracking as it tightened its grip on the club. Within easy reach lay a boulder large enough to crush the dragon's neck to bloody pulp. Moving slowly, almost imperceptibly, it inched its way closer to its chosen projectile.

Charynsanth watched them both, still unable to make up her mind which to attack first. Her tail lashed the sand in indecision. Her claws dug in beneath her, and fire bubbled in her chest. Her eyes narrowed, spotting the giant's movement and divining its intention. A low hate-filled growl boiled up through her throat. She moved one clawed foot ever so slightly through the sand, twitched her tail around in preparation for a lunge at the giant. Captain Hawser inched the crab closer, preparing to strike. The giant froze, its huge fingers twitching mere inches over the boulder it intended to grab and hurl at the dragon.

Water dripped from the stones overhead, plopping noisily in the water. The *Indestructible* lay just offshore, unnoticed by the dragon for the moment. Conundrum stood glued to the rail, waiting for something to happen, feeling as though there weren't air enough to breathe, as though he might suffocate before something happened.

And then many things happened at once. From behind the dragon, Sir Grumdish appeared in his battered, dented, no longer shiny, and bloodstained mechanical armor, already at a full run, bent broadsword raised above his helm as he shouted the Solamnic challenge to a foe. Charynsanth spun to meet this new threat, but Sir Grumdish dashed in beneath her upraised wing and sank his blade to the hilt into her exposed neck. She screamed in rage and pain, fire erupting from her gaping jaws to engulf the giant, who had grabbed the boulder and was lifting it to throw. The giant staggered back, a living bonfire, and dropped both its club and the boulder.

At the same moment, the crab rushed in to attack, one claw tearing into the dragon's sensitive and softer belly scales, the other clamping onto her rear leg. As Charynsanth beat her wings to maintain balance and keep the crab from flipping her onto her back, one wing swept up Sir Grumdish and flung him fifty yards through the air, out across the water and over the *Indestructible*. He hit the water with a loud, metallic bellyflop and sank quickly out of sight, a final glint of his spurs shining up through the black water.

Commodore Brigg grabbed Conundrum by the shoulder and screamed in his face, "Get below. Stand by to fire UAEPs on my order!"

Shaken from his paralysis, Conundrum slid down the ladder and through the hatch onto the bridge, stumbled through the half light provided by the glowwormglobes, and located the two big red buttons on the weapons console. Snuffling, he wiped one sleeve across his nose and waited.

"Flood aft ballast!" the commodore shouted. With a gurgling purr, the *Indestructible* began to tilt backward, lifting her streaming bow from the water.

Meanwhile on the shore, Captain Hawser dug the crab's legs into the sand and continued to push while Chief Portlost, at the controls of the pinchers, lifted with all his might. Charynsanth flapped like a trapped butterfly, her wings buffeting the crab like thunder, while her slavering jaws snapped at the metal braces protecting the two gnomes and tore off the last sections of its bronze shell.

The giant, its hair and beard smoldering, raw flesh showing through its cracked and charred skin, lunged in with a boulder and began to beat both the dragon and the crab. One blow caught Charynsanth across the snout, stunning her. Another broke off the crab claw gripping the dragon's rear leg. Recovering, Charynsanth lunged into the air, her mighty wings pummeling the wind. Commodore Brigg sank down in the conning tower as her wingtips brushed inches overhead.

With a roar of hatred, the giant launched its boulder. The huge stone cracked Charynsanth squarely across the brow as she banked round for an attack. The force of the blow snapped her head around as if she had come to the end of a string. Her wings fell limp and, tumbling backward in the air, she plummeted like a lead weight. With a tremendous thudding splash, she followed Sir Grumdish to the cavern's flooded floor, a storm of bubbles hissing and popping on the surface long after the waves of her impact had subsided.

With a victorious roar, the giant then turned on Captain Hawser and Chief Portlost, still inside the mechanical crab. They backed away, waving their one remaining claw before them. The giant limped across the sand and retrieved its club, then turned with a snarl and charged. Captain Hawser threw the crab forward, and the two came together with a deafening crash and roar.

Commodore Brigg had seen enough. Without aiming, he shouted "Fire!"

Conundrum slammed both buttons at the same time. The *Indestructible* lurched back as twin jets of water shot out from her bow. Two huge arrows streaked across the cavern. One struck with a quivering, meaty *thwack* in the giant's back, and the other glanced off the crab with such force that the mechanical contraption went spinning across the beach and slammed into the cavern wall. The giant clutched vainly at the enormous arrow in its back, then toppled face down in the sand. With a last groan, it breathed no more.

Commodore Brigg sighed with relief and turned his attention to the crab. It lay in a tangled heap of metal against the wall, no sign of life within its twisted remains. A thin blue exhalation of smoke curled up from its midst. Brigg's breath caught in his throat, and he turned and slid down the ladder to the bridge.

He landed with a thump beside Conundrum. "We've got to get to shore!" he cried, then turned and shouted down to engineering, "Engage the main flowpellar!"

The ship lurched forward.

"Steer her into shore," the commodore ordered, pushing Conundrum toward the wheel. "Run her aground. It doesn't matter."

"What's wrong?" Conundrum asked.

"My brother," the commodore answered, his voice tight with emotion, "and the chief. I'll get Doctor Bothy's spare kit. Just steer her in and put her on the beach." With those words, he ducked through the forward hatch and disappeared.

Conundrum gripped the wheel nervously, staring out through the porthole at the carnage on the beach. The giant lay with their arrow sticking out of its back like a tree. Beyond it, resting against the wall with a tendril of smoke rising from its midst, lay a heap of metal that Conundrum recognized after a few moments as the crab.

The sandy shore slid toward them, and Conundrum held the *Indestructible* on a steady course. Commodore Brigg banged around in sick bay like a gnomish percussion corps, all the while growling a string of dwarven curses vile enough to strip the rust from the ship's hull. Below him, the last four members of the crew cranked the ship's drive springs tight and saw to the oiling of the gears. They were good sailors, and Conundrum admired them. In the midst of this chaos, they kept to their duty, while he held the wheel of the ship as though, were he to let go, he might fly to pieces.

A dozen yards from shore now. A half dozen. Then the shore vanished in an explosion of water as Charynsanth rose up before the ship, like a leviathan, wings spread wide and streaming water in sheets. The *Indestructible* crashed to a stop against her belly, throwing Conundrum forward against the wheel so hard that it drove the air from his lungs. He hung on, gasping, watching in horror as the dragon's claws closed round the bow of the ship.

Charynsanth forced the ship's nose down into the water as he she leaned over the conning tower. The giant's boulder had only stunned her, but Sir Grumdish's sword was still embedded in her neck, her life's blood flowed out around it. She was dying, but she would see to it that everyone and everything died with her.

The conning tower hatch was still open. Charynsanth leaned over it, sucking her last breath in through nostrils frothing with her own blood. The fires boiled in her belly. Staring up through the hatch, Conundrum saw her jaws part, blood streaming out between her long cruel fangs to fall hissing on the deck of the bridge. He smelled the brimstone. He saw the moment of his death arriving.

And then he knew what he had to do. He crossed the bridge in three bounds as dragonfire boiled down through the conning tower. He leaped, grabbed the handle, and released the ram.

It shot out, impaling Charynsanth on its cold steel spike. She reared back in pain, screaming the dragonfire from her lungs in a white-hot plume that fountained upward. In her death throes, she kicked the *Indestructible* free, sending it skittering across the water, thick black smoke billowing from the top of the conning tower.

Conundrum's action had bought them only a little time. Enough of Charynsanth's dragonfire had poured into the bridge to set everything on fire, including Conundrum. His white guild robe went up in flames. He screamed and fell to his knees as the deck cracked and split underneath him. A column of fire shot up from belowdecks, and the floor dropped away beneath him.

Commodore Brigg picked himself up from the deck of the sick bay where he had fallen when the ship lurched to a stop against the dragon's belly. At first, he thought that Conundrum had run the ship aground, but then he heard the Toaster engaged and the dragon's roar of pain. He rushed to the door, jerked it open, and got a face full of fire for his trouble. Flames roared down the passage from the bridge and licked around the open doorway. Quickly snatching a blanket from a nearby examination table, he wrapped it around his body and lunged out into the inferno, his only thought to save his ship.

He arrived at the bridge to find half the floor vanished, swallowed up by a column of fire roaring up from below decks. Of Conundrum and his remaining crew, he saw no sign. The conning tower and its escape hatch were well within the flames and out of his reach, but through the forward porthole, he saw that the ship was still moving, that its engines were still engaged. Knowing that he had but one choice, he staggered through the flames to the dive control station. Grasping the scorching bronze levers in his hands, he jerked them down, opening the ship's fore and aft ballast tanks. Immediately, the burning wreck of the *Indestructible* dove beneath the waves.

The surface of the water crawled up the glass of the forward porthole. It seemed to take forever for the ship to submerge. Commodore Brigg gagged and choked on the smoke, waiting for what he knew would happen, what he knew was his only chance to save the ship, while flames crowded closer and closer around him.

Finally, the *Indesctructible* slipped beneath the waves, and as it did so, water roared down its open Snorkel. A fountain of chill water blasted across the bridge with the force of a tidal wave, knocking Commodore Brigg from his feet and washing him aft. He grasped the broken half of the Peeritscope as water continued to pour in, washing over the smoking decks and pouring through the hole in the bridge deck, dousing the fires in the crew quarters below.

Even as the fires were extinguished, the interior of the ship grew dark, dark as the blackest cavern in the deepest bowel of the earth. Commodore Brigg looked up. Outside the *Indestructible*, there was only inky blackness. The ship had sunk through the hole in the bottom of the cave, down through the hole the professor had explored, into the bottomless abyss that led to the underside of the continent of Krynn.

And she was still sinking.

CHAPTER

32

Conundrum awoke in a small bed, lined with soft white pillows, covered by a white blanket with blue ticking. A window near the bed was thrown open, and outside, a gentle afternoon shower pattered against the wall, falling in a hush through naked gray treetops stretching away into the distance. A cool wind flowed in through the window, stirring the filmy white curtains hanging to either side. The room contained seven other beds like the one in which he lay, but they were all empty, their linens neatly folded and stacked on the corner of each mattress. He sat up on his elbows and looked around in wonder.

It seemed an ordinary infirmary, only there weren't any nurses or doctors or engineers or mishaps officers scurrying about, taking peoples' temperatures and prescribing soapy water enemas and treatments of epsom salts. The ward was strangely silent.

He rose from his bed and walked to the window, staring out over the silver gray treetops dripping with rain. It was winter here—wherever here was. It had the look and smell of Darkember, as the Solamnics called it, Bleakcold to the kender.

Tears started in his eyes. At first he didn't know why, but then he remembered—the kender, Razmous Pinch-pocket. The memory of the *Indestructible*'s unflappable cartographer brought everything flooding back to him. There was the battle with the giant and the dragon, and the fire onboard, the deck collapsing beneath his feet, him falling, falling into a light that burned like a thousand suns. And then darkness. Nothingness.

How did he get here? Where was here? And where was everybody else—Commodore Brigg, Captain Hawser, Chief Portlost, Razmous, even Sir Tanar? He leaned out the window and scanned the ground below. A narrow path wound through the trees, beside which marble benches stood at regular intervals, but there was no one moving along the path, and the benches were all empty.

He turned away in frustration and scanned the empty ward once more. At the far end of the room, a single door provided the only exit. The walls of the room were made of stone, the floor of polished stone flags, the ceiling over-arched with thick wooden beams and roofed with timber planks. Three windows provided the only light.

The room had all the appearance of perfect order and sterility, neither warm nor cold, neither inviting nor forbidding. There were eight identical beds, four along either wall. Under each bed lay a shiny metal bedpan, and beside each bed stood a small table with a washing bowl resting atop it. Pushed against the wall opposite the door was a desk on which lay several thick books, a bottle of ink, and a feather. A simple wooden chair was pushed beneath it. Hanging on the wall beside the desk was a tall mirror. Conundrum saw himself in it, but it took him several moments to notice the difference. His flaming red hair, so unusual in gnomes, had turned bone white.

Conundrum turned away in shock. As he fingered his beard and ran his hand through the thin strip of hair circling his otherwise shiny, bald head, his eyes came to rest on a thick, black leather-bound book sitting on the table beside his bed. The edges of the pages appeared to have been burned, the cover warped and cracked as though doused with water and then carelessly allowed to dry without first oiling it. He picked it up, and a smell arose from its pages that brought choking sobs to his throat. He sat heavily on the edge of his bed, his fingers trembling as he stroked the cover, terrified, afraid to open it, afraid not to.

At last, he bent back the cover and examined the first page.

Ship's log — MNS Indestructible

Over the next few hours, Conundrum gingerly turned the cracked and brittle parchment pages, reliving each stage of his journey, from the day the *Indestructible* first sank in the harbor of Pax, to her second sinking and final successful launch, through the journey north and east around the continent of Ansalon. He read with a certain measure of pride and delight the commodore's account of his exploits with the chaos monster. He laughed at the antics of the kender, duly recorded in Commodore Brigg's own rough, masculine script and dispassionate scientific writing style, which only made them funnier. He then marveled at the description of the modifications installed during their period in Flotsam, and he learned for the first time of the commodore's misgivings about taking on the Thorn Knight.

The mention of the Thorn Knight seemed to lift a veil from Conundrum's eyes, and he remembered with painful clarity that moment in Sir Tanar's cabin when he planned to take over the ship. He realized then that the Thorn Knight had murdered his cousin, and that his own testimony about the "accident" had all been a lie planted in his mind by Sir Tanar's magic. Bitter hatred filled his heart then—hatred for the Thorn Knight for using him to cover his own crime and aid his attempt to wrest the *Indestructible* from the commodore's control.

Conundrum flipped through the last pages, only briefly scanning the contents as he searched for the answers now burning bright as dragonfire in his heart. What happened after the dragon set the ship on fire? How did he get here? Where was everyone else? Finally, near the end of the log, he found what he was looking for. He read:

Knowing that the flowpellars were still engaged and the Snorkel was in the open position, I did the only thing available to me. I flooded the ballast tanks. Ship sank straightaway and water from the open Snorkel quickly doused the flames, as I had intended. Unfortunate side effect being that we were sinking. Closed Snorkel and hatch, but the ship had already passed into the bottomless chasm leading to the professor's underside of the continent. Could only hope that he was right. Meanwhile, set about checking for surviving crew and pumping out the water.

Found Conundrum badly burned but still alive. Ensigns Dnat, Felthallow, Ruark, and Rimbortion burned almost beyond recognition, but still at their posts in the engine room. Recommend them for special recognition, if this ship survives. Unable to pump out the ship. Speculate that at such depths, pressure outside hull too great to expel water from inside ship through bilge valves. Used ascending flowpellar to slow and control descent, but main controls were shot. Had to do everything by hand.

Finally reached bottom of continent, found it much as Professor had described—a great roof of rock stretching away in all directions, millions upon millions of tiny glowing shrimp bumping their heads against it. It was at this time that I observed that the Indestructible *was leaking air, for bubbles were forming on the rocky underside of the continent. Noticed* that the bubbles did not stay in one place. Instead they moved like quicksilver along the undersurface of the stone, indicating upward slope, although slope was not detectable through normal observations. Concluded that upward slope led to edge of continent. Set course and engaged flowpellars.

It has been five days now since we sank, and I regret leaving behind my brother and the others, although I doubt that any of them still lived. Razmous Pinchpocket, if still alive, is a kender, and so I have little concern that he will find his way out eventually. The others . . . I would have preferred to confirm their fates before departing, but I had no choice.

The MNS Indestructible is nearly out of air and the lower deck is completely flooded, including engineering. Amazingly, the spring engines have continued to run, outperforming by several hours the length of time needed between windings. I have welded the controls into place to hold the ship on course, should I faint from want of air. My initial concerns about the bilge were unfounded. I effected repairs, and it is now working, slowly emptying the ship of its weight of water, and she is rising up toward the surface. Last night, we came out from under the continent and are now coursing through open sea, though deep beneath its surface. I think it is New Sea, but I cannot be sure without taking navigational readings.

The ship will live up to her namesake, I think, though I fear none of us will survive. Conundrum hangs on somehow. His burns seem to be healing with the help of some ointments I found in Doctor Bothy's spare kit—lucky for us that the Medical Sciences Guild has long known the best cures for burns.

Air grows thinner by the minute. We shall not reach the surface in time. This log shall be our testament to the endurance of the will of gnomes, if it and this ship are ever found. I pray to Reorx who is no more that it does. We should not die in vain.

Conundrum turned the last page and found it blank. He closed the log, sighed, and lifted his eyes slowly from its worn cover. Before him stood a woman wearing long white robes with the symbol of the sun emblazoned on the breast. Her long dark hair was pulled back in a simple ring of silver, revealing a sad, smiling face, soft and radiant.

"It is good to see you awake at last, Conundrum," she said, "but you should not tire yourself overmuch. You arrived here only seven days ago, and you were at the door of death."

"Here? Where is here?" Conundrum asked.

"This is the Citadel of Light," she answered softly.

"I've heard of this place," he said excitedly. "This is where the healers are. You must have healed me!"

"Not I," she corrected. "One more powerful than I. We have healed your body, but not your spirit. That is why we left your book here with you, so that you might find it and read it. There is much grief in your tale, and much joy. You needed to know its ending."

"But I still don't know its ending," Conundrum said. "How did I come here, and what happened to Commodore Brigg?"

"We found your ship beached on the eastern shore of this island, where few ever venture," the woman said. "You were the ship's only survivor, and only just. Your commodore, I am sorry to say, was beyond our ability to heal."

Conundrum hung his head in dejection. There were no more tears in his eyes, but his body shook with dry sobs.

"Does it help you to know these things?" the woman asked. "Some feared to reveal everything to you so early after your healing. I thought it best that you should know. I was born on Sancrist, you see, and have known gnomes before. I knew you would not rest until you knew all."

"Thank you," Conundrum said, clasping her hand.

She took it and gently helped him back into bed. She then set the ship's log on the table beside the bed. "You should rest now. Soon it will be dark. In the morning, you may meet your healer. She will be pleased to hear of your recovery, and perhaps she will show you the place where we buried your commodore. Dwarves built his cairn."

"I'd like that. Thank you again," Conundrum said as he sank back on his pillows. "I don't know how to thank you enough. I only wish . . ." but he did not finish the thought. Instead, he smiled.

The woman bowed and swept silently from the ward, softly closing the door behind her and leaving the room in silence. Outside, the last of the rain spattered on the windowsill, then the clouds lifted and allowed the setting sun to shine beneath, casting the chamber in a deep crimson glow.

Conundrum lay awake, watching darkness come. It was the darkness of his soul. Commodore Brigg had fulfilled his Life Quest to find his brother, as well as Snork's to subnavigate the continent. The professor had discovered what makes the continents float. Doctor Bothy found the cure for hiccoughs. Chief Portlost witnessed what had to be one of the greatest mishaps ever—several of them, in fact. And Sir Grumdish had slain his dragon.

He alone had not completed his Life Quest. In fact, he still hadn't even found his Life Quest.

Rising from his bed, Conundrum slipped from the dark chamber. The door let out into a long, echoing hall paved with glistening black stone. It stretched away into darkness in both directions. Picking one direction, he followed it, hardly even noticing where he was going. He had a vague desire to see the *Indestructible*, but he had no idea where it lay, whether they had towed it to their own docks or left it rusting on the eastern shore of the island.

He found his way to a stair and descended it, crossed a wide hall, and passed through a towering doorway that stood open, even at this late hour. Knights of Solamnia stood guard at either side of it, but they did not speak to him as he passed, and he barely noticed them except to remember Sir Grumdish with a sad sigh.

He wandered out onto the grounds of the Citadel of Light. His eyes were bent downward, watching his thin slippers shuffling through the neatly clipped, rain-soaked winter grass. He felt a chill and remembered that he had on only a hospital gown, but he merely tucked his hands into his armpits and continued onward, his head bent, consumed in brooding thought.

After a time, he came to an abrupt stop, his nose in a clipped hedge. He stepped back and examined it, then looked around. He found himself between two hedges, one of them running off to his left for a few yards before turning left again, the other stretched back the way he had come, passing beneath an arch and opening onto the lawn where he'd been wandering aimlessly. A pair of tall crystalline domes rose beyond the lawn, glimmering in the light of the newly risen moon.

Shrugging, Conundrum turned left. He followed the corridor to its next turning, then to a crossing of four ways. Still brooding on his own problems, he chose a passage at random and continued walking.

And continued walking. He began to shiver with a chill and wondered how long he'd been wandering between hedges. He glanced quickly around, found the moon and got his bearings, then set out to return to his hospital ward. He was sure he could find it. If only he could get out of this hedge maze.

The next morning, Conundrum's healer hurried on her way to the Citadel, for she'd heard her patient had recovered. As she crossed the lawn, she noticed a crowd of students gathered at the entrance to the hedge maze. They were laughing at something, and even as she looked, more hurried across the lawn to join in the fun. Shrugging, she diverted her course to see what all the commotion was about.

Seeing her approach, the crowd parted, many hiding snickers and chuckles behind their hands. What she saw filled her first with horror, but this quickly changed to relief and joy. Her patient was healed, body and soul.

Conundrum, still wearing his hospital gown, squatted at the entrance to the hedge maze, busily sketching it on a bed sheet with a chunk of charcoal.

"I got lost!" he said as he scratched a thick black line onto the linen. "Lost, if you know what I mean. Took me all night to find my way out, and even then only by accident!"

"Well, of course," one of the students said. "This is the magical Hedge Maze of the Citadel of Light."

"Yes, I know! Isn't it wonderful?" Conundrum beamed, his bald head glistening in the light of the morning sun.

The tales that started it all...

New editions from **DRAGONLANCE**® creators
Margaret Weis & Tracy Hickman

The great modern fantasy epic – now available in paperback!

THE ANNOTATED CHRONICLES

Margaret Weis & Tracy Hickman return to the Chronicles, adding notes and commentary in this annotated edition of the three books that began the epic saga.

SEPTEMBER 2001

THE LEGENDS TRILOGY

Now with stunning cover art by award-winning fantasy artist Matt Stawicki, these new versions of the beloved trilogy will be treasured for years to come.

Time of the Twins • War of the Twins • Test of the Twins

FEBRUARY 2001

New characters,
strange magic,
wondrous creatures.

ADVENTURE THROUGH THE HISTORY OF KRYNN
WITH THESE THREE NEW SERIES!

THE BARBARIANS
PAUL THOMPSON & TONYA CARTER COOK
Follow a divided brother and sister as they lead rival tribes of
plainsmen amidst the wonders and dangers of ancient Krynn.

Volume One: *Children of the Plains*
Volume Two: *Brother of the Dragon*
Volume Three: *Sister of the Sword*
August 2002

THE ICEWALL TRILOGY
DOUGLAS NILES
Journey with an exiled elf to the harsh, legendary land known as Icereach,
where human tribes battle for life and ogres search to reclaim lost glories.

Volume One: *The Messenger*
Volume Two: *The Golden Orb*
January 2002

THE KINGPRIEST TRILOGY
CHRIS PIERSON
Discover for the first time the dynastic history of the Kingpriest
and how his religious-political rule of Istar influenced the world
of DRAGONLANCE® for generations to come.

Volume One: *Chosen of the Gods*
November 2001

STORIES FROM
THE CHANGING FACE OF KRYNN

Bertrem's Guide to the Age of Mortals: Everyday Life in Krynn of the Fifth Age

NANCY VARIAN BERBERICK,
STAN BROWN,
AND PAUL B. THOMPSON

Countless legends, histories, and sagas have told of the great heroes and villains of Krynn. Now, delve into the life of Ansalon in the Fifth Age as seen through the eyes of the common people, through articles on everything from arms and armor to festivals and clothing!

TALES FROM THE WAR OF SOULS

Don't miss this new collection of short stories detailing the era of the War of Souls, newest chapter in the continuing saga of Krynn. Contains stories from Richard A. Knaak, Paul Thompson & Tonya Carter Cook, Jeff Crook and other popular Dragonlance authors.

BERTREM'S GUIDE: A WAR OF SOULS JOURNAL

The War of Souls has begun, and Ansalon will never be the same again. See how these world-changing events affect the lives of the everyday people of Krynn. Includes articles from Nancy Varian Berberick, Mary H. Herbert, John Grubber, and Jeff Crook.

THE DHAMON SAGA
Jean Rabe

THE EXCITING BEGINNING TO THE DHAMON SAGA

— NOW AVAILABLE IN PAPERBACK!

Volume One: *Downfall*

HOW FAR CAN A HERO FALL?
FAR ENOUGH TO LOSE HIS SOUL?

Dhamon Grimwulf, once a Hero
of the Heart, has sunk into a
bitter life of crime and squalor.
Now, as the great dragon
overlords of the Fifth Age coldly
plot to strengthen their rule and
destroy their enemies, he must
somehow find the will to redeem himself.

Volume Two: *Betrayal*

All Dhamon Grimwulf wants is a cure for the painful dragon scale
embedded in his leg. To find a cure, he must venture into the
treacherous realm of a great black dragon. Along the way, Dhamon
discovers some horrible truths: betrayal is worse than death, and there
is something more terrifying on Krynn than even a dragon overlord.

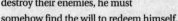

CLASSICS SERIES

THE INHERITANCE
Nancy Varian Berberick
The companions of Tanis Half-Elven knew of their friend's tragic heritage—how his mother was ravaged by a human bandit and died from grief. But there was more to the story than anyone knew.

Here at last is the story of the half-elf's heritage: the tale of a captive elven princess, a merciless human outlaw, a proud elven prince, the power of love, and how tragedy can change a life forever.

THE CITADEL
Richard A. Knaak
Against a darkened cloud it comes, soaring over the ravaged land: the flying citadel, mightiest power in the arsenal of the dragon highlords. An evil wizard has discovered a secret that may bring all of Ansalon under his control, and it's up to a red-robed mage, a driven cleric, a kender, and a grizzled war veteran to stop him before it's too late.

DALAMAR THE DARK
Nancy Varian Berberick
Magic runs like fire through the blood of Dalamar Argent, yet his heritage denies him its use. But as war threatens his beloved Silvanesti, Dalamar will seize the forbidden power and begin a quest that will lead him to a dark and uncertain future.

MURDER IN TARSIS
John Maddox Roberts
Who killed Ambassador Bloodarrow? In a city where everyone is a suspect, time is running out for an unlikely trio of detectives. If they fail to solve the mystery, their reward will be death.